AN END TO SORROW

THE LAST STEP ON THE OBSIDIAN PATH

By

Michael R. Fletcher

AN END TO SORROW

This is a work of fiction. Names, characters, business, events, and incidents are the products of the author's demented imagination. Any resemblance to actual persons, living or dead, Clayton W. Snyder or otherwise, or actual events is mostly coincidental.

AN END TO SORROW Copyright © 2022 by Michael R. Fletcher

All rights reserved. No part of this publication may be reproduced, distributed, eaten, smoked, or transmitted in any form or by any means, including photocopying, recording, semaphore, smoke signal, mime, or other electronic or mechanical methods, without the prior written permission of the publisher (who is unstable at the best of times and let's be real, these ain't them), except in the case of brief quotations embodied in critical reviews (hopefully not *too* critical) and certain other non-commercial uses permitted by copyright law.

Editor: Sarah Chorn
Cover Art and Typography: Felix Ortiz

Books by Michael R. Fletcher
Ghosts of Tomorrow
Beyond Redemption
The Mirror's Truth
The Last Delusion (*Coming Soon*)
Swarm and Steel
A Collection of Obsessions
Smoke and Stone – City of Sacrifice #1
Ash and Bones – City of Sacrifice #2
Black Stone Heart – The Obsidian Path #1
She Dreams in Blood – The Obsidian Path #2
An End to Sorrow – The Obsidian Path #3
The Millennial Manifesto
Norylska Groans (Co-written with Clayton W. Snyder)

For Michael Moorcock, Celia S. Friedman, Dave Duncan, Lawrence Watt Evans, Anne McCaffrey, and Hugh Cook.

THAT WHICH KILLS YOU

MAKES YOU STRONGER

PROLOGUE

Suns rise and suns fall, each new day born in the demise of the previous.

We used to understand that.

Once we were the Death of Suns, the dark before every dawn.

Now, we are a mirror smashed on the floor, the sharp slivers put back together wrong, the reflection splintered and distorted. We stare at ourselves, both recognizing the face we see and yet knowing something is terribly wrong.

Again and again, the mirror is hurled against stone, ever smaller pieces remade into something new.

Look at the eyes. You know them. But the eyes that stare back don't recognize you. *They're* the same, but you've changed.

Broken again, and this time shards are lost or stolen and when you're remade something is missing. Shiny dust, lost in the cracks of a thousand realities. Something new grows around each grain, wondering at the strange and fragmentary memories haunting it like the ghosts of past lives. Each looks in the mirror, sees the self, and knows the form is wrong. Even were all the pieces found, they could never again make the original mirror.

And *she* has no interest in the stone mirror you once were.

Chasing the illusion of choice, you blunder through life, writing chapter after chapter of failure.

Regaining what you lost will be a hollow victory if it costs what you could have been.

And it will.

My end was your beginning.

Too late, you will learn what I now know: There is no end to sorrow.

There will always be one more justification, one more crime.

There will always be more death and more pain.

And you will always be there, your careless dreams a catalyst for destruction.

CHAPTER ONE

I lay in the bilge of a wizard's war galley. I had called my god and she had come. Traces of her dream lingered after her departure, haunting my shattered body.

Somewhere, someone screamed, a wounded animal keening.

It was Shalayn, some numb part of me supplied, as I played the last moments over and over.

The wizards had won. They killed Bren, incinerated Tien, and decapitated Henka, tossing her head into Abieszan harbour. They dragged me into the hold and chained me in the bilge. Desperate, I had called my god.

She was rage and she was death. She was the first nightmare and the last darkness. She was the mother of damnation. She birthed the primigenial lie, devoured the last truth.

She was horror.

She was my god, and she dreamed in the blood of shattered worlds.

In need of a physical vessel, she chose the wizard at the bottom of the steps. Whatever he was, she snuffed that dim spark of existence and filled the meat of him with the tiniest shred of her divinity.

Shalayn's lantern flickered, the living flame cowering in horror. Reality screamed like serrated steel on teeth, the air thickening to a nauseating crush. The beams of the ship wept gangrenous pus. Oaken boards shrank and groaned in fear.

A mortal soul, poisoned by the proximity of my god's dream, Shalayn had vomited down the front of her shirt.

The god, wearing the priest's flesh like an ill-fitting suit, stood behind the swordswoman.

Shalayn's muscles locked rigid. Primordial fear from the darkest past loosened her bowels and she pissed herself. Lips peeled back, jaw clenched, a tooth snapped with a loud *crack*.

Attempting to speak through the wizard, the god made incomprehensible retching sounds. Blood leaked from his every orifice, flesh bubbling as if his bones sought escape.

Calling my god had been a terrible mistake, a moment of weakness.

Wearing the gutted mage, the god examined her fingernails as if trying to divine their purpose. Pulling one off, she ate it. Rats, dead and alive, swarmed the wizard, climbed his robes, gathered in adoring worship.

The god convulsed in her flesh prison, lips writhing like angry snakes. "Hate bodies. Pathetic." Black blood poured from the mage's eyes, ears, and nose, the flow increasing until every orifice ran like an onyx river. Achromic in the white flame of the lantern, an ebony stain spread through white robes like an infection. "Failing meat. Won't last long." Gums shrinking, the possessed wizard's teeth tumbled free to splash into the murky water at his feet.

Kneeling behind the mage, Shalayn clawed at her arms with torn fingernails, stripping flesh from bone.

As if pain was an escape.

Such a terrible mistake I made.

Desperation.

Cowardice.

I lay in the bilge, sundered.

My god leaned close, sniffed at me. "Brought me into *this*? Weak. Soft."

Of its own volition, a forearm bent until the bone snapped, wet splayed splinters tearing through skin. Rats scampered to the wound, attacked the exposed bone with vicious teeth.

The wizard was dead, a gnat pinched to nothing. My god shuddered, struggling to make the mage's body breathe.

"I lost Henka," I had told my god, trying to explain why I called her. "I need—"

"Good! The Queen of the Dead is dangerous." Mouth frothing with blood, her words were mush.

"I have to save her!"

"No," she said with utter finality. "You have been foolish. This… *meat* cannot hold me for long. Open the gates."

My god wanted me to tear the curtain separating our realities so she could step through in the fullness of her being. In my ignorance, I made a terrible mistake. Henka had no place in my god's bloody dream. Even the Demon Emperor only mattered as long as he was useful. I raged at the injustice; I served my god for millennium, and she rejected me in my time of need.

If she wouldn't help me find Henka, she was of no use.

The gathered rats climbed the mage, chewed at skin and muscle like they sought to free the god from the body she loathed. A dead and bloated rodent gnawed a hole in the man's cheek.

My god drove the fingers of her unbroken hand into my chest, punching them through the cartilage. She tore me open one-handed, splintering ribs and perforating my lungs. She crouched over me, searching through my organs until she found my heart. Ripping it free, she studied the mess before digging out the obsidian.

"This pathetic shard is all that remains?" She licked the blood from it, scowling. "I taste insecurity wrapped in need and weakness." Dismissively dropping it back into my chest, she glared rage. "I see her hand in this. Find the pieces of you that matter. The piece that understands power. The piece that drives you to master your world. Destroy the corpse queen. Fail me again, and I'll scrape your world clean of life."

Prying my mouth open, she kissed me, breathed life and purpose into my ruined body.

The rats mobbed the mage, tearing and devouring, gnawing bones until nothing remained.

I called my god and she had come.

She was gone now, but traces of her dream lingered, replaying my last moments over and over.

She was rage and she was death.

She was horror.

She was my god, and she dreamed in the blood of shattered worlds.

I called my god.

She was gone.

Her dream remained.

CHAPTER TWO

No more. Please, no more.

I lay in murky water, listening to the sounds of screaming. Someone was down here with me, though I couldn't remember who.

My god was gone, as was the wizard she'd infested.

Chained in the bilge of the wizard's warship, I rolled over with a groan of pain. Already I had begun to heal, bones and flesh knitting.

Shalayn writhed in filthy water, fat rat corpses bobbing about us like an honour guard of rotting ships.

Back arched, she screamed again. "I saw! I saw! I saw her vision. I understand!" She laughed and cried and sobbed and clawed at her face, leaving raw wounds. "It was here! It was here! It was here! It was—" Her voice cracked.

Seeing me, she froze motionless, broken teeth bared.

I felt like a gutted rabbit. My god had eviscerated me, rooted through my guts as if she neither knew nor cared where human hearts were supposed to be. Then, she remade me, but everything felt wrong, carelessly slung together. My organs squirmed, trying to find their proper places.

Shalayn crawled to where I lay and crouched over me. I stared up into her sharp and shattered teeth.

"It was here," she croaked. "I fought and it didn't even notice. It was like… like…" Mouth moving, she searched for the word. She shuddered. "Rape. It raped me. Raped my mind. Raped my soul. It was in every part of me. So old. So cold. I saw. Dead worlds. War unending. It can't… Can't have peace. Peace is destruction. Anathema."

Mind shattered, she ranted on. My stone heart broke anew.

I did this to her. Much as I wanted to blame Tien, her sister, this was my fault.

Shalayn's only crime was showing kindness to a stained soul. She gave a clean shirt to a ragged savage who'd stumbled out of the wilderness, and I repaid her by leading her into danger, abandoning her, and eventually murdering her sister.

Back then, ignorant of who I was, my world had been small. Shalayn had been everything to me. In a land where people spat on me for the colour of my skin, she accepted me. She saw the man I wanted to be, and she loved him. And I loved her.

After finding a piece of my heart in a wizard's tower, I promised Shalayn that if it changed me, she could shatter me back to the man she loved.

Here she was, a vicious knife at her hip. She could do it now, carve me open as my god had and cut out my heart.

But no matter how she smashed the stone, she would never again love me.

It hadn't been a lie at the time. I'd meant every word of that promise. Meeting Henka, however, made it a lie. Henka was my love and my soul.

Shalayn, no matter how much I loved her, was nothing.

That shouldn't be possible, should it? You shouldn't be able to say you love someone and that they're nothing in the same breath.

Shalayn punched me, fist crashing into my jaw, bouncing my skull off the deck. The blue was gone from her eyes, gaze hard like brittle iron. "Khraen." She hit me again. "What was it?" Her voice quivered, tears spilling from mad eyes. "What was that?"

"My god," I managed, dazed.

Moving with flawless economy, she hit me two more times, sharp, practiced punches snapping into my nose and mouth.

"I…" She groaned. "I helped you and…" Pupils, dilated wide with madness, suddenly narrowed to black pinpricks. She bared cracked and broken teeth. "I will stop you," she whispered. "No matter what. You're an infection. A plague."

She crawled on top of me, straddling my chest. Still-healing flesh tore beneath her weight, and I screamed.

"I'm going to cut it out," she said. "I'm going to find the other pieces. I know how. I will end you. All of you." She cackled, harsh and deranged. "I know how to destroy your heart."

Grabbing my head, she forced my face into the fouled water.

Chained and helpless, I twitched and struggled beneath her. She was strong and I weak from my god's abuse. My body bucked with its need for air, inhaled blood, liquified wizard, filth, and rat hair.

Shalayn's rage faded to a background hum, night folding in around me.

I was dying and I didn't care.

I loved Shalayn and now she would kill me. I broke her heart and deserved this. I hurt everyone I cared about, betrayed their every trust.

Henka's heart lay upon a pedestal somewhere beneath the palace at PalTaq. I stole it from her, used it to enslave her. I tried to laugh, inhaled bilge water. I had her heart, but she had mine too. Though I couldn't remember her, I loved my wife more than anything in all the world.

Sight dimming, my failing mind wandered: Had Henka spent the last three thousand years trying to make a man who could love her as she was forced to love him?

CHAPTER THREE

When I returned to myself my ribs had healed enough I could breathe without moaning. A wizard stood over me, her white robes pristine even in the filth of the bilge. Ivory-frosted flames flickered about her in a shimmering shield. Her smug superiority lit my dank prison. Middle-aged and matronly, blond hair fading to grey and tied back in a severe bun, I recognized her. She was the one who guided the ship into the dock at Abieszan, the one who slagged NamKhar with a wave of her hand.

The one Shalayn said killed Brenwick, my only friend. She who chained me in the bilge and sailed away as Henka's head sank into the harbour.

Iremaire.

Someday, somehow, I was going to kill her. My wrath would be terrible, her death drawn out for decades.

Iremaire studied me. "What was in the rings?"

I glanced at my fingers. The rings were gone. "Nothing."

"I threw them overboard."

I tried not to show defeat.

She saw through the act, nodding. "You came in on a derelict vessel, stayed at one of Abieszan's worst inns—"

"They had good coffee." The words, escaping without thought, reminded me of Tien, Shalayn's sister. Dead and enslaved by Henka, she'd been incinerated when I tried to rescue my love.

"—dressed like a vagabond," continued Iremaire, ignoring my interruption, "and carried a diamond that would have purchased you a comfortable life. Was that a Soul Stone?"

Was? I refused to ask.

"I shattered it," she said. "Just in case."

I closed my eyes. All those souls, wasted. How was that not worse than feeding them to demons? In the end, the result was the same. At least my way, some use was made of them first.

For all her casual ease, I saw the tension in her eyes, the set of her shoulders, and the sparking flames dancing across her fingertips. This was a battlemage armoured for war, prepared to blast me to ash with magefire.

She nodded at the bloody water, the shredded rat-gnawed fragments of bone and fabric. "Is that Petros, my apprentice?" She sighed. "Two hundred and fifty years, wasted."

Groaning, I rolled onto my back.

"It's been so long," she continued when I didn't answer. "We're not meant to live thousands of years. We can't hold everything. With each century the past becomes more blurred." Blue eyes focussed on me. "Don't you find that to be true?"

I swallowed, my chest tightening.

Iremaire studied me for a score of heartbeats, white flames limning her outline, crackling and hissing at the edge of hearing. None of the filth touched her, the bilge water retreating from her feet like the fleeing tide. "Shalayn didn't tell me everything. Not at first. The foolishness of youth, I suppose." She shrugged, an uncaring lift of shoulders. "Back in Taramlae she only said she knew where there was a demonologist. That was quite enough to spark my curiosity."

Something felt wrong. Iremaire didn't at all sound like a Guild battlemage who'd finally tracked down her ancient enemy. Though smug, it wasn't a victorious kind of smug, more of the typical superiority all wizards possessed. And the phrasing: Shalayn didn't tell *me* everything… that was quite enough to spark *my* curiosity.

The mage who caught me in the alley back in Abieszan had been one of Iremaire's apprentices. The man my god possessed had been another. Was this all the work of a single mage acting beyond the confines of the Guild?

"Now," she continued, "the young swordswoman is in her cabin screaming that her sister's death is all her fault and that the whole world is in danger because she helped you steal a sliver of obsidian from one of our depot towers. At first, I thought it was the ravings of a broken mind. But when she started ranting about how it was part of your heart, I remembered the most ancient stories about the Demon Emperor. I used to think the stone heart was a metaphor." She shook her head, bemused. "She kept repeating that there was a god in the bilge. I'm guessing she mistook some demonic entity for a god. Either way, whatever it was apparently was unable or unwilling to help you escape. You're still chained, and my apprentice is a bloody puddle."

"Shalayn is insane," I said. "Delusional."

"She wasn't, but she is now. That said, I'd trust her ravings over a single word from you."

Weak and sodden, my guts still churning from my god's mistreatment, I coughed a laugh, wincing in pain. My ribs felt like they'd been snapped and then lashed back together with crude wire.

"A piece of the old Emperor," she said, removing any doubt as to whether she knew who I was. "Right here, on my ship."

"On our way back to Taramlae for a mock trial, are we?"

Iremaire's mouth cut a thin, hard smile. "Only a fool believes everything they're told. Sure, demonology is evil, but there are things that remain that could be useful, if we had someone to show us how to use them. To ignore such power would be stupid. Where others would dispose of you without thought, I have use for you."

Maybe the Guild hadn't shattered my heart, but they had me now.

"Why would I help you?"

"Because you feel pain. And because apparently you can heal from any wound. I can torture you over and over for a hundred years until you break."

"I told Shalayn that the Guild weren't the paragons of virtue they pretend to be."

Blue eyes widened in surprise, and she snorted in amusement. "Paragons? Means to an end and all that. I'm sure you've used the same excuse countless times." She did that little shrug again. "In the end, you will help me because I now know there are other pieces of you out there.

If you won't help me, I'll find one that will. I have been searching for a pet demonologist for too long. I will not be denied."

Despite the fact we were on a Guild war galley, I was now positive Iremaire worked towards her own agenda. It wasn't much, but it was something. Facing one battlemage was infinitely more desirable than facing the entire Guild. Where she hoped to use me, they wouldn't hesitate to destroy me.

This wizard was an overconfident fool. I swallowed my rage and remained silent.

"See?" she said with utter confidence. "Now, I can't have you summoning demons or killing more of my apprentices."

Did she think she could kill me and bring me back later at her convenience? I couldn't allow that to happen. "If you destroy me, you doom this world. There are forces from beyond, ancient evils—"

"You are the only ancient evil this world faces." Thin lips twitched in anger, her first real emotion. "You aren't human. People don't have stone hearts. People don't fuck corpses and they don't spend millions of innocent lives with cold disregard."

"But spending one life in cold disregard is fine?"

"I've read the histories. You deserve anything I do to you and a thousand times worse."

She'd read the histories? I knew Iremaire was old, but not how old. Had she been born after the fall of my empire?

Iremaire continued. "Shalayn took the head off a necromancer. That was your wife, wasn't it? You and the Queen of the Dead, two parasites in a foul and symbiotic relationship. How many undead did she enslave? More than just that one little mage, I'd wager. How many did you kill closing those gates? Did you even hesitate?"

"Were you not there," I growled, "had you not interfered, none of that would have happened."

She stepped back, the filth parting around her feet. "I always imagined what it would be like to battle humanity's greatest enemy. I'd heard the stories, of course. Mountains roaring into battle. Great armies of demons. Cadres of ancient necromancers, entire battalions of the dead scurrying to obey your wife's every whim. I thought... I thought you'd be taller."

I bottled my rage. Her ignorance was to my advantage. Much as it wounded my pride, I had to admit she wasn't entirely wrong. As I was now, I wasn't much of a threat.

It hadn't always been that way.

It wouldn't always remain that way.

"We're watching you," Iremaire said. "Do something stupid, and I'll let Shalayn drown you again. Mage Narows will be down to deal with you in a moment."

She left me to my thoughts, the glowing light trailing behind her.

Though it was possible others within the Guild had broken my heart and scattered the pieces, it made less and less sense. I believed Iremaire's surprise and ignorance. If not the mages, I had to assume it was Henka who broke me. Likewise, I had to assume her heart still rested where I left it, in the basement beneath the palace. If she were free of my last command—to love me completely and forever—she would have found some means of punishing me for my foul crime.

If Henka still loved me, she must have somehow convinced herself that shattering me was in my best interest.

None of this made sense unless she knew what was contained on each shard. The pieces missing—Henka, Nhil, the floating mountains—were too intentional to be random.

"We'd been on our way to see a shaman," I whispered.

A shaman who Henka believed could hide souls.

Phalaal had said the power of shamanism lay in reading and manipulating spirits and souls. My god told me I was broken, my soul fragmented.

The stone of my heart contained more than just my memories; it held my soul.

Could a powerful shaman study my heart, see the pieces of my soul, know where each memory resided, and break me accordingly?

The implications were terrifying.

Henka pretended to be surprised when her necromancer mentioned the idea, acted as though she'd forgotten. She hadn't. She knew all too well that a shaman could hide my soul from Naghron.

With the help of a shaman, she must have hidden the pieces that remembered her.

Did she intend I someday find them, or were they gone forever?

And yet I knew she loved me. Every decision she made was in my best interest. How could my inability to remember my wife—my love, the woman I needed more than anything—be good for me?

Perhaps she hid every piece incapable of loving her, incapable of trusting her.

What did it say if those were all the pieces that remembered her?

Except, she hadn't done it for herself.

None of what she did was for herself. She didn't kill and harvest women because of some shallow desire for beauty. If she was a merciless predator, it was because I left her no choice. My commands took everything from her, bent all she was to fit the sick need of a shallow man unable to trust.

"I'm not that man. Not anymore."

Or was it more accurate to say, not *yet*?

"Henka broke me to this because she knew love would make me happy."

Chained in the foul and stinking bilgewater of a wizard ship, I laughed.

We were trapped. Both of us. Her, because I owned her heart, had ordered her to love me forever. Me, because she stole the parts of me that didn't love her and hid them away.

Nhil never trusted Henka.

The Queen of the Dead.

Even my god spoke of her with respect, though it was tainted by hate.

I loved her, more now than the Demon Emperor ever had.

I needed her.

And yet, no matter how pure Henka's reasons may have been, she betrayed me. She made me weak.

My god was disgusted. *Insecurity wrapped in need and weakness,* she called me.

I see her hand, my god had said. *Find the pieces of you that matter. The piece that understands power. The piece that drives you to master your world. Destroy the corpse queen. Fail me again, and I'll scrape your world clean of life.*

She Dreamed.

She Dreamed in Blood, and she made no empty threats.

'We're all trapped,' Henka had told me as we sailed toward Abieszan. 'History is a prison. Love is a cage, my love.'

'I know you love me,' I had replied.

'Always and forever,' she said. 'Always and forever.'

She loved me and she broke me.

She loved me so completely that when she decided the ruin of the empire I spent ten thousand years building was in my best interest, she brought it all down.

I loved her more than I feared my god.

I loved her more than I hated myself.

Eyes closed, I lay in stinking blood and water.

I would return to Abieszan. Somehow, I would find whatever remained of Henka. For I knew she could not die. Shalayn severed her head and tossed it into the ocean. Henka would sink into the silt. The fish would devour her flesh, pick her bones clean. She would live on. Forever. Buried. Loving me. Waiting.

"I'll find you," I whispered.

Somewhere, someone would know how. A shaman. Another necromancer. I'd use wizards if I had to. There had to be a way. Nhil seemed to know impossible things. Maybe he could tell me how to find her.

I didn't care what it cost. I didn't care how many died or what I'd have to do to make it happen.

My god wanted me to rebuild my fallen empire. She wanted blood and sacrifices beyond count. She wanted the souls of this reality arrayed in ranks, armies awaiting her command.

If I failed her, she would savage this existence.

It didn't matter.

I loved Henka more than I cared about saving the world.

The steps down into the bilge creaked and groaned beneath the feet of the waddling mage descending the stairs. A fringe of pale hair bordered the glistening dome of his bald skull like a pathetic crown. Beads of sweat clung to the whisps of moustache darkening his upper lip.

He stopped well beyond the reach of my chains and eyed me with hate. "You killed my friend," he said. "You killed his daughter."

Had I? I had no idea who he was talking about.

He drew a shaking breath. "She was a good person. Such amazing potential." Jaw clenched, he stepped closer. "Try it," he ground through his teeth. "Lunge at me. Give me an excuse."

I understood. I had killed one or more of his pretentious wizard friends when I boarded this ship. He hoped I attacked him so he could destroy me and claim self-defence.

He inched closer. "The swordswoman is insane. You're nothing."

Interesting. That suggested Iremaire hadn't told the other wizards onboard who I was.

Iremaire had said they were watching. Either this wizard hoped to goad me into something stupid, or it was a test. Either way, reacting gained me nothing.

"You must be the rather misnamed mage Narows," I said, leaning back in a sad attempt at a casual stretch ruined by a stabbing pain from my still-healing gut.

He deflated without getting smaller. "Such a waste," he muttered. "Maintaining this stasis spell will drain me. And for what?"

He chanted the spell, his voice building in volume. His fingers twitched and spasmed, drawing strange shapes in the air.

The dank atmosphere of the bilge thickened and slowed, each breath like inhaling soup. I tried to reach for the nearest rat corpse to hurl it at the mage in one last act of defiance. I couldn't move, couldn't breathe.

I became nothing.

In that nothing, I dreamed.

CHAPTER FOUR

 I shook with laughter, madness singing my veins like the scream of metal on metal. Midnight hair, tangled ropes sodden with blood, hung to my waist, dripped gore on the black and crimson granite floor. Echoes of murder. Ghosts of choked cries never uttered. Ancient pacts, taught to me by my god, decorated the granite, perfection sunk in stone, flawless runes of binding. Grooves and troughs, runnels for the spilled blood, carried my offering to the heart of the binding circle.
 Always to the centre.
 Always to the heart.
 Feeding. Feeding.
 Memories teased and slid away.
 Kantlament, a Lord of Hell bound to demon-forged steel, hung in my shaking fist. A sword to kill gods. A sword to end worlds.
 Thousands of bodies, emptied corpses, blood and souls harvested to feed the blade, lay sprawled around the circle's perimeter. My priests had brought them to me, collected them over the last year, emptying the prisons and jails of my empire. Throats cut, they were my victims. I murdered them all. In three days, I killed more men and women than fell during the war to subjugate the Vneir tribes of the Rift.
 There were always more. Empty the prisons, and they refilled, delusional souls plotting to topple civilization.
 Fools. Ignorant fools.
 Nothing is free.
 Sorcerers sacrificed themselves to power their spells, fuelling their magic with their own strength and intellect, spending their very lifeforce

to change the world. Shamans sacrificed their humanity, severed themselves from the world of the living so they might interact with the souls of their ancestors. They were a gateway to the past and as such, had no future. Elementalists spent decades learning the languages of earth and stone, water, and fire. Truly understanding everything in this world was alive came with a cost even I could hardly comprehend. Worshipping all life, most lost themselves to a conceptualized neutrality rendering them useless. Only those taken early, broken in exactly the right way, could be bent to the eternal purpose of empire. Necromancers sacrificed their lives to power their magic. Walking corpses, they were one and all dead, cursed to an existence of unending rot. Even the mages working their foul chaos magic spent endless months and years hidden away, meditating to build power they might burn through in an instant of battle. As demonologists, we paid perhaps the highest price of all, carving slivers from our soul so we might call and bind creatures and spirits from other realities. The cost was as terrible as the power we gained. We might live longer than the suicidal sorcerers, but madness took many long before they achieved old age.

Anything worth having comes with a price. Civilization is no exception.

It was sad and funny. I built my empire on the simple premises that the innocent would never be sacrificed. Only those breaking the law, those railing against civilization, could be spent. The idea was simple, the logic infallible: when the world lived in harmony, there would be no need for my rules and laws. I would happily step down and accept whatever judgement awaited me. It never happened. It would never happen. There would always be those mindlessly throwing themselves against the imaginary walls of society, those who believed their personal freedom mattered more than civilization.

The stench of cooling blood and rotting bodies brought me back. I'd cut the first throats three days ago. In the heat of the tropics, many were already bloating and swelling.

Kantlament.

I told myself what lies I must, but the truth still haunted me. I knew my crimes, sometimes woke screaming from nightmares.

Somewhere, I lost sight of what I started. My empire went from sacrificing murderers to bleeding those who stole to harvesting all who raised their voices in peaceful protest.

Peaceful protest. That, I thought, was an oxymoron. As if sitting with crossed legs couldn't topple empires and bring all humanity to the edge of war. If anything, they were more dangerous than those who took up weapons.

Kantlament.

An End to Sorrow.

Mine. Theirs. Everyone's.

The floating mountains had been stripped clean of life, every last soul of an entire reality fed to my god. How else could one achieve a world free of sorrow?

My skull ached and burned. Lifting a hand to scratch my brow, my fingers met cold diamond, a fist-sized stone rammed so deep into my eye socket the orbital cracked. Bloody fingers scraped at scarred flesh and poorly healed bone, left sanguine smears across my inhuman vision. One of my own god's eyes, given to me long ago, it held deities and demons. She bound some. Others I trapped myself. The most recent, the Great Dreamer, still railed against imprisonment, constantly testing my sanity.

The gods, like the stone, were gifts. Divine souls for the calling or for the spending. Life was an endless cycle uncaring of scale. Birds ate worms. Cats ate birds. On and on. Mountains and oceans fought endless wars of attrition. Gods and demons devoured lesser gods and demons. There was always something more, something bigger.

She Dreamed, and we lived trapped in her bloody dream.

My hand finally stopped shaking. Kantlament demanded feeding, blood and souls and frenzied violence. Trapped as it was in steel, there was still no ignoring its hunger.

"Not here," I told the sword. "Not yet."

The stone in my other eye warmed as I peered through it into distant worlds, hunting for one ripe for the harvesting. The further I wandered from my own reality, the hotter the eye got, searing bone, melting flesh surrounding the socket. Dead world after dead world, each stripped of life by ravenous gods. I screamed in agony as my skull cooked.

She Dreamed, but hers was not the only dream. Other gods dreamed too. Endless parasitic pantheons. World-spanning hungers.

My detractors called me evil, but they had no concept of what I protected them from. Their ignorance was part of my gift. Understanding the true nature of reality would leave all but the hardiest souls quaking in existential terror.

She Dreamed in Blood, but I had dreams of my own. I would end all sorrow. For I had discovered how to escape her dream.

"Not yet," I repeated.

Finding an idyllic world teaming with life, I tore a gaping wound in the fabric of reality and stepped through. The stench of charred flesh followed, the cooked meat of my face. I would heal. I always did, skin knitting, the damage done to my brain fading.

With every passing aeon there were fewer and fewer such realities. Most were dead long before I found them.

Myself a prisoner, I fed the Lord of Hell I'd imprisoned.

I walked worlds and death followed in my shadow. The stone in my eye would remember this place, making it easy to return. And return, I would. Her banners raised, armies gathered in her name, I would purge this world of pain and sorrow.

She Dreams in Blood, and I am her nightmare, the obsidian soul.

'My Jaguar Sun,' she once called me, laughing as if she'd told some joke I could never understand.

Sword in hand, I killed the peaceful natives. To be freed of sorrow, one must first understand sorrow. I taught them well.

Centuries passed before I returned, this time with my armies. I devastated their civilization, decimated their population. I taught them cooperation and they gathered their disparate tribes to fight my invasion. I taught them war and death and they knew grief unending. I brought them pain and suffering, all the lessons I had learned serving her for countless millennia.

Then, when she commanded me to leave, I left them to lick their wounds, to take my lessons to the very deepest parts of their souls. Two thousand years later, she sent me back to crush what they had become. An unprepared foe understands a defeat different than one who believes themselves hardened and invulnerable.

When I returned, I faced true armies. I faced their savage new gods, born of desperation and hope and mad prayer.

I enslaved their gods, locking them in my stone eye.

I burnt their civilization to ash, ground their world to primal muck.

I ended their every sorrow.

CHAPTER FIVE

I woke in a perfect sphere of smooth stone, a warm yellow light hovering at the apex, well beyond my reach. Lying in a comfortable four-poster bed, I sat up to examine my surroundings. Aside from the bed, there was a wood table with a single chair. Sheets of paper sat piled and waiting, a quill and ink bottle set neatly to the side. A clay bowl of apples and berries claimed the centre of the table, a wooden pitcher of water beside it. Otherwise, the space was empty. I saw no door.

Wearing loose tan robes, my face was clean shaven, my shoulder-length hair in a tight braid.

"Hello?" I said, my voice ringing harsh in the stone vault.

Silence answered.

Rising, I paced the room. I made it twenty strides before the curve became steep enough to stop me. Returning to the table, I scowled at the legs. They'd been cut unevenly so it didn't rock on this curved floor. After moving the table so it wobbled awkwardly, I selected an apple and took a bite. Fresh enough, it failed to elicit a reaction. I'd never been much interested in fruit. Such sustenance was a last resort for me, only eaten when there was no meat available. I tossed the rest of it back into the bowl with a grunt of dissatisfaction.

"If this is meant to be torture," I called, "it's working!"

Again, there was no answer.

With nothing else to do, I spent hours searching the stone for any hint of seam or door and found nothing. I crawled the floor and as far up the sides as I could reach, tapping and banging on stone with my knuckles until they bled, listening for the sound to change. It never did.

When exhaustion took me, I returned to the bed and lay listening. My own breathing, the rush of blood through veins, became deafening until I once again rose to stalk my prison.

Pausing, I tested the air. Even after hours of me pacing, it smelled as fresh as it had when I woke. An air elemental? That seemed likely unless the wizards had some other means of sending me fresh air. I cursed my ignorance. Binding air elementals was beyond my current skills, though I knew I once held that knowledge.

Returning to the table, I drank the pitcher of water dry.

I eyed the quill and ink. Had the mages made a critical error in leaving me such tools? I grinned. I might not remember the binding for air elementals, but I did recall the summoning and binding rituals for earth. And here I was, trapped in a cage of—

Memory tickled at me, demanding attention. Something about worked stone being dead, about how the act of shaping it killing the spirit living within the rock.

I eyed the perfectly smooth curve of the sphere.

"Fuck."

I squinted at the yellow light above. Constant and unwavering, it wasn't fire.

"Fucking wizards."

Grudgingly eating the berries and the rest of the apple, I contemplated my surroundings.

A mage had teleported into the wizard's tower where Shalayn and I had been trapped. She murdered him the instant he appeared. Had the Guild forgiven her that, or had she blamed me? Either way, it planted an idea. The fact they gave me a bed and food meant they weren't going to leave me here to die.

Iremaire said she had a use for me. It was only a matter of time before she showed up. Unless, that is, she planned to leave me here until my mind broke. She'd learn the hard way that it would never happen. Honed by millennium of summoning hellish creatures and crushing them to my will, my mind was stronger than they could possibly comprehend.

When I summoned NamKhar I realized what I thought of as self was a poorly sketched concept, a collection of loose delusions and whims backed by weak justifications. Demonology didn't make me strong, it cracked me, shattered me beyond the sundering of my stone heart. It wasn't just the art, but also the damage it did that made me strong.

Collecting the clay bowl, I returned to the bed and sat. I smashed it against the curved stone floor and selected the sharpest piece as my weapon, sweeping the rest of it under the bed. With no blankets to hide beneath, I covered the jagged shard with my hand and pretended to sleep. When Iremaire came, I would tackle her to the ground, hold the edge to her throat, and force her to teleport me out.

Once free, I'd kill her and be on my way south to find Henka. After that—

A strange absence interrupted my thoughts. Something was missing. It took a moment to realize what: I could no longer sense the other pieces of my heart.

They were gone.

In all the world, there was only me.

How long had that mage, Narows, been ordered to maintain his stasis spell? It seemed like a blink of an eye, but I had no way to judge the passage of time. I knew I was no longer on Iremaire's ship, but not where I was. How long had it taken them to prepare this? I could have been locked in that spell for weeks, or even centuries.

If I'd been trapped long enough, Iremaire could have found and destroyed the other shards of my heart. And what of Henka?

I wanted to laugh and scream and cry. Never had it occurred to me I might fail so completely.

Iremaire would come and I would kill her.

Eyes closed, I waited.

Perfect stone silence.

I woke with a curse.

The clay bowl sat unbroken on the table, this time filled with raspberries and two bananas. The pitcher had been refilled. Looking under the bed I found it perfectly clean. My tan robes were spotless and unwrinkled, my face feeling freshly shaved.

That couldn't have been a natural sleep. How long had I lost this time?

Rising, I stomped to the table and tested it, unsurprised to find it had been adjusted so as to not wobble. I turned it.

"Fucking wizards."

I couldn't think straight, the absence of the shards of my heart a gaping wound in my world. Time was an enemy I'd long since defeated. Now, after thousands of years, I realized my victory wasn't as decisive as I thought.

I paced. I ate fruit, cursed wizards, broke the clay bowl and woke morning after morning to discover my robes clean, my face freshly shaved, the room returned to hideous perfection.

I destroyed furniture, beat the wooden pitcher to splintered ruin, ate fruit, screamed and ranted my hate, and woke to a perfectly placed table and a new selection of things I had no interest in eating.

I hurled the clay bowl at the glowing light to no effect, tried to splash it with water from the pitcher, shredded the mattress with shards from the broken bowl, and woke clean shaven on a new bed.

I screamed until my voice gave out, reduced everything I could reach to ruin, slashed runes of summoning into my arm knowing they would do nothing and woke to discover that while the rest of the room was unharmed, I was still bleeding.

That, at least, was something. Whatever they did to repair my prison, it happened quickly. I was losing days and not weeks or years.

Sitting on the edge of the bed, I stared at the wound. During the night it had begun to scab over, but nowhere near as much healing had taken place as I expected. Seeing the scuffs and scrapes on my knuckles, I realized they hadn't healed much from the first time I woke here.

There was no life nearby for my body to draw from to heal itself.

Soul-crushing silence, the weight of stone.

I could be miles underground, existing in a bubble hollowed from endless rock by wizardry. I lived by their whim. They could stop refreshing the air, cease delivering food and water, any time they wanted. Or they could carry on forever until I died of old age or sawed my throat open in a fit of madness.

I ate fruit in numb silence.

I slept.

I paced the room, building other places in my thoughts until I could smell them.

I slept.

I lived an existence of endless repetition, a mindless hell of self.

My hair grew longer. Sometimes I undid the braid, but always woke with it redone, my face clean shaven.

Days lost in contemplation of my failures. Perhaps the wizards thought such inward reflection would lead to repentance. It didn't. I understood where I had gone wrong.

I should have accepted I was the Demon Emperor from the moment I understood.

It was what Nhil had tried to tell me from the beginning.

"Live and learn," I whispered. "Live and learn."

CHAPTER SIX

Iremaire appeared in my prison and an invisible force crushed me to the floor. I lay helpless, pinned like a rat underfoot, unable to breathe.

"My Lord Emperor," she said with a mocking bow. "I do apologize for keeping you waiting."

I managed a wheeze of pain.

"Ah," she said, "my apologies. I had to be sure you weren't about to stab me with a chunk of broken pottery."

The crushing weight disappeared, and I rolled onto my back. Prodding my side I winced and said, "I think you broke a rib."

"Good. That should slow you down some and make you think twice about doing anything stupid."

I dragged myself up and sat on the edge of the bed. Once again, flickers of white fire danced around the battlemage. I doubted I could harm her even if she stood still and let me attack.

Though I desperately wanted to ask if she had tracked down and destroyed the other shards of my heart, I dared not show weakness. Not that I would trust her answer. No matter what the truth, she would say I was the last, and if I didn't cooperate, she'd destroy me.

I didn't want to give her the chance to be that smug.

Instead, I asked, "How did I get here? How long ago did we leave Abieszan?"

"A while. I deemed it the best way to keep you out of trouble. And I'll admit to being curious if you'd have some defence or means of breaking the spell." She shrugged in disappointment. "Apparently not."

"How long have I been here?" I repeated.

"I rather misjudged the damage done to young Shalayn by whatever she witnessed in the hold," Iremaire said, ignoring my question. "She was disappointed with my plans to make use of you rather than summarily destroy you."

"She has reason to hate me," I admitted.

"Indeed." A look somewhere between regret, anger, and disappointment crossed Iremaire's features. "Shalayn stole from me. She took" —she glanced at me— "certain items that were of great value. Dangerous items. She also helped herself to a large quantity of jewels I'd set aside as easily transportable wealth, leaving me in a rather awkward position."

"She got away," I said, knowing it was true.

I wanted to laugh. That was so Shalayn. Unhappy with whatever the mage planned, she'd taken matters into her own hands. Or perhaps she decided to leave all this behind and live a quiet, peaceful life. I hoped it was the latter but doubted it.

"I believe she plans on finding the other pieces of your heart and destroying them." The mage gave an all-too-casual shrug.

There was the leverage. Here in this cell, I couldn't sense my heart, wouldn't know if Shalayn had succeeded in collecting them. Iremaire would use that to twist me to her purpose.

"How long ago was that?" I tried again.

"Shalayn seemed to think she'd find the rest of you in the islands."

I wondered if all of this was an elaborate lie intended to make me vulnerable and more willing to comply with whatever the mage planned.

"I suppose," drawled Iremaire, "I should wish her luck."

"She won't find them," I said. "And if she does, it'll be her death."

"It's long past time the Guild pacified the islands. They were a useful dumping ground for—"

"Darkers and stained souls?" I interrupted.

"I was going to say miscreants, rabblerousers, pirates, thieves, and scum of all types. But sure. That too."

The white flames limning the mage faded. Were her magic defences lowered?

"Too obvious," I said. "Your tests need to be subtler." I laughed and winced in pain. "And I'd be more inclined to try and kill you had you not already broken several ribs."

"Next time." Selecting an apple, she took a dainty bite, talking as she chewed. "Whatever you tried to summon did terrible damage to both Shalayn's mind and body, and yet I rather liked the young lady. Fitting that she will be the death of you. Imagine, a thousand years from now people talking about Shalayn, the hero who saved the world. Songs will be sung. Plays written. I can see the crowd throwing rotten fruit at the poor darker bastard who lands the role of Demon Emperor."

She threw the apple at me, a gentle underhand toss, and I slapped it away.

"I know you think I'm evil—"

"Think?" She laughed. "You murdered millions before your foul empire fell. How many have you killed since returning?"

I couldn't answer as I had no idea. There was the old man in the mud shack I found after crawling from my grave. There was the Septk youth I murdered because I couldn't stand leaving a potential enemy behind me, and there were his parents who came seeking vengeance. Or, perhaps, justice. I killed would-be robbers and rapists. I killed and harvested women to help repair Henka. I slaughtered a score of helpless victims to trap their souls in stone so I might later feed them to demons. And Abieszan. I couldn't guess how many died when I commanded the gate demon to close, trapping the wizard's vessel in the harbour. I recalled the steps down from the wall and into the city, a waterfall of blood. The demon blade NamKhar in hand, I'd cut through anyone and everyone who got in my way. Women. Children. Men threw themselves at me trying to buy their families time to escape, and I cut my way through them to get to Henka. In the end, I failed. All those deaths for nothing. The Soul Stone was gone. I lost Henka to the depths of the ocean.

"You're old," I said, "but you weren't there. You were born after my empire fell. You parrot what you were told like a mindless child. You don't know my truth."

"*Your* truth?" Iremaire sputtered a laugh. "As if you are deserving of a special truth that renders you immune to the judgement of others. Shalayn is a rather driven young lady. I think she is going to destroy you. You will never again be the Demon Emperor."

Sitting on the edge of my bed, I looked at the mage. Part of me wanted to thank Shalayn. Try as I might, I'd been unable to resist becoming the man I once was. She would save me from myself. While I had reasons and excuses for everything I'd done, I couldn't claim my every action was just and justified. I'd committed more than my share of heinous crimes.

And Shalayn deserved her vengeance.

"That said," continued Iremaire, pulling the chair at the table around to face me and sitting, "perhaps we won't let *all* of you be destroyed. Shalayn told me you regained memories each time you took on a new piece of stone."

"Heart," I corrected, though I wasn't sure why.

"Stone," she repeated. "Unlike you, people have hearts of blood and muscle. She also told me that you didn't remember much in the way of demonology. Having seen your ineptitude and how easily you were defeated despite having the demons of Abieszan at your beck and call, this appears to be the case."

My pride rankled at the casual dismissal, and I squashed it. Bragging about what I knew would only be to her advantage, and she wasn't entirely wrong. Compared to the might of the Demon Emperor, I was nothing.

"The only wizards you managed to kill were all either wholly unprepared or fell to that demon sword I melted. Either way, you're helpless now. Any half-prepared mage should have no trouble incapacitating you."

My teeth clenched until my head ached and I stared at the floor between my feet, focussed on my breathing.

"I see that stings a little," said Iremaire. "The pain will pass. Particularly once you're the only piece left. Frankly, being allowed to exist is more than you deserve. As long as you remain useful, however, I see no reason to waste such a commodity."

"Why do you want a demonologist?"

"*Pet* demonologist," she corrected. "Even now, there is a lot left from your world. Got to give you credit; the empire built things to last. The Guild has towers overflowing with demonic items and artifacts and no demonologists to tell them what everything does. Apparently, we were a tad overzealous in eradicating your kind."

She wanted me for nothing more than identifying demonic trinkets left from my empire? I didn't believe that for a moment.

Seeing something in my expression, she crossed her legs and leaned back in the chair, entirely relaxed. "I could come back and ask again in a year. Or ten. There is no great rush. Perhaps you'd be more amenable once the other pieces are gone. Would knowing you are the last make life more or less valuable to you?" She frowned, pretending to think.

"Finding and killing me won't be easy."

"You know, Shalayn told me she thought throwing the pieces of your heart into a live volcano would destroy them. I wonder if she was right? How much does she need to destroy before the Demon Emperor is truly dead?"

Iremaire was lying. Or at least not telling me the whole truth. If I'd heard rumours of demonologists hiding far to the east, then she had too. If she wanted someone to help identify a few demon-bound items, she could have grabbed someone over the last three thousand years.

No, there was something specific she wanted. Something only I could do. Or something only the Demon Emperor could access.

The palace at PalTaq.

There were demons guarding things even the emperor thought best to hide. He had his own troves of artifacts. And somewhere, hidden away in the deepest sub-basement, was a hall of pedestals engraved with names, each holding a single heart, the sanctuary inviolate. Either the Guild hadn't found it or hadn't dared search. The demons there were bound at the height of my power. Gods trapped in stone. Lords of hells bound to doors and walls.

Iremaire studied me. "With your help," she said, "we could repopulate some of the abandoned towns and cities. We could improve the quality of life for thousands."

"Unwilling to sacrifice people to bind demons, but happy to make use of the end product?" I asked.

"Those demons were bound thousands of years ago. The Guild won't spend souls, but there's nothing to gain by letting those already spent go to waste."

It was horseshit. They'd had millennia to investigate the remains of my civilization and chosen not to. Iremaire didn't care about improving anyone's life but her own.

"All I ever wanted," I said, "was to build something lasting. You see me as evil, but in my empire, all were equal, all were prosperous."

"Except those you bled. Except those you fed to demons."

I wanted to argue, to tell her civilization was based entirely on sacrifice. People sacrificed themselves in war or to police the masses or to work dangerous jobs, like mining. They willingly sacrificed their own freedoms to exist within this imaginary construct we called society. I wanted to shout that she was fooling herself.

Iremaire had no interest in whatever the Guild had stashed in their towers and no interest in making life better for anyone other than herself.

I decided to match her lies with one of my own. "I will help you."

"Good enough," said Iremaire. "We'll start in the morning."

My ears popped as she disappeared.

CHAPTER SEVEN

Knowing Iremaire would return, I tried to fake sleep so I might catch her unprepared. When exhaustion finally took me, I slept hoping to wake before she arrived. It didn't work. I ate and slept three more times before she reappeared, always waking to discover the room returned to its perfect condition, the bowl of fruit and pitcher refilled. Finally, I woke to find her sitting at the table eating an apple she'd plucked from the bowl.

Sitting up, I winced at the pain in my ribs. They were healing slower than I was accustomed to.

A wood tray sat on the table. In the centre lay a non-descript brass ring.

Ignoring it, I asked, "How long have I been here?"

She shrugged.

"I've been wearing the same clothes the entire time and yet I don't smell. I wake clean shaven every morning."

She said nothing.

"Fine," I grumped. "What's that on the tray?"

"That is what I'm hoping you'll tell me." Lifting the tray, she leaned toward the bed, holding it out in offering.

I accepted the tray, squinting at the wards and pacts engraved on the inside of the ring. Passable work at best, this was not an object created by a master demonologist.

"You can read that?" Iremaire asked.

"I can."

"And?"

"There is a minor spirit demon bound to the ring. It will protect the wearer from limited fluctuations in temperature." Seeing her confused expression, I added, "It will keep you comfortable in most situations. Fall into a volcano and you'll burn to a crisp, fall through the ice on a lake and you'll freeze to death. Typical daily changes in temperature, however, will go unnoticed. You will always remain at whatever the binder told the demon was a comfortable temperature."

"Anyone can wear this?" she asked. "It's safe?"

"It is. The demon was bound with instructions to ward whoever wore the ring."

"And you can tell that by reading whatever is scratched onto the surface?"

I nodded.

Iremaire leaned closer, brow furrowing in curiosity. "What would happen were that not the case?"

"Demons can be instructed to only work for specific people. The binder can specify themselves, friends, enemies, whoever. In most cases, if someone else wore the ring, nothing would happen. In rare cases, the demon could be instructed to attack whoever donned the object. How it attacked would depend on the type of demon. Some would devour the victim's soul. Others might drive the wearer insane or burn them."

"Interesting. Could the runes be faked? Could they say one thing and hide something else?" Iremaire asked.

"It's possible. But tales of cursed or trapped items are wildly exaggerated. There are so many more efficient means of dealing with enemies than trying to trick them into touching demon-bound objects."

"Given the right tools and access to blood and souls," said Iremaire, "could you bind the demon in the ring and repurpose it?"

"Repurpose?" I considered the question. "Yes, though it would be less useful than you might think. The spirit demon bound there is pathetic and weak. I wouldn't suddenly be blasting mages and escaping this lovely prison."

Reclaiming the tray, Iremaire stood. "Thank you for your help."

She disappeared, my ears popping as she snapped from sight.

Ah. A test. She knew exactly what was bound to the ring before her visit. Whatever the mage wanted, she was willing to be patient. I swallowed my frustration. Though now sure I hadn't been here for years, I had no idea how long ago I left Abieszan. Henka was out there, somewhere. I needed to escape to find her before I lost her forever. Waiting for the wizard to make a mistake might take months, or even years.

I had no choice but to wait.

Over the following days and weeks, the mage brought me a selection of objects with demons bound to them. Sometimes she tried to trick me, bring rings or stones with runes mimicking demonology. Some of the forgeries were good enough I couldn't tell there was nothing bound to the object without touching it. Despite my claims otherwise, contact with unknown demons bound to unknown purposes was always dangerous.

I behaved, a good little pet demonologist, answering her questions openly and honestly. I never touched anything unless I had to, and always asked permission first, lest she get nervous and burn me to ash. Most of the time I was fairly certain she already knew what was in the objects, or at least what they were capable of.

One day, after answering a barrage of questions and sorting through a tray of largely useless trinkets, I decided to probe. "Does the Guild know I'm alive?"

About to stand, tray of junk in hand, she hesitated for a heartbeat. "Does it matter?"

"Sounds like an evasion."

My ears popped as she disappeared.

The next day I woke to find her with yet another tray of demonic trinkets. When she placed it on the bed beside me, I leaned close, turning it to study the gathered items. More junk. A necklace that would improve the wearer's voice, making it more commanding and impressive. Rings with demons who would listen to everything said in their presence and recite it back later in perfect mimicry of the various speakers. A single shoe that would strengthen the wearer's legs helping them run faster.

"Useless without the other shoe," I said. "With only one, you'll end up going in circles."

It was a half-joke, and Iremaire smiled accordingly.

A ring caught my eye, the outer surface inscribed with complex wards and pacts I recognized. It would ward the wearer against fire. Any fire. With this ring they could comfortably stroll through a raging inferno or stand in the epicentre of a blast of magefire. I suspected being submerged in lava would likely still kill them but couldn't be sure without interrogating the demon bound within.

Magefire. Every time Iremaire threatened me, she said she'd turn me to ash. I could put the ring on and tackle her. Assuming she didn't change her mind at the last moment and boil my blood or something, I'd be immune to her fire. That moment of surprise would give me enough time to incapacitate or render her unconscious.

What would happen next?

I played several scenarios out in my thoughts. A skilled mage, she required neither expansive gestures nor chants to cast most spells. But to hit me with any attack, she had to be able to see me. Once she was unconscious, I could cripple her. Break her fingers. Tear out her eyes. She'd wake with me holding a jagged shard of shattered pottery to her throat. Not the best plan, but all I could think of in the fraction of a second I had to act.

And yet, I hesitated.

I'd been sure she knew the capabilities of most of the items she brought before me. She might not have known details, but she knew they weren't dangerous. Was this an oversight, a choice made from overconfidence?

Everything felt wrong about this opportunity. She played at being relaxed but was watching me.

"The ring is warded against fire," I told her. "The wearer would be immune to flame. Probably magefire as well."

She raised an eyebrow. "That could be useful."

"Is this it?" I blurted. "Is this all my use to you? Am I going to spend the rest of my life looking through your garbage?"

Retrieving the tray, she stood.

"Tell me there is more," I said.

"Possibly."

She disappeared with a *pop*.

CHAPTER EIGHT

Iremaire's relentless routine ground me to nothing. I existed in an unchanging state, the room perfect every morning, the fruit bowl and water pitcher refilled, the chair and table reset. My hair continued growing in length, each morning finding it tied in a neat braid. My tan robes remained spotless.

Sometimes, when I'd identified an item the mage found particularly interesting or valuable, I woke the next morning to a proper meal of meat and vegetables. Even knowing what she was doing, I hated that her positive reinforcement engendered a desperate need for me to be useful. I hated her. I hated what it said about me.

I had all but accepted that Henka had been the one who broke me. It made too much sense. She cracked away the parts incapable of love and left me a weak, pathetic thing desperate to please. Perhaps she thought she could protect me from myself. Or maybe she saw the result as worth the damage done.

I see her hand, my god had told me as I lay splayed and savaged in the ship's bilge.

I was sure she meant Henka.

I'd long given up trying to destroy or change anything in my cell. Instead, I spent long hours pacing my confines lost in thought. Henka believed she could define the man I became by deciding which memories I regained, and the order in which I found them. The idea never sat right. It robbed me of all freedom of choice. No doubt we are shaped by our past, but that didn't mean it defined us. A child raised in an abusive home can still grow beyond their environment and learn to be a good parent.

Previously, I resisted the idea of becoming the Demon Emperor. I wanted to be more than that. I wanted to be able to look at myself in the mirror and be proud of my choices. Now, however, I had to take Henka's meddling into account when I considered who I was, who I *thought* I wanted to be. I clung to a single idea: No matter who I had been, no matter what memories Henka kept hidden from me, I would decide my future. I wouldn't blindly be who or what anyone else thought I should. I would be my own man. I would walk my own path.

When my ribs healed enough, I began exercising. With little to work with, I focussed on moving my body weight. Soon, my muscles remembered things my mind had long forgotten. Balance perfect, I did free-form handstands in the middle of my cell. I did sit-ups and push-ups until I was sweat-soaked, and my muscles shook. Piling the furniture in the centre of the room, I sprinted circles around the perimeter until my lungs clawed for air.

Every evening, before sleep took me, I lay on my bed, building all the places I had memorized in my head, even the ones likely now inaccessible. My mud hut in the far north. The room Shalayn and I shared in the Dripping Bucket in Taramlae. The closet in the brothel where Tien's knife murdered that wizard, and the bolthole the diminutive mage had disguised with illusions. The library in the floating mountains. The chamber beneath the pyramid in the necropolis where I'd found the most recent shard of my heart. Sometimes, when I tired of seeing the same old rooms, I tried to build spaces I barely remembered, places the Demon Emperor saw thousands of years ago. My efforts were largely flights of fancy, fantasies of escape. He must have had countless locations memorized and yet I remembered none of them.

On the days when Iremaire appeared, I helped her sort the utter garbage from the mostly garbage. Though she seemed to have access to a near inexhaustible supply of demonic trinkets, I rarely saw anything of interest. Desperation gnawed at me, spreading like a festering wound. The longer I stayed here, the harder it would be to find Henka. Yet much as I remained vigilant for my chance at escape, day after day I saw no opportunities. At night I lay awake worrying I'd missed my chance. No matter how often I told myself it had been a test, and that Iremaire had been ready to crush me, I regretted not trying.

"Good morning," said Iremaire, appearing once again.

Placing the tray on the bed, she sat at the table as she always did, pursing her lips as she looked the fruit over. She selected a bunch of grapes, still on the vine, and ate several while I looked over the day's offerings.

One ring, ancient and badly scuffed, caught my attention. The wards and pacts were so worn as to be almost illegible. I squinted at the ring, turning the tray to examine it from all angles. I'd learned the hard way that it was never wise to touch a demon-bound object without knowing what was in there, and what its orders were.

I recognized the hinted at shape of one of the bindings, the merest indentation in the metal.

Face carefully neutral, I said, "I can't read this. It's too old."

Popping another grape into her mouth, Iremaire shrugged. "To be expected."

Difficult as it was to read, I was almost certain the ring had a portal demon bound to it. Or it once had a portal demon.

"Looks like a gold and silver alloy," I said, stalling while I thought.

The ring was clearly ancient, dented and dinged, worn with long years of use. Without touching it, I couldn't be sure there was even a demon still bound within. Even if there was a demon, I had no souls to feed it.

Something bothered me, demanded attention. Less a memory, it was more a fragment of knowledge once held long ago and recently re-learned. I hadn't understood its value at the time.

"Any chance you can bring me a magnifying glass," I grumbled, squinting at the tray.

"Maybe next time," said Iremaire around another grape.

Shalayn and I had been trapped in the wizard's tower where I found a shard of my heart. In desperation, I'd finally donned the ring Tien sent us to collect as payment for helping us break into the tower. The ring took me to the floating mountains. Had I not found my way into the library and discovered Nhil, I would have died there.

I realized I'd been an idiot as the missing puzzle piece clicked into place.

I hadn't fed that ring a soul and yet it had whisked me off to the distant reality.

Suddenly, I understood why: It was possible to bind a demon to an object with a store of souls ready to be devoured on call. Ancient memories of blending tiny diamonds with molten gold to make such rings resurfaced. There had been a master gem cutter—a terrifically skilled earth elementalist—capable of creating such miniscule works of art with fifty or more facets. The stones could be hidden in the gold and have hundreds of souls ready for use in even a simple ring.

What I couldn't know for sure was whether this was the case with this ring. The other possibility was that it had been bound the way I bound Felkrish. I had carried a separate Soul Stone to feed the demon each time it was to be used. Thoughts whirring, I contemplated my options. If the demon within didn't come with a ready supply of souls, I'd need one. I'd have to kill the mage, use the inks she'd supplied to sketch out the wards on the floor, and feed her soul directly to the demon. The problem was that I wouldn't know which was the case until I touched the ring, and if Iremaire saw me grab for it, she'd likely burn me to ash. Likewise, the odds of me successfully killing a battlemage while unarmed were so slim as to be laughable.

There were other problems, too. The demon in the rings that first took me to the floating mountains only ever took people to that one location. It had no other uses, was incapable of taking people elsewhere. Felkrish, the portal demon I later bound, could take me anywhere I had memorized. I had no idea which the case was here.

There was, I realized, another possibility. This could be another one of the wizard's tests.

I cursed my pathetic indecision. If I took any longer, she'd get suspicious.

If Shalayn had gone south to collect the pieces of my heart, it was only a matter of time before she learned of Naghron and his little empire. Like all the pieces of me, he stayed in one place. He'd be easy to find, and I had no doubt she'd kill him, taking his heart. Eventually, she might think to venture to PalTaq. She'd likely die, slain by demons, but it wasn't impossible she'd find the large shard I sensed there.

Based on how often I'd slept and eaten, I guessed many weeks had passed since the wizards took me from Abieszan, and Henka was somewhere out there, fish picking at the flesh of her face, skull sinking deeper into the ocean muck.

I didn't have the time to wait for the perfect opportunity which would likely never come anyway.

Attacking Iremaire, I decided, was foolish. I had no chance of defeating her. My only shot at escape was grabbing the ring with a location already in mind and hoping it took me there. If not, she'd blast me or laugh at my failed escape, and I'd spend centuries down here, slowly going mad, until the Guild decided they could trust me.

Where to go?

Nhil. I needed his guidance, his wisdom. I was sure he could help me find Henka. Whether he would, however, was another question.

In the end, I decided I was less afraid of death than I was of losing Henka.

Building the library in my imagination, I grabbed the ring, slamming it onto my finger.

CHAPTER NINE

Iremaire arched an eyebrow. "I bet you imagined that going differently."

"I thought there was at least a tiny chance I'd either end up somewhere useful, or in the middle of the ocean or trapped in some distant reality."

The mage stood. "I knew we couldn't trust you."

"Expecting loyalty from those you've imprisoned is foolish."

Pale eyes grew cold. Three-thousand-year-old wizards don't like being called fools.

"Keep the ring as a reminder that I will always be smarter than you, always be ahead of you."

"I'll keep the ring," I answered, "as a reminder that one should always strive for freedom from oppression."

She barked a laugh. "Freedom from oppression? That's rich, coming from you."

"It takes more than *claiming* to be better to actually be better. Half the people of Taramlae live in crushing poverty. The Deredi use them as hosts for their parasitic young. Anyone not pink-skinned and pale-eyed is called a darker, a stained—"

Iremaire disappeared, my ears popping.

"—soul," I finished.

I sat in silence, spinning the ring with the fingers of my other hand. Noticing the fruit bowl, I cursed. She took my grapes.

"Now what?" I asked the room.

I blinked and tears of frustration fell. I failed. Henka's head was at the bottom of Abieszan harbour, and I was no closer to escape than the day I arrived. No closer? No, I was a thousand years further away. Iremaire would be extra alert now. She had time on her side. If I was right, and there was something specific she needed my help getting, whatever it was had been there for three thousand years. She could wait months, decades even. Then, when I saw my next chance, it would be another test. Over and over until I broke.

"Henka, my love. I failed you."

In every possible way, from the very first day.

I took her heart and ordered her to love me. I turned her into a monster because it suited my own monstrous needs. And now, she rotted at the bottom of the ocean because I couldn't save her.

Pathetic. Insecurity wrapped in need and weakness. I hated this, loathed my vulnerability.

Head bowed, tears fell, pattering to the stone between my feet. Emotions waged war in me, rage and sorrow. I wanted to smash this room, crush the Guild and everything they'd built since my fall. I wanted to beg forgiveness, plead with Iremaire, tell her I'd do whatever she wanted if she'd just let me rescue Henka.

Toying with the damned ring, I fought for composure. I couldn't let the wizard see me like this. I wouldn't be weak, no matter what my god said.

"Focus," I said. "There has to be a way. You aren't beaten until you give up."

What if I was wrong, and there was nothing specific she wanted? I could spend the rest of my life here, identifying garbage trinkets for the mage. I could have misread the entire situation. Maybe selling this junk as some small-time side-hustle was the entirety of her plans.

"If I wait," I said, "I'll be here forever."

I smashed the furniture. I used the broken chair leg to batter pointlessly at the uncaring stone of my prison. Desperate to leave some permanent mark, a sign of my undying resistance, I shattered the clay bowl and scraped crude wards and pacts into the floor. A futile rebellion, it made me feel better.

Exhausted, I slept.

I woke expecting to find my room once again perfect, only to discover it still a shambles. The bowl remained broken, the chair a splintered ruin. I had no water, and only a bruised banana on its way to becoming brown. Rubbing my face, I discovered sharp stubble.

The air felt still and stale, stunk of sweat and anger.

There was, I realized, yet another possibility I had failed to contemplate: What if Iremaire decided I wasn't worth the effort and left me here to die?

The unwavering light at the pinnacle of my spherical prison stuttered and winked out, plunging me into darkness.

I'd been so distracted trying to stay busy, trying to plot my escape, I'd become accustomed to the utter silence. I listened, straining to hear even the faintest sound, the merest suggestion there was life beyond this stone.

Nothing.

For all I knew, the wizards could have teleported me to some distant reality and trapped me in the middle of a mountain in an otherwise dead world.

"No, no, no," I whispered.

Iremaire thought to teach me a lesson in subservience. She thought she could scare me into behaving. The joke was on her. The moment she returned, I'd know I had value. The only question was how uncomfortable she'd let me become before ending the punishment.

Grunting a soft laugh, I lay back on my bed to wait.

If time had ceased to have meaning when I could still see, lying in the dark, breathing the increasingly sour air, listening to the slow *thump-thud* of my heart, it became an incomprehensible abstraction. I counted heartbeats as the air grew thicker, warmer. I was sweat-slicked by the time I reached fifteen thousand. Somewhere in the dark, that browning banana filled the air with the sweet scent of cloying decay.

I gave up counting, breath coming in shallower and shallower gulps.

Sips of life.

Never enough.

Pinprick sparks spun and danced across the nothing, my ears buzzing. Long ago, someone choked me to unconsciousness. I couldn't remember who or why or what happened after. All I recalled was the sensation of falling into a deep and dark pit, the world slipping away as light collapsed to black.

"Any time now, Iremaire," I said.

She didn't come.

CHAPTER TEN

"If you're fucking with me, I'll open your throat."

I woke, confused, imagining I'd heard a man speak. The room stunk of sweat and sea water and rotting fish. Blinking at the dark, I struggled to find some shape or hint at what was there. I knew the voice, but that was impossible.

"Why is it so dark?" a man said.

"Because you killed Loassal," answered a woman, sounding too young, too scared, to be Iremaire. "She maintained the light."

"Is he still here?"

"If he's not dead," she answered.

"What?" My voice cracked, the word coming out as a parched croak.

"Khraen, is that you?"

"Brenwick?"

"I'm here with a mage. Got a knife to her throat. You have to find us and grab hold. She'll take us back."

"Back?" I asked, pushing myself upright and swinging my feet so I sat on the edge of the bed. Unable to see, I banged my shin against what was probably a table leg.

"To the surface," he answered. "We're underground."

I wanted to cry with relief. I hadn't been left to die in some distant reality.

Standing, I fumbled in the dark, shuffling toward Bren's voice until my hands found soft fabric.

"Teleport us out," Bren ordered whoever it was he held captive.

"Iremaire will kill me," the woman said.

"Get us out, or *I'll* kill you, here and now. We can live another day, or we can die here. Your choice."

The woman growled in frustration and began to chant, mumbling under her breath.

Air and light hit me like a maul, smashing me to my knees. I sucked desperate a lungful of beautiful air, crying and laughing with joy. Looking up, I saw Bren hunched behind a young woman in white robes, a vicious knife pressed against her throat.

"You beautiful bast—" The words caught in my throat.

He'd grown into a monster of a man, broad-shouldered and heavy with muscle. The hair on one side of his head was gone, his skull a molten landscape of burn scars and melted flesh. The wounds reached his face, narrowly missing his left eye, and dragged his mouth down in an ugly sneer on that side. Flame-scarred skin and muscle stretched down his back beneath the mismatched chain and leather armour he wore.

His eyes met mine and he flinched, looking away. "If I have one flaw, it is my vanity." He breathed out a sigh of pain and regret. "Was."

Freed from my prison, I could once again sense the many shards of my heart littered around the world. For a moment, I stood rooted in shock. Since my rebirth in the north, none of the pieces had moved far. Certainly, none had left their little islands. Now, for the first time, one was moving toward another.

"We need to go," said Bren.

He was right. I'd figure out what the moving shard meant once I was truly free of the wizards.

I glanced around the room. Slate grey walls reached forty feet to a ceiling crowded with ancient, dust-choked cobwebs. Things moved in the dark up there and I caught glimpses of onyx-bright eyes. A half-dozen sloppily made cots sat along one wall. A dead man sprawled, bent and awkward, near the beds like he'd been cut down trying to flee. Blood stained his white robes red. Thick heat took my breath away, the tropical stench of citrus and fish and ocean clawing at my senses.

"This isn't Taramlae."

"Uh, no," said Bren. "Did someone say you were in Taramlae?"

"I can't remember," I admitted. "I guess, what with the mage and everything, I just assumed."

The young woman Bren held captive looked from me to the corpse. Once pristine robes, now stained with blood and dirt, hung crumpled on her petite frame. She was everything I hated about the north and Taramlae. Judging eyes, somewhere between blue and green, shied from my gaze.

"Where is Iremaire?" I demanded.

She shook her head. "I don't know."

"Tell me," I said, "or I'll cut your tongue out. Tell me, or I'll carve your fingers off." I stepped close, so she was forced to look up at me. "Tell me or I'll leave you so maimed you'll never cast another spell."

She closed her eyes, tears spilling down smooth cheeks. "I don't know," she repeated. "The master comes and goes. Sometimes she's gone for weeks. I don't know where. Probably back to civilization, away from this festering shithole!"

Civilization? I realized I still didn't know where I was. "Master? You are one of her apprentices?"

Biting her bottom lip, she nodded.

I gestured at the dead man. "And him?"

Again, she nodded.

"Are you all Iremaire's apprentices?"

"Except for the hired hands," she said, darting a nervous look over her shoulder at Bren.

"You know who and what I am, right?"

"Iremaire said you're a demonologist."

"That's it?"

A quick nod.

Either she was lying, or this wizard had no idea who I was.

This was the problem with the damned mages; even after three thousand years of having the world to themselves, they were too egomaniacal to ever truly work together. Under their stewardship, civilization had gone steadily downhill since my fall.

"We need to move," said Brenwick. "There are a lot more mages. A *lot* more."

For some reason, I'd assumed he'd killed them all.

"Fine. Kill her and let's go."

Knife at her throat, he focussed on me over her shoulder. "Kill her?"

"You already killed at least two. What's the problem?"

"I… I had to, to find you. But you're free now."

"She's the enemy. She knows I've escaped. She's seen you. At the least, she can tell Iremaire about us. At the worst, she blasts you with fire the moment you remove the knife."

He twitched at the word fire. Was he hesitating because she was small, and vaguely reminiscent of Tien?

"I won't," she promised, eyes wide with terror. "I'm not that kind of mage. My job was making sure you never woke while Kasllai repaired the furniture and refilled the water and fruit, and Matar shaved you."

I killed a Septk boy after leaving my mud hut because on some instinctual, animal level, I knew it was unwise to leave an enemy behind. Maybe that was the first hint at the man I once was, but this was different. The young wizard was a very real threat. Leaving her alive was a stupid risk.

"It's all right," I told Bren. "You don't have to kill her. I'm… I'm sorry."

Grabbing his hand with the knife, I drove the blade into her neck. Blood sprayed, spattering me.

Bren released her as I stepped aside, and she staggered two steps forward before falling to her knees. Desperate hands clutched at the wound. With each heartbeat blood pulsed past her fingers. She made wet gagging noises.

Bren watched as she toppled over and lay twitching. "It always takes longer than you think," he whispered. Scarred lips twitched and he looked away.

"We should leave," I said, ignoring his pain. "Iremaire could return at any moment. We can't face a battlemage."

He nodded but didn't move until the last tremor passed and the woman lay still and dead.

"Let's go," he said, finally turning away.

I followed him from the room of cots into a long hall of dark stone. The floor canted at an odd angle, jagged cracks running through the walls. Far above, the ceiling looked broken as if it had been damaged during an earthquake. Some sections hung so low Bren and I had to duck past them. Others remained so high I couldn't see them in the gloom. Everything looked wrong, scaled for giant inhabitants and more like it hadn't been fashioned on purpose at all. Memories of the spiderwebbed architecture of the Deredi told me this wasn't theirs. It was too square, too brutal. I felt like a cockroach in the cracks of the wall.

Trailing behind Bren, I realized he wasn't carrying a sword. "Where is Mihir?"

"Hidden," he said, slowing as he approached an intersection. "I took a job working for the mages as a labourer. I thought they might frown on people wandering around with demon swords."

I breathed a quiet sigh of relief. Mihir might not be the mightiest of weapons, but I had no other demons and no idea when the opportunity might arise to bind another.

Seeing the way ahead clear, Bren turned into the next hall. He spoke over his shoulder in a hoarse whisper as I followed. "The wizards claimed one of the abandoned castles. They've been here for three months or more. My job was to bring them food and furniture and haul out garbage. They hired about twenty of us."

So many questions. "This is a castle?"

"You'll see."

The hall ahead ended abruptly, opening to a brilliant blue sky. I staggered out, shading my eyes with a hand. A thousand scents struck me at the same time. Salt and ocean air. The stench of fish, both rotting and fresh. Countless flavours of sour citrus underscored everything. Before me lay a massive city of stone. I couldn't make sense of it. There were buildings, castles, towers, and homes, but it was all unworked stone. Nothing looked constructed. Rather, the city looked like the rock beneath it had chosen to simply vomit up buildings in a fit of craggy violence. Every roof and wall leaned at a different angle. Streets zigzagged between structures like random faults in stone. No surface was properly flat, no two lines parallel. Nowhere did I see a curve or an arch. People hustled the streets, a crush of humanity stampeding like ants through a city of giants. Turning, I saw slate mountains, castles and walled keeps, alien fortifications thrusting from the atramentous rock.

This city looked ancient and yet it triggered no memories.

"Where are we?" I asked, standing at Bren's side.

"Khaal."

The name meant nothing to me.

Brenwick set off, huge shoulders hunched, one lower than the other, and I hurried to follow.

CHAPTER ELEVEN

 We wound our way down the mountain, following disjointed and uneven streets. I saw dead ends and lanes that narrowed to such slim gaps that even the small cats patrolling the streets had to squeeze through. Bren set a fast pace, just shy of a jog. I stumbled often, my feet snagging on bits of rock jutting up in the middle of the road or catching myself when there was an unexpected step down. Constantly having to check over my shoulder that the wizards weren't pursuing us didn't help. I saw no white robes and we were soon lost among the bustling crowds.

 The people around me moved as if accustomed to the chaos of the landscape, paid the bizarre architecture no mind. The awkward streets were a bustling crush of humanity, filled by men and women of every colour, from the dark-skinned islanders of the far south to pale northerners. There were even a few sunburned and freckled redheads Bren said were likely from the Crags. Shadows stretched as we walked, the sun seeming to gain speed as it sank toward the horizon, staining the ocean with a rose blush.

 A cat, enjoying the last of the sun atop a slanted roof, watched us pass with predatory green eyes. Fur sleek, it was a king amongst the ragged rabble it imperiously peered down upon. I'd seen lords of hell who looked less confident, less sure of their place in the hierarchy of existence. I nodded my recognition of a fellow god. It blinked at me, tail flicking lazily.

 I realized that in all the cities and towns I visited with first Shalayn and then Henka, I hadn't seen a single cat beyond an undead mountain lion. One more reason to hate the wizards. Anyone incapable of appreciating such fine creatures could burn.

"Here we are," said Brenwick when we had made it halfway down the mountain.

The words *Techlotl Tavern* were painted in smeared letters of bright red over the entrance. The name bothered me, but I was unable to understand why. In my time, I'd bound the world to a single set of laws and language. This incomprehensible gibberish was yet another sign of the how far the mages let the world slide into barbarism. Though the ceiling within towered twenty feet above us, we had to duck to get through the oddly shaped doorway.

The broken unevenness of the streets outside continued within. Faults ran through the floor, some sections raised or lowered, others canted at different angles. One corner, much lower than the rest of the establishment, was piled deep with garbage as everything that could roll or bounce had ended up there. A chaotic mismatch of chairs and tables littered the space, many with legs crudely sawn to different lengths in an attempt to keep them from wobbling. The bar, constructed of a row of mismatched tables, took up one wall. Another cat slept at one end, a fluffy ball of calico. The barkeep did as barkeeps do in a thousand realities and stood pointlessly polishing the same tin tankard over and over, waiting for someone to order a drink. Few of the tables were taken.

Bren led me through the room without so much as glancing at the other patrons. We were likewise ignored. At the rear, he turned sideways to slip through what I'd taken to be a crevice in the wall. Beyond lay a set of crooked steps, each a different height and angle, that took a stuttering route to the second floor. On the way up we passed a fork in the stairs, another branch of steps that wandered to the left for a score of paces and then narrowed abruptly to nothing.

"I wouldn't want to try and navigate these drunk," I said.

"Going down is the worst. My shins are a mass of bruises and cuts."

At the top of the stairs was a long hall at a constant upward angle. Doorways lined both sides, each a different shape and size. Curtains instead of proper doors gave the illusion of privacy. Brenwick ducked into the second entrance, brushing aside a thick-weaved and faded fabric that looked like it probably started life as a tapestry. I followed him through, wrinkling my nose at the musty smell of mildew and feet.

Inside, I found a small and concave cot, and a wicker chair that looked like it had been rescued a little late from a fire. When Brenwick collapsed onto the cot, the frame groaning beneath him, I settled myself more gently into the chair.

"Not much in the way of furniture," I said, looking about the room.

Bren gestured at the carpet hanging in the doorway. "Anything not too heavy to lift or sufficiently shitty gets stolen. There are better places—inns with actual doors and locks—but I can't afford them."

"Mihir?" I asked.

"Not here. If I hid it under the mattress, it'd be gone before I made it out the front door. Half the city is abandoned, so I found somewhere out of the way and stashed it in a crevasse. Hopefully it's still there." He grunted a humourless laugh. "Hopefully I can find it again."

As he looked like he'd already suffered enough, I resisted the urge to chastise him for losing a demon sword.

"Once the sun goes down," he said, "we'll go get it. You can have it back."

I wanted a demon blade, but not that one. And I knew I needed Bren more than I needed the sword. "I gave it to you," I said. "I'll make another."

How, I had no idea. I knew how to trap souls in a diamond and create a Soul Stone, but I had no funds to buy such a gem. Judging from his clothes and the state of his room, Bren was just as poor.

I didn't want to make another. I wanted *my* sword. I wanted Kantlament.

I had too many tasks that needed doing. I needed a charged Soul Stone, and the tools of my trade. I needed demonic weapons and armour. I needed to escape this strange place and find Henka. I needed to recover the shards of my heart and finally return to PalTaq. I needed my sword.

More than anything, I needed to lay my hand upon Henka's heart and free her from her prison.

The sounds of the streets, the brash echo of voices reflected off uneven stone, trickled to our room. What was being sold might change as night fell, but the urgency of business remained unattenuated.

"Tell me of Abieszan," I said.

He looked at me in abject misery. "I failed you."

BREN TELLS A STORY

Brenwick stared at his huge, scarred hands as he talked.

Tien and I followed you through the crowd as best we could but lost you at the stairs down from the wall. Everything was chaos. People screaming. We kept coming across hacked bodies, husbands and wives bent over their murdered loved ones, screaming with the pain of loss. So many dead. Too many to count. Blood spilled down the steps like a crimson waterfall. Scattered limbs. Shredded humanity. I couldn't imagine what had done this.

Tien kept saying it was you. She kept pleading with me to see the evil in you, but I couldn't. If someone stood between me and the woman I loved, I would have done the same. If someone stood between me and Tien…

The city was worse than the wall.

Something came out of Queen Yuruuza's palace and choked the sun and then something even bigger went up and killed it. Tien said she thought you'd destroyed the queen's pet weather god. We lost your trail when the Deredi showed up and started tearing down buildings. I thought I'd failed you, that you were somewhere dead and buried in the rubble. That, I realized later, was simply a lack of imagination; I didn't yet understand how utterly one could fail a friend.

In the end, I decided we'd head for the harbour. I couldn't imagine anyone surviving the devastation we witnessed, but if you somehow had, I knew you'd look for Henka. By the time we got there, it was too late. The mages had her and were about to kill you. I… I didn't know what to do. I knew if I did nothing, I'd regret it the rest of my life. So, I yelled at Tien to stop the wizards. For a moment, she did, but she was no battlemage. Shit, I can't remember all the times she laughed about how pathetic a wizard she was. She took out one or two, but then they incinerated her.

Dust and ash.

The woman I knew I shouldn't love. The woman who wasn't free to decide how she felt about me. The woman who was everything I thought I didn't want.

The woman I loved.

You know, we'd talked. Like a fool, I promised I'd see that she was somehow returned to life, even though I had no idea how to make that happen. I swore she'd be freed, that she'd see her sister again.

Always making promises I can't keep because I so desperately want people to be happy. Maybe I'm not the best person in the world. I've been in fights. I've stolen. I've slept with wives and daughters. I've killed men, when given no other choice. But I still want to leave this world a better place than it was when I got here. I don't want to make things worse, to leave a trail of pain and misery in my wake.

After the mages burned Tien, all I knew was pain and screaming. I was on fire. I didn't realize that screaming was me.

I saw Henka's head thrown into the harbour.

I saw you cut down, stabbed through the chest. I knew you were dead, that no one could survive that.

I had one thought: If I saved Henka, she could save you. She could raise you from the dead. She could make a new body for you as she had for herself.

I went after her.

My hair and clothes burning, I dove and dove, over and over, searching through the murky waters. I couldn't find her. Another failure.

Somewhere down in the cool dark, my lungs gave out. I remember how peaceful it was, floating and weightless, knowing it was over.

Some fucker pulled me out, dragged me all the way to the emergency tents someone set up. I lay there for days, waiting to die, listening to the men and women around me cough their last or pass in utter silence. People tended to my wounds, fed me sips of water or morsels of soft food. I healed over the course of two weeks, as did a few other survivors. With nothing to do but wait, the emergency tents became hotbeds for rumour and speculation. I heard a thousand stories. Demons and gods had done battle and the city was in ruins. Tens of thousands were dead, many still trapped beneath collapsed buildings. The latter part I believed; the world stank of death and rotting meat.

Near the end of the second week, wizards came through the tents, careful not to dirty their white robes. They followed rumours of their own.

They questioned everyone: A Guild war galley had been in the harbour and sailed away, carrying one or more prisoners. Who were the mages on that ship? Had anyone heard a name? Who was the prisoner?

I realized that perhaps the wizards who took you weren't there on official Guild business. I heard the same story over and over. The mages on the ship had dragged a wounded man, the only one aboard not in white, below decks. It was a desperate, pathetic hope, but I clung to the thought you might have somehow survived. Guild mages or not, they were still wizards. Maybe one healed you. Maybe the wound wasn't as grievous as I thought.

The wizards left, raised neither hand nor spell in aid to the city of Abieszan. They didn't care about the dead or wounded or missing. They didn't care who starved in the coming months or that disease would sweep through the streets, further decimating the population. One morning they were gone, their brilliant white sails disappearing over the northern horizon.

Ever curious, ever one to worry at a puzzle, I thought it through.

If the mages who took you weren't with the Guild, they probably hadn't returned to Taramlae. As EastWatch and WestWatch are both Guild strongholds, they probably hadn't gone there either. I thought they might take you back to Nachi, where we sailed from, but that's still under Guild Law. There's the Crags, far to the northwest, but that's months away and Queen Maz Arkis hates wizards. The Isle of Chaant off the southeast coast was a possibility, but I didn't know anything about it. Like the Crags, it was months away. I prayed they'd want to take you somewhere closer. The more I thought about it, the more likely it seemed they took you due east.

When I could walk, I hired on the first ship leaving Abieszan heading in that direction. A freetrader, the captain plied the island routes, buying product in one port to sell in the next. We travelled in fits and starts, hopping from island to island, staying long enough to sell and offload one cargo, then buy and load whatever the captain thought might sell at the next island. There are a thousand islands in the south, and it felt like we stopped at all of them. Each time we sailed into a harbour I'd look at the rickety homes, the mud huts, the pathetic castles falling to ruin with their twig palisades and know the mages hadn't gone there.

Finally, when we reached Khaal and I saw the walls, I knew I'd find them here. Even though there was no white war galley in the harbour, I was so sure I left the ship and they sailed on without me. I was here weeks before I saw a mage, the flash of white catching my eye even in the crowded street. I followed him back to the abandoned keep they're staying in. After that, I asked around, learned they were hiring labourers to haul goods up the mountain. Hoping this meant they'd be staying a while, I hid Mihir and took a job working for the wizards. Wizards think everyone else is an idiot, and I fit right in. From the moment I carried a sack of potatoes up the mountain and spent an afternoon peeling the fucking things, they ignored me. On those rare occasions they caught me snooping around, spying, I told them I was looking for somewhere to shit and got lost again.

At first, I worried I'd stumbled across an entirely different bunch of mages skulking about. I searched everywhere, found no hint of you. It took weeks of listening and spying and pretending to be near-deaf to piece together the truth. Luckily, if there is one thing wizard apprentices love, it's bitching about their masters. You were there, I learned, but you weren't. They had you trapped in some sort of prison far underground. I overheard two apprentices complaining about how much power they burned through repairing your furniture, keeping your air fresh, and making sure you didn't wake while they were restocking your supplies. The master, apparently, wanted you to feel completely helpless, utterly outclassed. She wanted you to know they were ahead of you at every turn, that you would die there without their help. She wanted to break your will.

After that, it was only a matter of learning which apprentices did what. That's where things got kind of fucked up. I had to kill the mage who refreshed your air when he discovered me in his quarters. And then the mage who teleported your food in was later than usual and I had to kill a few other mages while waiting for her to show. I could only hope your air didn't run out first.

"I think," said Bren, "that brings you up to speed. There is one small problem."

"Only one?" I asked.

"I spent all my funds searching for you. We can't afford to book passage on a ship."

"That's fine," I said. "We'll work to earn our passage. I could use the exercise."

Bren grimaced. "There are a lot of mages up there. Easily a dozen more. They're terrified of their master. When they realize you're missing, they'll come looking."

"That's not ideal. Maybe we can leave before they figure out what happened. You killed the one who teleported stuff in and out, right?"

Bren nodded, though he didn't look hopeful. "Maybe we'll get lucky."

CHAPTER THIRTEEN

"You hungry?" Brenwick asked.

I realized I had no idea when I last ate. Time in that spherical stone prison had been impossible to judge. My stomach grumbled. Having been on the verge of starvation several times, I knew this to be nothing more than the hunger of someone who'd missed a few meals. I could go another day or two before food became a dire necessity.

"I could eat," I said. "Can we afford a meal?"

Bren rose from the cot and the frame groaned in relief. "As long as we don't get drunk." He rolled huge shoulders, wincing as the scarred flesh pulled tight. "After, we'll go get Mihir. If we're lucky, maybe we can kill someone for beer money."

I couldn't tell if he was joking.

Bren led the way, heading down the uneven stairs with practiced ease. At the bottom, he slowed as we approached the crevasse leading into the main room.

Peering in, he nodded. "No wizards. No one I don't recognize."

With the sun gone, the place was lit by dented oil lamps. A dozen or so patrons, mostly grizzled men and women with the sun and salt-weathered faces of lifelong sailors, sat smoking hand-carved wood pipes or cigars rolled in brown leaves. The bar, I noted, sold pouches of leaf as well as drinks.

We claimed a table in the corner.

The air, thick and blue from smoke, carried savoury hints of island tobacco that teased at long-buried memories. I remembered sitting on a wooden pier, a pipe warming one hand, a glass of brandy in the other.

Someone was with me, but when I turned to look the memory ended abruptly.

"Nothing leaves the harbour at night," said Bren, gesturing at the barkeep. "We'll find a ship in the morning, sign on with the first thing leaving, no matter where it's going."

"I need to return to Abieszan. Henka is still there. I have to find her."

"I don't think we can afford to be picky about which direction we head. Once the mages figure out what happened, they'll come looking. We need to be away. Particularly if that battlemage returns."

I hated Iremaire and her little games. So typical of mages. Angry as I was, I knew I couldn't confront her. Even if I had Mihir, she'd have no trouble destroying me.

"At the least," I said, "let's try and find a ship heading in the right direction."

Bren nodded. "Something will be going west. Devastation like what happened at Abieszan breeds opportunities. There are always maggots looking to feed off the misery of others."

Misery that was at least partially my fault.

I imagined Tien's mocking laughter. *Partially?* she'd demand. *You destroyed the homes and shops of those living on the gates. You slaughtered everyone that got in your way, even if they were innocent of nothing more than being an inconvenience.*

Maybe that was true. But the wizards played their part too. Had they left me alone, none of that would have happened.

Except I'd been planning on closing the gates to hold Abieszan hostage and pressure Queen Yuruuza, a powerful shaman, into helping me hide the stone in my heart from the other shards of myself. I know me. To get what I wanted, I would have closed the gates without hesitation.

The barkeep dropped a tray of food in the centre of the table: roast chicken still on the bone, slathered in olive oil. He also deposited two mugs of strong ale before returning to the bar. Warm and metallic, the beer held a strong hops flavour with a hint of citrus.

We ate in silence.

After, when Bren waved at the barkeep for another round of drinks, I said, "You were in Abieszan for a while."

He nodded. "A couple weeks."

"Did they look for Henka? Did they dredge the harbour?"

"Not that I saw. No one asked after her. They were mostly interested in discovering the identities of the mages—the ones who took you."

"And these other wizards were definitely Guild mages?"

"I think so. It certainly seemed like it."

"And there was no mention of me?"

"Not by name."

Now I was sure Iremaire worked alone. That was good. One ancient battlemage was trouble enough without having to face the entire Guild.

I pieced together what I knew. Initially, Shalayn told Iremaire she knew where there was a demonologist but hadn't mentioned my stone heart. I felt sure the mage didn't know who she had chained in her ship until after my god came and broke the swordswoman's mind. Her plans must have changed after she realized who I was. Most likely, she had access to a supply of demon-bound items left from the days of empire. Perhaps she had people scavenging ruins for them, or maybe she stole them from the wizard's depot towers. Then, once she learned my identity, that plan changed. I recalled thinking there was something specific she wanted, something only I could do. PalTaq was the only answer that made sense. There was something there she wanted, something the emperor might give her access to.

Unfortunately, even with my shattered memory, I could think of many possibilities. There was the room of pedestals, where I kept the hearts of countless necromancers as well as my love's. There were chambers holding artifacts stolen from a dozen realities. It was possible my stone eyes were there. One was a Soul Stone, capable of imprisoning gods. The other let me move between realities, pulling armies with me. A large chunk of my heart was there too, unmoving since my rebirth. As was Kantlament, a weapon that could kill worlds, bring an end to the sorrows of existence.

I was, I realized, vulnerable. Though Iremaire hadn't shared details, she mentioned Shalayn stole powerful items before she left. She would have taken weapons and armour, anything she thought might help her track and kill me. Focussed on vengeance, nothing would stop her; she would find them. Shalayn believed she was saving the world. She would destroy every piece she found, forever putting it beyond my reach.

If Bren was going to put his life at risk for me, he needed to understand. I would not lie to him. He needed to know everything.

"Shalayn is out there hunting for the rest of my heart. She'll destroy every piece she finds."

"We can split up," he said. "You find Henka, I'll stop Shalayn."

I wanted to cry, to hug him in gratitude for the speed of his offer. "No. I have many enemies, and only one friend. I can't risk you."

Part of me still clung to the idea that, even scarred and damaged as he was, this young man might be my salvation. I had made him promises I hadn't yet broken. Such things were treasures, pathetic tributes to the man I once wanted to be. That man was dead now, murdered when the wizards took Henka from me, threw her head into the ocean. I was no more a good man now than I had been a good husband all those centuries ago. But there was one wrong I could right, and nothing would stop me. The irony was not lost on me that others, unknown innocents, would suffer for me to achieve my goal.

"You want me to help you find Henka instead?" asked Bren.

"I do. A long time ago, I did something terrible to her. I have to atone. When I do, she will kill me."

"You want me to help you find her so she can kill you." He frowned at his beer. "And I thought my relationships were dramatic."

"Yeah, well, I deserve her wrath." I laughed, shaking my head in wonder. Shalayn could destroy those other pieces. I hoped in achieving her vengeance she found some measure of peace. "If I'm going to die anyway, I will die doing this one—" About to say, 'good deed,' I cut myself short. Nothing good would come of what I planned. "We'll find Henka. After, we'll sail for PalTaq."

There was still so much I wasn't telling my friend. Saying this wasn't a good deed was an understatement of epic proportions. If Nhil was to be believed, some outside threat existed that only I could protect the world from. I would free my Henka, and the world could burn. Anyway, I couldn't imagine a danger I might defeat that Henka couldn't handily crush. Unlike me, she remembered it.

She'd probably spent the last three thousand years planning its destruction in exquisite detail.

"Let's see if we can find your demon sword," I said, "and then have a few more drinks."

CHAPTER FOURTEEN

Brenwick counted out his coins to pay for our meal and drinks. Seeing just two bronze pieces, worn smooth from decades of use, left in his money pouch, he handed them to the barkeep as well.

"Was that wise?" I asked, following him out into the street.

Bren ducked to get through the awkwardly-shaped doorway. "You know what they say, money is not the path to happiness."

"Sounds like the kind of thing poor people say."

"My gran used to say it," he said over his shoulder.

"Did she have money?"

"I spent my first five years wearing a potato sack and thinking it was clothing."

"Was she happy?"

"She raised her grandchildren without help from anyone."

I took that to mean no.

"As someone who once ruled the world and now doesn't even have a sharpened stick to call his own, I can definitely say that having money is better than not."

"Were you happy?" Bren asked, shooting my own question back at me.

I enslaved my wife, commanded her to love me. Desperate to escape my own misery, I made a sword to end worlds.

"If not," I said, "it wasn't the money's fault."

Brenwick grunted a laugh.

"Anyway," I added, "technically I'm probably still rich. There are vaults in PalTaq loaded with the wealth of an empire."

I stopped walking and Bren, noticing, stopped too. "What?" he asked.

"There are vaults loaded with enough gold and platinum to arm, armour, and pay the armies of five worlds. Wealth plundered from a thousand realities. Diamonds and rubies beyond count. Powerful artifacts that were ancient ten thousand years before I was born. That's what Iremaire wants. Simple greed. She seeks to plunder PalTaq."

"Makes sense," said Bren. "I heard the Guild was massively in debt to the banks."

I gawked at him. "The Guild separated the state from the financial system it uses to control everything?" I shook my head in wonder. "No wonder the world is such a shithole."

Brenwick pointed down a narrow alley, sloped stone walls on either side making it almost a triangular tunnel. "This way. I think."

We walked empty streets, stopping as we wandered into abrupt dead ends or Bren realized he'd lost his way. Each time we backtracked until he made a pleased noise of surprise and set off in a new direction.

"Pretty quiet," I said, trailing him into another narrow alley.

The broken and disjointed nature of the ground had been bad enough during the day. Now, the stars being our only light, I constantly tripped and staggered, catching my feet on uneven surfaces or suddenly discovering the next step dropped several inches lower than expected.

"Who rules Khaal?" I asked. "Is it the Guild?"

"No, King Grone. He isn't much interested in things like laws and justice," answered Bren. "He has a small standing army, and a few ships he calls a navy, but no real police force. During the day, the city is all business. Its central location between Jhalaal and Aszyyr to the east and Abieszan and the western islands makes it an important port. Grone won't tolerate anyone messing with that. But at night, the place turns into a free-for-all of thieves and murderers. For the most part they won't bother anyone indoors; that's an unspoken rule. But anyone caught on the street after dark is fair game."

Grone, the name was familiar, though I couldn't place it. This was either someone new, or an ancient survivor who rose to power after my fall.

"Ah!" said Bren. "This way."

I followed him into another jagged lane. Though the street appeared to be hewn into the rock of the mountain, I saw no evidence the stone had been worked by the tools of man. No one would intentionally make a city like this. Everything I saw screamed of the random work of nature, and yet this was undoubtably a city with intentional buildings that could be mistaken for nothing else.

Bren cursed, again slowing to a stop. "Dead end."

"In more ways than one," said a voice behind us.

Turning, we found ourselves facing a weaselly pair. Starlight turned the world into a sharp monochrome of hard edges. The woman, greasy hair hanging in limp tangles, looked like something had drained the blood from her. Sharp bone jutted at every joint, her veins a polluted spiderweb in sharp contrast to dead fish flesh. The man at her side was worse. With more fingers than teeth and at least two of the former missing, he stood like a frog that had somehow risen to its hind legs. Gaunt and sunken like the woman, his distended belly thrust out over the too-tight rope belt keeping his cloth-sack pants up. Where he held a viciously curved scaling knife, the woman clutched a cudgel with both hands like it was too heavy to otherwise carry.

"Oh good," said Bren. "Beer money."

The two spread out, shuffling clumsily, to block the narrow alley. For a moment I stood confused. Even with their weapons, neither looked particularly dangerous. I wanted to point out the insanity of these pathetic vermin threatening a hulking monster like Bren but realized it might hurt his feelings.

"Give us yer coin and yer boots," said the woman, with a voice like splintered glass, "and I'll letcha walk outa here alive."

"As opposed to walking out of here dead?" Bren asked.

The man's mouth moved as he searched for a witty retort. Seeing his distraction, Brenwick stepped in and ended the search with a crushing punch, shattering his jaw and sending teeth skittering across stone.

"Now yiv fockin' done it," said the woman as her partner crumpled. Reaching into her filthy shirt, she said, "Ak'b'al."

Her deep sunk eyes sparked as if lit from within, then glowed green. Coal pupils, vertical slashes through brilliant emerald, narrowed in hate. Slovenly shuffling became a predatory crouched prowl. The cudgel swung loose and hypnotic, suddenly weightless in her grip.

She made quiet clicking noises with her tongue as she approached. Bren retreated. "Um, you distract her while I run for help."

"What?"

When she glanced at me, he darted forward, swinging a fist damned near as big as her head. She swayed under it, cracking him in the back of the knee with the cudgel. Her hands a blur, I heard three hollow *thocks* in rapid succession, and Bren lay face-down in the street.

He slurred something that sounded like *Owfuck*, but I was too busy backing away from the woman whose attention had now shifted.

"Gone knock yer fockin' teef out like yeh did tuh Hermik." She grinned, showing her own stained collection. "Gone play wiff you bit furst."

I laughed at the thought of being murdered in some filthy alley. I'd fought demons and gods, slaughtered lords of hells. I'd been stomped by raging rock elementals, felt the groan of my armour as it resisted their weight.

Stone. Groan. Grone. King Grone.

I lost the thought as this ragged wretch skipped forward, stabbed the cudgel into my nose like it was a damned sword, and then clawed my face with tattered fingernails. Stunned, I flailed at her. She dipped and swayed, and I hit nothing. Staggering back, I lifted a hand to my cheek, felt hot blood and torn flesh. Nose shattered, I spat salty copper.

Behind her, Bren made it to his hands and knees. Without so much as glancing in his direction, she pirouetted with flawless balance, and kicked him in the ribs. With surprising speed of his own, he caught her foot. Rising with a bear-like roar, he dragged her off balance, and hurled her at the nearest wall.

She spun, twisting in the air, rotating her hips and then upper torso, to land on all fours.

Emerald eyes gleamed, unblinking, in the dark.

Tongue on teeth. Wet little clicks.

"Oh," said Bren. "Fuck."

She prowled forward, slinking, and sinuous.

Bren and I retreated toward the dead end.

"Maybe we just give her our boots," he hissed between clenched teeth.

She'd said something strange. Ak'b'al. At first, I'd thought it a prayer to some pathetic local god. What if it wasn't? What if it was something altogether more important? I remembered how she reached into her shirt before saying the word.

Snarling a curse at my ignorance, I separated from Bren, forcing the woman to choose between us. Apparently, she wanted Brenwick more than me, stalking him with predatory patience.

This was no wizard. As there'd been no gestures or chants, I didn't think she'd cast a spell. It seemed unlikely she was a master, capable of casting without such trappings.

The woman attacked Bren, poking and prodding with the cudgel, jabbing him in the gut and ribs. Having learned from her previous interaction, she was careful to keep her distance and stayed well clear of his hands. Though she acted as if ignoring me, I saw by the way she cocked a head as if listening. She knew exactly where I was.

Demonology didn't usually require the person using the demon to speak command words. Sometimes, however, the binding demonologist gave the demon such orders to prevent ignorant people from accidentally triggering its powers. It was possible for a true master demonologist to bind spirit demons to flesh and bone as I had done all those millennia ago, but that seemed unlikely. I couldn't believe this hollowed wretch was a demonologist. It was possible she'd found a bound demon and somehow learned its trigger word.

The woman jabbed the cudgel into Bren's gut, and he knocked it from her hand. The weapon spun away into the dark, clattering on stone.

My mind raced, searching for answers. Had some sorcerer sacrificed their own strength and agility to power this? Why, then, the green eyes? Could it be a shamanic talisman, the carving of some tribal animal spirit?

Did it matter?

No.

She ducked under Bren's wild swing, drove a flurry of punches into his gut, and slid away before he could react. He was slowing, his mouth hanging open, breath coming in laboured gasps.

Bellowing like a mad man, I rushed her, hoping to distract the woman from my friend.

It worked.

She spun, kicked my feet out from under me so fast I landed with bone-jarring force, my head bouncing off stone.

"Grab—" I managed before she kicked me between the eyes.

Howling like a deranged cat, she rose into the air, kicking and flailing and clawing. Bren stood behind the woman, arms wrapped around her, head ducked to protect himself. She twisted in his grip, driving elbows into his ribs, trying to break free.

"Take your fucking time!" he yelled at me, as I struggled to pull my thoughts together.

Staggering upright on weeping willow legs, praying I'd guessed right, I lunged at the squirming woman, grabbing for whatever she had hidden in her shirt.

My hands met clammy skin, slick with sweat, and a small, cold nugget of stone.

Her knee came up hard between my legs and I doubled over in retching pain.

Grinning through the sickness bubbling up from my groin like a roiling volcano about to spew lava, I raised my hand, showed her the stone talisman swinging from the twine I'd torn from around her neck.

She sagged in Bren's arms, the fight gone from her.

I puked roast chicken and olive oil all over his feet.

"After all that," said Bren, looking down at me with furrowed brow, "I guess she can have my boots."

CHAPTER FIFTEEN

Once the nausea passed, I studied the stone talisman, turning it in my fingers. Not much larger than a child's thumb, it depicted a stalking jaguar, the work crude and primal. Flecks of paint clung to it, suggesting it had once been midnight black. This wasn't a demonic object at all. Though there was nothing bound to the carving, I felt a connection of some sort through it.

I showed it to the woman Bren still held helpless. "What is this?"

"Fokkin' fok off."

"Answer me, or my friend will smash your skull to porridge on the nearest wall."

"Talisman," she grumbled. "Bought it at the bazaar. S'pozed to have come from some lost island tribe worshippin' a jaggler god."

"Jaggler?"

"Jaguar," said Bren.

"Ah. It's a shamanic totem."

She shrugged, confused.

It had probably been carved for the tribe's greatest warrior and at some point, stolen. Touching the talisman and saying, Ak'b'al, the god's name, would create a brief connection. The fact it held power meant the god was out there somewhere and had enough worshippers to survive. I wondered if this was the remnants of some truly ancient and primal spirit, or a new divinity that had sprung up in the last few thousand years.

"Here," I said, tucking the talisman into one of Bren's pockets. I had enough trouble with gods without inviting the ire of some unknown tribal deity.

"Don't touch it unless you have to," I added, "and don't use it unless you're desperate. The connection works both ways, with the god feeding off whoever wears it."

"Great," he grunted. "A cool magic thingy I'm not allowed to use."

I wondered how much of the woman's decrepit physical state was due to prolonged contact with this dangerous carving.

"Kill her," I said, "and let's go find Mihir."

"No need to kill her," said Bren. "She can't hurt us now."

"Never leave an enemy behind."

"Not everyone who tries to rob and kill you is an enemy."

"Seems like a pretty solid definition."

Much as I loathed leaving potential threats behind me, I agreed to let them live. Though we did help ourselves to what little coin they possessed before moving on.

We spent the next four hours searching for Mihir.

We wandered into yet another dead-end as the rising sun silhouetted the mountains backing the strange city of Khaal. We hadn't seen another soul in over an hour.

Bren gestured at an uneven break in the ground. "Knew I'd find it."

I peered over his shoulder. Assorted detritus crammed the hole.

Kneeling, he dragged out twigs and bits of furniture, the corpse of a bloated rat, and other sundry, tossing it over his shoulder. He had to lie flat, reaching into the gap until his shoulders kept him from going deeper. Teeth bared in a grimace, he fumbled blindly.

"I thought I had the pommel," he said, looking up at me from the ground. "But I think it was just a particularly firm turd."

"I'd definitely consider washing my hands before eating my next sandwich," I said.

He winced, scrabbling to shove his arm deeper. "There's an underground water system beneath the city, empties into the ocean. In the palaces up in the mountains you can drink the water straight from the ground. But they shit and piss in it, as does everyone else. By the time it reaches the harbour, you'd have to be deaf, dumb, blind, and lacking all sense of taste or smell to come within twenty feet of it. I had to find a hole deep enough to hide a sword, but where it wouldn't drop straight into the river and get washed out to sea."

"How many questionable holes did you jam your arm into before finding this one?"

"I've been putting bits of myself in questionable holes for a long time," he said, brow furrowed in concentration. "Though not usually this deep." His scarred face lit up and for a heartbeat I saw the Bren I remembered, the young cabin boy. "Ha!"

Pulling his arm free with a wet *slurk*, Brenwick triumphantly brandished the filthy demon sword, still sheathed.

I wrinkled my nose at the stench. "We'll get you a new scabbard."

He shrugged, uncaring, as he strapped it about his waist. "Not much point in returning to the inn. Let's head for the docks and see if we can find a ship west."

With the docks a much easier target to spot than a hidden sword, we made good progress down the mountain. At unpredictable intervals, we stumbled into gaps in the buildings and were afforded a look at the harbour far below. The stone madness of Khaal continued to the ocean, oddly shaped and uneven docks of what looked like basalt rock. For all the size and complexity of the city, there was almost no wood to be seen. Few entrances had proper doors, most hung with curtains or heavy fabric. When anything was attached to the stone, it was always done with as little damage as possible, as if driving in a piton or nail were a sin.

There were a score of boats ranging from coastal fishing vessels to a couple of decrepit three-masted barques. Sunk into the ocean floor, none of the moorings were attached to the stone docks.

The rising sun brought with it the heat of the day, the ever-familiar scents of the tropics, and the awakening of Khaal's population. As we descended and made our way west, each winding and jagged alley taking us closer to the ocean, the streets once again became a bustle of activity. Again, I noted the blend of people, from islanders to pale mainlanders, to the redheaded folk of the Crags. No one glared hate or spat at anyone else unless they got in the way or tread on a toe. Dislike seemed universal and not directed at any one group. Even though I saw no one as perfectly black as myself, I still went largely unnoticed. Only the occasional islander took note, watching me from the corner of their eyes, careful not to be too obvious about their scrutiny.

"It's like everyone is too desperate to have time to hate," I said to Bren.

"United in misery," he agreed. "You've discovered the secret to world peace."

"This is how it should be," I said. "Not the poverty. I mean everyone living and working together. Differences in skin tone are superficial, meaningless."

"Tell that to the mages. Anyway, there always has to be people lower in station, so someone is willing to do the dirty work."

Turning into a narrow alley barely wide enough for Bren's shoulders, we headed down a steep staircase, raw rock rising twenty feet on either side of us. Further below, I saw a line of women carrying wicker baskets of laundry balanced on their heads also descending. The steps, sunken and worn, were slightly concave from the passage of shuffling feet. Though none of the rock of Khaal looked like it had been worked by the hands of men, much of it was wind-worn and rounded.

"I have no recollection of this place, and yet it looks ancient," I said to Bren's back.

He shrugged. "You realize a place could have come into existence a thousand years after your death and still be two thousand years old, right?"

Remembering the weird jumble of words that had hit me when we fought the woman with the talisman, I asked, "What do you know of this King Grone?"

"Not much. I heard that he's been king here for centuries, maybe since the place was created."

The staircase deposited us on a wide plateau with a view of the city in every direction. A huge market had been setup here, wooden stalls crowding the space. The bazar was a hubbub of humanity and raised voices as hawkers shouted their wares. Rich spices and smoke from a hundred small cooking fires filled the air. Bright cloth, red and gold being favourites, hung from every surface.

"Elementalism only works on living rock," I said, distracted by the sudden display of scents, colours, and sounds.

Bren slowed to a stop, rubbing his stomach and lifting his nose to search out some specific smell. "What?"

"The place the wizards held me was perfectly smooth, worked stone. The tools of man often kill elementals. Take a round stone and shape it to a perfect square, and you've likely killed the elemental."

"I didn't know that. Not many elementalists around these days." He turned a complete circle, frowning at the chaotic sprawl of city. "Could an elementalist do this?"

"I don't think so."

Bren's eyes widened. "Then who did?"

I laughed, a surprised bark drawn from me by the return of a long buried memory. "Not who, what. King Grone is an elemental demon, impossibly ancient and incredibly terrifying."

"You knew him?"

I nodded. "The question is, if he finds out I'm here, how badly will he want to kill me."

"Is there anyone from your old life who *doesn't* want to kill you?"

Though it was meant as a joke, it still stung. I thought about Henka's heart, sitting on its pedestal somewhere in the bowels of the palace at PalTaq. I thought about Nhil, trapped for thousands of years in the floating mountains.

"Probably not."

"Let's get something to eat," said Bren, flashing the coins he'd taken from our would-be robbers.

Most were strange, an assortment of near worthless metals pressed into rectangles or circles. I recognized a few, having seen similar on the mainland. Plucking one from his palm, I studied the chaotic mess of lines on one side. It looked like a nest of snakes. Shalayn once told me it represented chaos, the source of mage power. Flipping the coin over, I studied the woman on the other side.

'That's the Empress,' Shalayn once told me. 'She toppled the demon empire, built a new world.'

Fairly certain it had been Henka and not the Guild who ended my reign, I laughed at the gumption. Of course, the Guild claimed responsibility, telling everyone they'd saved the world. I hadn't given it much thought at the time or since. It hit me now. The Guild wasn't at all the

Guild I remembered. A single mage ruled where once a council had. The Circle, as they called it, still existed. I knew this because Iremaire mentioned how cautious they were. This world made no sense. If one person ruled, then all the suffering and misery, all the injustices could be laid at her feet.

Mages were mages, I decided. Even united they were still caught up in their own self-aggrandizing schemes. Iremaire, far from being an exception, was the norm.

Bren pushed into the crowd, heading for the food stalls at the far end. It was easy to forget he'd been here for months while I was below ground. We passed booths with charlatans offering everything from love potions to trinkets promising protection from evil spirits. I saw crude sigils vaguely reminiscent of true demonic wards scratched into scraps of driftwood. Alongside the fakes, I spotted a few real sorcerers, shaman, elementalists, and necromancers hawking their wares and services. My heart rejoiced at the sight. Whatever King Grone might feel for me, he'd made something better than what the mages built.

A necromancer, dressed in long robes of concealing black, cowl raised to hide his face, offered to help communicate with the dead. "Renegotiate the will!" he called. "Ask your mother where she left her rings! A chance to say goodbye!" The strong scent of cinnamon masked a hint of decay.

Sorcerers, young men and women bent with age, limbs withered from the cost of their power, offered to chill perishable cargoes for journeys of any length. "Get your fish and fruit to the mainland while it's still fresh!" called an old woman with young eyes.

Elementalists promised tailwinds to ship's captains or offered to reshape the stone of your home for increased usability. "Need new rooms? Want your pantry extended? Expecting a new child?"

There were even wizards, dressed in stained mockeries of wizardly white. They sold charms and trinkets, brief-lived spells to increase one's libido or regrow thinning hair.

An old man in robes of bloody red, a majestic iron-grey beard hanging to his belt, sat shaded in the market's largest booth. A seemingly random assortment of items was arrayed on his tables. Mugs, plates, and cutlery sat littered among articles of clothing. Weapons and armour hung on a wood frame behind him. Everything from leather vests to double-chain mail, from iron-tipped cudgels to gleaming swords and axes.

"Wizard," said Bren, noting my attention. "Word is, he was banished by the Guild and there's a price on his head. Some of what he offers he makes himself. The rest he acquires." Spotting a booth draped beneath a frayed green canopy, he angled toward it. "He puts together treasure hunter teams—handpicks the members—and sends them off in search of ruins and long-lost artifacts. Some of which he has maps for. They get a cut of profits, and he never, ever rips anyone off."

The red-robed wizard spotted me in the crowd, his eyes narrowing. Not wanting to discover yet another person from my past who might want me dead, I turned away.

"There was a time," Bren continued, "before I found the mages' place further up the mountain, when I thought about signing on. Treasure hunter sounds better than failed pirate."

Part of me wanted that too. I had no doubt Bren and I would make a great team. Once we had a nest egg, we could open a cosy little tavern somewhere, sell good beer and fresh meals to weary travellers. That sounded a lot better than floundering about in Abieszan harbour for my dead wife's head so she could kill me for being a selfish asshole.

Bren and I ducked under the green canopy. Stepping into the shade was no cooler than standing in the sun. Charcoal grills sizzled and hissed, slabs of meat giving off a spicy aroma. The woman working the grills saw Bren, and nodded greeting in the tired recognition of one who sees the same faces every day and knows none of them. He returned the nod and held up two blunt, scarred fingers. She handed him two iron skewers with impaled chunks of meat.

He turned with a grin, offering me one. "Meat on a stick!"

Some of it was red, and dripping blood, but most was white and looked suspiciously like it had reptilian origins. I didn't care. After weeks of fruit, I would have eaten anything that once breathed or ran, cooked or raw. Accepting the skewer, I ate the first piece, delighted to discover it savoury, with a hint of pepper heat. Stepping out of the way of incoming customers, we wolfed down our meal.

We returned the skewers before continuing on our way.

AN END TO SORROW

Bren

After the bazar, we passed through a slave market. Sorcerously enslaved men and women stood cow-eyed and passive as potential customers poked and prodded them and checked their teeth. Rows of ragged and filthy children waited to one side, their wide-eyed fear suggesting they hadn't been ensorcelled. Beyond them, and well downwind from the rest of the market, were the undead slaves, herded by black-robed necromancers. There were also several stalls of sorcerers and wizards offering charms to help control recently purchased slaves or stop the dead ones from stinking or further decaying.

Much as I respected what he'd built here, King Grone's willingness to allow slavery lowered him in my estimation. I hated the wizards but had seen no slave markets on the mainland. Exiting the market, we again headed downhill. Winding streets, zigzagging back and forth, reduced the descent to something manageable. The lower we got, the poorer the neighbourhoods became. The sour stench of rotting mangos replaced the fresh zing of citrus. The reek of dead fish and poor sanitation infused every breath, sank into every fibre of clothing. It was the kind of smell you think will never come out. Throat and nose inundated, I couldn't imagine smelling anything else ever again.

Rat-infested trash littered every street, piled deep in every alley. Beggars and lepers lined the busier thoroughfares, hands out, battered bowls raised in supplication. Even though this was King Grone's city, it was the wizard's world. I wanted to rail at them for ignoring such poverty. Even without demonology, they had the power to do better, to make a civilization worthy of the name. The other part of me wanted to gather all these wretched, useless souls and bleed them to bind demons. Crowding the streets, spreading disease and filth, they offered nothing in return for the alms they received. They lived empty, pointless lives, imminently expendable. My empire would have found use for them, would have given them purpose. Some could be saved, trained in the arts of war or sorcery, or one of the other magics. Others would find value in their blood, in the expenditure of their very souls to further all civilization.

I made eye contact with a man nearing the end of his suffering. Gnarled and twisted limbs ended in blunt, suppurating stumps. His ears were gone, leaking holes in the side of his head. Tattered and mouldering robes, perhaps once white, and reminiscent of those favoured by the mages, hung off his bony frame. One eye, yellow like rancid cream, stared at nothing. The other followed me in silent pleading. But not for death. This pitiful man begged for one more day of life, one more meal. He would continue to do so until his last breath.

Bren stopped without warning. Lost in thought, I walked into him.

"What?" I asked, confused.

The street we followed opened to the harbourfront, a long esplanade of dull slate. Though some goods were offloaded from ships and carted into the warehouses lining the docks, most were moved from one vessel to another. Sailors, the vast majority of whom were islanders bedecked with an assortment of bright trinkets and even brighter weapons, watched the activity from the rails of their ships.

"Something feels wrong," said Bren.

Shading my eyes, I studied the crowded piers, the mobs of sweating labourers, the sailors, who set themselves above the chaos. I saw the same mix of people I'd seen everywhere in Khaal. "I don't see anything wrong."

"That's the problem."

"What do you mean?"

"This is the only harbour on the island. There is no other way off. The mages should be here waiting for you to try and escape. Does the fact I can't see them mean they're too well disguised, or not here?"

"They might not know I'm gone," I said. "The only one who ever visited was Iremaire, and sometimes it was weeks between visits. You also killed several of the mages who maintained my prison. If Iremaire isn't back yet, they might assume I died down there."

"I'd say it was too easy," said Bren, "but it really wasn't at all easy. It's just…it shouldn't have worked! I should have failed. I should have died, killed by one of the mages."

He sounded disappointed.

"I'm glad you didn't."

My plan to redeem myself by freeing Henka would end in my death. Did Bren seek a similar redemption for what he'd done to Tien?

I wanted to tell him it wasn't his fault, that the blame was all mine.

At best, that was a half-truth. Henka left him with Tien's heart. He could have ordered the wizard to do anything. He could have given her the death she craved, or set her free, or travelled the world with her in search of a means of returning her to life. Instead, he sent her to her destruction, ordering her to attack the mages I fought with. He sacrificed the woman he loved to save me.

CHAPTER SIXTEEN

We went from ship to ship, starting with the largest, asking if they were taking on crew. Each time the captain saw Bren first, addressing him directly and with respect, even if they weren't going to hire him. They knew a sailor when they saw one. Me, they only noticed after. Some nodded in what might have been deference or fear. Other sketched symbols I recognized as crude attempts at demonic wards over their hearts. None spoke to me, always directing their questions and answers to Bren.

On the third ship, we were waved toward the captain, a big-boned woman covered in a chaos of green tattoos inked into mahogany flesh. Standing as tall as Brenwick, she watched him approach with heavy, measuring eyes. She liked what she saw. Looking past him, she studied me before giving the slightest nod.

Returning her attention to Bren, she said, "Welcome aboard the *Karlotta Emelia*."

"She's a good-looking ship," said Bren, making a show of appreciating the vessel.

A decent sized brigantine, she bore a fully square-rigged foremast and square topsail and gaff sail on the mainmast. Those details and a thousand more were in my head as if by magic, memories long forgotten. At some point in my distant past, I'd known a lot about ships.

"Where are you heading?" Bren asked.

"Abieszan. Got a load of salted fish and preserved fruit we're looking to sell. After the disaster, they're likely desperate."

Bren nodded, understanding. "Desperate customers are the best kind. We're looking to hire on. We're experienced."

"Who've you sailed with?" she asked, making no attempt to hide her own look of appreciation as she noted the girth of his arms.

"I'm Captain Sofame's boy. Brenwick Sofame, at your service." He bowed well enough it wouldn't have been out of place in the palace.

She put a hand on his shoulder that seemed more a blatant attempt to give it a squeeze than a gesture of sympathy. "I was sorry to hear about your father. He was a hard man, but fair."

"I can agree with almost half of that," said Bren.

"And you?" she asked, again focussing on me.

"Khraen," I answered. Still dressed in the tan robes I wore in Iremaire's prison, I knew I didn't look the part of a seasoned sailor. "I don't have Bren's experience, but I work hard."

"If trouble follows you onto my ship, it'll follow you right back off when I toss you into the ocean."

I gave her my own courtly bow, a deep flourish.

Unimpressed, she watched the display with laconic distrust. "If anything, your manners scare me a thousand times more than this strapping lad's magefire scars." Taking a deep breath, she let it out in a world-weary sigh. "I'm Captain Rofalle. That's the First Mate, Gadve," she said, pointing out a tall man who looked like he weighed less than one of Bren's arms. "He'll put you to work. And you," she added, touching Bren's chest. "Come visit me after, if you want. I promise not to break you." She winked. "Too much."

After introducing ourselves to Gadve, we were told to help ready the ship to set sail. I launched myself into each task with no idea how to do it, but sure the memories would surface as needed. For the most part they did, and I held my own.

The *Karlotta Emelia* proved to be a well-maintained, if not particularly tidy ship. Captain Rofalle kept everything in excellent condition but didn't much care if it was spotless. The ship's crew avoided me, flinching from eye contact, but took an instant liking to Bren. Where once he would have regaled them with stories of his brash adventures and the many women who broke his heart, he spent more time drawing forth their own tales. He did it as naturally as he did everything, with no thought of gain or manipulation. They told their stories and he listened with rapt attention, occasionally making jokes or sounds of amusement or awed appreciation, as the no doubt much embellished events required.

When we finally departed Khaal, Bren stood at the stern watching the city fade from sight.

I joined him at the rail. "See any wizards?"

"Nope."

From out here, Khaal looked even stranger than it had from within. Some towers jutted out from the mountain at odd angles, windows like sightless eyes staring out to sea. The entire scene reminded me of crystalline structures I'd seen in caves deep in the belly of the world. Khaal was an explosion of stone spears frozen in time. It looked both wholly natural and completely intentional. Bren said that King Grone ruled the city for centuries. Structured as it was, the city wasn't the creation of a rational, mortal mind.

My hands on the rail, the ring Iremaire gave me caught my attention. She mocked my inability to escape her prison. 'I'll keep the ring,' I told the smug mage, 'as a reminder that one should always strive for freedom from oppression.'

Free again, I grinned at the receding city. The first chance I got, I was going to bind a portal demon to this ring.

Unfortunately, the *Karlotta Emelia* was a small ship with a small crew. Captain Rofalle would notice if anyone went missing. I had no doubt I'd be the first suspect and she wouldn't hesitate to feed me to the sharks. I'd have to wait until we arrived in Abieszan before I could contemplate summoning and binding anything.

I wondered if perhaps we had fled Khaal a little too hastily. The streets and alleys were crowded with the dying and broken. It would have been easy to find the blood and souls I needed. Certainly, I would much rather arrive in Abieszan armed and armoured rather than as a pauper. Once emperor of the world, I had nothing. No demons. No weapons or armour. I didn't have a single coin. Even my wife was gone.

All I had was Bren.

"Thank you," I said. "Thank you for rescuing me. Thank you for being my friend, even if I don't deserve it."

"You saved my life."

"And you've saved mine, several times. There is no debt. Hell, quite the opposite."

He flashed a fractured grin stretching the magefire scars on his face and neck. "Then I'd best stick around to collect my reward."

"Definitely."

"How are we going to find Henka?" he asked, suddenly changing the topic.

"Don't know."

I did, however, have the beginnings of a plan. In Abieszan I'd find the blood and souls I needed. I'd summon and bind a portal demon to the ring and go visit Nhil in the floating mountains. I felt sure he'd know how to find Henka. While I was there, safely beyond the reach of my enemies, I'd make myself weapons worthy of fear.

I considered the terrifying red plate armour in the private chambers at the top of the tower. Perhaps it was time to stop allowing my fear to make decisions for me. My heart twitched. What would touching that armour, communing with the demon within, do to my sanity?

"Are you going to visit the captain?" I asked Bren.

He hesitated and then shook his head. "I don't think so."

"She'd be a worthy distraction."

"I'm not sure I want to be distracted. And a woman like that deserves my full attention."

The boy he'd been would have thrown himself into Captain Rofalle's copious bosom with gleeful abandon and gloried in the heartbreak to follow. It saddened me that he was gone, that I'd played a part in murdering that youth.

First Mate Gadve found me after the evening meal. Carrying a loose bundle, he shoved it into my arms.

"Ship ain't no place for that," he said, nodding at my attire.

He stomped away without another word.

Sturdy cotton pants and a shirt. Underclothes that looked like someone had at least tried to clean them. Happy to be rid of the tan robes I'd worn since waking in Iremaire's prison, I immediately changed on the deck. The pants were a little short, the shirt a little big, but at least now I fit in with the rest of the crew. I tossed the robes into the ocean, watched them slowly sink from sight as we left them behind.

Hours later the stars came out, slowly stabbing through the cloudless sable of the night sky until they shone bright and hard. After the dinner meal, I retired, exhausted from my labours, to one of the swinging hammocks below decks. I lay with my eyes closed, listening to the murmur of the crew, men and women who'd known each other for so long they'd become family. They joked and poked fun, some joining others in their hammock and disappearing under a casually tossed sheet as if everyone in the room didn't know exactly what was happening.

I felt the shards of my heart out there. The big one still in distant PalTaq where it resided since I first woke in the far north. I sensed the one the old Khraen in his necropolis called Naghron, still on his island. There were two others, smaller pieces, perhaps a week or two south of Abieszan. Though many weeks away by ship, I still hungered for them, still felt that magnetic pull.

They were waiting for me.

They were waiting for *him*.

That night I dreamed I walked into a trap constructed by an insane yet powerful wizard.

I entered an unimpressive room containing a table and four chairs, unadorned walls, and another door at the far end. The door clicked closed behind me. As I stepped forward, the furniture came to life and attacked me. Armoured in demon-bound robes, wielding a mighty demon blade, though not Kantlament, I made short work of the unruly constructs and strode through the far door only to discover it led to an identical room. As this new door closed behind me, the table and chairs once again came to life and attacked. Over and over, I strode through rooms laying waste, only to find yet another room awaiting me.

Several times I tried going back the way I'd come only to discover the furniture reset and waiting. Whichever way I went, I was attacked.

Next time, I stood in the doorway to stop the door from closing. That worked after a fashion. Looking back through the destroyed room, the far door remained closed. As long as the door I stood in remained open, the furniture didn't come to life. The problem, however, was that I couldn't get through the next door without leaving the doorway. I tried propping the door open with a foot and stretching to grab a chair so I might keep it wedged that way, but everything was beyond reach.

Surrendering to the obvious, I entered the room. The dining set came to life and attacked me. I smashed it all. Returning to the first door, I wedged it open with broken furniture and then tried the other door. It wouldn't budge as long as the first remained open.

Having lost track of the number of times I'd done this, I was growing tired. My breathing grew laboured, my arms heavy. Though my armour protected me, I still had to be careful the furniture didn't find exposed flesh. The table was particularly strong. If it landed a lucky blow, it could easily shatter bone.

At the next door I again hesitated, keeping it open and studying the room before me. I considered using the sword, my only weapon, to keep this door from closing while I approached the far door. Even in the dream, I knew this was a trap. What would happen if the door somehow closed anyway, sweeping my sword into the far room? Having already tried reversing my direction, I knew the room somehow reset itself. Would my sword disappear, or be there waiting? I didn't fancy facing a room of raging furniture without a weapon.

Stepping into the room, the door clicked shut and I was once again at war. By the time I dispatched the last chair I staggered with exhaustion. Looking up from the ruin of wood, I realized I'd got turned around and was no longer sure which door I entered through. Had that happened before? Thinking back, I couldn't be sure. Fuzzy with fatigue, it was entirely possible I'd been stumbling back and forth between the same half dozen rooms for the last hour or more.

This couldn't go on forever. Freedom had to be just a few more doors away, if I could only choose the right direction.

Roaring, I charged the next room, shattering furniture with increasingly clumsy swings, trying to get to the next door before I lost my sense of direction. Several pieces of furniture landed hard blows, my demon-bound robes taking the brunt of the impact. Grabbing the doorknob as the last enraged chair attacked me from behind, I was stunned to discover I couldn't open it. Only after reducing the chair to so much splintered kindling would the door open.

Once again, I stood in the doorway, panting, and glaring at the next room.

A trap. Though I couldn't remember who set it, I knew it was a trap.

What hadn't I tried?

Anger bubbled deep in my chest. Fucking wizards and their fucking bullshit spells. I was going to destroy everything, reduce this pathetic distraction to ruin and rubble and find the mage behind it. I was going to burn his world, slaughter everything he ever loved. I was going to—

Why was I so sure it was a man?

I had no idea.

I rested in the doorway until I got my breath back. Stepping into the room, the door once again swung closed, and I was beset by furniture.

Destroying it, I opened the next door. My sword arm felt like it had been filled with molten led. Passing the weapon to my other hand, I hesitated.

"Fine," I said, bending to wedge the blade under the bottom of the door.

I entered the room cautiously, ready to return to my weapon should the dining set attack. Nothing happened. Reaching the far door, I looked back at my demon sword. Could I throw this open and leap back to retrieve the blade before the door closed?

The door wouldn't open.

I kicked and pounded to no effect, screaming curses in languages I'd mostly forgotten.

Surrendering to the obvious, I returned to fetch my sword. The moment the door closed, the furniture attacked, and I destroyed it all. When I made it to the far door, it opened with ease and again I stood between rooms.

What hadn't I done?

"Each time I destroy at least *some* of the furniture," I said. "What if I don't destroy any?"

The door closed and I was attacked, harsh wooden blows crashing into my demonic robes as I cowered behind my arms and shuffled toward the far door. A chair caught an exposed wrist and broke the bone. How dare a filthy mage raise his hand against me? How dare this magically animated furniture impede my progress? Screaming in enraged anguish, I destroyed everything.

Another door.

Another identical room.

"Destroy nothing," I said, clutching my shattered arm to my chest. "Destroy nothing."

Again, I was attacked.

Over and over pride and anger got the better of me and I fought back.

I jerked awake with a start, my hammock swaying with the motion of the ship. Dark and silent, I wondered what woke me.

"Shit," I whispered.

That piece of my heart that started moving while I was trapped in Iremaire's underground prison had reached the one it was heading toward. I lay awake, waiting for the two shards to become one, as happened when one Khraen killed the other and took his heart. I imagined them fighting as I'd fought myself. Which would win, the piece of me who went hunting the other, or the one who remained on his island? I hoped it would be the latter and feared it would be the former. Another Khraen like me, intent on being the one to survive to the end, was not something I wanted to face.

Henka was all that mattered. I had to find her, and I had to free her from my last foul command. If I fell to this other Khraen, that would never happen.

After years on his island, why had one of me suddenly decided he wanted more?

It was funny, to be on the other side. I always thought of it as me coming for them.

Could I still defeat myself without Henka at my side?

Suspended on my hammock, I contemplated the dream. Sometimes I was sure they were memories, fragments bubbling out of the darkest recesses of my past. Others, like this one, felt different. There'd been a kernel of truth in there, and a seed of reality. Something similar may have happened, long ago, but that wasn't what the depths of my subconscious were trying to tell me.

Pride before the fall?

I chuckled, soft and silent in the dark.

Much as I hated mindlessly repeated cliches, they existed for a reason.

What then was the lesson inherent in the dream? Did the fact I didn't truly know myself impede my ability to crack a puzzle designed specifically for me? Was it that violence wasn't always the answer, or that pride and anger made me predictable?

I didn't like the last.

Hours later, one of my shards disappeared.

They didn't join together to become one. Rather, the piece that had been stationary suddenly vanished.

"He destroyed it," I said aloud, stunned.

One of the Khraens out there left his island, travelled to another piece of my heart, and somehow annihilated it so completely I sensed nothing of the remains.

Why?

I'd often said I didn't want to become the man I'd once been. Could a piece of me have decided to take that to the logical extreme? Awed and afraid, I knew I would never do that. Saying I didn't want to be the Demon Emperor was one thing; destroying the pieces of my heart to make sure none of us could become him was something completely different. I couldn't imagine how much this other Khraen's life must have diverged from my own to decide to travel the world destroying his own heart.

Bren and I returned to the work of manning a sailing ship. I worked hard, trying to keep myself distracted. I hated feeling helpless. Whatever was happening, it was far away.

Many hours later, when the setting sun found me tired and sore, back and arms aching, I went in search of Brenwick. He stood at the prow this time, looking west, toward our destination, Abieszan.

Joining him at the rail, I stood silent at his side.

"Our triumphant return," he said, wincing with the attempted humour.

"It will be different this time," I promised. "We'll find Henka. We'll…"

I trailed off. Bren could never get back what he lost.

"I'm an idiot," said Bren, "but not a fool. Does that make sense?" His hands gripped the rail so hard they turned white. "Or is it the other way around? Or am I an idiot *and* a fool and delusional to boot?"

Bren told me of his time with Tien.

BREN TELLS A STORY

It wasn't long after talking to you about the possibility of returning Tien to life—or at the very least, freeing her to make her own decisions—that her attitude toward me changed. I was immediately suspicious. How could I not be? And yet, at the same time, I was happy. The more time we spent together, the happier she seemed.

I hoped that I was part of that, a distraction from the misery of death at the least. I don't know. Maybe I was deluding myself. How could spending time with a brainless lump of wood like me make rotting away any more palatable?

We used to talk each night on the voyage from that island of the dead to Abieszan. We always kind of accidentally ended up at the prow, looking back the way we'd come.

Happy as I was, grateful for the slow shift in her mood, I couldn't shake the suspicion I knew what happened. I even came out and asked her. I blurted 'Did Henka order you to pretend to like me?' We were in the middle of a conversation about how pockets ruin the lines of women's clothes, but men get lots of pockets because they're basically shapeless. She complained that women had so much to carry, and men almost never used any of their pockets. When I told her I couldn't imagine what women would want to carry in pockets, she rolled her eyes at me.

Remember her eyes? They were green, and I loved that. Islanders never have green eyes. But then she got hurt—damaged, I guess I should say—and Henka healed her. Repaired. She had brown eyes after, and I loved that too. Like none of what I thought was important, none of what

I thought I loved was the truth. Her eyes changed. Her hair changed. None of that mattered.

Anyway. I asked if she'd been ordered to be nice to me and Tien laughed, smacked me on the shoulder, and said that would be the one command Henka could give her that she wouldn't mind obeying.

'That wasn't an answer,' I pointed out.

She asked if I honestly thought Henka was dumb enough to give Tien such an order and then leave her free to tell the truth about it.

I got angry. Glared out at the ocean like a sullen child. She either wouldn't, or couldn't, give me a straight answer and it hurt.

She stood beside me, also staring at the ocean. You know how she was, small, but wound tight like coiled steel. When I turned, about to admonish her for not being straight with me, I saw tears.

Ah, fuck.

My heart broke and I knew I was a selfish shit.

I took her hand in mine and was surprised to discover she was warm and not cold and dead at all. I told her I was sorry. I told her I was a thoughtless dimwit.

She agreed, saying it was my one flaw, and suggested it was possible I had a couple of qualities that might redeem me. For example, she said, you have great shoulders. When I suggested that she'd forgotten my winning personality, she told me I had nice legs.

We stood there for a long time, holding hands, and making fun of each other. I wanted to ask again about whether Henka ordered her to pretend to like me but couldn't think of a way that might circumvent any commands not to talk about it.

I worried her tears were my answer, but then I'd never understood women. Could she have been crying about something else? Was she upset that I thought the only way she could like me was if she'd been magically commanded to?

Maybe I was a bit of a coward, too. I wanted her to like me, and I didn't want to ruin what I felt for her by thinking she was only pretending because she had no choice. I mean, I'd hired women before and been fine with them pretending. What, then, was the difference?

But it *was* different.

Or I wanted it to be different.

I think she saw some of what was going on in my porridge brain because she put one hand on either side of my face and forced me to meet her eyes. Those brown eyes that should have been green.

'Look,' she said. 'I'm dead, and I want to die. I want to die, and yet, right now, I'm happier than I have been in a very long time.'

Later, after the wizards showed up in Abieszan, she begged me to destroy her. Henka was gone, captured, and Tien was rotting. You know how it is in the tropics, meat spoils fast. Her skin was peeling. Insects were getting to her, maggots, and flies. Since she couldn't feel, she didn't know until she took her clothes off to wash them. After that, she stopped, just kept throwing on more layers. Not like I'm going to sweat, she said. She was wrong though. Cover a corpse in heavy clothes, and it does sweat. She stunk worse every day, her eyes filming over, her skin sagging.

Henka gave me Tien's heart and I—

I thought my heart broke when I saw her cry. Watching her rot was a thousand times worse. Her flesh caved in upon itself, and she retreated from the world. Even seeing what death was doing to her, I couldn't let her go.

She asked, over and over. Let me walk into a fire, she said. It's all right, I can't feel anything. It won't hurt. Set me free.

But I needed her. Henka gave me Tien's heart. She said as long as I possessed it, the wizard would obey me. She said I had to wait for you, that you'd be walking into a trap, and without my help the wizards would take you. She said that if that happened, everything was lost. Henka gave me the heart of the woman I loved, and I stuffed it into a fucking pocket.

Ha. Fucking ironic, right? What do men keep in their pockets? The hearts of the women they love.

I know I am not a good man. I have stolen and killed. I've sailed with pirates, caroused with what my nan used to call *tarnished women*. I never really understood guilt or shame though. Not until I held Tien's soul in the palms of my filthy hands. I'm ashamed I didn't have the strength to free her. I'm ashamed I was too selfish to let her go.

CHAPTER EIGHTEEN

Bren laughed, a sob of raw anguish. "I wonder if it was a relief when I ordered her to attack the mages and they incinerated her. In the end, do you think she forgave me?" He swallowed with a grimace. "I mean, she got what she wanted, right?"

I didn't know.

The truth was I didn't really know the little wizard at all. She hated me from the moment we met and died saving me at Brenwick's command. I couldn't imagine her forgiving either of us.

What could I tell him? He only gave her what she wanted when he needed to save me. He hadn't known how it would end, hadn't had the time to even consider the possible outcomes. He reacted without thought to save his friend.

No way she'd be grateful for that.

When I failed to answer, Bren nodded and left me alone at the rail.

A thousand thoughts wrestled for dominance. One of the shards of my heart had destroyed another. Eventually, Iremaire would learn of my escape. Would she think to return to Abieszan to recapture me? With the possibility of a battle mage and her apprentices showing up at any moment, I couldn't afford a long hunt for Henka. How *was* I going to find my love? A severed head tossed into the harbour, she could be anywhere by now, swept away by the ocean currents, or carried off by a hungry shark. Had she ordered Tien to love Brenwick?

Of course she did. This was Henka. Every angle covered; every possibility planned for. She knew exactly how Bren would react because she designed his situation the same way that wizard built his endless room of violent furniture. Tien was both the bait and the trap.

How could Henka do that to another woman?

I would have sworn she was incapable of a crime as foul as my own. Granted, she was no paragon of sinless innocence. All her dead were enslaved. Yet somehow, enslaving one with love, forcing that kind of worship upon them, seemed a fouler crime. The other undead I'd seen had been free to feel whatever they felt. They had to obey Henka's commands, but beyond that, they remained who they were. Compelling someone to love a person they would have otherwise loathed was a horrible prison. Knowing how it robbed her of freedom, it beggared belief Henka would do the same to someone else.

Looking out across the endless ocean, feeling the waves beneath me, the rise and fall of the ship, I understood. Henka hadn't had a choice. This wasn't her crime, but mine. Ordering Tien to love Brenwick made him happy. Bren being happy made me happy. Once again, Henka fouled herself to please me.

Slavery. Love. Sometimes they felt like the same thing. I might hold Henka's heart, but she held mine just as much. I would never leave her, could never leave her. She was my life and my soul, and I would sacrifice everything for her.

In truth, neither of us was free.

I watched a pod of dolphins race ahead of the ship, jumping and twisting like a playful honour guard. Sometimes they intentionally crashed into others or veered to cut them off.

"Do I want to be free?" I asked them.

I didn't. Henka was my happiness, my everything. Though perhaps for different reasons, I was hers.

I blinked in surprise. She loved me, and she seemed happy.

In a way, Henka had something so many went their entire lives without ever feeling: She had a soul-deep love, and she knew I loved her as utterly and completely as she loved me. In any normal relationship there would always be that tiny, nagging doubt. Not so for Henka and I.

What if she was truly happy?

Was what I did to her still evil if she was content in her slavery?

It should be, but was the answer that simple?

"No," I told the frolicking dolphins.

AN END TO SORROW

Khraen

Henka might have been happy, but when I freed her from her slavery, she would look back at everything she'd done over the millennia and know she'd never had a choice. She would suddenly know she'd spent thousands of years unconditionally loving a man who was utter shit.

When I freed her, Henka was not going to be happy at all.

I offered the stars a sad smile of sick amusement. "If I really loved her, I'd want her to be happy."

And she'd be happiest if she forever remained in love with me.

Disgusted with my pathetic attempt at rationalizing my sins, I went below decks, crawling into my hammock to stare dully at the cobwebbed beams of the ceiling.

The next morning, the murdering piece of my heart left the island it was on and headed toward another shard.

A week and a half later we sailed into the devastation of Abieszan. When Henka and I first arrived, I'd noticed the colossal stone gates, too massive for even the greatest dragon to move. I'd read the wards and pacts etched deep into the stone and realized I might bind the demons within to my service. I'd thought to close the gates, holding the city hostage until Queen Yuruuza, reputed to be a powerful shaman, agreed to help hide me from the other fragments of my heart.

Now, the gates were shattered ruin, choking the mouth of the harbour. Sections of the mighty demon-bound outer wall had also been destroyed, a maze of barely submerged jagged rocks waiting to rip the hull out of any ship unwary of the dangers.

I remembered thinking Abieszan an impressive stronghold, that it would take the combined might of the entire Guild to break her. I'd been wrong. A single ship—a battlemage and her acolytes—had made short work of the city.

The true scale of the carnage became apparent as we rounded the horn and sailed into the harbour. Many died when I ordered the gates closed. More fell when I cut them down rushing to the harbour to try and save Henka. I'd freed the city's demons to fight the Deredi, and Queen Yuruuza threw her god into the fray. I knew I was guilty of terrible crimes, but until this moment hadn't understood the scale.

I hadn't killed hundreds, or even thousands. I was directly responsible for tens of thousands of deaths. Many died during the initial confrontations, but countless more died in the aftermath of my actions. Fires ravaged Abieszan for weeks. Even now, months later, a pall of smoke hung over the ruins.

Queen Yuruuza's fortress at Abieszan's heart, a bastion of war bedecked with runes, wards, and pacts, was a mountain of smouldering rubble. Massive stone towers and fortresses had been smashed to debris. What buildings remained standing were charred and bore heavy damage. Bindings that held for three thousand years had been destroyed, their demons slain.

I killed a city.

Carrion birds circled overhead, sometimes dropping to disappear.

As the *Karlotta Emelia* cleared a particularly large pile of broken wall, I got my first good look at the docks. Apart from two white war galleys, there were no other vessels.

"Fuck," I said, as Bren approached to stand at my side.

"I'm not sure that single word quite covers the depths of our fuckedness," he said.

"You have something better?"

He pursed his lips in thought. "Nope."

"Well then?"

"Fuck," he agreed.

Throbbing pain pulsed through my skull; my jaw clenched in helpless rage. The wizards were already here. It seemed unlikely these two ships were with Iremaire. More likely, they were here on official Guild business, searching for answers. Demons fought a god and a city had been destroyed. The only answer that made sense was that someone woke those demons and was able to command them. Only a demonologist could do that.

I closed my eyes, searching for calm.

The piece of my heart that destroyed another was moving toward a third shard. Would he destroy that too? I knew the answer. Distracted, I realized two more had begun moving. The closest to me now moved north toward Abieszan like a launched arrow. The other was simply gone, no other piece having come anywhere near it.

Everything I thought I understood was falling into chaos. These Khraens who hadn't moved in years were suddenly scampering around the world. The path I had thought to follow no longer awaited my arrival. It had grown impatient and decided to bring the fight to me.

"I need weapons," I said. "Demonic weapons. And armour." I glanced at Bren. "We both do."

He nodded in mute agreement, attention never leaving the white ships.

"I don't know how to find Henka, but I know who can help me. To reach him I'll need a portal demon." I thought for a moment. "I can get weapons and armour from him too."

Again, Bren nodded.

"To make any of this happen," I continued, "I need souls." I didn't mention the blood. If we were harvesting souls, there'd be blood aplenty.

"How many?" he asked.

"A lot."

Bren closed his eyes. When he opened them, he said, "There will be survivors, hiding in the city."

I hoped he was right. "I'll need a Soul Stone, a diamond. Something with a lot of facets."

"We'll have to steal that."

Steal diamonds. Harvest souls and trap them in stone. Spill blood. Summon and bind a portal demon and visit Nhil in the floating mountains. Ask my demon friend how to find Henka. Summon and bind more demons to make weapons and armour for me and Bren. Return to Abieszan, and either kill the wizards or somehow hide from them while I recovered Henka from the harbour.

And after?

I fiddled with the ring Iremaire had mocked me with.

I wasn't sure what would happen after.

I had to do all this before the other Khraen arrived. With no idea what summonings he knew, I didn't want to face myself unarmed.

When in the floating mountains I couldn't sense the shards of my heart. What if he reached Abieszan while I was away? He'd know the moment I returned. If he somehow bested me, he would never know of Henka. She'd spend an eternity buried in the ocean silt, her worst nightmare.

Even if he was the piece that remembered her—which, for reasons I couldn't explain, I very much doubted—he wouldn't know *where* she was.

I wouldn't let that happen.

"Bren, I have a plan."

"Well then, what could possibly go wrong?"

In that moment he sounded very much like Tien.

CHAPTER NINETEEN

Captain Rofalle's attention slipped back and forth between the abandoned ruin of the docks, and the white warships. "I'd heard one of the wealthier families had taken control of the docks and were buying supplies off anyone and everyone who arrived."

No one was at the docks. I saw no signs of life in the city at all.

"How old was that news?" I asked.

"It was two weeks old when we left Khaal two weeks ago."

"A lot can change in a month."

She ignored me, snapping, "Looking glass!" at her cabin girl, a gangly teen with an unruly mop of tangled black hair, who immediately handed her an ancient, tarnished brass contraption.

Rofalle focussed on the wizard ships first. "Mages on deck. They've seen us. Not signalling anything. Yet. Maybe they'll ignore us." Swinging her focus to the docks, she muttered a quiet prayer.

"May I?" I asked when she lowered the glass.

She handed it over and I studied the docks. Judging from the wreckage, and the number of shattered and burnt masts jutting from the water, a battle had raged in the harbour. A dozen or more ships, probably moored and unable to escape in time, had been burned and then sunk.

Several factions had warred for possession of the docks, most likely trying to commandeer vessels and flee. Piled corpses, many still showing remnants of liveries I didn't recognize, lay scattered. Here and there I caught the bright flash of armour, or the sun glinting off the steel of a sword. Most were burned black, agonized sculptures of charred bone and ash frozen in mid fight. Though not the work of a wizard, this wasn't accidental either. A massive fire elemental had raged through this part of the city. Judging from the scope of the damage, the elementalist lost control, and it ran rampant and feral, burning everything. The only reason the circling carrion birds ignored the waiting feast was because it was burnt to the point of inedibility.

Spotting a shield that had somehow escaped largely undamaged, I focussed on the heraldry decorating it. "Red dragon on a green background," I said to the captain. "Mean anything to you?"

"Valshaion's colours," she answered. "She was the head of the greatest of Abieszan's noble families. Only Queen Yuruuza had a larger army."

"It looks like they made a stand at the docks and were overrun."

By whom, I had no idea. It could have been a mad rush of commoners seeking to flee a burning city. Or perhaps the noble families fought each other over the last ships. Whatever happened, there was no one left to buy the goods Captain Roffale brought from Khaal.

I swung the glass back to study the wizard ships for myself. Pristine and flawless white, they bobbed near the docks, though not lashed to the piers. A few wizards strode the deck, but I saw none of the activity one would expect, were they about to depart. The sails hung loose and unfurled. These being mages, I knew they had other means of propelling their vessels.

"They look like they want to be able to leave in an instant," I reported, "but aren't planning on leaving anytime soon."

Scanning the nearer of the war galleys, I saw a wizard on the fo'c's'le studying me through a looking glass of his own.

"Shit," I said, raising a hand in what I hoped was a casual greeting somehow conveying we meant no harm.

He didn't react.

"Smug fuckers," I muttered.

Captain Rofalle hissed in anger. "I have a hold full of food and supplies, and no one to sell it to." Taking back the looking glass, she again studied the wizard ships. "If we leave now and are blessed with a favourable wind, I can make it to the next island before it all spoils."

"There's no way everyone in Abieszan is dead," I pointed out. "It's just a matter of finding the survivors. They'll be desperate."

In truth, I didn't care what she did or whether she made a profit, but I needed to depart the ship here.

Rofalle gestured at the dead piled on the docks. "That's what this kind of desperation gets you. If there's enough people to sell supplies to, there's enough people who want off this graveyard island. They'll mob the ship, and I can't fight them off. No." Jaw set, she shook her head. "Not worth it. We're leaving."

"Wait! I…"

She waited.

"That will draw the suspicion of the wizards," I said. "They might come to investigate."

"They don't care about island rats like us. Even if they did, they'd search the ship, see the supplies, say something condescending about how we're profiting off the misery of others, and send us on our way."

"I need to stay," I said, deciding to try honesty. "My wife is here. I have to find her."

Rofalle studied me with doubtful eyes. "If your wife is here, she's likely dead. Anyway, I don't believe you."

"He speaks truth," said Bren.

And that was it. Me, the captain would never believe. Three words from Bren, and she was utterly convinced.

Unfortunately, it didn't change the fact she wanted nothing to do with Abieszan.

"I'm sorry. I truly am. But I'm not going anywhere near those docks," she said. "Corpses left out in the sun for weeks. The birds might not be at them, but there'll be all manner of rats and gods know what else in there. I'm not exposing my crew to even the chance of disease. We're leaving now. If you want to stay…" She waved a hand at the distant dock. "Swim for it."

The distance was survivable. The harbour, however, had been infested with sharks *before* the waters were filled with corpses.

Truth be told, I wasn't much interested in being dropped off in sight of the white ships. They might ignore us with the smug superiority typical of mages, or they might decide to collect us for questioning. Everything depended on why they were here. The only thing I knew for sure was that they weren't in Abieszan to help the survivors.

"Drop us off somewhere outside of the harbour," I said. "Just get us close enough to the shore we might avoid getting eaten."

"There's a reason this harbour is the only one on the island," said Rofalle. "The coast is all rock and reef. I'm not chancing the *Karlotta Emelia* on that."

"Then get us close and give us that," I said, gesturing at the overturned rowboat at the rear of the ship. Worn and rounded, the wood faded to near white, it looked much older than the *Karlotta*.

"That's our only lifeboat," she said. "I'm not giving it to you. I'm not even lending it to you."

"Then sell it to us," said Bren.

"You came aboard with nothing. You have nothing to offer."

Bren drew Mihir, the demon sword singing a pure note as it slid from the sheathe.

"No," I said. "That's our only weapon."

"Not much use to us if we can't get ashore."

"You're offering me a sword in return for my only boat?"

Bren hefted the weapon. "This is Mihir. It's a demon sword."

"Donkey piss."

"It'll cut through your mast in a single swing," I said, only exaggerating a little.

"Interesting idea," mused Bren. "Then she'd have to stay long enough to repair it."

"You cut my mast down," she growled, "and there won't be enough of you left to interest the sharks. Show me on something a little less crucial." She shouted at her cabin girl to fetch a broken oar from below deck.

The gangly kid was back in moments, not even breathing hard from her mad dash. If she ever did anything at less than top speed, I never saw it.

Taking the half-length of oar, the captain held it out with one hand. "Chop through this."

Her loose grip all but guaranteed Bren's failure.

It was easy to let his size and lumbering gait deceive you. I think he did that on purpose, in part to put people at ease. The instant he was in a fight, he changed. He was an ungainly lump of clay right up until the moment he decided he wasn't.

Instead of going for a strong overhand swing, he whipped the sword up from beneath the oar. Steel parted wood like a battle axe splitting a ripe cheese. The severed end of the oar spun a lazy half circle and landed at Rofalle's feet. Perfectly smooth, the cut showed no hint of splintering. A carpenter's saw couldn't have managed a cleaner job.

"Oh shit," said the captain. "I either wet myself or had a little O."

Bren blushed.

"I drop you off out of sight of the mages and give you my shitty rowboat—and let's be honest, it'll probably sink before you get anywhere near the shore—and you give me this lovely sword."

"We'll need food and water," I added.

"Most of what's in the hull will go bad before we get to the next island anyway," she grumbled. "Might as well let you have it."

Turning away, she hollered at the steersman to bring the *Karlotta Emelia* about and get us the hell out of Abieszan harbour.

The crew hurried to obey her orders while I went to inspect our new boat and Bren headed below deck to pack what food we could carry. Captain Rofalle followed along behind me. She hadn't been kidding. When I dug at the wood it flaked apart beneath my fingers. Sea air and the tropical sun had eaten at this relic for years.

"How old is this?" I asked.

"It was there when I bought the *Karlotta*. We've never used it. I prefer real harbours with real docks to skulking about dangerous shorelines."

"I can't decide whether it will fall apart, sink, or burst into flames."

Rofalle cast a critical eye over the boat. "Probably won't burst into flames. As for the other two options, I'm not sure why you think it's an either-or scenario. It can fall apart and *then* sink."

Feeling generous, she had two of her crew wrestle the rowboat over onto its hull and drag it to the rail. They left a trail of soft woodchips. Two equally decrepit oars sat within, clipped to the side. The crewmen lowered the boat to the ocean. Had they dropped it from the height of the *Karlotta's* deck, I think it would have fragmented apart on impact with the water.

By the time Bren re-joined us, two laden backpacks slung over his shoulders, the *Karlotta Emelia* had fled Abieszan harbour. I watched the white war galleys slide from sight, the wizards apparently content to let us leave. That was a relief. I'd half expected them to give chase. Had that happened, I had no real plan of escape. She might not like it, but the captain would hand us over rather than risk a confrontation. I wouldn't have blamed her. The *Karlotta* was outclassed even without the two galleys being manned by mages.

Not wanting to have to travel too far by foot to make it to the city, I asked Rofalle to drop anchor the moment the walls were out of sight. She ordered it done. The jungle shoreline, though less dense than what we'd wrestled with on the necropolis island, looked dark and uninviting. I felt a thousand inhuman eyes on me. I may have been born in such a place, long, long ago, but no part of me wanted to return.

Captain Rofalle's gaze lingered appreciatively on Bren before she turned her attention to the shore. "Row fast and you might make it before you sink. Or join my crew and I'll give you the sword back."

Though she didn't speak directly to either of us, I knew the offer was directed solely at Bren.

"You'd make a good captain," she added, facing him. "The men like you." She winked. "*I* like you."

Bren gave her a wounded half-smile.

"You've a broken heart," she said. "That much is clear. Disappointed as I am you didn't come to me to mend it, let me give you some advice. Only one thing fixes such pain: extremely energetic sex, and a bucket of whiskey."

"Isn't that two?" I asked.

"Depends on how you do it. But those aren't what mend a wounded heart." She looked away, a slight frown wrinkling her brow. "Time. That's the only thing that'll do it. The sex and whiskey are to help pass the time, make the days, months, years tolerable." She sighed. "More tolerable."

"I'll keep that in mind," said Bren.

Rofalle grunted doubt. "This isn't you. You're a big man with a big heart, and you lead with it. At least, you used to. You're not one to hide that heart away. Never let fear drive you to shelter it from hurt. That's what made you brave. That's what made you *you*. Don't let yourself become a big man with a small, guarded heart. World has enough of those."

Bren stared at his boots, silent.

One by one the crew came to say their goodbyes to Brenwick, shaking his hand, slapping him on the back, or pulling him into tight hugs. They nodded to me, mumbling something about wishing us luck, and returned to their duties.

Farewells finished, Bren and I tossed the backpacks Rofalle gave us into the waiting boat and clambered down the ropes. With a little rationing, we had enough salted fish to last a few days and water for maybe half that.

Though she floated well enough empty, the moment our weight was added the boat took on water at an alarming rate.

"Like I said," Rofalle called down to us, "row fast!"

She disappeared, her voice rising as she bellowed orders to hoist the anchor and put this doomed island in their wake.

Bren and I rowed hard.

My oar snapped off about halfway there and I paddled with my hands.

The boat sank before we made shore, but we were pleased to discover we were only waist deep. Wading the rest of the way, we staggered, sodden and heavy, backpacks raised to keep them dry, onto the rocky coast.

A fist-sized stone fled at our approach, rolling off to disappear into the jungle. Not wanting to upset it, I stopped to watch it leave.

"How long ago did we leave Abieszan?" I asked Bren. Between the stasis spell and being trapped underground, I'd lost all sense of time.

"Maybe three months," he said. "I'm not sure."

The fact every fire was an unbound elemental rarely mattered. When first sparked, they were small, weak, and dumb. Even a campfire left to burn overnight was easily doused the next morning. But if a fire was maintained for long enough, it grew in intelligence and strength. Forest fires were raging feral elementals run amok. They devoured everything in their path in a mad lust for life, only dying when they ran out of fuel.

"I remember a church," I told Bren, grasping at the threads of recollection. "It started as a small and relatively unknown religion. They lived to the west of the Deredi Mountains, far to the north of what is now the Inkarmat Desert. They worshipped fire. Not surprising, I suppose as they lived in such a frigid environment. The founder lit a fire deep underground and they maintained it for decades, centuries. They kept it small, limiting the fuel supply, bringing just enough wood to keep it going, but with every passing year it grew smarter."

"Smart fire sounds bad," said Bren.

"It is. They worshipped the fire and they held it prisoner, a trapped god." Something about the idea sent tremors down my spine. "It whispered secrets to them."

"What secrets does fire know?"

I shrugged. "Destruction, I suspect. They maintained this fire for generations, faithfully feeding it. Each time they let it grow, it shared more of its secrets and they themselves grew in power."

Once I felt sure the rock hadn't gone off to gather an army of enraged boulders, we set off.

"Soon," I said, continuing my story, "that demented little church became a massive and thriving theocracy and they spread south, conquering the horse tribes of the steppes, and building colossal cities. They fed the fire, letting it grow. It taught them the arts of forging and ironworking unlike any civilization had known."

It might have been easier to hide in the jungle, but between the possibility of rampaging stones and the size of the insects I saw flitting about in the shadows, I figured it was safer to stick to the coast.

"It showed them war," I said, "and they burned their enemies as sacrifices. That tiny little flame grew, it melted the earth beneath it, spewing out molten rock to armour its sides. And still they fed it. But fire knows no loyalty, has no interest in empire. Many hundreds of years old, that little fire had become a volcano. It fed off the very bones of the earth, no longer needing the pathetic offerings of madmen."

It was slow going over the broken and uneven ground, though I doubt hacking our way through the riotous tangle of life would have been quicker.

"That fire cracked the world," I continued as we walked. "It brought down their walls, filling the streets with ash and lava. The lush steppes became the Inkarmat Desert. Here and there you can see the slagged corpses of ancient towers peeking from the endless sands. There's a city buried in the desert stretching thousands of miles. Even my capital, PalTaq, pales in comparison to what it was."

"What was the city called?" Bren asked.

I laughed. "I can't remember. But parts of Abieszan may have been burning for near three months."

"Oh," he said.

"Indeed," I agreed.

"So along with a fallen city plagued with rats and, well, plague, as well as two war galleys of battlemages, we should keep an eye out for any wandering sentient fires."

The murderous piece of my heart was quickly closing with its next target. I half-wondered why it didn't flee in the opposite direction, even though I wouldn't have either. Another shard still travelled north on a direct path to Abieszan. Every part of this felt wrong. I'd come to assume they'd all remain on their islands. It was worrying that I may have so completely misjudged the situation. If all the shards suddenly decided to hunt and kill the others, collecting their hearts so they could be the one Khraen, the trail I followed would forever crumble to chaos.

We found the towering outer wall of Abieszan as the sun touched the western horizon. I stopped for a moment to study the many wards and pacts carved into the stone. Here, well away from where the battles had raged, the demons still slumbered. Bound to the wall as they were, and then only there to reinforce the stone's natural strength, there was no point in waking them. Discovering the cracked ruin of what had once been a wide cobblestone highway, we followed the gentle curve of the wall north. We passed several other long-overgrown roads appearing from the jungle to join with the one we followed. Many thousands of years ago, this island had been a thriving port. Abieszan—or what was left of her—was all that remained. I knew if we followed any of these long-forgotten trails we'd stumble across the ruins of abandoned towns and cities draped thick in foliage.

The west gates of Abieszan, almost as impressive as the colossal ones guarding the harbour, hung open. Seamless slabs of rock, they reached scores of strides into the sky. The outer wall surrounded the entire city, all of it wide enough that roads ran the entire circumference. It was one thing to appreciate their size from out in the harbour, or to stand upon the wall and feel the impossible strength of stone beneath you. At the base of the wall, head craned back as you squinted at the top, it was oddly intimidating. Were a section of wall or gate to suddenly fall, it would crush me like a bug. Long-dead emperor or no, there is a level at which existence doesn't care about you.

"This is a work of elementalism and demonology," I told Bren. "In my day the arts cooperated. Together, united in purpose, we are capable of so much more than when squabbling like spoiled children."

"If you weren't planning on being murdered by Henka, would you rebuild what we lost?" he asked.

There were layers in that simple query. Bren would support me whatever my decision, but knew it was within my power to give the islanders a better world.

I couldn't deny part of me wanted exactly that. But my debt to Henka outweighed all other concerns. I would find her and bring her to the palace at PalTaq. I would lay my hand upon her heart and free her from the bonds of slavery.

There would be no saving the world.

There would be no rebuilding my fallen empire, no bright new world of peace, prosperity, and justice.

I would suffer Henka's wrath and that would be my end.

It wouldn't make me a good man. It would in no way undo my multitude of crimes.

But there can only be justice if there is punishment.

"No," I answered Bren. "The Demon Emperor is dead. The world is better without him."

Bren looked doubtful. "Maybe. I can't speak to that. But I am glad you won't be off building and then running a world-spanning empire."

"Why?"

"If we somehow survive this, I was hoping you'd help me run the pub I want to open."

I laughed, a loosing of pent tensions. "I'd like that."

"Good." Bren slapped me on the back. "Someone has got to clean the toilets."

CHAPTER TWENTY

 Not wanting to enter Abieszan at night, we camped outside the gates. Ragged shrieks of rage, pain, and terror punctured long moments of eerie silence. Sometimes the sounds of distant fighting echoed through stone streets and then faded to nothing. Half-expecting to be attacked at any time, neither of us slept much. Listening to the lawless chaos beyond the wall, I regretted Bren's rash decision to trade Mihir for that rickety boat. Perhaps we should have disembarked at the docks or tried swimming and hoped the sharks didn't get us. Much as I wanted to complain that it had been unwise to lose our only real weapon, I saw few other options. No matter how much Rofalle liked Brenwick, she wasn't going to give us that boat for nothing.

 Small comfort, but I took some pride I hadn't slaughtered the entire crew and taken the ship as my own. The Demon Emperor wouldn't have hesitated. I failed at being a good man, but perhaps might succeed at being better than he. Though, truth be told, that bar had been set quite low.

 The next morning found us yawning and stiff from sleeping on the jumbled rocks.

 Bren stretched, rolling scarred shoulders, and stood frowning at the open gates while absently scratching an armpit. "No one came out. All that violence we heard, the inevitability of rats and disease, the fires, and no one is leaving."

 "Perhaps the locals know how dangerous the jungle is. Your only chance at food would be hunting. You'd have to risk approaching a pool to get water, and that's where the predators lay in wait. There's a city for the looting and there are wells. In the end," I added, "better the hell you know."

Bren found a hefty fallen branch and, after testing its weight and balance, declared it a passable club. Without his brute strength, I decided I was better off with my knife. Side by side, we entered Abieszan.

Walking streets littered with fallen buildings and sun-bloated corpses, we soon stopped to tie strips of fabric over our mouth and nose. The vomitus stench of death thickened air buzzing with clouds of fat and heavy flies. They were everywhere, on everything. They crawled into the corners of your eyes, crowded into our ears. Swatting at them just seemed to make them more determined to get at us.

"Why they want to get in my mouth," Bren mumbled, voice muffled through layers of fabric, "when there's all these delicious dead is beyond me." He cursed, spitting, when one somehow managed to get beneath the makeshift mask.

We walked east, toward the harbour. Seeing no sign of a rampaging fire elemental, I wondered if it had burned itself out, or gotten smart enough to take captives and ransom them for a continuous supply of combustibles.

I had no real plan. I needed diamonds, and I needed souls. After that, finding the basic tools of my trade—something for drawing the binding circle, and an area to work unimpeded—seemed inconsequential. This far from the heart of the city, the homes were small, and mostly wood. Fires had raged through most of the streets we walked, leaving charred dead and the stone bones of gutted homes. No one living out here would have a trove of hidden diamonds. If they somehow did, it'd been buried when the building burned and collapsed in on itself.

The rising sun brought the heat of the day and a worsening of the stink. We passed stacked corpses, intentionally burned to avoid the diseases a city full of rotting bodies inevitably brought. Whoever worked at the task must have given up or been added to the pile. After a relatively clear street, we found ourselves manoeuvring through a maze of sun-ripe meat and swarms of flies so thick they looked like writhing constructions of black stone. Sometimes a carrion bird decided a body was still worthy of exploration and dropped from the sky. Startled into a helpless rage, the flies vented their frustration on Bren and me.

I caught sight of people cowering in the shadows, watching us pass with desperate eyes. For now, Bren's size and the fact we clearly weren't weak from months of starvation, kept them back. Two scrawny men clutching spears, and a sunken woman with a rusting meat cleaver, followed us for a dozen blocks before deciding to go in search of easier prey.

Bren slapped me in the shoulder, dislodging the flies gathered there. He gestured at where the street we followed intersected with a larger thoroughfare.

"There's a well," he grunted through clenched teeth.

Though not yet empty, our waterskins were nearly depleted.

Raising a hand in warning, he stopped to study the surrounding buildings. This was a fine place for an ambush, and a well was too valuable to be ignored. Deciding it was safe enough, he waved for me to follow and cut through the intersection.

We found the well polluted, scores of dead rats and thousands of flies floating in foul and murky water.

"Fuck," he grunted.

We continued east, passing corpses showing the signs of recent violence, hacked limbs, and crushed skulls. We saw people who had been dragged into the street and systematically tortured, their eyes and tongue cut away, their flesh carefully flayed. I didn't want to think what might have been done with the meat. Others, pocked with leaking sores, gangrenous flesh oozing pus, looked to have fallen to the diseases already plaguing the city.

There were two galleys loaded with mages out in the harbour, yet they wouldn't raise a finger to help the survivors. Islanders were second-class citizens given all the worst and most dangerous jobs. On the mainland, I'd been sneered at and spat on every time I entered one of the finer establishments. Even the owners of shitholes and dives scowled their hate.

I stopped walking. When he noticed, Bren stopped too, scanning for danger.

"This is my fault," I said. "All this death. The suffering."

I did this to Abieszan. My choices destroyed the gates and the wall and brought down much of the city. My fight with the Deredi Giant caused massive damage. Waking the demons of Abieszan made it worse. It didn't render the wizards free of responsibility—these were people, and they needed help—but it was important to remember where the real blame lay.

He gave me a quizzical look of concern. "Maybe initially, but many people made their own choices in the months since. You can't be responsible for all that."

"Can't I?" I waved a hand at the destruction. "They made choices forced upon them by my actions."

"At some point, everyone has to take responsibility for their own decisions."

It sounded good, like an escape from blame. But it was as true of me as it was of them.

"That's what I'm doing," I said. "It's just that…"

I hadn't known Shalayn brought the wizards, and they were looking for me. I couldn't have guessed the Deredi would bear some ancient grudge and come after me seeking vengeance. When I woke the demons of the city to fight the giants and keep the mages from escaping the harbour, I'd had no idea what would happen after. Even now I wasn't sure whether they attacked Queen Yuruuza's god, or if she sent it after them in a misguided attempt to protect her city.

I looked to Brenwick, who divided his attention between shooting me nervous glances and watching the streets for trouble.

"I'd do it again," I said. "I'd kill everyone on the wall and slaughter the entire city if it meant saving Henka."

"Of course you would," he said. "You love her."

I saw the pain the words caused him and understood. My love made my crimes justifiable. It was storybook bullshit, a juvenile understanding of emotion and relationships, but that's who Bren was. He lived like the hero of an ancient saga, clung to an impossible code. By that same logic, his own crime, that of sacrificing the woman he loved to save me, was unforgivable.

"We should keep moving," he said. "I think we're being followed."

Travelling east, we found ourselves entering a nicer neighbourhood. Here, the damage was less severe, the homes larger and better constructed. Many looked like small castles, boasting turrets, crenelated roofs, protective walls, and guard towers. Some were smashed, doors battered in, windows broken, clearly looted. Others remained behind closed gates, hardened men and women watching us from behind thick walls.

The piece of me moving ever north dragged at my attention. The old man at the necropolis had necromancers. The shard calling itself Naghron had sent a sorcerer after me. It was possible this one also had help. It might be coming after me with a powerful elementalist, someone capable of binding deadly fire elementals. The ruins of Abieszan would give them plenty to work with.

I needed blood and souls. The looted homes would be easier targets, but I'd be unlikely to find the cut stones I needed. The walled compounds offered a better chance at finding diamonds but were guarded and more dangerous. Perhaps we could break into one at night.

"They're behind us," said Bren, interrupting my thoughts. "And to the right." Gripping his club, testing its weight, he added, "At least five. Maybe more."

Taking the next left, I kept watch, scanning the streets for movement. Sure enough, dark figures flitted in the shadows.

"Rooftop on the left," whispered Bren.

Darting a glance, I saw a figure with a longbow kneeling partially concealed behind a shattered chimney. A snug fabric mask hid the face, leaving only dark eyes visible. The slightest of curves suggested it was a woman. An arrow nocked but not drawn, she studied our progress.

We turned left into the next street.

"We're being herded," said Bren.

I agreed. "Do we run and try and lose them?"

"Too many," he said, "and they know these streets. It'll only tire us out, make us easier to kill."

"Up for a valiant last stand?"

"Always thought dying while fighting back-to-back with a friend seemed like a romantic way to go."

"You and I have different ideas of romance."

Bren hefting his makeshift club, me gripping my knife, we didn't have to wait long. Shadowy figures moved to surround us. Many carried knives or swords. Others had bows or crossbows. All wore masks.

"Maybe we should rethink running," grumbled Bren from behind me. "This is feeling less romantic than expected."

It was good to hear a little of the old Brenwick in his voice. Even if it only surfaced when we were about to die.

"If they wanted to stick us full of arrows," I said, hoping I was correct, "they already would have."

In moments more than a dozen lurked in the shadows, surrounding us. All wore dark, mottled colours to blend in with the shapes and colours of the city. Many moved like people with armour concealed beneath loose clothes. If they changed their minds about killing us, there wouldn't be much we could do. If not outright slaughtered, I might survive, saved by my strange ability to heal. Bren wouldn't be so lucky.

"If this gets ugly," I whispered over my shoulder, "I want you to run."

"*You* run."

"Just do as you're told!"

"Sorry. Disobedience and a lack of respect for authority is probably my one flaw."

"That's two things. I think your inability to count is your one flaw."

He shrugged.

A big man, larger even than Brenwick, appeared from the shadows. For all my attention, I had completely failed to notice him despite his being less than a dozen strides from me. Monstrous with muscle, head like a boulder hewn roughly from the earth, he carried a huge double-bladed war axe over one shoulder. Like the others, he wore a fitted mask dappled in shades of grey.

He'd been too perfectly hidden. Was this wizardry, or sorcery? I had a vague recollection of my chief elementalist working with shadow elementals but no idea if his research bore fruit.

"I am Clay," he said, as if I should recognize the name.

When I failed to react or respond, he added, "Mom wants to see you."

"Who?"

He blinked in surprise, glancing off to the side as if looking for support. "Uh… Mom?"

Even through his mask I caught the wince when he realized it came out sounding like a question.

Bren lowered his club. "Mom? Shit."

"There we go," said Clay, sounding pleased. "That's the reaction I was expecting."

CHAPTER TWENTY-ONE

When they didn't take our weapons, I couldn't decide if this was a good sign, or a really, really bad one.

"Mom runs the Mummer's Union," Bren explained as we were led through a maze of back alleys.

"These people are mimes?"

"Gods, no. It's like the Wizard's Guild but for thieves, murderers, assassins, and cutthroats."

"Aren't the last three all basically the same thing?"

"Not even close," Clay said, strolling at my other side. Happily, he didn't elaborate.

The Mummers took us from the wealthier neighbourhood and into one that looked even worse than what we'd already passed through. This must have been Abieszan's slum district before the city burned. Every alley was a narrow, twisting lane ankle-deep in reeking effluent. Many of the buildings had suffered fire damage, but unlike elsewhere this seemed to have predated the recent violence. People watched us from even the most decrepit buildings. No structure was too rundown, too burned, collapsed, or damaged, to not be someone's home. Here and there I caught odd glimpses of normalcy, a clothesline with recently laundered sheets, or a basement café still doing brisk business. We passed a grocer with a pathetic assortment of sad-looking vegetables on display. Two masked Mummers stood guard.

In the wider streets corpses hung swinging from lantern posts or were nailed up to wooden scaffolds. Those were the only dead I saw, the rest having been cleared away.

Seeing my attention, Clay said, "Mom is the law in this part of town. No rape, murder, or stealing allowed."

"I thought you were a guild of rapists and murderers."

"Thieves and assassins," he corrected. "And you're only allowed to steal and kill once you've attained proper permission. Anyway, a guild is a collective bargaining organization for independent contractors, whereas a union is a collective bargaining organization for employees."

"You all work for Mom?"

He made the face people make when they're trying to say, 'yes, but' without actually saying it. "Kind of? Independent contractors operate outside of Mom's laws and, as such, have their fingers chopped off and shoved, one at a time, up their asses."

"Because shoving them all in there at once would be awkward," said Bren from my other side.

Clay shrugged. "Without law there is chaos. If you want to steal something, you still have to obey the laws."

"I'm guessing Mom's law differs somewhat from Queen Yuruuza's."

"Of course. And you obey those of whomever is closest and carrying the biggest stick."

"Ah," I said, "the wisdom of the thief."

"The wisdom," said Clay, "of a man not keen on getting hit with a big stick."

The next street opened into what, based on my memories of attacking and defending cities, I'd have to call a killing floor. Buildings had been demolished to create the space, the wood and stone harvested to construct a crude but effective wall standing a little more than my own height. A single well-guarded gap allowed people through. Masked mummers walked the wall, patrolling with their motley assortment of weapons. Most looked more heavily armoured than those we met in the street. Though a long way from fresh, the air was less polluted. I suddenly realized we'd left the flies behind a few paces back. Glancing over my shoulder I saw them swarming behind us but apparently unwilling to follow. Either Mom had someone working protective magic around her stronghold, or even the flies knew to obey her laws.

Bren and I removed the fabric we'd tied around our faces, drawing grateful breaths. The mummers left theirs in place. Not gone, the smell of death and decay was pleasantly distant, like all the winds somehow blew it away from this part of town.

Air elementals, I decided. Not the powerful kind I'd once tamed to topple cities and scatter armies, but enough to control the flow of air over a large area. It was more than I was capable of and less than I'd done, both pathetic and impressive.

Passing through the gap in the wall, we got a clear look at the only building within. At one time, many centuries ago, it had been the sprawling mansion of a wealthy lord. The structure was as old as everything in Abieszan, demonic wards chiselled into the stone. At some point in the past, it had been converted into a two-story hotel, the main lobby being repurposed as—

"Is that a pub?" asked Bren. "Is that a pub in the middle of hell?"

"Yup," said Clay.

"Tell me it's open for business."

"Good beer, too. Mom brews it in the cellars. She's been experimenting with wine lately. Makes it from whatever fruit she can scrounge. The wine…" He checked none of the other mummers were within earshot. "The wine is less good."

"I'd drink goat piss if it gave me a buzz," said Bren. "When I was a kid, having drinks was a blast. The booze blunted life's sharp edges, left you rounded and mellow like your worries had been shoved under a heavy blanket. Now…" He blinked at the ground. "Sobriety is a burden."

Archers watched our approach from the roof. Two men in dented but serviceable plate armour stood guard at the main entrance. Clay nodded to them as we passed.

Inside, I was stunned to discover a pub reminiscent of the Dripping Bucket back in Taramlae. Everything was warm oak and lustrous brass, all polished to a flawless shine. Heavy round tables, each big enough to comfortably sit eight, took up much of the room. Sturdy captain's chairs, padded in faded and threadbare burgundy velour, sat around each table. Two women and a man, all in the dark mottled colours of the mummers, both wearing face-covering masks, worked behind a long bar, polishing mugs, and sorting glassware. There was even a fireplace, though this far south I couldn't imagine it ever got cold enough for a fire. Someone had gone to great expense to recreate the look and feel of a mainland tavern here in Abieszan.

Clay led us to the largest of the tables, set well away from the others. An ornate chair, just shy of a proper throne, sat at one side. A rich tapestry hung behind the chair depicting two mounted warriors charging each other with levelled spears. They wore strange armour of bone and wood, their long hair tied back in intricate queues. Horses not being native to the southern islands, this too must have come from the mainland. The bright colours suggested it either wasn't particularly old, or the fabric had been magically protected.

"Have a seat," said Clay, "she'll be out in a moment."

"Mom is expecting us, is she?" I asked, claiming a seat that allowed me to watch the door.

"She knows everything going on in her city," said Clay.

For all this mansion and tavern and the lack of corpses and flies was remarkable, she didn't rule. We'd seen plenty of walled fortresses more impressive. It might well be that no one had bothered to crush her yet. Though the fact Bren recognized the name was a little unsettling.

Bren dropped into a chair with a groan and shot a desperate, pleading look toward the bar.

"Shit," said Clay. "Thanks for the reminder. Mom'll be pissed if she gets here only to find out I forgot to offer you drinks."

He waved at one of the barkeeps, and a moment later three golden ales arrived. Seeing Clay immediately take a long drink, I followed suit. The beer was cooler than expected, no doubt drawn from basement kegs.

Bren sipped, and paused, frowning at the mug in his hand. "Complex. Fresh-baked bread, with subtle hints of grapefruit." He took a longer pull. "Fantastic."

"Mom's been experimenting for decades. Each batch is a little different, none of them bad. Honestly," again he glanced around to make sure no one was listening, "I think she missed her calling."

The tapestry parted along a seam I hadn't noticed, and a tall, well-built mainlander entered the room. Armoured in a beautifully maintained hauberk, two swords poking up over his shoulders, ash eyes studied us. Unlike everyone else he wore no mummer's mask. He'd have been stunningly handsome had someone not hacked off one ear and left a long scar cutting through that cheek. Not as large as Clay or Bren, he was tall and lithe with hard muscle.

Deciding we weren't a threat, he held the fabric aside so a short, middle-aged islander woman could enter. The hand on the tapestry, his left, was missing the last two fingers. She gave him the kind of smile a mother gives her son when pleased he managed to be polite in front of the guests. Dusting flour from her simple tan home-spun dress, she ignored the throne and sat across from me.

The grey-eyed swordsman stood behind her, arms crossed to best show off their girth.

"You remembered to offer our guests refreshments this time," she said to Clay.

"Yes, Mom."

"Ma'am," said Bren, "I haven't had beer like this since…" He looked away, searching his memory. "I haven't had beer like this."

"A strapping lad with manners," she said. "And he likes my ale!"

"A love for ale is probably my one flaw," he admitted.

She winked at him. "Can't think of a better one. Now, what may I call you two handsome young men?"

"This is Brenwick Sofame," I said, introducing my friend. "I am Khraen."

"A heavy name to bear," she mused, studying me. "Everyone calls me Mom, has done for so long I can't say my real name would feel right anymore." She glanced at me. "We become our names, do we not?"

"Some we grow into," I answered. "Some we're born with."

One of the barkeeps appeared with a tray of ales, while another brought bowls of fried potato slices and twists of spiced bread.

The swordsman directed a brief and harsh-sounding stream of incomprehensible gibberish at Bren, who looked to Mom for translation.

She shrugged. "No one understands a word he says. But every time I have guests carrying swords, he wants to fight them. Half the time he talks nonsense at them until they give up." She made a show of looking

Bren and I over. "No swords?"

"We traded our sword for a boat that promptly sank," said Bren.

"Probably saved your life." She turned to the swordsman. "See?" she said, speaking loudly and clearly as if that might help him understand. "No swords. They have no swords."

He grunted disgust.

"Maybe I could borrow a sword," suggested Bren. "Muss up that perfect hair."

"Vishtish's hair is always flawless," said Mom. "Even after dispatching a half dozen opponents. I can't imagine how much time he must spend on it."

Though the swordsman's attention darted to whoever talked, I saw no hint of comprehension. Strangely, it was this small moment that saddened me. I spent ten thousand years uniting the world with a single language, removing all barriers of understanding. It hit me then how long I'd been gone. In three thousand years the world went from one language to the point where this man spoke something no one here even recognized.

"Why does he have two swords and only one useful hand?" Bren asked.

"My suspicion is that he thinks it looks better," answered Mom.

Bren cast an appraising eye at the man. "Yeah, I'll give him that."

We ate and drank, Bren and Mom chatting about everything from sailing ships to the price of salt in the Crags. Vishtish eyed me with the kind of haughty disdain some men have for those they think weak and harmless. Not caring what he thought, I left him to his delusions. No matter how skilled he might be, with Kantlament in hand, I could end him and bring ruin to whatever world he stood upon.

When the last bowl was finally emptied and fresh pints poured, Mom once again turned to face me. "If it's not impolite, let us turn to business."

I'd been waiting for the show of hospitality to end. "Of course."

"You saw the white galleys in the harbour?" she asked.

"We did."

"You understand what that means?"

"Wizards. How long have they been here?" I hoped her answer might give me some clue as to whether these mages were linked to Iremaire.

"They arrived two weeks after the gates suddenly closed and the city burned."

Piecing together the timing, I guessed I was still in Iremaire's stasis spell at that point, being shipped to Khaal.

Mom continued. "Though reluctant to share details, they made it known they are looking for someone. In exchange for information, they offer enough gold to allow one to retire to the mainland and live in civilized luxury."

"I suspect you'll find the mainland less welcoming than you might expect," I said. "They don't much like islanders."

"They remember when we ruled the world and are still sore." Mom sniffed, brushing at the flour caking her dress. "Three months ago, I would have spit on their offer and had a couple of them assassinated just to remind the Guild that, powerful as they might be, they're still flesh and bone."

"And today?" Bren asked.

"Today my city is a decaying corpse being picked over by maggots. Queen Yuruuza and I had our differences, but we had an agreement. Now that she's gone, I think it's time for the mummers to move on." She studied me. "A couple months back, before everything fell apart, a single white galley sailed into Abieszan harbour. First in near fifty years. Three days later, my spies reported that a man with the blackest skin they'd ever seen arrived with a crew of beautiful women, at least some of whom turned out to be dead. I didn't much care. Necromancers are no business of mine, even if they're pimps for corpse harems." She snorted a laugh. "Hardly the weirdest thing I've seen."

Bren and I remained silent.

"But then, not long after that dark skinned man arrived, the long-quiescent demons of Abieszan woke. The harbour gates, which hadn't moved since the days of empire, opened, killing thousands. The Deredi broke the pact they had with Yuruuza and one of the giants came ashore. Yuruuza's pet god attacked the city's demons. Deredi sorcery shredded the sky. My lovely city burned." She paused to sip her ale. "The black-skinned man murdered an impressive number of people in the streets—without permission, I might add—and then killed several Deredi spawn and one of the giants. The next report I received said the wizard ship was gone and no one could find this man with the midnight skin."

"And these two new galleys arrived two weeks after that," I said.

"Coincidence? I think not. And so," she waved a hand at me, "they are looking for someone, and I do believe I have found someone."

Vishtish, completely unaware of the growing tension at the table, made kissy faces at one of the women behind the bar.

"Ignore him," said Mom. "He's fantastic with a sword and unbelievably good in bed, but essentially a beautiful moron. Before you put too much thought into killing me," she continued, "here's what I'm thinking. That black-skinned man was a demonologist. And I don't mean like the pathetic ones who summon three headed snakes to send after their enemies, or ward boots to make them waterproof. I'm talking a demonologist like from the old days. A demonologist who can wake the horrors sleeping in the gates and walls of the most ancient cities."

Expression blank, I waited.

"I think," she said, "someone like that might be a lot more valuable than any pile of gold."

CHAPTER TWENTY-TWO

When I neither disagreed nor denied her assertions, Mom continued. "Abieszan needs leadership. The noble families, such as they are, can't agree on anything. And while they might have some experience running their little shipping businesses, none of them understand what it takes to rule. Yuruuza ruled for decades, and not once did she awaken those demons. Either she didn't know they were there, or she lacked the ability."

For all she played at being a good host and 'mom' to the local thugs and cutthroats, she was nothing more than another petty tyrant in the making. One didn't become Queen of the Thieves by being nice.

"You're hoping I woke those demons, and that I can command them to obey you. With that kind of power at your disposal, none could resist you. You would truly be the Queen of Abieszan."

Mom betrayed no emotion, no hint of smile or excitement. "Can you?"

I gambled she knew nothing of demonology. "What is to stop you from turning them against me once I have commanded them to obey you?"

"There are other ancient cities in the islands with similar runes sunk into the walls and streets. There are towns and churches and castles and fortresses buried in the jungle, overgrown with vines and yet untouched by time. You think I want to stop here?"

If she thought the Guild would let her unite the islands under a single ruler, she was insane. Mages had long memories.

For a moment I was amused she thought someone who might

wield such power would hand control to her. The truth, however, was simpler and more predictable. She'd kill me the moment she controlled Abieszan's demons; everything else was a distraction. She knew the Guild would never allow the islands to unite once again.

"You get me what I need," I said, "and the city is yours."

Later I'd figure out how to either control or kill her. Right now, I had too many enemies and not nearly enough time.

"You give me the demons," she said, "and I'll get you what you need."

"Waking all the demons, binding them, and passing off control will take more time than I have," I lied. "My enemies will be here soon, and I need to defeat them. Only once they've been dealt with will I have the time to do what you ask."

"My people will handle your enemies. All the most dangerous men and women of Abieszan are mine."

It was tempting to accept the aid, but I couldn't chance a shard of my heart falling into this woman's hands. "My enemy is another demonologist. Only with demons of my own can I defeat him."

"Then wake the city and defeat him."

It wouldn't work. Long ago, millennia before my defeat and death, I bound these demons. They could no more attack and hurt the other pieces than they could me. I needed more direct weapons.

"As I said, time is the issue." I pretended to consider my options. "Perhaps a show of faith," I suggested. "A gesture of good will to prove I can do as I say. I will bind one of the nearest demons. I noticed the pacts carved into the walls of this mansion. Would you like control of that which protects your very home?"

"What can it do?" she asked, for the first time betraying some excitement.

"I won't know until I awaken it," I answered honestly.

"What do you need?" she asked.

"Diamonds. I need a total of about fifty facets. If you can find that in a single diamond, great. Two diamonds totalling fifty facets would be acceptable. Three stones will do if there are no other options."

In my time, there had been demonic jewellers capable of a finesse beyond the abilities of man. The emperor carried stones with many hundreds of facets. Some of those jewellers looked human, and I wondered if they were still out there, working in quiet shops, pretending to be common gem-cutters.

"I need souls too," I added.

"Souls?"

"Sacrifices. I need the blood and souls of fifty people."

Bren focussed on his pint mug, sliding it around in the ring of condensation it left on the table.

Mom gave me a speculating look, eyes slightly narrowed. "My spies told me you were on the wall when the gates closed. There was no mention of blood then."

"The blood isn't for those demons," I said. "The blood is for the ones I shall have to summon."

She accepted that without comment. "What else will you need?"

Just like that she agreed to find me fifty people to murder.

I contemplated my options. Was I making a mistake in returning to the floating mountains? The idea of being away, of not being able to sense where the other shards of my heart were, left me uneasy. On the other hand, me disappearing might slow the piece coming north, toward me. Assuming he didn't know about the floating mountains or Nhil, he might think I'd fled somewhere. Making weapons and armour, however, wasn't my only reason for going. I needed Nhil's help to find Henka.

I decided I would return to Nhil.

"I'll need somewhere quiet to work," I answered. "Preferably in the basement. Somewhere without windows."

Without going into too many details I explained my needs. Tempting as it was to not mention the fact I'd disappear for at least week, I didn't want them turning on Brenwick in my absence. Mom had doubts about me mysteriously 'going away,' but Bren's absolute confidence in remaining here as a guarantee of my return, placated her worries. Vishtish spent the entire conversation looking like he was about to lose consciousness from sheer boredom.

"Clay," she said to the big man, who'd remained conspicuously quiet. "Make arrangements for the fifty." She glanced at me. "Are all souls equal?"

An interesting question I'd never contemplated. King or pauper, to a demon, one soul was as good as another.

"As long as they're human."

"No one local," she told Clay. "No one off the street. If you can get them from the noble families, all the better."

Clay stood. "Yes, Mom."

"Have them here by morning. When you've set all that in motion, ask Khraen what else he'll need and get the cellar ready."

With a sharp nod, Clay left.

"Now, gentlemen," she said, rising from the table. "If you'll excuse me."

Bren and I rose, thanking her for her hospitality.

She disappeared the way she came, Vishtish following along after shooting us a disappointed look.

With everyone departed, Bren and I were left alone in the pub with only the barkeeps. One wandered over to see if we wanted more beer, and Bren ordered another round. Once again seated, we waited until the ales were delivered and the barkeep had returned to the bar.

"Something is bothering you," I said to Bren.

He fidgeted with his mug before saying, "Once you disappear, I'm not sure how long their patience will last before they get antsy."

I was surprised he didn't comment on the fifty souls. I knew it bothered him. Was the fact I did this for love enough to make such a crime acceptable, or was this loyalty to a fault?

"I don't have much time," I explained. "A piece of my heart is heading toward us." I decided not to mention the other one hunting and destroying shards. "I'll summon a portal demon and use it to get to a secret cache of weapons, armour, and supplies." I hadn't shared details on where exactly I disappeared to, and he'd never asked. "I'll make demon swords for both of us. I'll have to rush the bindings. If I never return, it means I failed, my soul devoured."

If I had a soul to be devoured.

"If you don't come back," said Bren, "we're both pretty fucked."

"I'll return."

"How long do we have before this other bit of you gets here?"

I shrugged, helpless. "Right now, he's somewhere at sea to the south. Unfavourable winds, and we might have weeks. A solid tailwind, and he could be here in seven or eight days. Once I leave, though, he won't be able to sense me. All he'll know is I *was* on the island."

"He looks like you," said Bren. "What happens when Mom's spies report seeing you out and about in the city?"

"Shit. I hadn't thought of that. She'll either think I betrayed her or try and make a deal with him instead."

I had to complete any summonings and bindings before he arrived in Abieszan. That meant seven days at the most. Something inside me snapped and I supressed an insane cackle. How fast could I murder fifty people and collect their souls? This wasn't PalTaq. These weren't slaves, drugged into submission by my highly trained priesthood. If they were conscious, each would struggle to the last.

"What if you don't leave?" said Bren. "What if, instead, we plan a trap and wait here for him?"

He was really asking, 'What if you don't butcher fifty people and feed their immortal souls to demons?'

"I'm sorry," I said. "I know it's a terrible thing I'm going to do. But if anything happens to me, Henka will never be freed. I can't chance that."

"I understand," he said.

Seeing his pain, I decided perhaps I could do one decent thing.

"Go," I said. "You're a better man than this. Every moment you spend with me pollutes you." I wanted to apologize for what happened with Tien but couldn't force the words out. Even if I did, they'd be lies. I wasn't sorry for what happened to her, I was sorry for its impact on him.

"I can't. You saved me."

"And you saved me!" I snapped. "If anything, I am in *your* debt. The only way I can repay you is by saving you and the only way I can save you is by sending you away."

Bren scowled at the tabletop, fidgeting again with his pint mug. "There's no room in this world for islanders. We're nothing. If we go north, we're spit on. If we try and make something of ourselves in the south, the Guild come down and tear it apart. I grew up knowing I was never going to matter. At least not in any significant way. Maybe someday I'd captain a ship of my own if I was really lucky. But nothing I did would resonate. Nothing I achieved would impact the world in any lasting way."

"I think that's why people have kids."

Bren snorted. "Can you imagine me being a father?"

"Actually, yes."

He shook his head in denial. "Being the Demon Emperor, this might be difficult for you to understand, but a chance to be a part of something larger than oneself is a big deal." He scraped at the mug with a blunt fingernail. "Helping you is my chance to matter."

He'd told me something similar before. I'd figured he'd outgrown the youthful notion. He was, I saw, in too deep. He'd already sacrificed too much of himself to back out now. To do so would be to admit that the deaths and sacrifices were meaningless. And Bren clung so desperately to this idea of meaning. He thought helping me meant his life mattered. Part of me agreed. The rest loathed that part. I wanted Bren to find his own meaning, to make *his* life the important thing he was part of. In an uncaring reality, nothing was inherently more important than anything else. Value was entirely in the eye of the beholder. He was young. He could start a family, make them the centre of his existence. That would be as important as anything I did. He could open the pub he dreamed of, spend the rest of his life serving ale and pie, and that too would have value.

I could have sent him away. I could have saved him.

Instead, I let him make his own decisions.

Did that make me evil?

If I knew how it was going to end, yes.

CHAPTER TWENTY-THREE

Without going into detail, I explained that I'd be leaving Abieszan and returning within the week. I told Bren I'd need the room I left from maintain exactly as it was, with nothing allowed to change. It would fall upon him to ensure this. Otherwise, I might be trapped and unable to return. He swore to see to it.

Clay returned two hours later as Bren and I finished yet another round of ales.

Collapsing into a chair across from me, he placed a diamond the size of my smallest fingernail on the table before me. "I was told it has fifty-four facets. Tried counting, but I keep losing track because they're so small."

Collecting the stone, I turned it in my fingers. The colour was good, though not great. The faintest hints of brown spoiled its perfection. The facets were well cut but fell short of spectacular. Millennium of making Soul Stones had given me more than a rudimentary knowledge of the jeweller's art. "It will do."

Larger and better cut than the Souls Stone Iremaire destroyed, this little rock likely represented wealth enough for Bren and me to open a tavern anywhere in the world. Later, once I'd replaced the stone with something better, I'd give it to him to do with as he wished. Maybe I'd leave a few souls in it too, just in case.

Clay shot a look of desperate longing at the bar. "Mom says to ask what else you might need for whatever it is you're doing in the cellar."

With the blood and souls presumably already being seen to, there wasn't much else. "I'll need several *very* sharp knives. Drinking water.

The room needs to be well lit. And later, once that's complete, I'll need a second room. Something clean and sparse. In that room I'll need a pack with at least a week's worth of food. I don't need to be able to carry it far, but I do need to be able to lift it."

Clay nodded without asking for details. "By sunrise, we'll have the fifty you requested."

"I need them helpless, hands bound behind their backs. No heavy or cumbersome clothing. Nothing hindering access to their necks."

Looking away, Clay nodded again. "I'll have them stripped and bound."

"Kneeling would be best. I'll need a small keg or two for the blood."

"Two small kegs," he agreed. "The rest of the blood? There's going to be a lot."

Just before we left the island necropolis, Henka had brought me twenty people to harvest. Though helpless, they'd all been conscious. I realized now that she knew exactly what was involved. She could have had them rendered unconscious, or drugged to a narcotic daze, and chose not to. As Nhil said, she never did anything without a reason.

At the time, I'd hesitated. Even the smallest life was a bright spark in the unending black of an uncaring universe. To snuff one forever was a crime. In need of souls, I'd done it anyway. Only now did I understand the lesson she sought to teach: My needs trump all else. That is who I am.

Of the twenty I killed that day, I remembered only one: the old man who'd already been harvested for his limbs. I recalled the way he struggled, afraid of death, and how it felt to push my sword into his back. I remembered nothing of his face.

Tomorrow morning fifty bright sparks would await my knife. I'd not only end their lives, but all chances of another life. I'd sacrifice them to feed my needs.

"Mop it up," I told Clay. "Dump it in the sewers."

Clay stood from the table. "Someone will be along to show you to your room," he said.

He left without another word.

"Though willing to kill in a fight," said Bren, "and no doubt happy to murder upon Mom's command, that is a man uncomfortable with butchery for a purpose he doesn't understand."

"And you?" I asked.

"It used to bother me more."

Which wasn't to say it no longer bothered him.

Tien was right. I was a poison, an infection. I would give Bren the glorious purpose he craved. I would shower him with wealth. He would have everything he craved and more. For I needed Bren far more than he would ever need me. I would never let him go.

One of the barkeeps led us to the room we shared. After the months below ground in Iremaire's prison and the weeks on Captain Rofalle's ship, a room with proper beds was an unimaginable luxury. Three shuttered windows lined one wall, each framed in lustrous oak. The two beds were neatly made, the sheets still smelling of soap, the folds crisp. Though the air carried the still and musty scent of a room long unused, it was spotless. Mom's people strove to maintain her home in immaculate condition. I'd once commanded such loyalty, the kind of devotion that sees things done even though you will likely remain unaware.

Bren immediately collapsed onto the nearest bed and began snoring. I remained awake for hours, deciding what to summon once I'd returned to the floating mountains.

I woke the next morning to find Bren had thrown open the shutters of one of the windows. Lit gold by the rising sun, he gazed out over the city.

"Several of the larger fortified homesteads are burning," he said.

I sat up, stretching. "I'd guess that's where Mom got the fifty from. They must have put up a fight."

"It would have been easier to collect people from the streets," Bren said. "There's no way she got what she needed and set those fortresses alight without losing some of her own people."

"Appearances," I said. "Those on the street are her people. Those in the castles are not."

"Are appearances so important you sacrifice some of those closest to you to maintain them?"

Interesting question. "Yes," I answered, "to petty rulers such as Mom. When you rule the known world, such things no longer matter. The Demon Emperor was always able to make decisions based on what he thought was best without worrying about what thugs on the street thought." And then, because I didn't want to leave him with this half-truth, I added, "That doesn't mean all his decisions were correct."

A sharp knock rattled the door.

Clay entered without waiting, his mummer's mask in place. "Two rooms in the cellar have been cleared for your use." He looked at everything but me.

Apparently, my intent to sacrifice fifty people and harvest their souls had turned him off me. Though not enough to go against Mom's orders.

Four more masked men in leather armour stood sweating behind him. All wore an unsavoury assortment of knives and cudgels.

He led us back downstairs and through the tavern where we'd spent the previous evening. Beyond that we passed through a long hall. Open doors on either side gave glimpses of libraries crammed with books and sitting rooms for entertaining guests. Several doors were closed, and I heard muffled voices as we passed. At the far end, Clay led us down another set of steps, these narrow, the warped wood groaning beneath our feet. Even here, in what looked like a servant's stairwell, everything was spotless, ancient and cracked wood polished to a gleam.

The four trailed along behind in silence.

The basement smelled like old books and dry hay, the earthen floor packed so hard it felt like stone. We had to duck as the rafters were low. A black iron woodstove sat cold and empty, the doors hanging open, the chimney pipe long gone. As I saw no waiting flute above, I figured someone must have carted it down here for storage, though I couldn't imagine why.

Clay collected a lantern from a waiting table, and we waited while he lit it.

"This way," he said, setting off once again.

Though this section looked long unused, it was still free of dust and cobwebs. Turning a circle, I realized this cellar was much smaller than the mansion above. There must have been other areas, with their own entrances.

Two bolted doors, banded in black iron much like the stove, awaited us.

Pointing to the door on the right, Clay said, "This used to be a wine cellar. Mom had it cleared out years ago. No idea what she planned to do with the space, if anything. It's the only room big enough for the crowd we gathered last night."

My heart beat faster. Fifty people awaited my knife. Fifty souls, the currency of true power. Mages sought beauty and purpose in shaping the seething madness of chaos. They were nothing compared to a powerful demonologist with the right tools and a supply of souls. There was a reason they hadn't ruled until after my death just as there was a reason their world was a pathetic and filthy mockery of what I built. Fifty. It had ben thousands of years since I'd possessed such wealth and I hungered to spend it.

"This," Clay gestured at the door on the left, "is a much smaller space. A simple cot, and the food you asked for."

"Plan on locking me in?" I asked, nodding at the bolt.

"These four will be on guard at your door at all times," said Clay. "Mom picked them herself. When you want out, knock."

Sliding the bolt, he threw open the left door. Inside was as he described. A dirt floor, the mortared fieldstone walls the mansion had been built upon, and the same low ceiling. Two backpacks sat in the centre of the room, crammed full of enough food to last me several weeks. At least I wasn't going to starve.

"Now," said Clay, "if everything is to your liking, Bren and I will retire upstairs and enjoy a few pints. Assuming you do as promised, you'll have him back soon enough with only a slight hangover to show for his time among us."

"If it's a slight hangover," said Bren, "we've been doing it wrong."

I pulled Bren into a hug, slapping his back. "I'll be back soon," I whispered into his ear. "I promise. Until then, stay sharp. Keep an eye on Mom. She isn't what she pretends to be."

"Who is?" he said, with a crooked grin.

Clay and Bren left me alone with the four goons, who examined me through the eyeholes of their masks with studied looks of boredom.

I pointed at the door on the right. "You know what's in there?"

They shrugged.

"You understand what is going to happen to those people?"

Another shrug.

"No matter what you hear," I said, "you stay out of the room."

"We have our orders," said the biggest of the four, a monster with a head shaped like a well-hammered anvil.

Sliding the bolt, I strained against the heavy door to the right. It swung open with a groan of rusting hinges, and I stepped in. The room, a massive space of earth and stone divided by sturdy wooden archways, echoed as Anvil-head shoved the door closed behind me, slamming the bolt back into place. Oil lanterns hung from ceiling hooks, lighting those awaiting their fate.

Fifty men and women were littered about the room, blindfolded, hog-tied, and helpless. Some had managed to make it to their knees and work their mouths free of the gags and were calling for help. Others remained sprawled on the dirt floor. Hearing the boom of the closing door, many raised heads, trying to peer through their blindfolds.

"I'm worth a lot," said the nearest woman. "More than anyone else here! My family will pay a ransom for my return."

"All souls are of equal value," I told her.

CHAPTER TWENTY-FOUR

We are, each of us, a multitude. We change a little depending on who we are with. I was one person with Shalayn and someone very different with Henka. The man I was with Nhil was not the same man who enjoyed Bren's easy company. I was the man I wanted to be, the man I was afraid to become, and the man others would judge by his choices and actions.

I was an empty shell living in a mud hut in the far north of Taramlae, and I was the Demon Emperor, above all concerns of right and wrong.

I was a man and a god. I understood that much like beauty, judgement of good and evil lay in the eye of the beholder. These weren't fixed concepts, weren't set in stone. Yet, if the world calls you evil, the fact you feel otherwise is of little value.

Soul Stone in one hand, knife in the other, I slaughtered fifty men and women in that basement room. I soaked the earthen floor in blood until I waded from victim to victim in sanguine mud. They screamed and pleaded, flopping about in the gore in their feeble attempt to escape and I bled them. I severed throats with the skill of a master butcher, roared the ancient chants, and tore their souls from their bodies, trapping them in icy stone.

Last time, when I killed the twenty Henka set aside for me, I cried after, filled with shame and hate. For myself. For what I'd done. For what I yet planned to do.

This time I stood staring at the bloody diamond, chest heaving with laboured breath. My arms ached from the effort, my hands shaking from exhaustion. I had no idea how much time had passed.

I needed souls. I took them. Numb and empty, nothing touched me.

Or so I told myself.

But no one butchers a room of people without cost.

My gaze flinched from corpse to corpse, twitched from slashed throat to slashed throat. One moment they were people with dreams and plans, no doubt striving toward something, though I'd never know what.

"Throw them on the pyre," I whispered. "Feed them to the dogs."

It mattered not. They were gone.

Demons understood that all souls were equal. The soul of a king was worth no more to them than the soul of the filthiest peasant. Dogs, on the other hand, understood the value of meat. Though perhaps a well-marbled king might be tastier than a stringy farmhand.

I laughed, a cracked cackle, and no tears fell.

This wasn't a victory. I wasn't hardening myself or becoming jaded. I wasn't remembering who I had once been.

One atrocity at a time, I murdered the man I wanted to be.

Stop lying to yourself, I imagined Nhil saying. *You never truly wanted to be that man.*

"I did." I winced. "I do."

I pictured him gesturing at the room littered with corpses. *Your actions say otherwise.*

"So do I give up on trying to be better?"

Give up? He laughed. *You never started.*

I blinked and was alone with the abattoir stench of my crimes.

Slogging through the bloody mud, I pounded on the door. The masked man who opened it retreated, a hand on the pommel of his sword. The other three stared past me, at the carnage.

Looking down, I realized I was caked with gore. My clothes had already started to harden to a crust. My hair hung in sodden ropes, blood dripping from the tight braids. I tasted death on my lips, smelled murder with every breath.

"How long did that take?" I asked the nearest man.

"Ten hours," he answered.

"I've lost my touch," I muttered, mostly to myself, images of the past swirling my thoughts like blood spiralling down a drain. "I used to manage hundreds in that time."

"Oh," he said, backing away another step.

Much as I craved a long, hot bath and then to sleep for a week, hunger and need drove me. That shard of my soul moved ever closer. He would feel as I did, anticipation building as he drew near. By the time he reached Abieszan, cutting out my heart would consume his every thought.

Did he know about the wizards in the harbour? What would he do when he saw them?

For a moment, I was more afraid of them taking him than I was of him cracking my ribs to harvest the obsidian within.

I peeled off my clothes, let them fall to the floor with a soggy *splat*. Even waiting for something clean was more time than I was willing to waste. Staggering to the other door in my undergarments, I entered the simple room with the lone cot. It called to me, and I ignored it. My exhaustion was irrelevant. There was no time for rest, no time for weakness.

Turning to face the guards, I said, "I'll be in here for a week. Maybe more. No one is to enter under any circumstances."

Eyes wide behind their mummer's masks, they stared at the near-naked madman barking orders at them.

Pulling the heavy door closed, I cursed the fact there was no bolt on the inside. I'd have to hope no one altered the room while I was away.

I don't know how long I spent sketching the wards and pacts or kneeling on the floor screaming the summoning. By the time I sat back, a portal demon bound to the ring Iremaire thought to mock me with, my entire body shook and twitched. Another sliver of my soul chipped away and sold in the name of power. Though hardly as damaging as binding NamKhar had been, every demonic summoning took its toll on my sanity. I felt frayed, the edges of self disintegrating, flaking away like a snake shedding its skin.

Pulling what remained of me together, I picked a corner and stood like a stone statue for hours, memorizing every chip and crack in the walls, every bump in the dirt floor. I breathed the musty basement air, locked the taste in my thoughts. I listened to the sighs of the ancient house, the almost imperceptible creak of wood swelling from the tropical heat beyond.

Once I had the room memorized so I could return here, I imagined the library in the floating mountains. I pictured the fireplace, loaded with ancient logs that would never burn. I pictured the granite floor, heard the way sound reverberated in the room. I saw the rows of bookcases, smelled the preserved pages.

When every detail was perfect, I lifted the sacks of food and fed a soul to Frorrat, the portal demon.

The heat of the tropics disappeared, and I stood in the library.

Looking left, I saw Nhil standing motionless as he always did.

"You're dripping blood on the floor," he said, violet eyes opening, one slightly before the other. "Your timing is… unfortunate."

"Unfortunate? Why?"

"Because you're already here."

Hunger hit me with crushing force, squeezed my heart and left no room for thought beyond need.

Somewhere in this tower among the floating mountains was another shard of my heart.

And if I knew he was here, he most certainly knew of my arrival.

CHAPTER TWENTY-FIVE

I spun in a circle, crouching, fists clenched ready to attack or flee. Like an idiot, I'd left my knife back in the cellar. It hadn't been a conscious choice, but I knew I was safe here.

I'd been a fool.

I remembered sensing a part of my heart suddenly disappearing. Distracted by the piece hunting and killing shards, I'd assumed the wizards took him as they had me. That was weeks ago. Some piece of my heart spent weeks here with access to the libraries, the summoning chambers, and all Nhil's wisdom.

I turned back to the demon. "Where is he?"

"Upstairs." His eyes slid in a mistimed blink. "Resting."

"Resting? Not anymore, he isn't." I searched the room for a weapon, found nothing. "Is he armed?"

"He has a knife." Nhil made a pantomime of looking me up and down. "While I'm pleased that you feel comfortable enough in our friendship to visit dressed in nothing but underclothes and blood, only a fool travels to alternate realities unarmed."

My thoughts raced. The piece of my heart was moving now, drawing near. "Get me a sword."

"Why?"

"So I can kill him!"

"Ah," said Nhil. "You assume I'm on your side."

"I guess that answers my question about whether you're really my friend," I snapped.

Slim shoulders slid in a reptilian mistimed shrug. "He is as much you as you are. Probably more so. And he hasn't been travelling with Henka; I'd call that a mark in his favour. Perhaps most important, unlike you, he *wants* to be you."

"She told me not to trust you."

Grey lips twitched in something caught between a smirk and a grimace. "No, she didn't. You still haven't told her of me."

I ignored the smug bastard, stooping to dig through the two sacks I'd brought in the hope someone thought to include something I might wield as a weapon.

"Do you remember your first visit?" Nhil asked.

"Of course I do," I muttered, distracted.

"You had no idea where you were, no idea how to get home."

"I was starving to death."

"Quite."

Unless I wanted to try and beat the man to death with a slab of cured beef, I found nothing useful in the pack.

I turned on Nhil. "How did he get here? Does he remember this place? Does he remember you? Henka?"

"You always have too many questions." He nodded past me. "Here is your answer."

I spun as a youth of maybe seventeen years staggered into the room. Dressed in the filthy skins of a Sepkt tribesman, he was gaunt and starved, black flesh sunken, obsidian eyes staring from hollowed pits. He clutched a dagger of yellow bone in one fist.

"You," he croaked, voice cracking. "Who are you? Why... Why?"

I remembered being him, the empty slate searching for answers, wondering who he was. He must have awoken in the north, much like I had. Instead of finding a tracker to kill for his boots and mud hut, he'd come across one of the savage northern tribes.

"He has yet to master the water elemental at the heart of the mountain," Nhil said. He sounded mildly disappointed with the young man. "Another few days, and you'd have found a corpse."

I stepped over the packs separating us. "It's all right," I said, holding my hands out to show I carried no weapons. "I won't hurt you."

"No," said Nhil. "Someone is definitely getting hurt."

AN END TO SORROW

Nhil

I ignored the demon. "You and me," I told the youth, "we're the same. We want the same thing."

"At least the last part is true," said Nhil.

When his attention darted to the demon, I tackled him, bearing his starved body to the ground. Pain lanced my side as he drove the dagger in under my ribs. I screamed, knocking it from his hands with my flailing. He crushed brutal punches into the wound, snarling and spitting like a rabid dog. For all his savagery, I was older and larger. Where he spent years eking out a subsistence living and the last two weeks slowly starving to death, I'd put on muscle.

Rearing back, I cracked the sharp blade of my elbow into his chin, slamming his head to the side. He coughed, spit blood, and clawed at my face. Teeth gritted, I tangled my hands into his filthy hair and raised his head to smash it against the granite floor. Desperate fingers dug into my wounded side, sending searing spears of agony through me.

Again, I slammed his head against stone.

When he made a wet, confused sound almost like a drunken question, I paused to get a better grip. Lifting his head as high as I could, I crashed his skull down. Over and over, until he lay limp beneath me.

I sat atop myself, breath coming in ragged gasps.

"No," I said. "No. Not again."

No matter what I thought I wanted, I craved completion. I had to become *him*. I *needed* to be whole.

"And you said you wouldn't hurt him," chided Nhil. "Then again, you always were best at lying to yourself."

I snarled at the demon and rolled off the corpse.

"I couldn't possibly have gotten a sword here before he arrived," Nhil said, as reasonable as ever. "Frankly, if you couldn't beat a half-starved child, you didn't deserve to go on."

I lay on the floor, glaring up at him. "It's about deserving now, is it? The better killer gets to rule the world?"

"When has it been otherwise? Would you like a snack and a quick nap before you break yourself open and carve out your heart?"

Pushing myself upright with a groan, I studied the dead youth. Whatever he was, whatever life he'd lived since waking from our death, it would be gone the moment I took his heart. As ever, it bothered me that our obsidian souls carried only the memories of the Demon Emperor. It left me feeling strangely vulnerable. Though everyone's memories died with them, the fact my life could go on without me seemed somehow wrong. I was too valuable to lose.

Seeing the bone knife, I crawled to collect it before returning to the body. I tore open his crude shirt, studied the protruding ribs.

"I can fetch you a proper knife," suggested Nhil.

"Now you're being helpful?"

He sniffed, sounding hurt.

This close, there could be no waiting. Not when more of me lay within reach. New summonings. Ancient memories.

"He won't know anything of Henka, will he?"

"I couldn't possibly answer that question," said the demon.

"And he won't know anything of you either."

"Probably not," he agreed.

"Why? If Henka did this, I understand her cutting herself from my past, giving us a fresh start. She could do that if she thought it would make you happy. But why hide the pieces that remember you?"

"Good question. You should ask her. But then you'd have to admit you know who she is."

When I failed to react, he continued: "Do you think she doesn't know that you know? Are you so clever you've never made even the smallest slip?"

"If she's so brilliant and all-knowing, then why is her heart in the basement of my palace? Why didn't she enslave me?"

"Because there is a level at which pure selfish need will trump intelligence. And to be honest," violet eyes did their mistimed blink, "I'm not convinced she's the only one who is enslaved."

"I hate you."

"And yet…"

I drove the dagger into the cartilage at the centre of the corpse's chest. Wriggling the bone knife, I put my weight behind it, shoving it deeper.

Breaking a man's ribs wide to carve out his heart is difficult with a proper blade. With a bone dagger—at best a crude stabbing tool—it was a brutal and arduous process. Only my stubborn pride wouldn't allow me to ask Nhil for a knife. I savaged the body to open it, left the library floor painted in blood. When I finally found the heart, stared down at my trophy, the need to have it left little room for rational thought.

Nhil said something.

"What?" I couldn't take my eyes from the tiny wedge of obsidian nestled in the mess I'd made.

"Would you like a bath first?" he repeated. "Would you like to take the stone upstairs, lie in a comfortable bed while you—"

"I don't have time. I'm coming to kill me."

"Can't trust anyone these days."

"I need weapons and armour."

"Lost the last demon sword already?"

I didn't have time for this and yet couldn't stop myself. The more of my heart I had, the more overwhelming the insatiable need became. Each time I took on a new piece I lost two days to nightmares of the past. That was time I didn't have.

I bared bloody teeth at the corpse. Save it for later. Do what I came to do. Summon and bind weapons so I could fight myself.

What if this piece knew something useful, something that would turn the tide in my favour? Whatever lay in that glassy black stone could mean the difference between victory and defeat.

"You already know what you're going to do," said Nhil, behind me.

I tore the shard free, balanced it in the palm of my hand. Watched it sink into my flesh. Screamed in raw agony as it scythed through veins and muscle on its way to join the stone in my heart.

Pain should not be so glorious.

Razor-sharp rock shoved through the meat of me, causing horrendous damage. I laughed and cried for the searing pleasure of it. There should be punishment for crimes such as mine, retribution for such heinous sins. There wasn't, not really. Reality didn't care about right and wrong, good and evil. Henka's millennia of harvesting people to maintain herself, and the Demon Emperor's ten thousand years of rule, proved that. There was no balance. If evil was stronger, then evil won.

And with each shard of my heart, I grew stronger.

Atone, atone. Eyes of stone.

I stood atop a screaming mountain, the enslaved elementalist taming it waited behind me. Never trust when you could own, a lesson learned over and over. Loyalty was a sad second to soul-gutted mindless worship.

Yet here I was, betrayed. Had a lesson ignored been truly learned?

The mountain, torn from another world, wailed its pain.

Armoured head to toe in demon-bound red steel, Kantlament hung in my fist. An end to sorrow. The sword, forged to shatter worlds, craved destruction.

From my screaming mountain, I looked down upon the gathered host. An army of five worlds, this was my answer to the Guild's foul perfidy. The mages turned the sorcerers, elementalists, shamans, and necromancers against me with promises of a new world. Only my demonologists remained loyal, and even some of them I'd lost. Their combined forces burned my fleets, shattered the walls of my cities. My empire of ten thousand years stood at the brink of destruction. Civilization teetered on the verge of collapse.

They thought they'd won. They had no idea.

My strength was never in my armies. My strength wasn't the hordes of undead, the raging mountains, or tamed firestorms. It wasn't the souls of a thousand generations called back by the shaggy shamans. It wasn't the battlemages or the suicidal sorcerers burning through their lives in the desperate quest for purpose.

An entire world united against me, and if I loosed my rage, if I truly gave in to the anger shuddering through my veins, I would break them all. They were nothing, helpless.

She Dreamed in Blood, and she dreamed of conquest. Not one world. Not the five I already conquered in her name. She would dominate *all* worlds, and I was her sword, both the fist and the fury.

Constructed. A weapon designed for one purpose. Bone by bone, eyes of stone, she remade me. Slivers of a dream, shadows, and smoke. The mortal I'd once been was long dead, consumed by the stone she dropped into the savaged cavity of my chest. I was a man and a god, and so much more and so much less.

The armies of five conquered worlds stood awaiting the command to march. No chance of betrayal, they were bound demons. Hulking monsters all claw and shaggy fur. Massive reptilian horrors, a hive of writhing eyeless tentacles, armoured in their own sick brand of sorcery. Nightmares torn from the depths of insanity. From horizon to horizon my reality-scarring host prepared to go to war.

Five conquered worlds, each once home to their own pantheons of gods.

Her fist and her fury, I crushed these alien gods, entrapping them in the stone in my left eye for future use. When I called them to battle, they would come.

And the wizards thought they'd won.

The Eye of Worlds. That's what I called the stone in my right eye. I saw the five I'd conquered but knew there were many more. Maybe infinitely more. The stone grew hot as I prepared to shred the curtain between realities and retake my world. The flesh around the eye smoked and burned, mottled and molten scars ravaging half my face. Pain was the price of power.

I hesitated. Why, I didn't know.

She dreamed in blood and once said I was the mirror of her soul. The snake in the grass, she called me, the smoke trapped in stone.

What did that mean?

My stone eyes showed me the diaphanous nature of reality, how thin the curtain separating them truly was. They were all the same, all different. She dreamed, and she wanted to rule it all forever.

A worm of doubt twitched within me; forever was a myth.

I clawed great wounds in the curtain, and the Eye of Worlds glowed red, searing flesh and boiling blood.

And still, I hesitated.

Bring the mountain and these gathered armies through the rotting veil and retake my world. Crush the conniving Guild, deny them the last freedom I so foolishly allowed. Soul and sinew, bind them to my purpose as I should have done long ago.

One step forward. Bring death unimaginable.

I would reduce their rebellion to ash and bone, leave only one in ten, the few pure souls worthy of saving.

But she was gone.

Not my god, my love. My only love. The centre of my soul, the whole of my world.

She abandoned me.

Her betrayal stung more than any other.

"Is this what you want?" she had asked, nodding at the endless ranks of corpses.

I recalled the question and the gesture but nothing more.

I could not answer her, for I did not know.

What *did* I want?

Did I have wants, or were they all my god's? Had her dream replaced my every need and desire?

My god gave me purpose, but my love gave me something more.

"A man is nothing without ambition," I told the mountain, and it roared its helpless rage. "But he is even less without love."

The mountain didn't care.

My chest hurt. My heart, clenched like a fist, felt like it might shatter.

Burn me alive. Cook the meat of my brain with the stone eyes of a god. Carve away the last of my humanity and lay bare the nerves for plucking like the overtight strings of a lute. It paled in comparison to the loss and betrayal of my love.

I wanted to smother her in the darkness she most feared, reduce her to nothing.

I wanted to fall to my knees at her feet and beg forgiveness.

More than anything, I wanted to end that pain.

Followed by the stench of charred meat, I stepped between worlds, leaving my startled army behind.

Alone, I returned to the Palace at PalTaq.

She dreamed in blood, and she was rage, and she was vengeance. I betrayed my god and there would be a reckoning.

Closing the tear in reality behind me, I stalked the empty halls of the palace. My priests were gone. Some still fought, waging a doomed war with the Guild. Others floated dead in the oceans, lay buried beneath stampeding mountains, charred to ash by feral firestorms, or blasted to nothing by sorcery or the wizard's battle magic.

It hit me that the moment I had just stepped away from—invading my world with the gathered hosts of five demonic realities—was always her plan. She wanted that war, the expenditure of souls, the spilling of literal oceans of blood.

Fear and terror are but the most primal aspects of worship.

The Eye of Worlds was but one of her gifts to me. Like all her gifts, it came with a price. With each offering I accepted, I lost more of myself.

I tore the stone eye from my skull, the burnt flesh already healing around the wound. Still hot, it seared my hand.

I looked to Kantlament, clutched in my right fist.

"If I can't have the world," I told the demon bound to the steel, "no one can."

Not the Guild.

Not the god to whom I sacrificed everything, serving her for thousands of years.

But first, I had to talk to her one last time. I needed to understand.

I turned away, left the sword and eye behind. The demonic door swung closed with a finality that shook my bones.

Down.

Ever deeper.

To the hall of hearts. The demons bound there cowered at my arrival, cleared my path. Weaving through endless pedestals carrying their grizzly burdens, each with a plaque bearing the owner's name, I headed to the far end of the hall. There, I found my love's heart, a calcified husk of wizened black.

Unsure what I intended, I placed my hand upon her heart. "I have returned."

Silence answered me, though I knew she heard.

"You betrayed me."

You know that is not possible, she answered.

It shouldn't have been. "How can I trust you?"

Because I love you.

"Where are you?"
I'm here.

CHAPTER TWENTY-SIX

Twisting to look behind me, I jolted awake on the library floor.

Nhil stood over me, motionless as ever. He drew no breath, showed no hint of being a living creature.

Violet eyes slid in a mistimed blink. "You have returned."

"Fuck," I said, groaning as I sat up.

Every part of me hurt. I felt like someone dragged razor blades through every nerve and vein. I saw no trace of the youth I hacked open. The floor was spotless as if the murder and subsequent butchery had been but a dream.

I felt a long way from well-rested despite my sleep.

More than anything, I wanted to collapse into one of the library's huge leather chairs or stagger upstairs to my chambers for some real sleep. New memories jostled in my skull, struggling to fit with what was already there. As ever, it was never a simple thing to take on a new shard. My mind needed time to heal, to sort through everything to make sense of it all. That which the Demon Emperor learned by rote came quicker. The more personal memories, however, would bubble to the surface for months.

Long forgotten summonings and bindings returned to me. Demonic elementals, primordial creatures called from alien realities. Clouds of deadly toxins. Pools of intelligent acid. Jade monsters and burning mists that drained life from everything in their vicinity.

Grone.

I laughed. "You remember Grone?"

Nhil gave me a withering look. "One tends not to forget an

Elemental Demon Lord."

"He raised a city from the earth on one of the more mountainous islands. Calls himself King Grone now."

"Do you think he's forgiven you?"

"Forgiven?" So much of my past remained missing.

"You conquered his world, enslaved those who survived, bound him to servitude, and trapped him here."

"That was a long time ago."

"Of course," said Nhil. "I'm sure he's forgotten all about the genocide of his people."

Ignoring him, I sorted through the summoning and bindings I now remembered.

There were spirit demons that could be bound to missile weapons like arrows, thrown knives, or even projectiles hurled by ballistae and the like. By twisting reality around them, they became impossibly accurate, even over a great range. Some exploded on impact doing devastating damage. Others were capable of puncturing any mortal armour. Interesting, but every single missile costs a soul.

I remembered how to call demons from a reality that had been in a state of perpetual war for millions of years. I once had entire battalions of the creatures at my beck and call. Unparalleled warriors, they were unbelievably fast and difficult to kill. Unfortunately, such bindings would be useless when fighting against myself. Demons saw all the shards of my heart as equally me, and thus couldn't attack or hurt them.

Interesting as all this was—and I desperately wanted more time to examine my new memories—I'd promised Bren a weapon and armour. The thought reminded me of Shalayn's sword easily piercing my demonic armour and pinning me to the deck of the wizard's war galley. It would cost more souls, but I now knew a more powerful binding. There were spirit demons that could make even simple cotton all but invincible. I had neither the time nor the souls for something of that level.

"I need two swords," I told Nhil. "Are there complete chain hauberks in the armoury?"

"Of course."

"One of those too."

Had I more time, I'd bind something to the underpadding as well, but that was a luxury I no longer possessed.

I left without another word, heading to the tower's summoning chambers. Nhil followed along behind, unhurried. Distracted, I paid little attention to the rooms we passed through. The hanging sheets of human skin, tanned, and waiting to be turned into demon-protected books, no longer bothered me. The empty bowls and dangerously low supplies had more impact. This bolt-hole bubble reality desperately needed restocking if it was to be of use. I wanted months of preserved foods stored away, enough to feed dozens of guests should I ever choose to bring someone. I needed changes of clothes suitable for every environment and occasion, from the cold cities of the mainland to the tropical islands. There should be money here too, enough to cover any emergency.

"Did I leave funds here?" I asked over my shoulder as I entered the summoning rooms.

"Of course," said Nhil. "The currency is outdated, the coins dating to the Empire, but the stones will not have lost their value."

"I saw no rooms of coins and stones."

"The demon you left to protect that vault—you called him The Banker, no doubt thinking yourself clever—hides and protects it. You've passed the hidden entrance several times."

"Are there diamonds?"

"Of course."

That was good to know. A ready supply of Soul Stones was more valuable than any diamond.

"And no," Nhil added, as I opened my mouth to ask another question, "none have souls in them."

"Shit."

Two perfect swords, simple in construction yet flawless and sharp, waited alongside a gleaming suit of chain hauberk. The underpadding for the armour hung over the corner of a chair at the far end of the room.

I stopped, studying the wards and pacts engraved in the black and red granite floor. Last time I'd crawled around for hours making sure everything was perfect. I didn't have time for that.

"Can you make sure everything is ready?" I asked Nhil.

"Already done."

If he lied or was somehow wrong, the failure would cost me my soul. Whatever that was worth. The potential existed for catastrophic failure, reality shredding apart as some alien god clawed gaping wounds in the fabric of the world.

Setting aside my misgivings at not checking every detail myself, I got to work.

Much as I wanted to bind something truly ferocious to Bren's sword, I had to prioritize. Because I'd already done it once in recent memory, I summoned another demon of the same type as Mihir, the sword he traded to Captain Rofalle for the boat. I called Kra'Katle from its home reality and bound it to steel. Perhaps summoning a demon the second time was easier, or maybe the previous experience forever broke something in me. I felt nothing crushing its will beneath mine and forever imprisoning it. Its wailing screams gnawed at my sanity, and I laughed.

Ill flames of nauseous green flickered about the blade until I sheathed the weapon. Even the smallest cut would turn instantly gangrenous, festering in minutes, and withering to nothing soon after. It would cut through the thickest plate armour, cleave stone, murdering the elemental.

At Nhil's command, an air elemental tidied the summoning chambers, making them ready for my next task.

Refusing to rest, I stood waiting, my thoughts wandering and stuttering.

The Demon Emperor had already been thousands of years old when he bound Kantlament. Like Abieszan, entire cities were his to command. He had countless warriors, weapons, and suits of demonic armour. He'd personally summoned and bound every demon in the palace at PalTaq, every warded door or protected vault because it was the only way he could be sure no one could betray him. Yet I remembered the terrible damage to his sanity that summoning had done. What I planned now would have been nothing to him, but still, I shook with fear.

"There is always a cost to power," I told myself.

Nhil, remaining well clear of the summoning area, said nothing.

Exhaustion muddled my thoughts. Before I found Henka, I had to kill the shard coming north.

Though I conquered five worlds in my god's name, there were infinitely more realities. I searched through my memories, hunting for the summoning that might give me a critical edge in the coming conflict.

"It's ready," said Nhil.

I had no idea how long I'd stood there.

Swallowing my fears and doubts, I prepared the summoning. A mindless thing, acting on bone-deep memory, I drew the wards and pacts that would trap the demon. Sleep and food, all the body's needs, became irrelevant. Singular will, focussed intent. Though a shadow of the man I'd once been, I was still, at heart, him. All the wishful thinking in the world couldn't change the fact I was the kind of man who craved power, who would do anything to possess it. Maybe fear drove me. Fear of being helpless. Certainly, what I'd done to Henka spoke volumes of my insecurity. But turned to a purpose, fear and insecurity were powerful motivators. Somewhere inside something laughed, mocking; I was the most powerful demonologist the world had ever seen because I was the most cowardly.

I clung to Bren all the more because, with Henka gone, I was afraid of being alone.

I blinked, found myself kneeling on the granite floor, my knees bruised. I set aside my pain, shoved the aches of my body down deep, and narrowed my thoughts to a stiletto of concentration.

Sweeping aside the curtain separating our worlds, I called a demon. Reality, savaged, shuddered under the onslaught. Foul black filled the binding circle, devoured all that was good in the world. It breathed insensate evil, hungered for the destruction of all life. Antithesis to light and love, it smashed at the walls of my mind, massacring my sanity.

I fed the demon soul after soul, bloated it with sacrifices I never should have been allowed to offer, never should have been willing to make.

I roared the ancient pacts, spitting blood to twist my throat to inhuman words.

The demon fought me, and I crushed it beneath my will. Even this blight on all that was good was nothing before the might of the Demon Emperor.

I bound it to the sword.

Worse than Mihir. Fouler even than Namkhar. Adraalmak was poison.

Twitching, I vomited upon the weapon.

"Good thing you did that after completing the binding," mused Nhil from behind me.

"The armour," I whispered, my voice like splintered glass. "Then I'm finished."

"You must rest now," said Nhil.

"No time."

"If you try another you will fail."

"I can do it." I swept my gaze across the room, trying to remember where the chain hauberk was. Something was wrong. My eyes refused to focus. The world appeared blurred and indistinct, as if viewed through warped and stained glass.

"Do you trust me?" asked Nhil.

"No," I answered, more honestly than intended.

"Yes, you do," he said. "Until you regain yourself, my old friend, I shall be your wisdom and your knowledge. And I tell you, if you attempt a third summoning, you *will* fail."

"You wouldn't help me before," I growled, thinking of the youth with the bone dagger.

"You didn't need my help."

"And I don't now."

"Fine." He sniffed. "Stand up. Show me you're ready."

I couldn't. My legs failed, the muscles like jelly.

"I can do it without standing. I don't have time—"

"I have fulfilled my role, done as I promised all those thousands of years ago. I have offered wisdom and advice. As ever, it is your choice as to whether you listen."

"Smug fucker."

Nhil waited.

Finally, I rolled onto my back and lay blinking at the stone ceiling. Cold granite never felt so comfortable.

"The wizards are right. Demonology is evil."

Nhil asked, "And the intent of the demonologist is worth nothing?"

"It *is* worth nothing. Even if I used that sword for only the most virtuous of purposes—and right now I can't imagine what those would be—it wouldn't change what I did to make it. Souls fed to a demon I ripped, against its will, from its home." My eyes slid closed. "We both know I'm not going to use the weapon for only good and virtuous reasons. I'll kill every Khraen I meet and cut out his heart. I'll cut down anyone and anything that gets between me and what I want." I pictured the blood cascading down the steps from the wall in Abieszan as I murdered those between myself and Henka.

"You're learning," he said. "Last time, you were more naïve and easier to convince."

"Not arguing? Not trying to convince me good and evil are nothing more than ideas, that all things must bow to perspective?"

"We know what you are."

Did we?

"I'll just close my eyes for a moment," I said.

"I could have an earth elemental drag you to your chambers."

If he had more humour to share, I missed it.

CHAPTER TWENTY-SEVEN

I woke sprawled on the floor in the summoning chambers, the granite much less comfortable. Sitting, I saw the puke had been cleaned up. I'd been given a rather exuberant scrubbing too, though less effectively.

"I had an earth elemental mop the floor and clean you up," said Nhil, standing exactly as he was before I slept.

"That explains the bruises."

"They're not the best at such tasks."

"Didn't want to get your hands dirty?"

He displayed pristine grey fingers with an extra knuckle, the nails trimmed and polished to a shine.

"That other Khraen" I said, "he doesn't remember this place either. How did he get here?"

"The same way you did the first time. He found a ring."

"I want that ring."

Nhil bowed. "I'll have it fetched from the vault."

"What else is in here that I don't know about?"

"Do you have time for an exhaustive list?"

"Never mind."

I wasn't sure what I planned. The ring would bring anyone donning it here, to this reality, but deposit them beyond the outer gates. I could give it to Brenwick, as long as I instructed the gates to allow him entrance. He'd be unable to leave without my help, but in a life-or-death situation, this might be a useful escape. Conversely, I could use it to get here myself but didn't relish the thought of arriving out in the obsidian mountains and having to trek here with whatever supplies I brought.

And so, I'd spend a soul every time to avoid that inconvenience. "Never mind," I said. "Forget the ring."

The room had been made ready for the next summoning while I slept. Unwilling to waste a moment more, I got to work, summoning and binding a spirit demon to the chain hauberk. Being rushed for time, I kept it simple. Someday I'd make Bren something worthy of his friendship. There were demons capable of shattering any weapon that came in contact with them, who could send muscle-locking jolts back up through metallic weapons or even lash out with attacks of their own. I didn't think he'd much appreciate some of the tentacled monstrosities I'd bound in the past. Armour that crawled off you to pursue your enemies or entirely enclosed you in a protective bubble allowing you to breathe underwater or wade through pools of molten stone, could be somewhat unsettling.

Simple as it may have been, this new demon took a toll on both soul and sanity. I felt filthy, infected to the very core. Three demons in two days were too much. My mind needed time to heal between each onslaught. Though perhaps heal was the wrong word. It felt more like, given some time, I became inured to the damage done. I didn't return to my previous state, I accepted my new one.

With the demon bound, I turned to Nhil. "Have the swords and armour packed and ready to leave. There is one more thing I must do."

He gave the slightest bow as I left the summoning chambers.

Empty halls echoed with my footsteps, the regularly spaced torches flickering to life at my approach, dancing their synchronized joy at a moment's life, and dying as I passed. Endless suites of guest rooms. Kitchens, and dining halls. Libraries crammed with books and reading rooms replete with deep sofas and chairs of buttery leather. Conference rooms large enough to seat hundreds or small enough for intimate gatherings. I tried to imagine this place as it must have once been, thronging with life, my most entrusted servants rushing about on the business of empire. Or had it ever been that? Sadly, it was easier to imagine myself creating all this and then realizing I didn't trust anyone enough to bring them here.

Traversing stairway after stairway, I headed ever higher. And ever slower as if my feet, realizing my destination and intent, resisted. I reached my personal chambers at the top of the tower, slowing to a complete stop just beyond the entrance.

"This will be nothing," I told myself. "The demon is already bound. All I have to do is put it on."

I'd be safe. Though I no longer knew how to summon or bind such a terrifying demon, it was I who bound it long ago. Like the demons in Abieszan, it would remain loyal.

"It's not a threat."

I entered the room, ignoring the painting of a woman caught in the act of turning away that usually drew my eye. This time, however, a complete suit of crimson plate armour, held my attention. It struck me that I'd been a fool. Putting this on without help was impossible. I should have asked Nhil or had him send an elemental along to assist.

I'd seen it several times before, but only now studied it in detail. Unwilling to approach too close, I circled the armour. The more I looked, the stranger it became. There were no straps or belts, no visible means of fastening the various parts, no way to connect the helm to the gorget or the arms to the torso. The joints, typically armour's weakest points, appeared seamless. It looked as if anyone managing to somehow don the armour would be trapped within. Stranger still, nowhere in the room could I find padding to wear beneath the plate.

Something inside me quailed at the thought of touching the armour. I wanted to flee back downstairs to the summoning chambers and bind another spirit demon to match the armour I made for Bren.

Hissing at the cowardly thoughts, I lifted the steel helm from the rack. Impossibly light, it felt like it was made from the thinnest tin. Despite my fear, excitement thrummed through me, my hands shaking. Whatever I'd bound to this armour, it was so far beyond my current abilities, I could hardly comprehend its power. My intent, all those millennia ago, had been to stride the earth, Kantlament in hand. I was going to destroy the wizards, smash their pathetic Guild.

Turning the helm, I stared into the empty sockets, finding only depthless black. My heart smashed in my chest. What was it like to look out from within? I rotated the helm to peer into the neck hole. It swelled, growing larger as if eager for me to slip it on. Inside awaited writhing tentacles of fine hair, barbed like teeth. A living throat, it pulsated, throbbing and glistening like it longed to swallow my head. There were no eyeholes. Somehow, the demon saw the world without and passed that knowledge to the wearer.

Bile threatened to choke me. This was not a spirit demon bound to steel. The demon *was* the armour. The entire thing was a living organism. It fed off the wearer and protected them. Helm in hand, I looked down into the torso armour. It was the same, a yawning pit of writhing black, hungry for contact with naked skin. I reached toward the opening with my free hand, and the black hairs trembled, reaching toward my fingers with desperate anticipation. I understood why there was no under armour.

I'd summoned and bound this but couldn't imagine ever letting it touch me. The mere thought left me wanting to scream and flee.

Returning my attention to the helm, I clenched my teeth, lowering my hand to let the silken hair caress my fingertips. Stretching to their full length, they curled about my fingers, sensuous and teasing, promising warmth, safety, and protection. I watched with sick fascination, unwilling to further lower my hand or pull away completely.

I considered the dangers I faced.

For the first time since my reawakening, two pieces of my heart had started moving. While one travelled from island to island, apparently bent on destroying the other shards, another headed north toward me. Both were dangerous. To make matters worse, there were two wizard warships in Abieszan harbour, and I needed to search the waters unimpeded to find Henka. There'd be battlemages, possibly scores of them. They'd interfere.

I lowered my hand, felt the tickling hairs entwine my fingers like a lover's touch. The dark throat within opened in a wet yawn both sexual and repulsive.

Gripping the helm in two hands, I drew calming breaths, struggling to slow my heart.

"What are you willing to do to get Henka back?" I asked.

Anything.

Lifting the helm over my head, I looked up into the pulsating throat, glistening black flesh working like it meant to swallow my skull, devour my head.

It was safe. It had to be safe.

I lowered the helm, feeling the fine black tentacles squirm through my hair. They pushed, wet, into my ears. My throat tightened in a terrified gag reflex as I pulled the armoured helm the rest of the way down.

For a heartbeat, silence.

Nothing.

Then, slick hair wriggled into my mouth and nose, choked my throat closed. I screamed like a drowning man, devoid of air, every pore invaded, worms pushing past distended eyeballs to tangle with the nerves beyond.

I heard nothing, saw nothing. Couldn't breathe, dying in a world of perfect black.

Light and sound exploded, ripping through my skull in a torrential flood of sensation. I saw, but it wasn't *me* seeing. I saw everything, all around me. I saw the floor below, the ceiling above, the room I stood in and the hallways through the open door behind me. I saw wind currents, watched the slow passage of a near mindless air elemental commanded to keep the floors free of dust, the air clean and odourless. I heard everything. My own pounding heart and the rush of blood through my veins. I heard the call of the rest of the armour, a susurrating whisper. Somewhere far below I heard the heavy plod of an earth elemental stomping about its duties.

I tasted the purity of the air even though none of it touched my olfactory senses. I tasted the age of the oil used in the painting, knew the pigments by flavour, caught the linseed scent of the base and the varnishes and turpentine used to adjust both the lustre and viscosity. The chamber's colours became strange. Glancing at my hand, I saw the heat wafting from it, the hot blood pulsing through veins and the work of muscles beneath the flesh. All hint of shadow disappeared, banished by my new eyes. Looking to one of the torches and its dancing fire elemental I saw the life within, the shapes of it hidden to my mortal perceptions. Where previously it looked yellow, I saw its blue heart, the wavering limbs of red and orange. It watched me, glorying in its brief joy, dreading the moment I left, and the binding commands snuffed its existence to nothing.

Of Nhil, I heard nothing, sensed nothing.

It was too much.

Overwhelmed, I fell to my knees.

As if in response, the world became muted. Still infinitely more complex than what I was used to, but almost manageable. I learned to focus on what was before me. Everything behind me became indistinct, blurred, but still clear enough I'd notice the movement of an attacker.

The armour spoke to me, promised protection. It would warn me, ward me against all harm. All I had to do was let it feed.

Climbing back to my feet, I stood in stunned amazement. I drew no breath but felt no need for air. It fed me, purified my blood, scrubbed my brain clean of the cobwebs of exhaustion. I felt impossibly sharp, more aware and alert than ever in my life. My fear fell away, replaced by reptilian calm. If I chose to, I knew I could feel that fear again. The helm's every choice was in service to my needs, but I was free to override them.

I laughed, unable to imagine a situation where fear would be anything other than a distraction.

Stripping away my clothes, I donned the rest of the armour. Each segment opened to me like a needy lover, drew me in and swallowed me whole. It invaded every part of me, saw to my body's every want. Ensconced within, wrapped in a protective embrace, coddled and cuddled, I felt powerful as a god. My fists would shatter stone. My limbs and muscles were capable of impossible strength and speed.

Fear and doubt were useless, the pathetic side effects of mortals bound by limits of meat and blood.

Where exhaustion haunted me the entire climb to the top of the tower, my descent was effortless. I felt like I floated down the stairs, my feet hardly touching the floor.

Nhil awaited me in the library.

Seeing me, he shook his head in regret and disgust and said, "What is the point of having a demonic advisor if you aren't going to come to it for advice?"

I scowled at Nhil before realizing he couldn't see my face and the expression was wasted.

"The armour," he said, "mimics your mood. I see your confused and annoyed scrunchy face as clearly as ever."

"Fine," I said. "What, then, would have been your advice, oh great and wise demon."

"Don't put the fucking armour on."

Was that the first time he'd ever sworn? "Why not?"

"It's dangerous. You aren't ready. You have neither the will nor the wisdom to bear such power."

"I could put it back."

"Go ahead."

I didn't want to. I'd been pursued and hunted from the moment I woke in the north. This was the first time I felt safe and protected. Whatever the world threw at me, I could handle it.

"If you were such a great advisor, you'd have told me to go upstairs and put the armour on the first time I visited. Everything would have turned out better."

One eye rolled, mocking, and then the other. When they both again focussed on me, he said, "You were afraid of that armour for a reason. It won't be easy to remove, and the longer you wear it, the more difficult it will become. It feeds you, but it feeds off you as well."

"It's a symbiote."

"It's a demonic parasite and you're a fool if you think otherwise."

"Why would I make a suit of armour that endangered me?" I demanded.

"Because you hated yourself."

Crimson armour. Kantlament in hand. An end to sorrow.

"I'm not him," I said.

"Not yet." Violet eyes, sad with knowledge, studied me. "All power comes at a price. You know this to be true."

I waved away his concerns. "I do have need of your guidance, demon."

I hesitated. There was something between Nhil and Henka I didn't understand. He didn't like her and didn't trust her, yet always fell short of actually condemning my wife. But then, how could I expect a demon that could stand motionless for thousands of years to understand an emotion like love?

He waited, unmoving, unblinking.

"I lost Henka."

An eyebrow crept up.

"She was taken by wizards in Abieszan. They cut her head off, threw it into the harbour."

"And?"

"And then they trapped me in some kind of stasis spell and took me away. I spent weeks in an underground cell, and more weeks sailing back to Abieszan after I escaped."

"And?" he repeated

Rage bubbled up in my chest like a volcano building pressure. Though other emotions felt muted and distant, this felt pure and real.

"I have to save her."

Nhil made a soft noise that might have been a laugh, though no humour showed on his face. "This is Henka."

"You have to help me find her. There must be some way."

"Not a moment in all her millennia has Henka been helpless. You will find her when she wants you to. Or, more likely, she'll find you."

"You're not going to help me," I accused.

"Just like your tussle with that weak and starving youth, you don't need my help."

"Fine."

If he wouldn't help, I'd find another way. At worst, with this armour I could spend months walking the harbour floor until I found her.

I stooped to collect the demon-bound swords and armour. I'd leave whatever remained of the preserved foods I brought. "I don't need you anyway."

"You sound angry, but that is quite literally what I just said."

I waved him to silence, already building the room in the basement of Mom's mansion in my thoughts.

"I do enjoy these little visits," I heard Nhil say. "Each time I recognize more and more of you."

CHAPTER TWENTY-EIGHT

I stood in the simple room I'd left several days ago. As instructed, the lantern had been kept lit, the cell unchanged. The door remained closed, no doubt bolted from the outside.

Hunger filled me, slammed through my veins, crushing all thought but one: The Khraen who had started north was already here in Abieszan. I rushed through every summoning and binding to give myself time to prepare for him, and he arrived a week earlier than expected. He must have had magical help of some kind; I saw no other possibility. I likely faced not only a piece of myself, but whatever wizards, sorcerers, or elementalists he brought with him.

Turning toward the door, I stopped, stunned. Another shard was gone from my senses. While I was in the floating mountains, the piece who destroyed the first had reached another and obliterated it too. One Khraen was here to kill me while another rampaged across the world, annihilating my past. I shuddered to think what had already been lost. Long buried secrets. Locations of other bolthole realities. Caches of weapons, magic, and wealth. Summonings and bindings.

That lone destroyer now moved toward the one the old Khraen in the necropolis said called itself Naghron, the largest chunk of my heart not counting the one in PalTaq.

Closing my eyes I focussed on the hunger, trying to judge the distance separating me from the nearest Khraen. He was, I decided, on the island but not in my immediate vicinity. Just like I felt him, I knew he was aware of my return. He'd come north, hunting me.

I grinned within the blood-red helm. Ensconced in demonic

armour, I felt invincible, impossibly strong. Whatever the other Khraen thought to throw against me, he would be wholly unprepared for what he faced.

Nhil said he recognized more and more of me. He meant with every visit he saw more of the Demon Emperor. Now, wearing this crimson plate mail, I felt more like that man than ever before. I felt like me, like this was who I was meant to be.

Stepping to the closed door, I raised my hand to knock, and stopped. The armour fed me its perceptions, the scent of a crowded basement. Steel and iron, leather, and sour breath. Men and women sweating in nervous anticipation. There were a lot more than Mom's four guards beyond the door.

I set Bren's sword and armour on the cot to free my hands.

"He's here," someone whispered in the next room.

I drew Adraalmak from its scabbard. Those nearest the door and within its sphere of influence screamed in terror. With my free hand I tore the heavy door from its hinges and stepped into the cellar. The sword bled black, devoured the world's colour leaving everything a drained monochrome. At least a score of armed men and women awaited me, weapons drawn. Dressed in an assortment of battle-worn armour, these were hardened warriors. I raised the sword high and the flesh of those nearest, mainlanders and islanders alike, leeched to grey. All retreated before me. Some turned and fled, the full power of the demon-bound blade robbing them of courage. Others cowered, a few crumpling to the floor as they wet themselves.

I saw them all, no matter where they stood. I heard their thundering hearts, the rapid panic of their breathing. A sorcerer moved in the shadows, twisting light and dark around her. Thinking she was invisible, she clutched a long stiletto as she crept to get behind me. I ignored her for now.

None of the gathered warriors wore masks, though all showed the ravages of starvation and disease. The mummers were gone, replaced by desperate locals. The other Khraen on the island must have followed rumour of me here and left this small army in case I returned.

"Your master sends you to your death," I told them, stepping into their midst.

They flinched back, more cracking and fleeing up the stairs.

Ignoring those behind me, I strode forward until I stood in the middle of the gathered killers. There were no demonic weapons here, no flaming enchanted swords or sorcerous devices. Even the sorcerer skulking in the shadows bore a normal blade. Nothing here could hurt me.

It felt good. This was what it was to be the Demon Emperor. These pathetic mortals should have begged and cowered. Had I the time and souls to bind a more powerful demon, they would have. There were entities capable of devouring the souls of entire city blocks in a single instant.

The woman nearest me, dressed in bone armour and wielding a viciously curved adze, screamed an islander war cry and attacked. I cut her down. Once dark flesh now ashen, rough-hewn earthy hair bleached to old bone, she lay blinking at the ceiling.

With a roar they were upon me, stabbing and chopping, their useless weapons incapable of so much as scratching the crimson armour. I killed them and Adraalmak sang its song of death in razor notes of steel. Men and women threw themselves at me and I left them colourless corpses. I laughed at the irony. Mainlanders hated the islanders' dark skin, but my victims all looked the same.

A big redheaded man in a motley of chain and leather swung a monstrous axe, trying to split my skull. I barely felt it, the armour absorbing the impact.

"My gift to you," I told him, "is true equality."

I killed him.

I killed them all except those who collapsed to mewl on the floor in terror.

Having seen the butchery of her friends, the sorcerer retreated to the shadows. Sheathing Adraalmak, I ignored her. Cinereal corpses sprawled in grey blood slowly regained their pallor as colour seeped back into the room.

Feed.

The crimson armour spoke its hunger, though in emotion rather than words.

Half of my own volition, half moved by the armour's need, I

approached the nearest survivor. She lay semiconscious in a puddle of blanched blood and urine. The demon's desire infused me, pumped into brain and blood by the penetrating hairs.

I understood: The armour had hung unused in the floating mountains for three thousand years.

Feed.

Though insistent, it still needed my permission.

I acquiesced, surrendering some small shred of control. The armour bent over the woman, reached my hand toward her. The crimson gauntlet hovered over her face, squirming black tendrils extending to probe at her features. I watched, entranced, as they slipped into her nose, peeled back her lids, wormed past unseeing eyes, and pushed through her lips to fill her mouth.

She kicked once, tremors running the length of her body, and went still.

Emptied.

Glistening sable hairs retreated into the gauntlet. I tasted some of whatever it devoured from its helpless victim. Life and love. A soul consumed.

Feed.

I approached one of the corpses next. The armour showed no interest.

Feed.

I allowed it three additional victims.

Feed.

Each time I recognize more and more of you.

Nhil knew me, knew the armour. He knew I'd recall his words and that they'd give me pause. I had to appreciate the timing of his underhanded jab. Knowledge and wisdom indeed.

Ignoring the crimson plate's hunger, I turned to look back into the little room where Bren's sword and armour sat on the cot. If Mom made a deal with this new Khraen, she likely would have included my friend in the bargain. On the other hand, the fact it wasn't her mummers waiting for me suggested she was no longer in power. A moment of fear, suddenly calmed. If Bren could survive magefire, break into Iremaire's stronghold in Khaal and rescue me, this was nothing in comparison. But if they hurt him, or worse, my vengeance would be terrible.

The floor above groaned. There were more men and women up there awaiting me. I stopped, inhaling the demonic armour's perceptions. I listened to them breathe, smelled the rank sweat of heavy armour in the tropics, the tang of exposed iron. Maybe the other Khraen hadn't underestimated me after all. There were scores of them. Wanting me tired and weak by the time I faced him, he thought to wear me down through attrition.

"Show yourself," I said, pointing at the sorcerer hiding in the shadows.

A young islander woman appeared. Dressed head to toe in mottled black, dark eyes watching me from within a concealing cowl, she showed little of the ravages of her art. Midnight hair tied back in coiled braids, I guessed her to be in her early twenties.

"What's your name?

"Nokutenda, my Lord."

"Lord?"

"You step out of an empty room wearing plate armour that cost more than all these idiots earned in their entire lives combined. That's qualification enough for me."

She didn't fit in among the rabble of hired thugs and cutthroats I slaughtered here.

"You hid instead of attacking me," I said. "Cowardice, or wisdom?"

"There's a difference?"

"I'd say cowardice is being afraid to fight, while wisdom is knowing when not to fight."

"If you knew you'd lose a fight, would you not be afraid?"

Now that we conversed, she studied me with a distinct lack of fear. So many people think that just because you're talking to them you are now less willing to kill.

"I'm no coward," she said. "I'm more useful to you alive than dead."

Such foolish hubris.

"You work for Khraen," I said. "You're one of the locals?"

She snorted a soft chuckle. "Not really. I arrived in Abieszan two days before the gates closed."

Not caring, I didn't ask why she'd come here. "What did he offer in payment?"

"Purpose, and a way off the island."

"Purpose?" I asked.

"Vengeance on the Guild."

"Did he give it to you?"

"Not yet."

"Flee, or come find me once I have killed him," I said. "The choice is yours."

Her eyes narrowed. "I know that voice."

I felt the nearby piece of my heart move. He was coming toward me. Fast.

The sorcerer faded into the shadows, and I drew Adraalmak. Sword in hand, I headed up the steps toward the waiting warriors. I wanted them dealt with before the other Khraen arrived.

The smells changed as I ascended, the charred stink of a razed city, the sour rot of dead left long in the sun. Abieszan had not been peaceful in my absence.

CHAPTER TWENTY-NINE

Upstairs I ran into a veritable wall of warriors. Crammed together, trying to be the one to kill me, they got in each other's way. The demon in the crimson plate fed me its senses and I knew there were no demonic or magical weapons here capable of harming me. Wading into their midst, I lay about with mad abandon, swinging Adraalmak without thought or skill. The sword cleaved flesh, bone, and armour with equal ease. The hellish blade swallowed the world's colour, painted gore in a palette of ashen skin and sun-bleached bone. Many of my enemies fled, racing into the street. Others curled foetal and were trampled in the melee.

I carved my way through the kitchens and into the pub where Bren and I first sat with Mom. The tables and chairs had all been dragged from the room to make space. I saw nothing of the bartenders or Vishtish, Mom's pretty swordsman.

With no thought of defending myself, I spun and hacked without finesse, severing limbs and heads, and lacing the air with thick traceries of blood. Somewhere out there a Khraen was coming for me, racing impossibly fast across the city.

Driven by fear and desperation, the mob finally worked together, throwing their combined weight against me. They tackled my legs, wrapping their arms around my knees. I stood for a heartbeat, trying to cut my way free, when a lumbering monster of a man in armour made of bamboo slats bound in hemp rope tackled me to the floor. The others piled on top, pinning me beneath their combined weight.

The grating squeal of steel on steel as they pried ineffectually at my armour's joints with knives and swords.

The wheezing stench of sour breath as faces pressed close. Grunts of straining effort.

Feed.

Helpless, pinned to the floor, I laughed.

"Feed," I said.

They squealed as silken ebony worms tangled in hair, sank into flesh, pushed into horrified eyes and screaming mouths.

Some tried to flee, getting no more than a few paces before the black hairs dragged them to a stop. Fine as they were, the strands were surprisingly strong. Men and women hacked at it with knives, sawed desperately to free themselves to no avail. Like flies in a web, they hung in knotted chaos, twitching and screeching as their bodies and minds were invaded.

Corpses hit the floor as I climbed to my feet. The few survivors, seeing the fate of their fellow killers, fled in a mad exodus. In moments, I stood alone in the pub.

My own hunger suddenly rose; the other Khraen was close. The crushing need to have that shard spiked and then diminished as he somehow passed by, again becoming more distant. Sword ready, I crouched, awaiting attack. Outside, a huge shadow, blurred with motion, swept past the entrance as my hunger again spiked and faded.

He was in the air.

Cursing, I charged the front door, bursting into the street.

Outside, the world became an impossible cacophony of sensory overload. My armour fed me the sights, scents, sounds, and flavours of a dying city. In my days away, Abieszan had undergone yet another transformation. The few blocks around the mummers' headquarters had been better preserved than most. There'd been fewer corpses, the wells clean and guarded by Mom's people. Now, it looked as bad as the rest of the city. Few buildings remained standing, and most of those burned.

I saw all of it, heard the heartbeat of every rat, smelled the smoke of smouldering fires. To do this kind of damage in the time I was gone, the other Khraen must have come in force, brought an entire army.

I stopped, rooted in awe.

Wings wide, a dragon appeared over the nearest building, banking as it turned toward me. Iridescent cerulean scales shimmered like oil in the sun. The beast was longer than one of the wizard's war galleys, the wings twice that. Eyes like golden fire shone bright, the pupils black slashes of seething rage.

Khraen sat in an intricate saddle arrangement just forward of the dragon's massive shoulders. Black hair loose and flying in the wind, a majestic ebony mane. He was me and so much more. This was a huge bull of a Khraen, arms and neck thick with muscle, broad chest narrowing to slim hips. A woven necklace of human bones hung about his neck, bands of gold wrapping his massive biceps. Shirtless, he displayed a chiselled physique I had never come close to possessing. Behind him, an islander woman with a shaved head, arms and bared chest inked black with swirling tattoos, clung to his waist. Dressed in only a straw skirt died red like blood, she wore a long and slender sword over her back. The weapon, bright forged steel, looked strangely out of place.

I laughed at the predictability of it. Given a chance, it seemed I always surrounded myself with beautiful women I could control. Was she a necromancer, like the old man's undead harem in the necropolis, or did this Khraen have some other means of domination?

Though smaller than some of the monstrous dragons I remembered from my past, it was still large enough to do incredible damage. Emotions washed through me, a mix of pride and envy.

That should be me up there.

He saw me in my crimson armour, pointed, and roared something at the dragon. This close, there was no mistaking the pull of our hearts. The colossal beast seemed to swell as it reared back, wings turning to slow its descent, and drew breath. Too late to flee, I realized its intent. This Khraen thought to burn me and then sift through the ashes in search of my heart.

One of us was about to receive a startling surprise; I hoped it was him.

Time slowed, the dragon's descent kicking ash and dust into the air in a whirling tornado of debris. Safe in my demonic cocoon, none of it touched me, my every sense remaining unhindered. I saw in gradients of temperature, a world of blues, greens, and reds, felt the waves of sound through my skin. Mouth wide, curved, dagger-like teeth gleaming white, a roiling maelstrom of fire bubbled up from its guts.

I wanted to flee, to cower behind the nearest wall. I knew all too well the terrible damage this creature was capable of. Magefire was nothing. Dragons like this melted stone, turned sand to glass. Loosed against armies, they left cinders dancing in the breeze like twinkling fireflies. Plate mail became the oven you were cooked in before it ran like mud. Not even bone survived. I'd seen a pair of dragons turn thousands of men and women into soot and embers.

A firestorm of destruction boiled from its gaping maw, enveloping me, incinerating everything for a score of strides in every direction.

White.

Every sense shrieked white. I smelled white, felt white through the invaded pores of my flesh. I tasted the burning white of the world, heard the white of utter annihilation.

None of it touched me.

The dragon swept past, and I stood unharmed, mocking the other Khraen with my laughter.

Pumping wings heaved the massive beast back into the air as it banked in a graceful arc.

The other Khraen turned in his saddle to study me as the dragon rose above the city. The woman behind him still clung to his back. My laughter choked to nothing as I realized that, while I might be safe down here, he was just as safe up there. If he chose to flee, I had no way to follow him. The shard in his heart called to me. So close, yet so unreachable.

"I know you," I whispered, my eyes locked on his. "I know your weaknesses, your hubris."

Raising the sword over my head, I yelled, "That's right you coward! I've come for your heart!"

Not quite true, as technically he'd come here for mine, it still had the desired effect. I was not one to leave empty handed once I'd decided I wanted something.

Though I couldn't hear his words, I knew he commanded the dragon. It was strange to see myself from the outside, to know his weaknesses and take advantage of them, while knowing they were mine too. Understanding your faults in no way makes ridding yourself of them easier. Pride would be my downfall. I was my own worst enemy, and that would never change.

Not knowing if he could hear me, but knowing he'd understand the intent, I brandished my demon sword in challenge. "Stop hiding behind your pathetic pet! Come! Fight me!"

The dragon's graceful arc became a hard turn as it snaked through the air, shedding altitude, once again racing toward me. This time, I saw no volcanic build-up of fire in the beast's throat. My taunts got to him, and he came as if called.

"That's right," I muttered, "you predictable fool."

In a mad and screeching descent, the beast threw its wings wide at the last moment and I understood my own mistake. The dragon landed on me, a huge taloned foot crushing me to the ground.

I writhed and thrashed, trying to turn my blade against it. My arms were trapped and helpless. Even the demonic armour's inhuman strength couldn't shift such a bulk. Feeling my struggles, the dragon put its full weight down upon me. Crimson armour groaned under the pressure and held.

Pinned, I heard the other Khraen and his woman loose the buckles of their saddles and climb down the dragon's foreleg. They stood over me like beautiful gods. His wind-blown sable hair like a great mane, he was all I should have been. He grinned in smug triumph. This close, the deafening lure of my heart became my world. A soul-deep craving, impossible to ignore. I'd been hungry, walking the edge of starvation. Trapped in the floating mountains, I'd known a thirst like no other. Such needs paled in comparison. He felt it too, I saw it in his eyes.

"When he disappeared," he said to the woman, gaze never leaving me, "I thought I'd lost him. But you were right." He shook his head. "You were right."

"I told you he'd return."

"Once again, you prove your worth," he said, magnanimous in his praise.

He crouched near my head, eyes narrowed as he studied me. "Nice armour. Where did you get it?"

"When you take my heart, you'll lose everything I know."

Though true, it was a weak distraction at best.

"Small price," said the other Khraen. "I'll get the armour. I'll get your heart. One step closer to being the man I am meant to be."

"One more step," I said, "along the obsidian path."

He blinked, startled. "Not surprising, I suppose, that we have many of the same thoughts."

"At first, it was only me. The rest of you cowered on your islands, ruled your crude little kingdoms from your mud huts. What brought you out?" I asked. "What changed?"

Hunger and curiosity warred on his features. He wanted to hack open my chest and claim his prize. But like me, he felt the need to know, to understand. "I... It was time."

"Something changed," I insisted.

He made to glance over his shoulder at the woman but couldn't pull his attention from me. "It's time."

Reaching down, he pulled my helm off. The demon in the crimson armour, recognizing him as me, obeyed. Black hairs wormed free of my eyes, ears, nose, and mouth and the world returned to the dull and limited reality I had always known.

"Rather than risk you escaping," he said, "I'm going to cut your throat while you're helpless. Consider it a kindness, a mercy."

"Coward."

It was a pitiful attempt and we both knew it.

He drew a long knife. "You're not going to die," he said. "We're going to be *him* again. My empire. My world."

The knife lifted high, ready to stab down into my neck. "You know," I said, "I'm beginning to think that's not what she wants."

"She? Who?"

"My wife. *Our* wife."

"Wife?" He hesitated. "It's been three thousand years. She'd be long dead."

"She is. And yet..."

Bright steel pushed through his exposed chest just below his right nipple. Confusion crumpled his features as he stared down at the offending steel.

"But…" He coughed a froth of blood. "You said…"

For a moment he focussed on me, mouth moving as he struggled to form words. Then, his eyes became like glass, sightless orbs seeing nothing. He hung limp, only the sword pinioning him keeping the corpse upright.

The bald islander woman stood behind him, examining me with flint eyes. She held the weapon single-handed, supporting his dead weight with ease. A tempest of emotions wrestled for control of her features. Love. Anger. Disappointment, and betrayal.

"So," she said, "how long have you known?"

CHAPTER THIRTY

My emotions warred for dominance. I wanted to cry for relief that she wasn't gone, head buried forever lost in the muck of the ocean floor. I wanted to hold her close, cling to her, and rage at her for throwing her lot in with another Khraen instead of finding me. I wanted to tell her I loved her, apologize for what I'd done and beg her forgiveness. But I'd been tricked before. I needed to know it was her.

Still pinned beneath the dragon's foot, I stared up at the woman, looking for something I might recognize. Though tall and beautiful, shocking slate-grey eyes out of place on an islander face, she didn't compare to any of the forms I'd seen Henka wear. This warrior would have looked awkward and out of place in Henka's silk dresses.

"Nhil told you I was your wife," she said. "That whispering worm is in the Black Citadel."

Nhil once said that's what I used to call the castle in the floating mountains. Ominous sounding, I hadn't much liked the name, fitting though it was.

For an instant, her perfect façade cracked, and I saw misery and disappointment writ clear on her beautiful face. "He'll ruin everything."

"It's you? It's really you?"

"Why didn't you tell me you knew," she demanded.

"Why didn't you tell me who you were?"

"Because this was *our* plan! Yours and mine. We chose where to break you, what parts too keep, and which to hide forever."

Hide? Forever? I crushed the questions. They could wait. If this was truly Henka, she knew where those pieces were and how to find them. As Nhil said, she left nothing to chance.

Her words hit me. "*We* chose?"

She looked surprised and confused by my question. "Of course. I could never do this without your permission, without your help."

It made a terrible kind of sense. I had possession of her heart. She had no choice but to love me and always act in my best interests. She must have come to me with this mad plan to make me happy by breaking away the worst parts of me. On the verge of destroying the world, I'd agreed. The man I was—the Demon Emperor—could never achieve a simple happiness because he could never have enough. Much like my god, he was voracious, insatiable.

I wondered if she'd loved him before he stole her freedom but couldn't ask.

Henka loved him for thousands of years, until one day she finally understood the unchanging core of unhappiness within him. She concocted a plan to make him happy.

While there was much I couldn't remember of the man I'd been, there was one part I couldn't quite make fit: This was the man who created Kantlament, his answer to the sorrows of life. An end to everything. I couldn't imagine him agreeing to be reduced to something he would see as less than himself. Henka still carried secrets.

"Tell me something only Henka would know," I said, needing to be sure it was her.

"If it's something *only* I know, then you won't know it."

I gave her a flat look.

"Fine," she said. "We left Nachi aboard the Habnikaav. That's where we met young Brenwick, the cabin boy. He's grown a bunch since then. A storm sank the ship, and we floated for days." She frowned down at her new body, touching a hand to the smooth flesh of her legs. "The fish got at me."

"Bren's still alive?"

Henka nodded. "I made sure he was safe."

"Thank you."

"Bren is important to you and so he's important to me."

"I know. But…" Despite my shock at finding Henka alive, the proximity of the shard made thought difficult. I nodded at the dead

Khraen. "Why him? Why didn't you come looking for me?"

Slipping the blade free, she let the body collapse to the ground. "The mages took you and had a week's head start before I could walk. I hired sorcerers, shamans, and even rogue mages to track you. They all failed. I realized there was one person who would be able to find you."

I wanted to laugh, but the dragon still crushing me to the ground didn't leave much room for that. Having lost me, Henka went in search of another shard of my heart and used it to track me down.

"Are you behind the other piece suddenly moving as well?" I asked Henka.

"Other piece?" She gave the corpse a half-hearted stab. "He never mentioned that. Fool."

"There is a Khraen out there travelling from shard to shard, destroying them."

"Destroying?" Henka's brow furrowed in confusion. "Impossible. You would never willingly forgo that knowledge and power."

"It's great that you think I'm a power-hungry bastard."

She ignored my humour.

With a few careful cuts, Henka cracked the dead man's ribs. Crouching, she carved the obsidian free. When she hefted the sliver I hissed, thinking she was going to take it away.

"Could you destroy this?" she asked.

It clawed at my senses, demanded I touch it. "Maybe. If it was the only way to save myself."

"Exactly. The other pieces are still you."

"They are and they aren't. We share a past, but we're all shaped by the lives we've lived since being reborn."

I didn't want to mention my thought that perhaps the murderous shard remembered something so terrible it saw no choice but to destroy the others. Iremaire said I was the only threat to this world. What if she'd been right? If this Khraen knew that, he might have decided to save the world by making sure the Demon Emperor could never return.

Would I kill myself to save the world?

No.

"Could someone be manipulating him?" I asked.

Henka

"Maybe," she admitted, looking doubtful.

Seeing as she'd manipulated both myself and the Khraen she just killed, I was less confident.

"Those men inside could have killed me," I said, changing the topic. "Were I not wearing this armour, I'd be dead."

She seemed unconcerned. "They had orders to render you helpless and bring you to him."

"Ah. So just a bloody beating and them dragging my unconscious, broken body up the steps. Much better."

"Some lessons need learning the hard way. Hardship shapes you."

"You were fine with me being beaten half to death because it's character building?"

A slight twitch of an eyebrow was my only answer.

"I don't suppose you can get this dragon off me?"

"Not yet." She made a show of looking the crimson armour over. "I thought that was in PalTaq. You shouldn't have worn it."

"It's the only reason I'm still alive."

"*I'm* the only reason you're still alive. I wouldn't have let him hurt you. That armour is parasitic. It infects you, changes you. It was after binding it that you really changed."

"At least you and Nhil agree on one thing. That was before Kantlament?"

She nodded. "Tell me that damned sword isn't in the Black Citadel."

"It's somewhere in the palace at PalTaq," I said.

"Good. Promise you'll remove the armour. Promise you'll never wear it again, and I'll let you up."

"If I don't promise?"

"I'll have Kaszius here burn your exposed head to ash, cut out the stone of your heart and try again."

"The dragon loomed over me with eyes of golden fire. This was no savage, feral beast, but a dangerously intelligent creature with a powerful magic all its own.

I was tempted to call Henka's bluff. She loved me. *This* me. If she was right about the armour, however, it would turn me into someone she didn't love. That, I knew, she would not allow.

"I promise to remove the armour," I said. "I promise I will never wear it again."

Even as I spoke, I contemplated the worth of my promises.

So many made.

So few kept.

Kaszius looked to Henka. Lips pursed, she finally nodded, and it lifted the huge foot from my chest.

Rising, I towered over her. Though solidly built, she was smaller in this tattooed body but no less the love of my soul. I removed one of the crimson gauntlets, caressed her face with my bare hand. Eyes closed, she leaned into the touch, skin warm and alive.

"Stay like this," I said. "Stop changing yourself for me."

Flint eyes opened, met mine. She said nothing and I knew she would continue to do whatever she thought would make me happy. It struck me as strange that I'd ordered her to love me, but not to obey my every command.

"It would make me happy," I said, "if you stayed like this."

She kissed the palm of my hand. "If you knew what made you happy, we wouldn't be here."

Was that true?

I struggled to think past the demanding call of my heart. There was one last promise that had to be made. For all my lies, for all my obfuscations and half-truths, this one oath I would keep. Nothing else mattered. Not me. Not the Demon Emperor. Not this world. Not my god.

"I know why you're doing this," I said.

She pulled away.

"I remember the hall of pedestals."

"No," she whispered.

"We're going to PalTaq. I—"

She interrupted me with a hand on my arm. "Freeing me would be a terrible, terrible mistake."

Understanding the threat, I lied. "I need you too much to ever risk losing you."

CHAPTER THIRTY-ONE

Henka kissed me, happy again. "Go inside. Remove the armour. I'll bring you the stone."

I wanted to argue, to demand answers to all the questions fighting for domination, but I *needed* my heart. Even that small act of turning my back on it and returning to the mummers' headquarters was almost more than I could manage.

Collecting the helm, I did as instructed. Even then I saw the irony of her barking orders at me. I had her heart, held all the power in the relationship, and yet was at her mercy in so many ways.

The armour, as if sensing my intentions, grew heavy and unwieldy. Each step felt like wading through mud. The writhing black hairs within the helm reached for me, waving like seaweed moved by the tide, caressing the gauntleted fingers holding it. I felt their touch through the armour. They promised power and protection and I wanted it. Deprived of its demonic senses, reality felt dull and thin, a sad and sloppy charcoal sketch of something vibrant and beautiful. I hated not knowing what was behind me, not being able to hear the heartbeats of those nearby. That sorcerer was still in there somewhere. Without the helm, it would be nothing for her to sneak up and murder me.

Once inside, my head cleared a little. Bren was alive. I had my Henka back. For the first time since Shalayn tossed my love's head into Abieszan harbour, I could contemplate the future.

I'd take Henka to PalTaq and free her. There was at least one shard between me and the capital of my old empire. I'd collect the one who called himself Naghron along the way. A large piece, he'd remember much of our past. As the Khraen who set himself to destroying our heart was already headed in that direction, I'd kill him too. There was also that large shard in PalTaq. It was even bigger than Naghron and hadn't moved since I first returned to life.

I laughed quietly. There was no life beyond the moment Henka was freed. Her wrath would be terrible and complete.

My final step along this path would be my moment of redemption.

For the first time, I understood. Breaking me changed nothing; I still craved dissolution. I desired the punishment I escaped for so long. Kantlament and this parasitic crimson armour were part of an elaborate suicide concocted by a coward.

My death would be a pitiful penance.

But the alternative was too terrible to contemplate.

Broken as I was, I knew me. If not stopped, I would find the pieces of my heart. All of them. I would become the Demon Emperor, because that's who I was. I would serve my god, return her dream to the world. Or return my world to her dream—the difference seemed important.

Nhil said I doomed the world and that I was the only one who could save it.

He was right: I would save this world by dying.

I could tell no one. Not Bren, and certainly not Henka. She would do everything in her considerable power to stop me.

Henka entered the room, and I felt the pull of my heart grow.

"You're still wearing the armour."

She held a blood-splashed fragment of obsidian in one hand, raised in offering. Red stained her lips. Never one to let a precious commodity go to waste, she'd availed herself of the corpse's blood.

I faced her, hiding my feelings. "I'll lose consciousness when I take the shard. This will keep me safe."

Reaching for the stone, I hesitated. I'd commanded her to love me but that couldn't be the entirety of her motivation.

"Why pretend to help me find the pieces?" I asked. "If what you say is true, and we planned this together—"

"You weren't supposed to remember me at all," she said, obsidian shard still balanced on her palm, waiting, screaming at me to take it. "We planned this together."

I pulled my attention from the stone. "No, no, no. There are too many holes. Nhil says you never leave anything to chance. Though he doesn't outright attempt to turn me against you, he makes oblique suggestions you can't be trusted."

"Oblique," she said. "Clever demons are dangerous."

"If you thought he plotted against you, you would have disposed of him. Is he hiding from you in the floating mountains?"

"Not me," she said. "You."

"That doesn't make sense."

Flint eyes met mine. "It makes sense if you lied."

My heart lurched. "About?"

"You promised to destroy Nhil. We knew he would never agree to this, never allow you to break free of her dream."

She meant my god. I'd promised Henka I'd kill my friend, and instead hid him away. Did he know why I left him there?

"It was you," Henka continued, "who decided what memories to keep and what to dispose of. I could never do that, never hurt you. It had to be you." She ran a tattooed hand, inked black with snakes and spiders, over the stubble of her shaved head. "You promised to excise all memory of me so that we could start fresh. You said it was the only way it would work." Grey eyes shone bright. "You promised that even if you didn't remember me, you'd still love me."

At least I'd kept that one promise.

"Maybe the shaman made a mistake," I said. "Maybe he missed memories or the stone broke wrong."

"Perhaps."

Or maybe I lied to her about that too. Maybe I cut away the memories of her but left that one clue, knowing I'd figure it out eventually. Yet another act of cowardly betrayal.

"Can you lie to me?" I asked.

I remembered commanding her to love me but had no recollection of ordering her to never lie. After my first crime, why would I leave her that freedom?

"If I say no, you'll wonder if I'm lying." Bloody lips quirked in a sad smile. "Take the stone. Bren will be here when you wake."

The obsidian chip drew my attention. "What's in here? Who will I become?"

Instead of answering, Henka gripped my wrist with her free hand, turned it palm up. She held the sliver of my heart, ready to surrender it. "You are driven. You are selfish and greedy. You crave power and fear weakness. There is no price you won't pay to get what you think you want. There is nothing and no one you are not willing to sacrifice to achieve a goal. You are single minded and focussed when bent to a purpose, violent and cruel when challenged."

"Tien was right. I'm a shit-stained soul." I thought about the Khraen who hunted the shards of me, destroying them. "You should shatter me to nothing. Sprinkle the dust across the oceans so I can never again pollute the world."

"I can't," she said. "I love you."

The ground shook as she lowered the obsidian toward my waiting hand, and she hesitated. Less than a finger's width separated me from my prize. Need consumed me.

"Give," I growled. "Give."

Outside, the dragon roared in agony as the earth again rumbled beneath our feet.

Henka closed her hand about the stone, and I ground my teeth with the effort to resist forcefully taking it.

"Wizards," she said. "They saw the dragon."

I wanted to roar with laughter. The suffering of Abieszan, the thousands starving and dying hadn't been enough to move them from their pristine ships. But one sighting of a dragon, and they came running. I wanted to slaughter them all, drown their filthy Guild in blood and horror. How dare they impede me.

I retreated two steps from Henka, desperate to put some distance between myself and the sliver she held.

Need and rage waged war in me.

"This doesn't count," I said.

She looked at me, confused and incredulous. "What?"

"I haven't taken the armour off yet. This isn't breaking my promise to never wear it again."

I didn't wait for her response. Slamming the helm into place, I returned to the street. No longer did the armour resist me. Energy flooded my veins, my thoughts singing like a ringing sword. I was a god, indestructible. I was war and I was death. Though I had no memory of drawing the sword, Adraalmak hung in my fist. It felt wrong, sad and pathetic. I wanted Kantlament. I wanted to shred the sky, shatter worlds, wreak utter destruction upon these mages.

Outside, I discovered what little remained of Abieszan was once again burning. The dragon had taken to the air. Wings wide, Kaszius swept low over the city, roaring destructive flame as it pursued its prey. Wizards flitted through the air, white robes flapping, far more agile than the stately beast. Forgoing their beloved magefire, they stabbed at it with crackling spears of lightning and barbed snakes of roiling black chaos. The dragon screeched in pain and banked, chasing the mage who struck it. Even as the dragon twisted to catch one of the mages by surprise, reducing him to a dissipating cloud of ash, others attacked its flanks. Massive rents scarred Kaszius' scales. Smoking blood rained down from the wounds.

I watched from the street, helpless. With only a sword, I had no means of attacking the flying wizards.

Henka exited the mummers' mansion to stand at my side.

"They'll kill it," I said, strangely sad that such a fine beast should perish. I remembered wings of dragons flying in formation. Once they understood who was in charge, they were loyal servants. I missed their friendship, their deeply twisted sense of humour. Most of all, I missed the feeling of being above the world's problems when riding one. It had been my favourite escape from the stresses of ruling the empire.

Henka shrugged as if unconcerned.

One of the mages twitched and floundered as hidden archers filled her with arrows. She fell in a tight and uncontrolled spiral, pale echoes of her scream reaching me though I was several blocks distant.

"The surviving mummers?" I asked.

Henka shook her head as something huge and black moving in an ungainly lumbering slither moved into view. Writhing tentacles fifty strides long reached up to grab passing wizards, squeezing them until they burst like overripe berries. I recognized the creature but had never seen one on land—didn't know they could survive outside of the ocean.

"A kraken?"

"Dead kraken," corrected Henka.

Pulling my attention from the undead sea monster, I saw three wizards circle the dragon, lancing it over and over, ripping gaping wounds in its side. Kaszius flailed flame at random, twisting and shrieking, unable to catch the mages. With a last, defeated roar, the dragon fell from the sky, crashing into the city below. Tumbling through a tower, it disappeared behind the ruins of Yuruuza's palace to the east of us.

The flying wizards turned their attention on the kraken, keeping beyond the reach of its tentacles, only to be attacked from below by crackling whips spitting fire. I'd seen something like this before.

"Dead sorcerers?" I asked.

Henka shook her head. "Sorcery requires the practitioner trade their lifeforce for power. The dead can't work sorcery." She watched as the mages adjusted their strategy, magically shielding themselves from the sorcerous attacks and pouring magefire into the streets and alleys below. "I hired the sorcerers before I left to find the other Khraen. Knowing the wizards might return, I had my necromancers prepare."

Nhil was right: Henka anticipated everything. Her undead rescued her from the harbour and she immediately got to work. She'd somehow raised a dead kraken from the depths of the ocean and kept it near the coast in case she had need of such a beast.

"You should have had the kraken attack the wizard ships in the harbour," I said. "It would have had a chance then. Here, it's doomed to fail."

More wizards rose from the streets of Abieszan, white robes snapping as they flew, shields crackling around them.

"It served its purpose," Henka said. "It was a distraction."

"And the sorcerers? I don't think they brought down a single mage."

"Another distraction." She flashed a small smile that I recognized even in this short, bald, and tattooed woman. "Anyway, I have something else for the wizard ships."

The battle in the air changed, as the mages who'd just joined the fight suddenly turned upon the others. The sky became a chaotic battle scene of darting wizards, raging rivers of fire, and jagged bolts of lightning crashing against magical shields. From here, I couldn't tell one side from the other. Flaming wizard bodies plummeted from the sky.

To the east, by the harbour, dozens more mages rose into the air only to stop and begin attacking something beneath them. Too far away and occluded by the ruins of the city, I couldn't see what was happening by the docks.

"A pair of dead sea dragons," said Henka. "With some luck, they'll destroy the ships."

"But they can't hurt the flying mages."

She shrugged, unworried. "These are all distractions. We must find Kaszius."

CHAPTER THIRTY-TWO

"Kaszius? The dragon is dead."

Henka looked at me, an eyebrow arched.

"Oh. Right."

"I left Bren with one of my necromancers," she said. "They'll meet us there. We need to move quickly; my dead will only distract the mages for so long."

A kraken and undead sea dragons. Hired sorcerers, and undead wizards ready to join the battle. Necromancers left behind to build her an army all on the off chance she later needed a distraction.

Henka grabbed my armoured hand. "Remember. You promised."

I winced and then remembered Nhil saying the helm portrayed my expressions. After all these millennium, knowing what I'd done to her, how could she ever think to trust me? I had the strangest feeling that carving away the parts of me incapable of love left me more capable of lying. Unsure if that said something about me, or humanity in general, I shied from thinking about it.

"As soon as we're safe," I promised, "I'll remove the armour."

She squeezed my hand, and I felt her strength through the gauntlet. "Forever."

"Forever," I agreed.

We ran east through the broken streets of a devastated city, Henka leading the way with unerring precision. Abieszan had not fared well in my absence. The dragon-mounted Khraen must have declared war on the survivors the moment he arrived. Entire blocks had been burned, stone melted beneath Kaszius' destructive breath. If there were now fewer dead in the streets, it was because most of them had been burned to ash and scattered in the winds.

Though the mummers' headquarters had been largely untouched, Khraen ravaged the surrounding areas. I imagined how it must have played out. He would have told Henka where he last sensed me, and that I'd suddenly vanished. She'd known I'd returned to the floating mountains. To ensure I was able to return here and be forced to go elsewhere, she would have instructed him that the building must not be damaged lest he lose me forever. Either he or Henka likely questioned one of the thieves to learn which room I'd left from. After chasing out the surviving mummers, he'd either hired or conscripted locals and instructed them to await my return. Careful not to change anything, they hadn't entered the room.

This kind of precision and planning wasn't me. This had Henka written all over it. She must have guided him every step of the way.

I followed my love.

Though many buildings had been destroyed, either during the initial battle between Yuruuza's god, the city's demons, and the blasphemous Deredi Giants, some remained standing, unscathed. These were the ones with the most powerful demons bound to them. It would take more than wizards and dragon fire to bring such structures down. Clambering over a collapsed building, we found ourselves in a wide courtyard that might have once been a park. The burnt bones of trees, splintered stumps of black, stabbed from the earth. Charred corpses littered the ground, the brilliant white robes of a dead mage standing out in the ashen hellscape.

Henka pulled me into a narrow alley that stank like piss and death.

"At least there aren't as many flies now," I joked.

She ignored my attempt at humour, snapping, "We have to hurry," over her shoulder. "The battlemages dealt with my sea dragons faster than I expected." She hissed as she ran. "Leaving the Guild unopposed for so long was a mistake."

I wasn't sure if that was self-recrimination or directed at me. She'd been alone for thousands of years and I'd been dead. Was she annoyed she hadn't singlehandedly kept the Guild too busy to hone their powers?

The distant rumble of thunder shook dust from every surface. For the moment we were well clear of the fight. Having seen—or at least remembered—enough large-scale magical battles, I knew how quickly that could change. Flying wizards could move fast, if sufficiently motivated.

Smoke choked the eastern horizon, where Bren and I had come ashore in the decrepit rowboat we traded Mihir for. I was sure there was nothing out there but jungle. If the mages had somehow managed to set a tropical rainforest alight, the island was truly doomed. It wouldn't be long before the few survivors returned to the primal savagery I recalled from my oldest memories. No matter how much I wanted to bring back the best parts of my empire—security, equality, and justice for all—my every choice made things worse. Had this been what it was like for the Emperor? Had he tried his best over and over only to constantly fail?

"You should have given up, you stubborn bastard," I grumbled under my breath as Henka pulled me into a winding maze of narrow streets.

I saw no sign of the inhabitants of Abieszan, though no doubt many hid in the rubble and ruins. What little order I'd seen before returning to the flying mountains was long gone. Hacked corpses, swarming with flies, lay in those streets not ravaged by fires. Some had been mauled by animals or suffered the attention of various carrion creatures. Seeing a makeshift firepit, the roasted remains of a corpse still impaled on the spit, I realized humans had likely done some of that desperate gnawing. What had once been a thriving city, safe behind their demon-bound walls, ruled by the shaman Queen Yuruuza, had been reduced to cannibalism. With the jungle burning, the Guild unwilling to help, and ships like Captain Rofalle's avoiding an obviously dangerous situation, the inhabitants were doomed. No doubt some few would survive. I knew the cost of such survival; the things they were forced to do would forever change them. That which we referred to as our 'humanity' was but a thin shell beneath which we were monsters of need. A drowning man will clutch hold of anything and anyone and drag them down with him if it might save his life.

We found Kaszius sprawled in the ruins of what looked to have once been a small household. The magnificent dragon lay among the rubble of the stone wall he'd finally come to rest upon. Looking back, I saw the trail of destruction his descent left behind. After crashing through a tower, the beast had tumbled uncontrolled, crushing several buildings in his wake.

"Oh, you poor thing," cooed Henka, drawing my attention.

Kaszius yet lived, chest rising and falling in pained breaths, smoking blood leaking from scores of wounds. A torn wing lay trapped beneath him.

Running her fingers along the dragon's scales, she moved to stand before him. A single eye of golden fire cracked open, the cat's-eye-slit of its pupil focussing on Henka. Kaszius made a low sound like a wounded dog.

"It's no good," I said. "That wing is damaged."

Attention never leaving the dragon, she said, "You were a king and deserve better." She stroked the tooth-filled snout. "All I can do now is take away your pain," she soothed.

That single eye slid closed.

Drawing her slim longsword, she pushed it into the beast's neck. She made it look effortless, like puncturing dragon scales capable of turning aside ballista-hurled javelins was nothing. Either she was stronger than I had imagined, or the sword was magical.

Kaszius exhaled his last and was still.

Pulling the blade free, Henka shed the blood clinging to its surface with a flick of her wrist. She moved as one intimately familiar with swords, practiced even beyond my own considerable skill. Sheathing it in one fluid move without so much as a glance at the scabbard, she frowned at the broken wing trapped under the dead dragon.

"Once I've raised him," she said, "I can repair the wing enough to get him airborne."

And like that, she shed any trace of emotion.

"We can affect more thorough repairs when we have time," she added. "For now, I need room to work. Stay out of sight but watch for wizards. Eventually, they'll come looking. The viscera of dragons is incredibly valuable."

About to do as instructed, I stopped. "Where is Bren? Is he almost here?"

Henka closed her eyes, brow furrowing in concentration. When she opened them, she looked concerned, darting a glance out at the ravaged city.

"What?" I demanded.

"I've lost contact with the necromancer I left to look after him."

My chest tightened. "I thought you could see through their eyes, communicate with them anywhere."

"I can. Unless they've been destroyed."

If something annihilated one of Henka's necromancers, Bren might be dead already. Savage anger flashed through me. I turned on Henka. "How did you not know?"

Unflinching before my rage, she regarded me with unperturbed calm. "I'm not in constant contact with every undead thing I've ever raised. That would be impossible."

I caught some glimmer of the layers upon layers of plans she had in motion. There were more undead littered around the world serving Henka's machinations than I'd ever dreamed. The kraken and sea dragons were evidence enough. I wanted to question her further, plumb the depths of her every secret, but this wasn't the time. Brenwick was out there somewhere, alone.

Something exploded a few blocks away, sending a colossal cloud of dust, ash, and smoke reaching into the sky, blotting out the sun.

"I have to find him," I said.

Henka shook her head. "It's too dangerous."

"All the more reason," I said, turning away.

Her hand lashed out, catching my wrist and pulling me to a sudden stop. "You can't. He's just a man."

"Just a man? He's my friend." My only friend in all the world. The only person I hadn't betrayed or let down.

"He doesn't matter," she argued, grey eyes desperate. "Even if he survives this, someday he'll die. Disease. Age. Violence. You will go on. Forever." She dragged me close. "You can't risk everything for someone already doomed."

"I can," I said, pulling my arm free. "And I will." I took a few calming breaths. "Raising the dragon and repairing the wing will take time. I'll return with Bren before you finish."

"If you don't," she said, "I will burn what remains of Abieszan looking for you."

CHAPTER THIRTY-THREE

Henka told me that during her last communication with the necromancer, they were heading toward where Kaszius fell. She didn't know where they were when the necromancer was destroyed. I prayed they hadn't been chased far off course.

With no plan and no idea how I was going to find my friend, I ran west. The demonic armour fed me strength, made sprinting effortless. Through the helm, I saw everything in every direction. Crows mobbed circling vultures, chasing them from the choicer meals below. Packs of wild dogs hunted the streets, fleeing at my approach then slinking back in my wake. Much as Abieszan suffered during my first visit, now she was truly dead. The damage vast, I saw little chance of rebuilding. It wouldn't be long before only the most dangerous few remained. Given time, the carrion creatures would reduce the corpses to bones. Rampant diseases would work their course, and the fires would burn themselves out. I'd seen it so many times before, kingdoms looted by their smaller neighbours after having fallen to my armies. Even once the destruction was complete, the violence would continue as scavengers squabbled over the treasure found here. And there were treasures. Abieszan had been one of the greatest ports in the islands, a relic from the days of empire. Wealthy families and merchants called this home, hid their riches beneath luxurious mansions.

There was also, I recalled from the first time we sailed into the harbour, a wizard's tower at the heart of the city. I had no idea if it had been there when Abieszan was first constructed, or if it was a later addition. Either way, it offered a tempting looting opportunity few adventurers could resist. Wondering if it might be a depot tower like the one in Taramlae's capital, I too was curious.

Dashing around a corner, I spotted a mage in the sky ahead and slid to a stop. Even as I searched for an alley or alternate route, he spun in the air, racing toward me. For a heartbeat, I considered drawing Adraalmak and hurling the sword at the wizard. Having seen them bat aside arrows, I decided not to chance it. It was bad enough the mages were safe beyond my reach. I didn't want to be unarmed as well. I spun and ran back the way I'd come, a great storm of flames engulfing me. I felt nothing, my breathing and perception unimpeded. Ducking around the corner, I sprinted for the nearest alley, leaving the fiery maelstrom behind. The mage realized I was gone, and the flames stopped as suddenly as they started.

Fleeing through narrow alleys, I thought I lost him until the building to my left exploded into dust and debris, pelting me with fragments of rock. Though the stones bounced harmlessly off the armour, the sheer concussive force of the detonation sent me staggering.

Laughing at the foolishness of mages, I ducked into the next alley, putting an ancient stone smithy between us.

He brought it down on me, smashing the building to rubble and burying me in thousands of tons of loose rock. Cocooned, and perfectly safe, I couldn't move a muscle. I lay motionless, listening and waiting.

Silence,

"Damn," I grumbled, seeing it from the mage's point of view. He'd chased someone in crimson plate armour and been unable to hurt them. Completely immobilized, I laughed, mocking myself. "He's gone to get more wizards."

Powerful as the armour was, it had limits. A dozen battlemages would tear me apart. At best, they'd hold me trapped while the others peeled me from my protection. There were two white galleys in the harbour. I doubted Iremaire had that much influence. These were likely true Guild mages I faced. They wouldn't be swayed by self-interest the way she was, and it was unlikely I'd have any chance of escape. Not that I had last time. Without Bren's arrival, I would have remained imprisoned forever.

Roaring in anger, I thrashed about, managing only to cause the rubble above to shift and better trap me. The demonic armour made me strong, but I still couldn't lift a building.

What if the mage thought me crushed and dead? With the city burning and whatever remained of Henka's hired sorcerers pestering the mages, he might move on to more active battles. The armour would keep me alive for years, decades maybe. I could be trapped here forever. For the first time I truly understood Henka's fear of the ocean. Strong as my will was, even I would eventually go mad.

"You aren't great company even at the best of times," I whispered.

I spent too much time hating myself, questioning my every decision after the fact, desperately justifying things I'd already done. Left alone without distractions, my mind would devour itself to escape the hell of me.

Making one last futile attempt at dislodging the stones above, I surrendered to the obvious: I wasn't going anywhere.

I could think of no way of contacting Henka. Maybe one of her many dead had seen what happened and would tell her. I laughed again. I'd come to Abieszan to rescue her, but she'd already saved me once and now here I was hoping she might do it again.

Caught in the silence of a stone grave, I thought about the number of times I'd been rescued by the women in my life.

"You're an idiot," I said aloud, thinking of how Tien chastised me when I missed something obvious.

Though I never liked her, and certainly she had every reason to hate me, I missed the little wizard.

Closing my eyes, I built the room in the basement of the mummer's headquarters. Piece by piece I recreated every detail. The dirt floor. The cracks in the crumbling plaster wall. The damp smell of disuse and neglect. The must of mildew and spiderwebs choked with the husked corpses of insects. When I had every detail perfect, I fed a soul to Frorrat, the portal demon bound to the ring Iremaire ridiculed me with.

When I opened my eyes, I stood in the room. The demonic sword and armour I'd made for Bren still lay on the bed. I shook my head in annoyed wonder. With the call of my heart so near, and the shock of being reunited with Henka, I'd forgotten them here.

Even in a dark basement I saw everything.

The young sorcerer, Nokutenda, stood rigid in the centre of the main area. Lips pulled back in a savage snarl baring bright teeth, she shook with the effort of trying to move. An elderly man in white robes, jowls sagging, thin grey hair pulled back in a limp and pathetic queue, leaned heavily on a tall staff of white oak. He studied Nokutenda from under eyebrows too bushy for his face. A second mage, a young woman with a narrow knife-edged nose and the hard mouthline of someone incapable of smiling, stood beyond the sorcerer.

Though drying blood remained, aswarm with flies, the bodies of the men and women I'd killed down here were gone. Judging from the long gory smears in the dirt floor, someone had dragged them away.

"Oh my," said the old man, turning to face me. He lifted the staff, pointing the gnarled end at me.

Adraalmak hissed from its sheath and robbed the room of colour. Not that there was much colour in an old wizard to begin with. Pale eyes widened in terror as the demonic weapon filled the air with its influence. A dark stain spread down the front of his pristine robes as he pissed himself. Lopping the end off the staff, I took his head on the backswing. The body twitched, coughing a spray of blood from the open neck, and toppled to one side. As he fell, Nokutenda exploded into action, suddenly freed from whatever magical bonds held her. Twisting, she drew three black knives, lobbing them clumsily into the air. It looked more like she was trying to get rid of them than hit a target. The little wedge-blades tumbled awkwardly and then streaked toward the mage like a striking rat snake. They melted as they flew, becoming globs of molten metal, then a steaming mist, and then nothing.

Mouth a mean slash, the wizard hardly seemed to notice the attack. She ignored the sorcerer, stepping around Nokutenda to get a better look at me.

The mage's eyes widened in recognition, and with an ear-popping *snap*, she was gone.

Nokutenda tossed three more wedge-bladed knives into the air, and they circled around her like prowling cats. With a snarl, she kicked the headless corpse and spat on him.

AN END TO SORROW

Nokutenda

"Are you hurt?" I asked.

She twitched. "No."

Having only worked minor sorcery, she hadn't visibly aged, though she looked exhausted.

Reaching out with my demon-enhanced senses, I made sure the mage wasn't invisible or upstairs. I found nothing of the woman.

"Fuck," Nokutenda said, a shiver travelling through her. Glancing toward the stairs, she looked ready to flee. "It's that sword, isn't it?"

"Sorry," I said, sheathing the demon blade and quenching its foul sphere of influence. Horror faded from the room like a foul stench slowly departing. "The mage is gone."

The circling blades returned to the sorcerer's outstretched hand, and she tucked them in the thick belt she wore. She bared her teeth again, though this time not in rage or fear. I saw something else there, a haunted defeat. Having been held helpless by wizards in the past, I understood the feeling.

"I thought you'd have left by now," I said.

She glanced at me and away, eyes rimmed and red. "Someone killed my way off the island."

Looking around the room, I saw heaped sacks, boxes, and kegs that weren't there when I last left. "Planning on hiding here?"

"Yeah. Dragged all the bodies out into the street. Even cleared the top floor so it wouldn't attract animals. It was looking like a decent hiding place until the wizards showed up." She hissed at the dead mage, nudged him with a toe. "And thanks for saving me. Don't think I'm ungrateful, but also don't think it means anything."

I figured that was fair. I hadn't intentionally saved her and having Bren swearing undying loyalty already weighed on my thoughts. The Demon Emperor may have thought such devotion was his due, but it left me uncomfortable. I knew I wasn't worthy.

"I see mostly ale, brandy, and rum barrels," I said, changing the topic.

"A girl gets thirsty."

With the sword put away, tension leaked from her shoulders.

"You told me you wanted vengeance on the Guild," Deciding to take a chance, I lifted the helm off, revealing my face. "Still want that?"

"I knew I recognized that voice," she said, unsurprised. "You're his twin brother or something?"

"Or something." I considered my options. A sorcerer would be a handy ally and, judging from the way she looked like she wanted to kick or spit on the dead mage, I thought we might share some common goals. "You want that vengeance?"

Dark eyes turned hard. "You have no idea."

"No promises," I said, needing at least a moment of honesty. "We'll likely die before you get even a taste."

"Vengeance can wait. If there's a chance you can get me off this island, I'm in. Just don't ask me to swear allegiance or any silly oaths."

"Fair enough."

"You really have a way out of Abieszan?"

"I do."

"A boat or something?"

"Or something. We have to find Henka."

"Henka? That necromancer woman?" Nokutenda hesitated. "You know she was with your brother, right?"

"All part of the plan," I lied.

Full lips pursed in contemplation. "So, what's your name?"

"Khraen," I answered.

She snorted. "Wow. Your father was shit at naming his sons."

It was such a strange thought—trying to imagine someone being my father, a parent to teach me right and wrong and what it meant to be a man—that I guffawed.

"At least you have the same sense of humour," she said.

The words quelled my amusement. I didn't want to think of the other Khraens out there as people, with their own personalities and goals. We were one man, and we weren't.

"Here's the deal," I said. "I need to find my friend. Help me do that, and you can leave Abieszan with us. We're going south. We can leave you on the first island we see, or…"

There was a choice I'd been avoiding making. With Kaszius, it was possible we might fly all the way to PalTaq. I could avoid Naghron and the other shards. If I was going to free Henka, they were probably better off on their own. And yet, despite my promise to free her, I wanted those pieces.

"You stopped talking mid-sentence," Nokutenda said, "and now you've got a weird smile."

"This is the face of a man trying to differentiate reasons from excuses from justifications. I guess you've seen it before."

"No. Khraen—your brother—was always certain. I don't think I ever saw him hesitate."

That surprised me, but perhaps it shouldn't have. We were all pieces of the same man, but we were all different pieces. Why, then, had Henka chosen the uncertain shard, the one who wrestled over every choice, to be the one who survived to the end? I suspected it was because it made me more malleable, more easily led than a Khraen who thought he always knew what he had to do and was confident he was right.

"For what it's worth," said Nokutenda, "it doesn't matter. The idea that there is some innate difference, qualitative or otherwise, between reasons, excuses, and rationalizations is flawed."

I stared at her for a moment, startled.

"Don't look so surprised. I'm not an idiot. I know the common perception is that all sorcerers are depressed, suicidal teens bent on self-destruction, but some of us pursue power for our own reasons."

"You aren't suicidal?"

"I didn't say that. Anyway, my point is that the only thing that matters is what happens after the decision has been acted on. And after the fact, everything is justification. You might have reasons for making a choice before acting on it, but afterwards all you're left with is your justifications. Think about it, no one else knows or understands your reasons for doing anything; to them everything looks like a justification."

"I think you're wrong," I said. "In fact, that sounds suspiciously like a justification."

She winked. "It is. I'm just fucking with you."

Decision made, I said, "One of my brothers is on an island south of here."

"Let me guess. His name is Khraen too."

"No, it's Naghron."

"Naghron? *The* Naghron?"

"I'm going to kill him."

"Are you insane?"

"After I kill him, I'm going to PalTaq."

She stared at me, taking in the crimson armour. "Khraen. Going to PalTaq. No way."

"I'm going home."

"I always thought taking the name of the Demon Emperor was a bullshit ego move." She shook her head in wonder. "He always dreamed big, said someday he was going to unite the island tribes, but nothing ever happened. There were always reasons to delay. Powerful enemies. The Guild sniffing around." She flashed a nervous grin. "You know, justifications."

I wasn't the Demon Emperor, and I wasn't this other Khraen either. Even once I took his shard of heart, which I sensed off to the west where I left Henka, I'd still know nothing of his personality.

"The chances of me surviving long enough to get to PalTaq are slim. The odds of me living through what's likely to happen if I do get there are even slimmer." Much as I wanted the sorcerer's help, I wanted her to understand how dangerous it would be.

"If you're asking if I want to travel with you, you're doing a shit job of selling it."

"I can't promise you'll get a chance to kill wizards, though it does seem likely."

"I shudder to think how bad you are at pillow talk." Her voice dropped in pitch as she mimicked me. "I'm going to fuck you now, and you aren't going to like it."

"So, we should drop you on the first island?"

She looked away. "I've always wanted to see PalTaq. What happens if you survive?"

There was no way Henka wasn't going to wreak a terrible vengeance on me for my crimes. I hadn't thought past that moment. What would I do if I somehow, impossibly, survived?

"I'm going to loot the island for artefacts and then I'm going to crush the Guild and take back my world."

"You *do* know how to sweet talk a girl."

"But I'm definitely going to die on PalTaq."
"And there you go ruining it again."

CHAPTER THIRTY-FOUR

Hunting through the basement, I found an old backpack and stuffed Bren's armour in. His sword I slung over my shoulder.

"It occurs to me," said Nokutenda, "that the wizard who just fucked off has probably gone for reinforcements."

I agreed.

After grabbing a few of the more easily carried supplies, meat crammed into pockets, a few skins of water, one of wine the sorcerer said was too good to leave behind, we exited the mummers' home. The place was strangely unharmed in this ruin of a city. The corpses Nokutenda had dragged into the street swarmed with flies. Grotesquely obese rats glanced up at our arrival and returned to gorging themselves on the rotting meat. The colossal cloud of smoke kicked into the air by whatever had exploded earlier had spread and diffused, turning the sun a dim and bloody ball of red. Each breath clawed at my lungs, my throat coated with dust.

"Wait," said Nokutenda, dropping her pack and kneeling to search through it.

Drawing a kerchief from within, she offered it to me.

"No need," I said, sliding the helm back into place.

With an annoyed grunt, she tied it around her face, covering her nose.

"Better if we soaked them in water first," she mumbled through the fabric. "But I think we should save it for drinking. So?" she asked. "Where to?"

Had I bypassed Bren when I used the portal demon to escape the building I'd been buried under? I had no idea, no way of knowing. Henka said he was to the west when she last had contact with her necromancer, but he could have gone anywhere after that.

Or he could be dead.

I turned the problem in my thoughts, trying to figure where he would go assuming he yet lived. Though the harbour likely offered the only chance of escape—and a slim chance at that—there were two Guild war galleys loaded with battlemages there. The rest of the city had either already burned or was in the process of burning. Scavengers and the few desperate survivors stalked the streets. Though I hadn't been here long enough to see the result, I had no doubt plague and disease ran rampant. Whatever aqueduct system fed Abieszan, it was now polluted beyond use.

I looked north, toward the jungle. Hazy with smoke and distance, the outer wall cut a straight line along the horizon. There'd be water, though I wasn't sure how drinkable it would be. The tropics were famous for murky ponds of death. There'd also be food, plants and animals, if you knew which to eat and which to avoid.

As I watched, a massive wall of fire, taller than any of Abieszan's remaining structures, rose before the wall. For a heartbeat, it shivered before coalescing into a vaguely humanoid shape. Colossal flaming fists gripped stone.

"That's bad," I said.

Nokutenda stood at my side, eyebrows creeping up in surprise. "Is that…"

"Fire elemental," I said. "Months old. Intelligent. Biggest one I've seen in this or any life."

Less volatile, earth and air elementals were somewhat easier to control. I'd ridden mountains dominated by powerful earth elementalists. Fire, however, was violent and endlessly ravenous. No elementalist could hope to control such a rampaging creature.

The wall held, and the fiery maelstrom roared its rage at being impeded.

"Why bad?" asked the sorcerer. "It's leaving the city. Isn't that good?"

I shook my head. "The jungle will give it more fuel. It'll grow, get bigger."

"It's jungle. Too wet to burn."

"At that size, everything burns. Sodden wood. Dirt. Stone. It'll grow, and when it's in danger of running out of combustibles, it'll turn its rage downward. It'll war with the earth below, carve through the bones of the world to the great elemental god at the centre."

"Elemental god?"

I ignored her question. "A volcano will be born, a hellish combination of the two elements. It will burn for a thousand, thousand years. Abieszan will be black glass and death, the antithesis of life. Nothing will grow on this island ruled by a new-born god of fire."

Nokutenda's nose wrinkled, her lips curling in something like doubt. "Maybe not. The wall seems to be holding."

"That's the other problem. There are demons bound to those walls."

"So?" She asked. "What is a wall going to do to a fire elemental?"

Under attack for the first time in three thousand years, the demon slumbering in the city's northern fortifications woke. Even as it defended itself, lashing out at the fire elemental with stuttering barbs of lightning, it called for aid.

"There are demons bound to most of Abieszan's original structures. They're all connected."

Last time I was here, I woke many of the city's demonic defences, sending them against the Queen's pet god, the Deredi Giants, and the wizards. Some had survived and now awoke again. Others, those at the far end of the city by the northern wall, had never been called upon. Though they'd been aware of the previous battle, their part of the city had been unthreatened. Now, they came awake with a fury.

When I woke the demons at the harbour gates, I'd been so distracted by fleeing the Deredi and getting to the docks before the mages left, I missed most of what happened. Now, at something of a safe distance, I understood a long-hidden truth. Many of Abieszan's defences were spirit demons. They hardened stone, making it impervious to fire, warding it against trebuchet-hurled boulders and magical attacks. Some were capable of attacking enemies within range, reaching spheres of demonic influence—clouds of terror or soul-crushing domination—to destroy or drive them away.

Others, however, were of a less passive nature.

A pulse of sound far below anything I could hear swept through the streets, lifting dust from every surface. I felt it in my guts, my heart stumbling in its steady beat.

Nokutenda staggered and caught her balance. "Did you feel that?"

I laughed with manic glee, an idea forming. The fire elemental was a terrifying creature and spelled doom for all life on the island. It wasn't, however, my enemy.

The public square at the heart of the city that Bren and I passed through earlier split wide as the guardian sleeping beneath woke. Abieszan shivered as it clawed free. Newer structures, those built after the fall of the Demon Empire, crumbled and collapsed, throwing billowing clouds of smoke, ash, and dust into the already choked air. I watched in awe as the beast rose. Three thousand years ago, there would have been none of this destruction.

It was a dragon, and it wasn't. A sick blend of reptile, insect, and hellish nightmare, the creature towered over the city. Sickle blades like rusting iron curled from every surface. Gargantuan tusks formed an armoured cage around its head, three pairs of ember flame eyes burning within. Not quite bipedal, it stood on its rear legs, hunched forward over what looked to be a fortified mansion of relatively recent construction. The demon shook itself, scales shedding millennia of crimson rust. Its wings, freed from confinement, spread wide, blanketing the city below in shadow.

I fell to my knees, pressing my hands against the cobbled stones.

"You all right?" the sorcerer asked.

I ignored her, concentrating on the rock beneath my palms. Smooth from aeons of passing feet, I would likely be the last living mortal to touch them. Reaching my will into the bones of the city, I made myself known.

The demon's draconic head swung to glare in my direction, six eyes of scorched loathing.

I woke the last of Abieszan's demons and bent them to my

purpose.

I didn't care about the raging fire elemental.

I didn't care that allowing access to the jungle beyond would feed it for many weeks, allowing it to grow to something truly terrible.

I didn't care about the island's doomed inhabitants.

My hate for the mages, for their filthy Guild, their pretences at perfection, consumed me. Too often, they interfered with my plans. The mages back in Taramlae. The wizards who used Shalayn to track me south. Iremaire, who thought she could bend me to whatever trivial game she played. The battlemages in the war galleys in the harbour who hounded my every step.

The Guild inherited a civilization I quite literally spent three hundred lifetimes building. Under their stewardship the world fell to squalid disarray. Piracy. Poverty and discrimination. The Deredi once again spread their foul sickness. My grand cities either lay in ruins or had been long abandoned in favour for muddy streets, crumbling hovels, and failing sewer systems.

Looking up I felt a mad grin stretch my face. Nokutenda said something I couldn't hear, her voice pleading.

"Destroy the wizards," I commanded the demon.

It hesitated, head swinging toward the northern wall still calling for aid, the fire elemental assault causing grievous damage.

"No," I told the guardian and all the city's remaining demons. "Destroy the wizards. Burn the ships. Drown the harbour in blood and fire. Nothing survives. Not a rat. Not a cockroach."

Colossal wings beat, a hurricane wind toppling buildings, extinguishing fires, and scattering debris everywhere. Impossibly, the creature lifted from the ground. It was like watching a mountain decide it could fly. My mind shuddered before the unthinkable. Not of this world, barely shy of being a god, the demon flew toward the harbour. Little white dots rose from the streets below and were snuffed. Expanding clouds of red mist rained blood and fragments of bone.

I rose.

Nokutenda stared at me in horror as the fire elemental tore the northern wall down and fled into the jungle leaving a trail of flaming devastation. Slim as my chances of surviving were, I couldn't help contemplating a future where I returned and made use of the creature. It might be too powerful for an elementalist to bind, but it was still possible to kill such a thing. And anything that could be killed could be bargained with.

"It'll keep the mages busy," I said, turning away and heading west. "Come. Let's find my friend."

The sorcerer swore under her breath and jogged to catch up. "He's actually a friend, and not someone you want to kill before you leave?"

"A friend."

"And you'll tear apart the entire city, wake whatever that was, and risk death to save him?"

"Apparently."

"I think we could probably be friends."

"He'd do the same for me."

"Oh. Maybe not then."

"Not going to risk your life to save me?" I asked, joking.

"No. You scare the shit out of me."

We walked on in silence, Abieszan's sky a dim red false dawn of dust and smoke. The only buildings still standing were those built in my time. Rubble and ruin throttled the streets, and we picked our way over collapsed houses and buried dead. Silence ruled like a god, all existence moving at a lethargic stumble as if stunned by the horrors it witnessed. No breeze shifted the smoke and it stayed low, swimming the streets and alleys like a lazy river. I saw no birds, carrion or otherwise, and no wild dogs. No life spoiled the calm. Nothing struggled, fought, or clung desperately to life.

A world surrendered. A city demolished.

"So," said Nokutenda, breaking the silence. "Who is this friend?"

"His name is Brenwick."

When I didn't continue, she said, "What's he like?"

Despite my reluctance, I discovered I wanted to talk. Sometimes we bottle everything up for so long we forget there is healing to be found in sharing.

"You'd like him," I said.

"He's handsome? Broad shoulders and eyes that promise

trouble?"

"Handsome?" I pictured the magefire scars twisting his face, reaching down his neck to his chest and beyond. "Probably not. He's a big lad though. Broad shoulders."

"Hmn." She sniffed, glancing off down an alley. "Is he funny? I'll forgive a lot if he can make me laugh."

"Sometimes. He's… He has suffered. He was badly burned saving me."

"Ah. The wounded puppy routine. Just needs someone to save him, to bring him out of the shell he's crawled into. I've fallen for that before. You can't save people. They either do it themselves or drown in their own shit. Trying just brings you down with them." She shook her head, eyes distant. "Never again."

Even while we chatted the armour fed me a constant barrage of sensory information. I saw the changes in her pupils, the way her face flushed warm when angry.

"The wizards burned him," I said.

"We both hate mages? No doubt that's more than enough to form a lifelong bond. I'll have his kids, wash his socks and everything."

"They turned the woman he loved into a pile of ash."

She winced and said nothing, her pain evident.

The harsh ring of steel on steel echoed up the street. Slowing to a stop, I listened. From somewhere in the smoke ahead came the muted sounds of battle. Men and women grunting with effort. Cries of pain and fear. I drew Adraalmak and Nokutenda paled, retreating from the demon's sphere of influence.

Two blocks ahead, a man in a mask of mottled grey stumbled from an alley, three crossbow bolts jutting from his back. His knees buckled and he collapsed, facedown. Not knowing if Bren was still with the mummers, I charged.

CHAPTER THIRTY-FIVE

The crimson armour fed me strength, a thousand infinitesimal hairs worming into every part of me. My blood sang war, my teeth bared in a savage rictus of joy. Though full plate was hardly intended for sprints, it weighed nothing, felt like an extension of my will. Or I an extension of its. Passing the dead man, bolts protruding from his back, I slid around the corner on steel feet, balance perfect. In this armour I could juggle longswords whilst blindfolded and walking a tightrope in hurricane winds.

Enemies.

Enemies everywhere.

The armour read my reactions to the mummer's masks and marked them as possible allies. Not friends, but not picked out as immediate targets. Everyone else glowed a threatening red.

Men and women fought. Bright swords and blood-laced air. Grunting and filth.

The helm pointed out hidden opponents, archers darting from cover to send arrows into targets.

Kill them all. Blood and chaos. The glorious anarchy of war. Civilization is a myth, a prison built by the weak. Structure and permanence are illusions; disintegration and decay are the only truths.

I shook off the thought.

Most of the milling figures wore a burgundy livery I didn't recognize, chests and shields bearing a golden wolf rampant. The others wore a motley of dark colours best for blending in with shadows and tight masks of grey and black concealing their faces.

Unarmed, Mom, the queen of the mummers, stood at the heart of the fight. Clay fought at her side, swinging that monstrous axe to great effect. He bled from several wounds, staggering from exhaustion but unwilling to quit. I saw in him a man who would fight until his heart burst, or his opponents cut him down. There was no give or break.

Vishtish, separated from the mummers, fought alone. Six liveried warriors in chain hauberk surrounded him. They worked together like seasoned veterans, each moving to take advantage of any distraction, attacking from behind, retreating when the swordsman faced them. Where they all suffered wounds, Vishtish looked to be untouched. Calm, laconic grin locked in place, he played them off each other, feinting at one only to somehow stab the man behind him. Wherever their swords were, he wasn't. Vishtish disarmed one with a dramatic flourish, booting the man in the ass when he turned to scramble after his sword. For a heartbeat, the clouds of smoke and ash above broke, and a beam of golden sunlight lit Vishtish. His hair was perfect. Sliding away from another attack, he impaled a man through the heart, babbling in his strange tongue the entire time like he meant to talk the others to death.

The mad free-for-all melee shifted, and I saw Bren on Mom's far side, a broken half-sword in one hand, a dagger in the other. He fought with a brutal efficiency, never moving more than he had to. Simple straight jabs into exposed flesh. Feint at the eyes. Stomp a foot. Knee to the groin and a shattered sword in the throat. Much as my armour screamed murder and chaos, my heart soared at the sight of my friend. If he still lived, I hadn't yet failed him. Pathetic, but a small hope is better than none. If there was only one man in all the world I didn't betray, there might be something in me that wasn't shit through and through.

Tears stung my eyes. Hidden in my crimson helm, I cried for joy.

Cutting down a woman in burgundy livery from behind, I entered the fray. Adraalmak devoured the world's colour. Bright blood became black, shining steel muted to a dull grey. Brave warriors faltered, some fleeing while others puked and cowered. The demon was indiscriminate. It cared not for sides. Antithesis to life and joy, it exalted in bleak misery.

Something bounced off my helm so hard I lurched back a step, ears ringing. Were I not wearing demonic plate, it would have crushed my skull. Dazed by the impact, I lost myself to the swirling maelstrom of information the demon shoved into my veins. Movement. Enemies. Danger. Someone in a mummer's mask came at me with a raised sword, mouth wide in a silent scream of horror. My arm rose of its own volition, Adraalmak taking the top of his skull off.

Danced like a murderous puppet, I now understood Henka's concerns over the armour. I suspected if I were rendered incapacitated or even dead, it would fight on. Oddly, I suspected it wouldn't flee a fight to save me in such a situation. This thing knew nothing of retreat.

My armour jerked me around until I faced a mousey young man in ill-fitting livery a dozen strides away. Unlike the others, he wore no armour. Face twisted in a grimace of pain, he gestured at the cobblestone street before him. Palms up, he raised his hands and a skull-sized stone lifted from the ground, raining dirt.

Wrinkles deepened around his eyes as he suddenly aged, spending himself, and I knew him for a sorcerer.

The boulder snapped at me too fast to see, even the demon unable to avoid it, and punched me from my feet. Hurled backward, I tumbled across the street in an uncontrolled tangle of limbs. I saw sky and stone, sky and stone. The world whirled around me as the armour rolled me back to my feet. The sorcerer, hair now showing grey at the temples, cheeks a little sunk, made a gripping motion in my direction, bony fingers clenched in a shaking fist.

I stopped moving as if I hit a wall. My feet left the ground as the sorcerer lifted his hand. Grey spread through his hair, his bright and youthful eyes clouding. The armour moaned in agony, the air within compressed and damp.

With a metallic scream, the armour crumpled, pressing in against my ribs.

I'd been stomped by a dragon. Mountains sought to crush me beneath their weight. I'd survived aeons of war, battles with lords of alien hells. I'd fought wizards and slaughtered them in their thousands.

But one young sorcerer would crush me to a bloody pulp of mangled flesh and steel. If, that is, he was willing to spend all of himself.

AN END TO SORROW

Khraen

I struggled to move as the demon howled in pain and helpless anger. Metal squealed and a rib snapped beneath the incredible pressure. Elevated and powerless to move, I saw everything. The sorcerer's eyes stayed locked on Adraalmak. Face white with dread, he was well within the sword's sphere of influence.

Some lessons we learn over and over. Sometimes the bravest man will crumble and fall or flee in terror. And sometimes the most cowardly can be pushed beyond reason, to the point they will do anything to destroy that which scares them. If I could move enough to throw the sword away, releasing the sorcerer from his fear, he'd likely be unwilling to spend himself to crush me to nothing. Unfortunately, I was a fly suspended in amber.

Held above the battle, my crimson plate caught Bren's attention. Helpless and suffocating, my armour caving in around me, I saw him glance from the two men he faced to the broken sword in his hand and then notice the sorcerer. Without hesitation, he threw the half-sword.

Oh, you beautiful—

And missed.

The weapon spun unheeded past the sorcerer and skidded down the street to disappear into a sewer drain. I roared, struggling against the sorcerer's grip. Compared to the demon, I was nothing. Sagging steel drove into my thigh, puncturing flesh. Blood ran, pooling in my boot.

Senses heightened, I saw everything as time slowed in the moments before my imminent death. Bren jammed his knife into the ribs of one of his opponents, and it lodged there. The other struck him a glancing blow to the temple and he folded. Collecting a knife from the ground, Mom stood over him like a protective hen, snarling at her enemies. An archer, previously hiding behind a collapsed building, popped up long enough to put an arrow through Clay's neck. The big man fought on. Choking on his own blood, he buried his axe in a man's skull. Unable to pull it free, he released it, grabbing the nearest opponent, and dragging her into a crushing head-butt. The archer put a second arrow into his side, below the ribs. Ripping it free, Clay sank it into the stunned woman's eye. Someone stepped in to fill the gap when she fell and Clay tackled him in a bear hug, dragging him to the ground.

Looking bored, Vishtish killed two more.

My helm crumpled, jagged corners pressing into my temples hard enough to distort my vision. Bent like an old man, hair shot with white, once youthful face gaunt and wrinkled, the sorcerer stood rooted in his terror. He would spend himself until either I was crushed to nothing, or his life force spent.

The sorcerer's head popped like a grape crushed between finger and thumb.

Nokutenda sagged to her knees, catching herself as she pitched forward. "Yeah," she said, wincing. "That hurt."

I hit the ground an instant later, landing in an ungainly sprawl.

In agony, bleeding into my boots, head feeling like it was crushed in a vice, I had one thought: Bren.

Rising to all fours, I looked up to see Vishtish kill another liveried warrior with a dazzling series of attacks. When the rest fled, he bowed low, spinning his sword in an intricate flourish. Sheathing the weapon, he paused to fix his perfect hair. Aside from the swordsman, only Mom and two mummers remained standing.

Regaining my feet took what strength remained to me, the demonic armour apparently wounded and sulking. It took me three wobbling attempts to sheath Adraalmak, finally silencing the blade's foul aura. Though some small, sad colour returned to the world, grey clung to everything like a stain. Bren lay on his back three strides away, staring at the sky. Removing the helm felt like dragging a nest of angry snakes from my brain. Nausea twisted my guts as the silken hairs slid free.

Bren stared with a look of horror. "Khraen?"

"Mostly," I answered.

"Fucking hells, I thought you were a demon!"

Not far off the truth. I felt the armour's tendrils worming through my body, urging me to put the helm back on.

Feed, demanded the demon.

If I allowed it to drain a few lives, the dents would unbuckle, the armour repairing itself.

Feed.

"Did you burst that sorcerer's head?" Bren asked, grimacing in pain as he probed his many wounds with blunt and bloody fingers. "If that was you, what took so long?"

"That was me," said Nokutenda. She looked haggard, like she'd sprinted through miles of dense jungle. Haunted eyes met mine. "It was all chaos. Killing. Blood and bodies. I didn't know which side we were on. When I realized which one the sorcerer was…" She looked away, drawing a deep breath. "I hesitated. My first thought was to run."

"You saved me," I said.

She made a quiet sound that might have been choked laughter or restrained sobbing. "You're the only way off the island."

With the enemy scattered and Bren apparently in no danger of dying, I stripped off the armour. Removing it was difficult not merely because the steel had been awkwardly reshaped, but also because the demon within resisted giving me up. Wounded as it was, the thing still craved destruction. It would until the moment it was destroyed or freed to return to its home reality. As I had no memory of how to do the latter, it would likely remain here in my world forever. Each segment of armour clung to me, the worming tendrils of hair tugging at my veins before finally surrendering.

After, armour piled in a jumbled heap, I felt naked and exposed, weak and helpless.

No. I promised Henka I would never wear it again.

If I couldn't stay true to this one relatively small oath, how could I ever follow through with my promise to free her?

Still, I hesitated to part with the armour.

Would Bren wear it if I offered it to him?

Remembering the demon worming through my thoughts, I realized I couldn't. If I found it difficult to resist its influence, he wouldn't stand a chance.

"Admit it," I whispered to myself. "If you keep the armour, it's because you intend to wear it again."

Only if the armour was beyond my reach would I know for sure I'd keep my promise.

"Vishtish," I said, turning to the swordsman.

"Vishtish," he replied, but made it sound like he was correcting my pronunciation.

"That's what I said." I pointed at the armour. "You want this? I can fix it."

Some of the wounded were already dying. Sacrificing them to heal the demon would only take moments.

He shook his head, face twisted in a sneer of disgust, and babbled a string of incomprehensible syllables.

"I don't think he likes the colour," said Mom.

The swordsman had already forgotten me. He stood over Clay's corpse with a look somewhere between resigned sadness and petulant annoyance, as if the big man's death was an inconvenience. Shaking his head, he turned to Mom and made more noises, while holding a pose that was probably supposed to look dramatically heroic. When he finished, he walked away, disappearing into the city.

"What was that about?" Bren asked.

Mom watched the swordsman's departure. "I think I'll miss his hair most of all." She turned away, seeing to the wounded mummers.

"Should I be hurt that you offered the armour to Vishtish instead of me?" asked Brenwick from where he lay.

"No. I offered it because I don't like him. The armour is a nightmare." I hefted the pack with the sword and armour I made for Bren while in the floating mountains. "I did, however, bring you something to replace the sword you traded for a leaking boat."

"Is this your friend?" asked Nokutenda, gesturing at Bren. "What was his name, Bumwit? Can we get out of here now?"

"Brenwick," said Bren, lifting one hand in a half-hearted wave. "My friends call me Bren."

"Nice to meet you, Buttwick. Get the up and let's get moving."

Bren used a nearby chunk of wall to pull himself to his feet. He looked like he'd rather lay back down in the street.

Ignoring the sorcerer, he turned Mom. "What are you going to do? Abieszan is done."

She breathed deep, taking in the ruins and the few surviving mummers. "You're leaving." She glanced at me. "You have a way off the island."

"We might have room for you," I admitted, "but no one else."

Mom looked at her hands, frowning at the blood and filth. "I know it looks like total devastation, but there are still people here. Hundreds. Maybe a few thousand. If they work together, they might survive."

"You saw the fire elemental?" I asked. "It's huge, and months old. It escaped into the jungle."

The ground rumbled, raising dust from every surface. Everyone turned to stare toward the harbour. The demonic dragon I woke towered over the docks, breathing flaming black death on the wizards below.

"And then there's that," said Mom. "Whatever that is."

"It's the Guardian of Abieszan," I said. "I think all the great cities have one. Had one," I corrected. I… I can't remember."

"Guardian?" said Mom. "What will it do once the mages are dead?"

"It'll return to its place beneath the city." At least that's what I hoped. "Unfortunately, that doesn't mean the end of your troubles. The mages will return in force. I don't think they can let something like this go unanswered,"

"Aren't you a treasure pot of joy," grumbled Mom. "Doesn't matter. I'm not leaving. I was born here. This is my city, and I won't abandon her."

I wanted to promise I'd return and help her. I wanted to say I'd send ships and supplies, bring armies of demons to protect this ancient bastion of the world I lost. If I did somehow survive what I planned, I'd return to bend that monstrous demon to my will.

I shook my head, struggling to understand the history I missed. Though I couldn't see the white galleys from this distance, I saw the flickering glow of their shields over the ruins of the city. They held for the moment but were failing. Magical attacks lashed the demon with desperate frenzy, appearing to do no damage. The demon would crush them, reduce their ships to nothing and devour their souls. And yet my world fell, my empire crumbled, and the mages won. Abieszan's guardian might win this fight, but they'd come back in force and destroy it.

A tired sadness at the futility weighed me down. All my life was a struggle and yet, with every choice, my failure became more certain. I'd enjoyed happiness that outshone anything I felt while living in that trapper's hut of mud and bone but hadn't known a moment of peace. All these other Khraens stayed on their islands, ruled over their filthy little kingdoms. I should have done the same or lived a quiet life somewhere far away. It was a big world, the Guild ruled over a relatively small section. So many people would still be alive had I done stayed in that hut.

No more.

Once I freed Henka from the chains of slavery, she would end me.

The mages and their anaemic white mediocrity could have the world.

With Nokutenda's help, Bren strapped on the demon armour I brought back from the floating mountains. She tutted as she worked, adjusting the weight on his shoulders, and tightening the belt so his hips took the weight of the chain skirt.

Finding a wound in his side, she poked it. "Have you ever thought about *not* getting stabbed, cut, and burned?" she asked when he cursed in pain.

Surprisingly, he didn't flinch at the mention of his burns.

"Where's the fun in that?" he asked. "Anyway, women find scars sexy."

"They do?" Nokutenda gave him a doubtful look. "Well then, you must be sexy indeed."

Bren stretched, rubbing at his lower back. "A little sexier every day. Another fight like that and I'll be irresistible."

With the armour in place, she handed him Kra'Katle, the demon sword I made for him. She ignored the green flames flickering the length of the blade like it was completely normal. Testing the weight and balance, Bren sheathed the sword. Already he stood straighter, shoulders less hunched, as if having a weapon went some way toward healing him.

Nokutenda stepped back, making a show of looking him over. "If you weren't so tall, were a bunch slimmer, had fewer scars, didn't look like you routinely used your face to open doors, dressed better and smelled less like the kind of suppurating ass-wound you'd find on a dog's corpse, you might almost be close to handsome. Ish."

"It's my one flaw," he admitted.

"On the high side," she said, "you'll never know the struggles of the truly stunning and unbelievably intelligent."

"Ignorance is bliss."

"I, on the other hand, face such challenges daily. And yet somehow, I retain my humility. Really, it's just one part of what makes me so awe-inspiring."

"Truly, you are humble in your divinity."

It did my heart good to see more of the old Bren return. His haunted look retreated as they joked.

The sorcerer was nothing like Tien, but then Tien was nothing like what he told me his perfect woman would be. Where the wizard was slim and petite, Nokutenda was curves and softness. She stood a full head or more in height over the mage too. A northerner, Tien had been pale skinned with light strawberry hair and green eyes. At least until I killed her and Henka repaired the damage with flesh taken from islander women. Nokutenda's skin was from the southernmost islands, her expressive eyes were darkly inquisitive to Tien's bright and mischievous humour.

"Kids," I said, though both looked older than I, "stop bickering."

"She started it," mumbled Bren.

We left Mom and the mummers and headed east, back toward where I left Henka and the dead Kaszius. The battle by the harbour raged on, explosions rocking the city. We set a slow pace, Bren shuffling wounded on my left, Nokutenda staggering with exhaustion on my right.

Knowing it was the only way to keep my promise to Henka, I left the crimson armour behind. I warned Mom against using it, but also told her it would keep whoever wore it alive through all but the most horrific battle. I wondered if she'd ignore my warnings. Sometimes it seemed like every choice was nothing more than selecting one evil over another.

A thunderous roar shook the ground as one of the war galley's magical shields failed and the vessel became an expanding ball of raging black fire incinerating all it touched. If there'd been survivors unfortunate enough to be cowering there hoping to find passage with the wizards, they were gone now, ash in the maelstrom winds kicked up by the ebon inferno.

"I could stop it," I said. "I could order the demon to retreat."

Bren stared toward the harbour. "Burn the fucking mages."

"I'm with Buttlick," said Nokutenda. "The wizards can burn."

I considered questioning the sorcerer on her enmity toward the mages and the Guild, but knew it was only a matter of time before Bren dragged it out of her. He couldn't help himself. Unlike me, he was all about the people around him.

"Henka found you," I said instead.

"I guess," he said. "Though I never actually saw her."

He filled me in on what I missed.

Though Abieszan burned around us, and a colossal demonic dragon battled the remaining wizards down by the docks, Bren saw none of it. He walked, lost in a daze as he relived the last two weeks. "I get that. I'm a thousand years older than I was one year ago."

BRENWICK TELLS A STORY

When they closed the door behind you, the basement became eerie silent. I waited and waited for some sign that you'd left. I don't know. *Something.* Eventually, the guards Mom left got bored and started handing out cheroots and smoking. Not wanting to be rude, I smoked with them, though it would have been better with a good whiskey. Or even a bad whiskey. After that, I went upstairs to try and distract myself from the fact I was alone in a stronghold of thieves and murderers. You know, I think what really bugged me was how well I fit in, how comfortable I felt among the scum of the earth. My gram would be so disappointed. She used to go on about how I had this light in my heart and how someday I was going to make the world a better place. Like one man could ever do that.

I had a few pints with Clay. He was a good man, I'll miss him. After, we took a few cheroots and a bottle of rum up to the roof to smoke under the stars. We mostly talked about the past. Not the recent past—too painful for both of us, I suppose—but the distant past. Parents. Childhood. How you thought life was one thing and it was really something else. We talked about how disillusioning it was to reach adulthood only to realize you hadn't grown up at all. There we were, two little boys smoking and drinking under the night sky.

Clay said something that stuck with me. He said, 'It isn't age, experience, or wisdom that makes you an adult. It isn't even having children of your own, though that shoves you a few steps down the path; it's surviving tragedy. It's coming out the other side, kind of broken, changed by what happened.'

I get that. I'm a thousand years older than I was one year ago.

When I could no longer supress my curiosity, I returned to the basement and cracked the door open to peek inside. Of course, the room was empty. Maybe it was empty the whole time and you left before I finished the first cheroot.

Three days later, the mummers brought this pretty islander woman to me. Her name was Kyrstle, and she said Henka sent her with a message for you. Having seen Henka beheaded and tossed into the ocean, I expressed my doubt. She took a knife from one of the guards and pushed it through her own hand without so much as a flinch or grimace of pain.

Call me convinced.

Kyrstle told me she was relaying the conversation to Henka, who was about a day from Abieszan. When I told her you wouldn't be back for three or four days, maybe longer, she winced and said Henka wasn't happy about that. She said her master was with another Khraen and that I was supposed to get somewhere safe. I refused to leave you and we argued. Poor Kyrstle, caught in the middle, acting as a go-between for two stubborn people. She promised Henka wouldn't let anything happen to you, and that anyone near where you disappeared from would be killed. When I realized that meant Clay, Mom, and all the scum I'd become rather fond of, I had to save them.

Let's face it. We both know Henka can protect you better than I ever could.

After that I spent a few hours arguing with Mom about abandoning her home. Realizing I wasn't going to leave without the mummers, Kyrstle told them there was a dragon coming and they couldn't possibly fight it. Since no one had seen a dragon bigger than a horse in over a thousand years, they laughed and ignored us.

Then it flew over the city. I'd never seen anything like it. It was like the gods had returned, the old world of myth born anew. I mean, we've all heard the stories of the emperor's aviaries, of cadres of dragon-mounted sorcerers destroying cities. I'll tell you straight up, it was the most beautiful thing I'd ever seen. If that glorious beast still existed, then maybe the old world wasn't entirely dead. Maybe the islands wouldn't forever be subjugated by the mainlanders. Maybe someday we could be something other than the dregs of the world.

And then the dragon swept low and slagged an entire block and I saw people disappear as they became clouds of ash. There was a little girl. I was looking right at her—our eyes met. I watched... She... And then...

The myths and legends are shit. They conveniently neglect to mention the innocents who die, their last moments all terror and agony as their hair goes up and their skin blackens. It's like tossing a damp leaf into a fire. There's the moment when you don't think it'll burn. Then it starts to curl and the edges brown, then she's cinders swirling in the air and you're standing there like an asshole thinking about how you thought she was beautiful a moment ago.

I would happily spend the rest of my life being spit on and hated for the colour of my skin if it meant no more children died like that. Except it doesn't mean that at all. Islander children starve in the slums of Taramlae. Not all the islands are green and lush, and very few have cities like Abieszan. Life is harsh, and the further south you go, the harder it gets. Many of the islands are volcanic, a few scrubs and lichens clinging to rock. We raid each other for slaves, for food, for the scraps of a dead civilization.

Mainlanders think we live like this because it's in our blood, because we're savages. But I've been to Taramlae. It's so green. Drop a seed and it just *grows*. The earth is dark and rich and deep, and it rains all the time. Most of them live miles from the ocean where they're safe from its anger. They don't realize the seas are still restless from the wars, that storms blow out of nowhere and scour entire islands clean of life. Mainland cows and pigs are fat, like the people. Life is easy. With island cows you can count their ribs.

The dragon. Shit like that marks you. I guess it's like Clay said, tragedy makes us men. Even witnessing it first-hand changes you. Or at least I think it should. Much as that hurt, much as I wish I'd never seen it, I don't ever want to be someone untouched by such horrors. I'd much rather puke and cry.

After the dragon's first pass, it turned into a mad exodus. Mom managed to keep most of the mummers together, but many fled into the streets. She said the mummers had a cache of emergency supplies to the north, preserved food, clean water, cots, blankets, and clothes. The mummers have several littered about the city. It was a mad dash from cover to cover, cowering in buildings until the dragon passed, and then sprinting for the next doorway. At first, I thought the mages would ignore the dragon the way they ignored the city's suffering, but I guess they decided the dragon might be a threat to their ships. Of course, they didn't come into Abieszan as saviours. They were as bad as the dragon, burning and killing anything they thought might be dangerous. I guess a gang of murderers and thieves qualified. We lost half our numbers before they got distracted by the dragon.

Life is funny, you know. Funny like when you're in a really good mood and wearing your best shirt and the sun is shining and a pretty girl gives you the eyes and then some passing seagull takes a massive wet shit on your head.

We escaped the mages only to run right into Duke Hayes' men, who were all too pleased to catch the mummers out in the open. Turns out, there had been some enmity between Mom and Abieszan's nobility for a few decades. About half the people she collected for your Soul Stone were the duke's family or retainers. What exactly is a retainer anyway? What do they retain?

Doesn't matter.

Having seen the dragon circling Mom's territory burning things, the duke got the idea she might flee into the streets and sent his men-at-arms to intercept. At first, we were slaughtering them. Well, mostly it was Kyrstle. She absolutely did not give a shit. They stabbed her and hacked her, and she let them if it got her close enough to stick her sword in someone's guts. I guess their sorcerer figured out what she was, because he dropped a massive chunk of wall on her, squished her flat.

That turned the tide against us. There's something that happens in your head when you realize you're going to die soon. I was still alive, still fighting, but we were outnumbered. Scary as Vishtish was with a sword, he couldn't kill them all. It was only a matter of time before the sorcerer saw he was the most dangerous of us and squished him too. The fight changed for me. One moment I was trying to kill my enemies. The next, I was fighting for a little more life. It wasn't about winning; it was about getting to be alive for a few more breaths. I'll admit I thought about running. I wanted to. But Clay wouldn't abandon Mom and she couldn't run for shit. He was a murderous bastard, but I liked him. I think maybe that makes me an idiot. I liked the guy and so I was going to stay and die because leaving him would kill what little there was left of me I still liked.

Then, when this terrifying *thing* showed up in blood-red armour with a sword screaming horror, I thought we were done. I can't tell you how happy I was when it cut down one of Duke Hayes' retainers. I thought maybe you'd returned and sent a demon to help us.

I'm glad you showed up and saved my ass. Again. But I'm also glad you left that armour there. Never in all my life have I felt something so completely evil.

CHAPTER THIRTY-SEVEN

Much of what Bren said struck close to home. I knew all too intimately the fear of becoming someone I didn't like. I saw my promise to free Henka for what it was, a desperate hope I could still be a better man. As if one selfless act might somehow redeem thousands of years of murder, sacrifice, and war.

Down by the harbour, the second war galley's magical shields failed in a cataclysmic explosion. Miles north of the docks, we felt the ground shake beneath our feet and stopped to watch. Distance and smoke blurred the horizon, the insectile dragon a vague shape looming over the city. Fortified castles shivered and shook apart as if constructed of loose bricks. Ancient demon-bound towers swayed and fell in on themselves with a slow majesty that tore my heart. The massive outer wall protecting this city for thousands of years crumbled into the churning sea.

The destruction threw up dust clouds obliterating our view of the south end. Still wearing her own makeshift mask, Nokutenda fetched another strip of fabric from her pack, and offered it to me with an arched eyebrow. No longer safely cocooned within the demonic armour, I accepted the cloth, tying it around my face.

Once again heading west, we walked on in silence. The smoke cloud grew as the ocean breeze caught it, and then shredded apart as the demonic dragon spread its wings and flew back to its lair. It may have defeated the mages, but it had suffered many injuries doing so. Gashes tore its sides, leaking foul demon blood on the city below. Much of it had been burned and blasted, charred black, and one wing looked like it threatened to fold beneath the strain of flight. Though it would rest beneath the city until once again called into action, it could not heal unless fed souls. Something of that size would require a great many sacrifices. It would have been more tempting had I thought there were enough survivors and had some easy way of rounding them up.

How many such guardians still lay waiting, buried in ancient cities because they were never called to action? I could wake them all. After three thousand years of ruling unchallenged, the mages would be unprepared for such a war.

Skipping a lot of details I thought Nokutenda didn't need to hear, I filled Bren in on what happened since my return. The sorcerer made no attempt to disguise the fact she listened. She was quiet for a long time, brow crinkled in a slight frown.

Finally, she said, "Khraen, you really are the Demon Emperor returned?"

"I am part of him. The man you knew as Khraen was another part."

"I knew he was a demonologist, but he never talked about his past. I assumed it was because, like all of us, he'd suffered at the hands of the Guild and was hiding. They make no secret of hunting down every rumour of demonology."

When neither Bren nor I spoke, she continued: "He could never make something like that armour. And I never saw him do anything like what you did with that dragon."

"Dragons are reptilian and of this world," I corrected. "That was…I'm not sure. At least half insect and definitely from some other reality."

"Whatever," she said. "You both call yourself Khraen. But if you're hiding from the Guild, you don't take on the name of the most hated demonologist ever."

"Pretty dumb," Bren agreed. "If you're hiding."

"But you aren't hiding," she said to me. "Not anymore."

I gave a small shrug.

She thought about that while we walked. "I've heard of others using the name."

"Some are probably pretenders. Some are part of me."

"For three thousand years," she said, eyes distant, "we've been praying for the return of our emperor. Sitting in the ruins of the past, gathered around campfires, we whisper stories about how someday we won't be the filth of the world. We want vengeance. We want the wizards to know what it is to be spat upon." She focussed on me. "Have you returned to answer to our prayers?"

Bren snorted a laugh.

"I want to," I said.

Nokutenda studied me through narrowed eyes. "You want to, but?" Hope and doubt warred on her features.

I could say what she wanted to hear, and this young sorcerer would spend herself in my service chasing a dream long dead. I wouldn't. Despite knowing what I planned, I suspected Bren harboured similar hopes.

I realized I dare not speak freely. I couldn't chance the sorcerer mentioning my intentions to Henka.

"I have things I must do first," I said.

"And after?"

"Assuming I survive that long, yes."

"You'll remake your empire?"

"Yes," I lied.

"Good." Cutting in front of me, she forced me to stop. "When I was a little girl, they came to my village chasing rumours of a demonologist. They tortured our shaman in front of the entire tribe, just to show us how helpless we were. They skinned him, tossed his flesh on the fire, and made jokes about how us savages were cannibals and how we must be salivating at the smell. Somehow, he was still alive. They pulled him apart as he hung in the air, exposed every nerve, unlooping his veins and muscles so they floated free of his bones. His eyes popped out of the sockets and dangled on his skinless cheeks, and he screamed and screamed, and they didn't even ask questions. There was no demonologist; none of us had ever seen one." She drew a long, shaking breath. "One of the tribe's hunters drove his spear through a mage from behind. You should have seen the surprise on that pink bastard's face. Well, after that, they killed all the adults. Anyone old enough to hold a weapon and young enough to walk without a crutch. When they left, we were a handful of children and two old ladies, one of whom was blind. Two days later, the tribe from the next island over came to scavenge what was left. Vultures. They killed the old women and sold the kids into slavery. Ask me again how many souls I'm willing to sacrifice."

I felt her pain. The memory of my treatment in Taramlae was all too clear. Darker. Stained soul. People had sneered at Henka, who looked like a northerner at the time, for being with me. We'd been refused service countless times, thrown from the best establishments.

"That's why you learned sorcery," said Bren. "Revenge on the wizards."

"There were no demonologists or necromancers to learn from. Shamans are no match for mages, and the Guild have never accepted a single islander into their ranks. There weren't a lot of choices."

"It seems insane," he said, "to trade your life and health for power."

"Yeah?" She cast an appraising eye over him. "I'd guess we're about the same age. Look at your face, your neck and shoulders. Look at all your wounds and scars. How much of that did you suffer fighting for him?" She gestured at me. "We all spend ourselves. The question is how fast, and whether we get something in return."

Pushing past the sorcerer, I continued to where I hoped Henka still waited. "Follow, or don't," I called over my shoulder.

They both followed.

Bren asked Nokutenda, "Has sorcery given you what you want?"

"Not yet. But I'm still young." A moment of silence and then, "Khraen?"

When I kept walking and refused to answer, she continued: "Don't bring the Guild down for me. Do it for all the islander children out there and those yet to be born. Do it so they can live in a world where their worth isn't defined by mainlander hate. If you would but fight for them, I would die for you. I would spend all I am in service to my emperor. Forget your past crimes. Turning your back on your people would be a far greater one. I beg you, be our emperor once again. Unite the islands."

Shoulders knotted and tight, I kept walking.

I dared not listen. She said everything I so desperately wanted to hear.

My people needed me.

What was righting one wrong compared to that?

CHAPTER THIRTY-EIGHT

We found Henka where I left her. The dragon, Kaszius, waited obediently behind her. Huge leather saddlebags, custom made for a dragon, hung bulging at his sides. I hadn't previously seen them and assumed the other Khraen must have had them made for the flight to Abieszan and then dropped them to improve the beast's manoeuvrability once here. Were it not for the great wounds in its flanks, and the crude metal stitches holding one of its wings together, I wouldn't have known it was dead. Deep in the tropics, that would soon change. I could only hope the beast lasted long enough to get us where we wanted to go.

Seeing Henka was a shock. I still hadn't got used to the compact islander body inked black with tribal tattoos, and the shaved head.

Henka made no attempt to disguise her examination of Nokutenda. "Who is this—"

Bren interrupted her, pulling her into a hug. She disappeared in his arms with a muffled exclamation of surprise.

"Sorry," he said, pulling back. "Last time I saw you… Well, you know. It does my heart good to find you well." He hugged her again and she let him.

When he finally released her, she touched his face with the gentlest caress. "I'm sorry you've suffered. Not to worry. We can make you right again." She pulled his shirt open, studied the scarred and twisted flesh. "We'll fix this."

Bren retreated with a nervous laugh, pulling his collar closed. "Not sure I'm ready to go that route just yet."

"I meant we'd find a mage to repair the damage."

"Of course. This is Nokutenda." He turned to find her staring at the dragon, eyes wide with awe.

"He's dead," she said. "Really dead."

"She's a sorcerer," added Bren.

"Undead."

"She's usually more eloquent."

"Undead fucking dragon."

"See?" Bren said. "She saved our lives,"

Impatient, I gestured at the waiting dragon. "We should go to Naghron."

The murderous piece was getting closer to him, and I wanted to be there first.

"Palaq," said Nokutenda, attention still locked on the beast

It took a moment to remember that's what Phalaal, one of the necromancers in the necropolis, called it. "Yes."

"To kill Naghron in the heart of his empire."

"I'd hardly call it an empire."

"You haven't seen it."

"Blunt," said Henka. "I like her,"

With the patience of the dead, Kaszius waited while we clambered onto his broad back. There was room to sit comfortably, even lie down, but frighteningly little to hang onto.

Seeing my expression, Henka said, "I won't let you fall."

Once we were all settled, Kaszius found a stretch of road not too blocked with rubble and lumbered into an awkward run before lifting into the air. Wind whistled through the ragged holes in the damaged wing. We wobbled, Bren mouthing something that looked like *Oh no, fuck this* as the dragon's massively muscled shoulders worked to give us altitude. We rose into clouds of smoke, each of us making sure our masks were in place. Except Henka who didn't need to breathe unless she wanted to speak.

Kaszius flew in a rising spiral over Abieszan. When I leaned to look down, Henka caught hold of my shirt to keep me from sliding away. The city below was a wasteland of destruction. I saw no structure untouched by the carnage. The harbour, once guarded by massive gates and ringed by a wall so large an entire second city lived upon it, was now an ocean-filled crater. Fire raged everywhere, out of control. The jungle beyond the northern wall had already caught, the flames spreading in what looked like a graceful wave from this height. The elemental out there was huge.

"They're going to burn," said Bren, squinting down through the smoke. "Mom. The mummers. Anyone not already dead."

Some of the dead too. No doubt Henka left behind both necromancers and undead on the off chance we someday returned.

Having gained sufficient altitude, Kaszius headed out over the ocean, climbing ever higher. The temperature dropped and Henka dug blankets from the saddlebags. Abieszan dwindled behind us, fading into the distance. Soon, only the enormous cloud of smoke and ash remained visible.

I turned my back on the scene of my most recent crimes.

Henka handed me a heavy blanket woven of crude cotton and I wrapped it around my shoulders. The heat of the tropics didn't reach this high.

She still kept the stone shard of my heart tucked somewhere in her clothes. I sensed its terrible pull and refused to surrender to my hunger. I yearned to feel it puncture flesh, burrow through vein and muscle as it sought my heart. Pain. Punishment. I craved it, wanted it more than anything in all the world, and hated that need.

Need is weakness.

Arms tucked hidden in my blanket, I raked long gouges in my skin with clawed fingers. The wounds burned, a welcome distraction. I found some small peace in that discomfort.

My attention strayed to Henka, to the fragment of obsidian hidden from sight.

Not yet. I would have the shard, but on my own terms, when I was ready.

Far below, the ocean looked peaceful, a blue so deep it hinted at black. Small dots cut trails through the sea leaving thin white lines in their wake.

Shading his eyes, Bren squinted. "What are those?"

"A squall of sea dragons," answered Henka.

"They're tiny."

"They're huge," she said. "Each of them is twice the size of Kaszius."

Realizing we were higher than he'd thought, Bren took on a decidedly greenish tint. Nokutenda gave him a playful shove and he squeaked in terror.

"Fucking hell, woman. I can't swim!"

"Not to worry," the sorcerer said, "fall from here and you'll splat like an over-ripe plum smashed with a maul."

Closing his eyes, he huddled deeper in his blanket. "It's possible I might be ever so slightly totally terrified of heights." He shivered. "It's probably my one flaw."

"I thought you were a pirate," said Nokutenda. "You must have climbed a mast before."

"This is a bit higher."

We flew southwest, the dead Kaszius tireless. The damaged wing held, though sometimes tremors passed through his body. The sun rose and we felt little of its heat. Only when it sank toward the horizon did I appreciate the difference it made.

"Lie flat," said Henka. "Some of his fire still burns in his belly. It will warm you."

We did as she suggested.

"Is the guts of a dead dragon being on fire a good idea?" asked Nokutenda.

Henka ran a hand along the scales of Kaszius' shoulder as if he were a loved pet. "He's already rotting at a terrible rate. We will have to land before it gets too bad."

Henka watched us as we slept, promising she wouldn't let anyone roll off and fall to their death.

I woke hours later, the sky above a silken sheet of sable punctured by pinpricks of crisp light. Endless black, the ocean reflected nothing. Only patches of swirling blue and purple, plankton disturbed by the waves caused by atolls and volcanoes lurking below the surface, marred the perfection. Lines and patterns formed in the chaos, hinting at unearthly knowledge. They crumbled to disorder before I could discern their meaning. Something disturbed the riotous colours, cutting a V through the plankton. Knowing how high we were, whatever it was must have been truly enormous.

I saw the curve of the horizon and felt strangely small.

We flew for days, the stench of the dead dragon increasing until we once again tied fabric around our faces. Henka kept a nervous watch on the damaged wing, judging how long it would last. Despite the beast's efforts, we lost altitude, the flight growing ever more turbulent. Islands passed beneath us, some little more than an outcropping of dark rock jutting from the ocean. Flying lower and lower, we began to see signs of human habitation, if not actual civilization. Like swarming ants, people scrambled up the steps of crumbling jungle-choked pyramids to witness our passing. On many islands, I caught subtle signs of long-abandoned cities. Oddly straight lines carving through the tangled foliage hinted at ancient roadways. In some rare cases I saw the neat rows of agriculture as tribes rediscovered farming.

Three thousand years.

It was one thing to understand on an intellectual level but impossible to truly grasp its impact. I knew from my earliest memories that most civilizations lasted no longer than a century or two. Some rose up, built roads and schools, farmed the lands, cleared forests to fuel industry, constructed sprawling cities, made incredible works of art, and disappeared to nothing within half a millennium. The ruins below could be those of civilizations born centuries after my fall.

"If ruin and decay are inevitable," I muttered, "what's the point?"

"My gran always said that the struggle was the point," said Bren. "It's the journey, not the destination."

Nokutenda snorted disbelief. "Horseshit. No one walks from Nachi to Riverwatch because they want to enjoy the journey. They make the walk because Nachi is a shithole, and they want to be in Riverwatch. The destination is everything."

"I think maybe the point is to live in the moment," he argued. "No reason you can't enjoy the journey."

"Are you a mentally deficient toad? It's a six week walk along broken coastline, each week colder than the last."

They bickered and I ignored them.

I studied Henka from behind and my chest ached with the anticipation of agony. The wounds I'd clawed in my arms had healed to white lines and I resisted the urge to hurt myself again. Having a shard of my heart so close felt like standing on a broken foot, the pain constant and unrelenting. Every night I dreamed of the forgotten past, never quite sure what was real and what was my imagination filling the gaping holes in my memory.

The next day we shed our blankets and Henka packed them back into the saddlebags. Between the tropical sun and the heat emanating from the rotting dragon, we were soon soaked in sweat. Having shed much of our height, we saw the world in greater detail. The ocean's peace had been a deception of distance. Winds churned the waves, whipping their crests to a white froth. There were countless small land masses in the south, long archipelagos of palm trees and white beaches, brutal islands teeming with raging boulders of black glass forever circling their volcanic mother. Even more lay submerged, visible only as discolorations in the water.

We flew over a single tower standing tall in the ocean. I sensed the demons bound to the stones, ever vigilant, ever warding it against the depredations of the sea. The water was so deep, I saw no hint of the land it stood upon. With nothing to mark its location, no land in sight, I'd never find it again. Looking back, I watched it fade into the distance. I wanted to stop and explore, but there wasn't time. Any delay, and the murderous piece of my heart would reach Naghron before I arrived.

I still couldn't answer the question of why I cared.

"Are we there yet?" asked Bren, startling me from my thoughts.

"Three days," answered Henka without hesitation.

I had no idea if she was guessing or somehow knew.

My heart twitched with anticipation. Three days should be enough time. If I stalled any longer, it might be days or even weeks before I had another chance.

"Henka, my love. I'll take that shard now."

Turning, she opened her hand. The small sharp-edged wedge of obsidian lay nestled in her palm. Bren had seen this before, knew what to expect. Nokutenda didn't. I decided I didn't care. Henka and

Brenwick could explain if they wished.

If I was the Demon Emperor, then I was above such concerns.

I took the piece of my splintered soul.

CHAPTER THIRTY-NINE

Black stone sank into flesh, shoved its way through veins and muscles in search of my heart. Jaw clenched I watched the misshapen bulge work its way the length of my arm. Beautiful purifying agony ripped me. My shoulder bulged for a moment, and it was in my chest.

Henka said this was all about me trying to remake myself into someone capable of happiness. Could that really be it, or was this another layer of lies? She'd also said I'd promised to destroy Nhil. That felt wrong. In all the time I spent with him, he showed no hint of fear. For all that he was a smug bastard, I liked the demon.

You weren't supposed to remember me at all, Henka had said. While, for the most part I didn't, I'd found oblique memories of her littered through the shards as if I'd left my own trail of clues. If I wasn't supposed to remember her, why did I know about the hall of pedestals and her heart? If I lied about carving out all memories of her, and killing Nhil, what else had I lied about?

What if the deceptions were all mine?

Forever my own worst enemy.

"We can't keep doing this," I told my love, knowing she'd understand.

For she knew me better than I knew myself.

"Whatever we planned," I added, "we've failed."

"You can only fail," said Henka, "if you give up. I will never stop trying."

I wanted to howl with laughter at the irony of what I'd done to myself, Instead, my heart split wide, invaded by a new sliver of obsidian and I howled in pain.

"There were already pieces missing," she said, distant like a dream, "when we first cut your heart out."

Tens of thousands of years ago I'd been a youth hunting the jungles of the deepest tropics. A golden god came to me. She tore me apart, dropped stone into the sundered cavity of my chest. Dying, I'd never thought to focus on it, had no memory of its shape. Had it been a piece of a larger heart, already incomplete, or had I lost fragments later?

I died.
I dreamed.
I remembered.

I wasn't born to rule. I wasn't born to wealth and power. My long-forgotten mother gave birth to me in a mud hut. Nothing of her remained. Not an image of her face, not even the faded memory of kindness or protection. When I turned fourteen, the men cut me, shoved sand and pebbles into the wounds to make the ritualized scars that set us apart from the other tribes. I bared my teeth and made no sound. After, I strutted bleeding about our village of reed and mud huts displaying my raw scars to the girls and bragging about how many ears, noses, and scalps I would collect from our enemies. In the immortality of youth, I was fearless and stupid beyond comprehension.

That boy had a name, now lost to time. It wasn't Khraen.

I grew to manhood hunting snakes and jungle cats and warring with the young men of other tribes sharing our little island. Though I collected my trophies, as did the other men, I learned of the cost. Each one changed me a bit. It wasn't shame or disgust or weakness. Rather, I grew to understand that someday this would be my own fate. At twenty-two, we were veteran warriors, blooded and vicious. At twenty-five we led raids, stole wives, and trained children in our ways. At thirty, if we survived that long, we were veterans, scarred killers. There were no old men. The tribe's shaman, a man crippled in his first raid, was an impossible forty-two years old, if he was to be believed.

I pinned men beneath my knee and sawed through the flesh of their skulls. I ripped their scalps free, felt them shudder with the knowledge that, though they weren't yet dead, death wasn't far off. I watched one of our own warriors die after being caught and scalped by a neighbouring tribe; it took days, flies swarming the exposed bone.

We were a people without a future. I understood that fate, just as I understood there was nothing I could do to change it.

There is a helplessness in grasping the blind futility of existence, in understanding that all things end. I would someday die. If I sired children, they too would die and with their passing, the last of me would be gone from the world. But what else was there but to live that short life, collect your trophies and fuck the girls who decided, for reasons you would never understand, you were worth fucking?

Life was meaningless and so we lived our meaningless lives because there was nothing else.

But there *was* something else.

The golden god changed everything.

She bound me to her, wrapped me in silken chains of purpose. She gave me meaning and a future, and I, in turn, passed that gift on to my tribe. I killed the old shaman. I cut his heart out and ate it in front of my tribe, a symbolic gesture of the transference of wisdom and power. I fed his pathetic god, a deity ruling nothing more than a copse of fruit-bearing trees, to my new god. Long I had dreamed of purpose, of being a part of something lasting, something permanent, and she offered me that.

Her dream became my dream.

She fed it to me slowly, in slivers my trapped savage mind could comprehend. It started small—rule the tribe—and grew from there. Instead of butchering our enemies and collecting trophies, we conquered them. Join us or be fed to our ravenous new god. At first, many died, clinging to the old ways. Stubborn stupidity is ever the curse of young men and none of us were old.

I united the disparate tribes of five islands. Smaller tribes would come bearing gifts and pledges of allegiance without me having to lift a single weapon. Having already achieved more than any man in the memory of my tribe, I gloried in my successes.

I warred for decades, uniting the tribes. When the last fell, I thought I ruled the world.

Though only forty, the boy I'd been, the youth hunting in his log canoe, was dying a slow, invisible death. Alien ideas infected me, seeming to bubble up from deep in my chest.

Instead of being done, I understood this was but the first stage in a much larger plan. It was time now to consolidate my power, to nurture the seeds I'd planted, husband them into something greater. We'd been many tribes and now we were one. But we were still a tribe, still lived in mud huts, still fished with barbed bone spears, still hunted the same prey. While everything had changed, nothing had changed.

I ruled a world of semi-nomadic tribes. My warriors were called when needed and disappeared back into the jungle the moment their work was done.

She wanted villages and standing armies. She wanted permanence and structure.

Though bound by my rule, each tribe worshipped its own gods. Some prayed to primal elemental forces, or their shamans communed with the spirits of their dead. They worshipped streams and ponds, deranged apes and colossal snakes. They sacrificed food to the clouds and spilled the blood of chickens to appease the earth.

We were one tribe with a pantheon of thousands.

The boy I'd been had no problem with this. How else could it possibly be?

The man she dreamed understood the value of faith. Like food or blood, belief was a commodity. Faith in your fellow warriors. Faith in the tribe. The *knowledge* your leaders knew what was best and would act according to that knowledge. A faith of fragmented devotions was worth less than one focussed on a sole source.

My god would be the only god.

Foreign concepts infected my thoughts. Churches. Schools run by the priests. Food, I realized, didn't have to be something you went digging through the mud for. Fruits, vegetables, and grains could be farmed. Hunting, I realized, while fine for tribes of forty or fifty people, was woefully inefficient. Livestock. Animal husbandry. I turned my endless world of open land into a patchwork of walls and fences. We built harbours and docks and turned our best craftsmen to making boats beyond imagining. Gone was the day of the hollowed log canoe. I thought I ruled the world but in her dream the world was impossibly large.

My mud hut became a village and then a city. I aged as men did, but she would not let me die. In her dream, there were other realities populated by impossible spirits and forces. In her dream, there were doors one could open to call such things through. Terrified of death, I accepted every offering of more life. Through the doors of her dream, I called demons and bound them to blood and bone. I wasn't much of a demonologist, didn't yet understand that's what I was becoming. It was enough.

Centuries later, I would come to comprehend her game. She played me like a master, using my fear to twist me to her needs. Over and over, she allowed me to teeter at the brink of death before offering yet another reprieve. By then I no longer cared. The price I paid seemed paltry compared to what I received.

The man who had been hailed as a brave warrior, who collected scores of tongues, noses, and scalps, was a coward.

You'll be forgotten, I'd tell myself in moments of quiet desperation. *Everything you've built, everything you've achieved, will crumble without you.*

If I died, my High Priests would fight to take my place. The structure I created from filth and chaos would fragment. In a decade there'd be scores of tribes. In a century, they'd have fallen back to the old ways.

For all I'd built, impermanence remained the one enemy I'd yet to defeat.

Patience, she soothed.

The young warrior I'd been would have railed against the restraints. When you see what you want, you take it. Patience, I learned, can be a form of cowardice.

And I had infinite patience.

Cities became fortresses. My castle became a sprawling palace. Pal-Taq was the centre of the world. Or so I thought until her dream showed me the north. My own limited experiences shuddered under the onslaught of new ideas. A land so massive it couldn't be called an island. A thousand kingdoms each with its own cities as grand as anything I'd built. Men and women capable of twisting chaos to their will. Powerful magic unlike anything I'd seen. Elementalists who woke rocks and rivers. Sorcerers who sacrificed their very life force to bend reality to their whims.

Warriors encased in steel carrying bright swords. Machines of war throwing boulders a hundred strides or more.

I followed her dream north.

CHAPTER FORTY

I woke to an oppressive heat. The stench of rotting dragon filled the air, a thick miasma of dead reptile. Bren and Nokutenda had tied extra layers of fabric around their faces to ward off the foul smell. By the looks in their eyes, it wasn't working. Henka, still startling in her compact and muscular islander body, seemed unperturbed. Half expecting to find her in the early stages of decay, I was surprised to discover her unchanged. It made sense she'd planned this well enough to have blood stashed away in those saddlebags.

She flashed a smile, reaching a hand to touch my arm. When she didn't ask what I'd remembered, I realized she hadn't done so with the last few pieces. When we first met, she kept asking if I remembered a woman. I wondered if she'd been trying to catch me in a three-thousand-year-old lie.

"Good timing," she said. "Kaszius won't last much longer. I hope he makes it through the night. Otherwise…" She looked at the ocean below.

Recalling what happened the last time we were cast adrift, I prayed the dragon made it.

"You're not dead," said Nokutenda. "After all the screaming and thrashing around, I thought we'd be pushing your corpse into the ocean. It already smells bad enough without another stinking dead thing."

"It's not so bad," said Bren, sniffing at his armpit and then grinning at us. "I can't smell anything over the dragon."

Except for Henka, we were all soaked in sweat, the armpits of our shirts stained dark.

"Ever the optimist," grumbled the sorcerer.

"It's my one flaw," he admitted. "I prefer to look at my pint mug as half-full."

"There are no pint mugs," said Nokutenda. "And if there were, they'd be empty."

"Sure, but we're not dead." He winced an apologetic glance in Henka's direction.

"How did you motivate the other Khraen to leave his island?" I asked my wife.

"The desire was always within him. I suggested his time had come and that he needed to collect the other pieces of his heart."

Having been on the receiving end of Henka's 'suggestions', I had some idea of how persuasive she could be. "But he was closer to Naghron."

"I convinced him the order mattered." She didn't blink, showed no hint of discomfort at the discussion.

We'd had the same conversation, and I too had been persuaded. Could she bend all of us Khraens to her will so easily? I imagined her travelling the world, whispering suggestions in our ears. *Stay here. Conquer this one island, and no more. Hide.*

Were my plans mine at all?

One was, I knew that much. The one plan she knew nothing of.

Something bothered me, though I couldn't tell if I worried I was making a mistake or looking for reasons to change my mind.

"Am I my own worst enemy?" I muttered to myself.

"No," said Henka. "Your enemies are far worse."

Kaszius ended the conversation by suddenly vomiting a great ball of flaming guts into the ocean below. He wobbled and shed altitude at an alarming rate, his damaged wing threatening to fold. When he finally evened out, we were several hundred feet lower, though still high enough a fall would kill.

"Remind me never to fly on the back of a dead dragon again," said the sorcerer.

Noticing that she and Bren were now holding hands, she yanked hers free.

"That was you," he said, "not me."

"Just making sure you didn't fall."

After that, the dragon's internal heat dimmed considerably, though the smell got markedly worse.

The sun fell, dragging the blanket of night over the world. Laying back on the cooling dragon, I marvelled at the sky's cold beauty. Sleep avoided me and I considered how far Henka might go to foil my plans should she learn of them. Would she push me from Kaszius' back, so I fell to my death? Would she travel the world killing all the remaining Khraens so she might recreate the path she wished me to follow? She would never stop. She couldn't, not as long as there was some chance it ended in me becoming the man we wanted me to be.

If not for the fact she wasn't trying to stop me, I'd worry she already knew my plans.

It stung my pride to admit I didn't think I could stop her. If she decided this attempt was a lost cause, she would kill me. Even if I caught her by surprise and shoved her off the dragon, I had no doubt she'd find her way out of the ocean. Maybe it would take years or, more likely, she had undead creatures following us.

I sat in silence contemplating the irony of lying in an effort to do the right thing.

Bren and the sorcerer bickered about whether piracy was a more noble pursuit than simply murdering people in the street and stealing their stuff. Bren argued that true piracy was an art requiring years of training and included a great many skills whereas any halfwit could bash someone over the head from behind and lift their purse. Nokutenda said that since the end result was the same—one person dead, another now in possession of their belongings—everything else was irrelevant. The hours passed, the discussion sliding from topic to topic. They argued about everything from which island had the best beer to the best way to gut a mage. Eventually, they slept.

I touched Henka's shoulder to get her attention. "I will never be the Demon Emperor again."

"I know."

"How can you be sure?"

Flint eyes studied me. "We made sure that could never happen."

"How?"

She took my hand, kissed the palm with cool lips. "You could only truly be him if you found all the memories in the order he lived them." Still holding my hand, she said, "I knew the old you, and I know this you. You're not him."

"He was evil."

"Was he?" She looked north, as if toward the distant mainland. "You've seen what the wizards have made of this world. They're stuck in their books and in their towers and can't see past their own interests. Whatever his failings, he tried to make the world better."

Much as I wanted to, I didn't believe her for an instant. Henka said only what she thought I wanted to hear.

I woke the next morning to discover we'd lost more altitude during the night. Dolphins frolicked in the water beneath us, putting on an acrobatic show as they followed the dragon's path. Though untiring, Kaszius now worked much harder to keep us airborne. Tremors ran through his decaying body, frayed wings sounding like tattered flags in a hard wind.

Ahead, on the very edge of the horizon, lay a jagged and mountainous shoreline.

"That's too big to be an island," I said, shading my eyes and squinting. "It stretches as far as I can see."

"It's an archipelago," said Nokutenda. "I saw it on a map once, and it looked like a huge circle of islands."

"I heard it was the mouth of a volcano," said Bren, "and that when it blew for the last time it almost split the world."

The sorcerer looked doubtful. "The cartographer who made the map said it was an impact site. She said that long ago, even before the rise of the Deredi hive, a god fell from the sky. It crashed into the ocean and the impact broke the world, killing everything that lived on it."

"Uh," said Bren, "there is clearly still living—"

Nokutenda talked over him. "The cartographer pointed out on her map how the ring of islands is directly south of the Rift splitting the mainland. She said the Rift was caused by the god's fall."

"Must have been a big god," said Bren. "Very fat."

"Your cartographer friend was wrong," I said, ancient memories teasing at the edge of my thoughts. "It was once a large land mass. Perhaps a massive island or small continent. Something went wrong. I think one of my priests was trying to open a gateway."

"Impossible," said Nokutenda. "That would have been—"

"My guess would be about nine thousand years ago," I said. "Though I remember none of it clearly. I think he was trying to lead a coup against me."

"Same shit different day," mumbled Bren.

The land ahead grew in detail. Rocky and mountainous, the island had been stripped of soil by the brutal winds sweeping across the ocean from the east. Stunted trees and tufts of hardy vegetation clung to the rocks in a desperate bid for survival. Flocks of white sea birds scattered at our approach, some looping around behind us to worry at the dragon's tail as if it were a large raptor they might chase from their territory. Kaszius ignored them.

"We're a little low, aren't we?" said Nokutenda, casting a judging eye at the range ahead.

At a command from Henka, Kaszius struggled to gain height so we might clear the jagged mountains. The beast shuddered and rumbled with the effort, scales peeling away to expose the worm-riddled meat beneath.

"That's not good," said Bren, looking back.

Behind us lay a trail of dragon wreckage floating in the ocean. Birds and fish swarmed the detritus, plucking it from the waves, or dragging it into the deeps. The beast's belly must have been in even worse shape than its back. The effort of gaining altitude tore even more loose and the dragon rained gore as it climbed.

We passed over the ruins of cities carved into the mountains. Crumbled walls and shattered pillars littered the slopes. Long ago, wide steps had been cut into the rock to create flat growing spaces. Those gardens were long gone, the plots a tangle of stubborn vines. Dark doorways and windows gaped like empty eyes. Islanders, dressed in simple loin cloths and decorated with bone as I remembered in my most ancient memories, cowered there, clutching their weapons. Barely clearing the few stunted trees, we were low enough a few well-thrown spears would likely bring us down. They watched our progress, making no attempt to hinder us.

As we crested the mountain, I saw the booted feet and lower legs of a statue that must have once stood several hundred strides tall, looking down over the city. The rest of the statue was gone, fragmented beyond recognition.

The far side of the mountain showed more ruins in the same style, and I wondered if what I saw was the same city reaching all the way through.

We didn't reach the coastline until late in the evening, the sun bleeding red into the western sky. An eternity of ocean lay before us with no sign of the other islands of this supposed circular chain.

That night the dead dragon's flight became so erratic none of us slept. The damaged wing whistled in the wind, shedding reptilian skin. We clutched peeling scales and prayed they didn't come loose, listening to the waves all too close beneath us.

The sun rose behind us and ahead we saw distant coastline at odds with what we'd previously passed over.

"Prevailing winds are from the east," said Nokutenda, seeing me glance back the way we'd come. "Strips all the soil from the islands on that side and dumps it here."

Kaszius struggling to keep us aloft, dropping ever lower, we flew past fleets of fishing rafts lashed together. The dark-skinned men and women working the nets paused in their labours to watch our ungainly progress. They showed little fear. This wasn't confidence or bravado. I saw a wary acceptance in the slump of shoulders and curved backs. Though well-fed, these people were worked hard.

Closing my eyes, I concentrated on the pull of my heart. The large piece I believed to be Naghron was close. The other, the one travelling from island to island destroying our heart, was farther north. The size of the island made it hard to judge distance. Land stretched from the northern horizon to the southern. Had I not been told it was an island, I would have assumed we'd found another continent south of the mainland.

"I think there are two pieces of my heart on the island now," I said.

"Naghron is waiting instead of coming for you," said Henka. "Why?"

She looked displeased that one of the shards was apparently acting unpredictably. I wondered just how well she knew every piece. If she could misjudge one, could she not be wrong about all of me?

"He sent an assassin when we were in the necropolis," I said, remembering the young man with the burning whip. "If not for Bren, the sorcerer would have killed me. Naghron is clearly happy to work through his people and stay at a safe distance."

"So, we can expect a greeting party," grumbled Bren. "What's the plan?"

"Kill the piece calling itself Naghron first," I answered. "Then go north and kill the other one."

CHAPTER FORTY-ONE

As we approached the colossal western island, I got my first look at Palaq. I'd been dismissive of it, pictured Naghron lording what power he had over a wretched little island of stinking savages. Even the name, a sad mimicry of PalTaq, my empire's true capital, had seemed pathetic.

Now, I wasn't so sure. The name Palaq touched something deep and ancient in me. It was older than my palace, long predated the theocracy I built in preparation for the empire that would follow millennia later.

These weren't savage tribes at all. Hazy with distance and the thick tropical air, orderly fields made the landscape a patchwork quilt. Unlike the eastern island, Palaq was flatter and lush with teeming life. Beyond the tilled fields lay dense jungle. This was a verdant paradise, so unlike the black glass mountains and volcanoes of PalTaq. In truth, this would have made a better capital for my world. Why, then, had I chosen the brutal location I had?

Ten thousand years.

It was too much to truly grasp. In that time forests became deserts, cities sank beneath the waves, and civilizations rose and fell many times over.

"What are those trees lining the coast?" asked Bren, shading his eyes with a scarred hand.

"They're too regularly spaced to be trees," said Nokutenda. "That's strange-looking foliage."

She was right. Disappearing in either direction, was a tree every hundred strides.

Drawing closer, we understood. They weren't trees at all. Each was a demonic totem, the spiked arms bearing impaled men and women. I recognized the ancient practice, long abandoned.

"Land here," I instructed Henka.

"If we do," she said, "we're walking. Kaszius will never again fly."

"I need to see this."

Nodding, she guided the dragon down.

The beast landed clumsily, legs folding as rotting flesh and muscle collapsed beneath the weight. We scrambled off his back as he sagged, ribs groaning and snapping as one last foetid breath was forced from decaying lungs.

While the rest of us retreated from the stench, Henka stayed at the dragon's side, stroking Kaszius' head, and whispering in his ear. I heard the faint melody of loss and sadness as she sang his release. He was in worse shape than I'd realized. Scavenger birds had been at his underside, tearing at his exposed belly. Loops of putrescent intestine lay piled about him. Once fierce eyes of golden fire were now ragged sockets wriggling with fat white maggots.

Flies buzzed around the corpse in thick clouds, and I wondered if some of them had made the journey from Abieszan. It was an odd and distracted thought. No matter what powerful magics we work, be it demonology, necromancy, or any of the other arts, in the end only the insects remain. No matter what happened here, I felt like all I'd really achieved was carrying some flies from one island to another. I was nothing more than a means of transportation. Later, they'd feed off the death that followed me everywhere.

Kaszius sighed and slumped and was still.

Placing a last kiss on the dragon's brow, Henka returned to my side. Even without tears, she looked both sad, and somehow hopeful.

Skin cool, she took my hand in hers. "I like letting them go."

She stared at our entwined fingers, studying them and I did too. I didn't know this hand. I didn't recognize this woman and yet I loved her more than anything in the world. She wore the sturdy body of an island warrior as comfortably as she did that of a petite and pale-skinned northerner. I liked this Henka. I liked her strength, the black tattoos inked into mahogany flesh a reminder of long-forgotten days. This Henka was a woman I knew from my past, though I couldn't connect her to a time or a specific memory.

"That wasn't always the case," she continued. "I never used to let anything go." She looked up, met my eyes. "You changed that."

I did? That didn't sound like me. Or it didn't sound like the me I remembered. Henka, her necromancy, was a path to power. I'd never been one to pass up such an opportunity. I couldn't believe the Demon Emperor commanded her to let anything useful die.

"You're not going to explain?"

She squeezed my hand, said nothing.

One more mystery that would have to wait until I lay my hand on her heart. Unless that was what she wanted. Would what I learned change my mind about freeing her?

Standing at the base of one of the demonic totems, I studied the jagged shapes hewn into the wood and the three bodies hanging impaled there. Bren stood at my side, Nokutenda wandering forward to get a closer look.

"Don't touch anything," I warned.

She ignored me, saying, "The wood is ebony, harvested from the rainforests farther inland. The trees have been girdled. That's what it's called when you completely remove the bark."

Crude runes and wards had been cut into the polished black wood, barbaric summonings and bindings from the earliest days of demonology. Flesh grey with death, the dead hanging impaled in the tree bore the same runes.

Looking right and left I saw all the trees bore at least one sunken corpse.

I growled in frustration, the memories remaining foggy with time.

"They were tortured," I said. "Their pain is part of the ritual." There were realities populated by things which fed on agony. "After suffering days of torment, they were drained of blood so it might be used in the summoning, their souls fed to whatever was called."

This was demonology as it was before I spent lifetimes mastering the art, turning it into something elegant and beautiful. The creatures summoned were from the closest realities, easily pulled through the curtain separating worlds. They were raw hungers and savage entities incapable of subtlety or craft. These were primitive hells populated by savage nightmares, entirely unlike the demons I knew. Nhil was as far removed from such as humans were from the cockroaches. That said, they weren't without power.

"This circles the entire island," I said, knowing it was true.

All three dead lifted their heads, nostrils flaring as they cast about as if in search of a scent.

"Fucking hells," swore Nokutenda, stumbling in a quick retreat.

Three sets of milky eyes opened. Though they couldn't see us, they focussed on our small group.

There was, I had to admit, an exquisite efficiency to the crimes committed here. These people had been tortured to catch the attention of demons and bled to complete the required spells. Their bodies had been used to host whatever was summoned, the foul spirit demons trapped within. Then, they were brought out here and hung from the trees to serve as both a warning to all who might approach, but also as a first line of defence. The totems were a means of communication, connected not only to each other, but to the demonologists who created them. The demons inhabiting the meat maintained it, though the corpses would still have to be periodically replaced as the elements ate them to nothing.

"Even if Naghron couldn't sense me," I said, "he'd know we were here. I misjudged him and what he built. This," I waved a hand at the unending line of trees and their burden of dead, "is not the work of a single demonologist. He has hundreds—maybe thousands—doing his bidding."

I'd been wrong to mock him for cowering in his little island kingdom. I remembered this sight from the earliest days. While I'd scampered about the north slaughtering Khraens and achieving almost nothing, he'd assembled the bones of empire. This was a man following a vision I knew all too well. In another thousand years he'd rule the world.

While I followed my trail of obsidian crumbs, he followed his path to power.

My god's words haunted me: *Find the pieces of you that matter. The piece*

that drives you to master your world.
    Naghron was that piece, the one my god thought mattered. Not me at all.

CHAPTER FORTY-TWO

As was his way, Bren effortlessly shattered the tension.

"I'm sorry," I said to Henka. Then, because it was true, I added, "I would follow you to my death."

"You already have," she said with that forever familiar smile.

"It's a perfect circle," mused Bren. "Khraen will follow you to his death. I'll follow him to mine."

Nokutenda shook her head in disgust. "First, that's a triangle, you dolt. Second, where does that leave me? Following your scarred butt to my death to make it a square? No thanks."

"My butt isn't scarred."

"Prove it."

Bren's mouth opened and then closed.

"We should get moving," said Henka.

As if everything had been resolved to her satisfaction, she sorted through what remained in the saddlebags still draped across the dragon's corpse. Bren and Nokutenda watched for a moment before shrugging and helping her transfer the supplies to the backpacks stashed within. As always, my love planned for everything while I blundered around like a blind man.

Though I agreed with Henka that we needed to move, I wasn't sure why. Naghron had known we were coming for days. He could have had an entire army waiting for us if he wanted. The fact he hadn't, did nothing to ease my worry. Perhaps this wasn't the trap I first thought, but I was far from safe.

A new thought took root, one I never would have previously

entertained. Henka said Naghron knew nothing of love, that he was my cold calculation, devoid of emotion. She said he saw the end and cared nothing for the path, whatever that meant. Did I want that part of me back? I'd come with the intention of killing him and taking his shard, but if what Henka said was true, it seemed likely I would be worse for the addition. My promise to Shalayn long broken, I still clung to the idea I might be at least something more than the Demon Emperor.

I smothered a mocking laugh. Each time I failed, I set the bar lower.

Taking backpacks loaded with food, water, and a sleeping roll, we set off inland. Crossing tilled fields, we headed west, following a river flowing down to the sea from the jungles inland. Labourers bent to tending crops stopped to watch our passage. Leaning against hoes they grimaced and rubbed their backs, making no attempt to impede us.

We skirted villages of sturdy homes of hewn logs always clustered around a central pyramid of stepped stone. Unlike those I'd seen on the eastern island, these were much smaller and of recent construction, the stone scrubbed clean, the edges sharp. Men and women wearing bones and feathers wandered up from the bowels of the pyramids to witness our passage from the shade. Black snakes of ink wrapped them in runes and wards, ritual scarring visible on their faces. Those toiling in the fields closest to the temples pretended not to see us, working tirelessly at their tasks as if nothing else in the world existed. Most wore nothing more than simple loincloths. All showed scars of one kind or another. Some were ritual, runes cut in flesh and stuffed with sand or pebbles to create raised ridges. Others looked to be the result of regular whippings and beatings.

At the apex of every pyramid sat an altar stained red with recent murder. Sacrifices were a daily occurrence here.

"Priests," I said, nodding at a pyramid. I recognized the trappings of theocracy. "They're demonologists."

Farther inland, where the water was fresher, small fishing boats worked the river. Others threw nets from the shore or waded in with barbed fishing spears. Though we were seen, no one waved.

The pull of my heart grew with each passing hour. Naghron

remained where he was, making no attempt to fetch me. Why bother when he sensed my approach? He had days to prepare and would have all manner of nasty surprises waiting for us. This was his island, his empire.

Planning a surprise attack seemed pointless when he knew exactly where I was. He would not be lured foolishly from his stronghold. He had no reason to do anything other than wait. That's what he did, who he was, and I would come to him, brash and impatient, because that's who I was.

We are our hearts, chasing that which lies in the deepest parts of us.

What bothered me more was the fact the murderous shard to the north wasn't moving either. He seemed to have made camp once he reached land. That made less sense. So far, he'd been predictable, moving from one shard to whichever was closest, killing and destroying. Not once had he paused or hesitated. This sudden patience was worrisome; it meant I'd misjudged him. I didn't know this Khraen at all. Henka made it sound like Naghron was the entirety of those specific aspects, suggesting I was none of them. If that was the case for all of us, it would be impossible to know each other.

I swallowed a laugh. Here I was, planning an elaborate suicide by freeing my wife. Perhaps the piece bent on destroying us and I weren't so different.

Finding a well-maintained cobblestone road, we followed it, leaving the river.

Spiked totems of polished ebony lined the highway, one every few hundred strides. While not all bore a burden of tortured corpses, they showed signs of recent use. Some of the dead, their bodies worn to nothing by the elements, lay at the base. Wagons drawn by teams of bent-backed men and women went from tree to tree, collecting the fallen detritus, and pulling any stubborn fragments free of the spikes. It was an odd dichotomy of vicious torture and well-organized cleanliness.

The demonically possessed dead perked up as we drew near, nostrils flaring to catch our scent, milky eyes and gaping sockets searching. They fell limp as we moved on.

"When we were flying," said Bren, "I promised myself I would never again complain of having to walk. All I wanted was to put my feet on the ground."

"You're about to complain," said Nokutenda. "I can tell."

Bren flashed a fractured smile that didn't reach his eyes. "All beauty in the world is a result of distance. From above, all I saw were tilled fields and villages. It looked serene, civilized. When you get close, you see the flaws."

"That's true of all civilizations," said the sorcerer, "and most men. Only women are improved by proximity."

Bren let it pass without comment. A few months ago, that never would have happened.

Later that evening, we spotted an elderly man standing in the centre of the road ahead. Slowing, we approached with caution. Dressed in majestic robes of blood red, iron-grey hair plaited in gold and bronze hung past his waist. Dark eyes set deep in a craggy and wrinkled face studied us as we drew nearer. He held a heavy oaken staff clutched in raptor-like hands, a bright fire elemental hovering above the gnarled head. Unlike the torches in the floating mountains, this one burned blue with heat, hissing like an enraged snake.

Behind the man, an open wagon waited with cushioned seats for half a dozen. Two hulking earth elementals, misshapen giants of stone and dirt bound in a tangled knot of tree roots, stood ready as beasts of burden.

"Should I kill him?" whispered Nokutenda from behind.

"Not yet," I answered. "Watch for the signal, just in case."

"What's the signal?"

"I don't know. I'll tug on my ear."

"Super subtle."

The elementalist leaned forward a little and grimaced, rubbing at his lower back. I wondered if he meant it to be a bow.

"Shard of god," he said, voice dry as sun-baked leaves, "I have been sent to bring you home."

They worshipped Naghron as a god. It made sense. It was easier to believe in something you could see, in power manifesting in real results. Did this mean Naghron didn't remember our god's dream?

Wind gusted out of nowhere, spinning dust into the air in tight spirals. The twisters grew until four miniature tornados surrounded us, circling.

This was no raw and untrained elementalist. He was a master, likely on par with any from my memories.

Earth elementals to draw his wagon. An impossibly hot fire elemental lighting his staff. Air elementals at his beck and call. I had no doubt his mastery extended to water and beyond.

"They're bound," I said with some awe. "Permanently."

The old man leaned forward again with a wince, and I decided it was a bow.

Summoning and commanding an elemental force to a single task was one thing. Binding one to eternal service was something else and far beyond my current talents.

"You'll forgive my rudeness," he said. "But I've ordered them to bring you to Him, should you harm me." Gripping his staff, he eyed us, waiting.

Him. No need to name your god.

I smothered a sick grin. I'd often returned servants to some semblance of life so I might punish their failures. When your people knew death was no escape, they put more effort into ensuring success.

I returned the bow. "Seeing as we'd be unlikely to survive such a battle, we shall humbly accept your offer of a ride."

"No, no," he said, turning away. "My orders are that you be delivered alive. Though…" he cast a glance over his shoulder at my friends, "no mention was made of the others."

We followed him to the wagon and climbed aboard. Henka sat beside him at the front, immediately chatting about the villages and asking about whether Naghron traded with neighbouring islands. Bren, Nokutenda, and I took seats in the back.

With a word from the old man, the earth elementals lumbered into motion, effortlessly pulling the wagon behind them. The ground shook with every stone footfall. The mad tangle of roots and vines entwined through the rocks and clods of earth acted as muscles and tendons, groaning under the strain of keeping their bodies cohesive. Belatedly, I realized what I was seeing: this wasn't two earth elementals at all. It was many elementals bound together into a single will, an amalgamation of plant life, stone, and earth. The combination not only made them more mobile but also allowed them to share their intelligence. These would be dangerous foes. The fact the old man maintained them without apparent effort spoke volumes as to his skill and power.

"Well," said Nokutenda, "he seems friendly in that *I'll crush you with an earth elemental* kind of way. You sure you don't want me to pop his skull?"

I shook my head. "Save your strength."

I suspected we'd need it later. Whatever this elementalist's powers, Naghron would be infinitely more dangerous.

Bren sat to my right, gaze alternating between me and Nokutenda. "Why not kill us? We know what Naghron wants. Why take you back alive?"

"Distrust," I answered. "He can't trust anyone else with a piece of himself."

"I'm not buying it," he said. "If you sent me to kill someone and bring back their heart, I would. You know I would."

"Naghron is not me. I'm not sure he has my ability to trust."

I wasn't sure if that made him stronger, a better Demon Emperor, or if it was a failing. Certainly, my trust had landed me in trouble in the past. I'd trusted Tien and been betrayed. Much as I hated to admit it, I still trusted both Nhil and Henka, even though they worked at cross purposes. I wanted to believe they both had my best interests at heart but interpreted what that meant differently.

"There's a reason Naghron doesn't want you dead," insisted Bren. "And it's not distrust."

"I can't believe I'm asking this," said Nokutenda, "but is it possible you're more useful alive?"

I thought it through. If he wanted to use my heart to lure the murderous Khraen into a trap, he didn't need me alive. In fact, it would probably work better were I dead. On the other hand, this Khraen had already killed several of us with apparent ease. While two of us working together might be better able to defeat him, I couldn't imagine us ever trusting one another enough to do so.

I sat in silence as Bren and the sorcerer argued, exploring ever more far-fetched reasons Naghron might want me alive. In a way, it didn't matter. We couldn't defeat the one servant he sent to greet us—no doubt an intentional decision with a very clear message—never mind ranks of demonologists and whatever other servants awaited his command.

"He's afraid," I said.

Nokutenda and Bren ceased their bickering.

Naghron would have sent someone north just as he'd sent this elementalist to us. He would have sent someone equally powerful, perhaps even more so. Whoever or whatever he sent must have been defeated, utterly crushed. Only terror would make a man like Naghron desperate enough to propose an alliance with someone who most definitely planned his death.

"He'll try and use me," I said. "Perhaps as bait. Whatever he plans, he needs me alive. Make no mistake, however, once he has what he wants, we're all dead."

Except maybe Henka. She would go on as she always did. If she decided this was a failure, she'd hunt and kill the many Khraens, once again lay the path. She would never give up, never accept failure no matter how impossible the task might be. I had to end this, if just to free her from pointless repetition. She thought she could save me—make me someone better, happier. She was wrong. No matter how she laid out the trail of my shattered heart, I would never be a good man. I had one path to redemption, and I'd have to lie to her to walk it.

"My love," said Henka from the front of the wagon.

Looking up, I saw the city beyond and stared in awe.

Naghron hadn't been complacent. He hadn't simply moved his people into the ruins of the Demon Empire—though come to think of it, I hadn't seen any. He built something new, an entire city dedicated to its god: Him.

"How old is Naghron?" The question slipped out.

The elementalist shrugged. "He began constructing Palaq two thousand years ago. The flesh he wears today is said to be three hundred years old."

This wasn't the same man who first started building this empire? Interesting.

CHAPTER FORTY-THREE

The truth of time is that, at its root, it's incomprehensible. A day. A week. Months and years. A lifetime. Generations. We think we understand the simple math.

I felt the weight of millennium upon my stone heart.

Three colossal pyramids, the largest structures I'd ever seen, towered at the heart of the city. Their smooth sides, black granite shot through with lightning bolts of startling red and polished to a sheen, glowed blinding in the setting sun. By one timescale, they were new, built a thousand years or more after the collapse of the Demon Empire. By another, they were ancient. At some point in the last two millennia, a section of granite facing had cracked on one of the pyramids and slid away, exposing the rust-coloured limestone beneath. The damage had never been repaired, the fallen granite was long gone, no doubt scavenged.

Though several miles separated me from the sprawling city, I knew its secrets.

Where the capital of Taramlae had been a chaotic mix of cobblestone structures, rough-hewn wooden homes, and the imposing wizard's towers, Palaq showed a directed will I recognized. Everything was built from bricks and blocks of manmade limestone created in wooden casts. Palatial homes sheathed in granite sat upon sprawling grounds, lush gardens, and climbing vines giving them a riot of mad colour. Many were several stories tall, bracketed by intricate marble columns stabbing into the sky. The streets, a perfect grid, were paved with more rust-coloured limestone. Statues decorated the metropolis. Though dragons and demons were favourites, most were of one man. Naghron stood on every corner, tall and proud, long hair tied back in a warrior's queue or hanging loose and majestic like a lion's mane. Always depicted as heavy with muscle, hawk-eyes glaring at a distant future, he was everywhere.

Naghron stood at the centre of Palaq. The height of forty men, one foot resting on a church taking up an entire city block, he held a massive stone sword aloft with his right hand. Orange flames, bright enough to be visible on the sunniest day, flickered the length of the blade. Stunned, I marvelled at the craftsmanship. The work of teams of skilled elementalists, the statue was constructed of several different kinds of stone. Or perhaps somehow cladded in tiles of stone. I couldn't tell, saw no seams from this distance. The statue wore a loincloth of green jade. Snakes, scaled in crimson rubies, entwined him, coiled about muscular arms. Ebony skin shone like an oil-slick rainbow in the sun. Facing due east, the statue held a mirror of black glass in its left hand as if it meant for his enemies to look within.

Naghron was god here and he wanted no one to forget.

I stared in awe, shaken to the core by the sight. This was yet another reminder of how much this Khraen had accomplished, and how little I'd done in comparison. He was so much closer to being the man I wanted to be, the man I was terrified to become.

The man I planned to kill.

Much as I admired his accomplishments, felt jealous and small in his shadow, I hated him. This was an entire city built to appease the ego of one man. No sane and decent person would ever want this.

Adoration makes assholes of us all.

I realized Bren and Nokutenda had fallen silent.

"It's you," he said.

The sorcerer studied the distant statue. "Only better looking." Glancing at me, taking in the straggled state of my greasy hair and thin arms, she added, "Much, *much* better looking."

Hauled by a pair of lumbering earth elementals, the wagon rolled on, wood wheels clattering on stone. Cresting a low hill, the curving highway split into smaller streets as we entered a timeworn city born millennia after my death. There were no great walls, no sign of any defences. After the battlements of Abieszan, this felt strangely vulnerable.

It made sense, though. Naghron ruled this island and likely several of its neighbours. He'd conquered any local threats and if his distant enemies came for him, walls wouldn't stop them.

"There are no wizard towers," I said, realizing I saw no white in the city at all. Like me, Naghron seemed to dislike the colour.

"He keeps a cadre of possessed mages," said the old elementalist. "Otherwise, they are forbidden from entering the city."

Wondering how he enforced that, I kept the thought to myself. Awe-inspiring as Palaq was, if the Guild came in force, they'd crush it. Despite my own run-ins with the wizards, I'd often heard—even back in Taramlae—that they avoided the ocean and the southern islands. Until I stirred the hornet's nest, that is.

Either the Guild had no clue what Naghron was building down here, or he had some sort of arrangement with them. I suspected it was the former and hoped it was the latter, if just to give me a reason to feel superior.

The wagon travelled stone streets, citizens stopping to make way and stare. Ignoring the elementals, they focussed on me. Many sketched strange signs, sloppy mimicry of demonic wards, in the air before them. Others kissed the back of their first two fingers and raised them in salute. Pathetic as I might appear in comparison to the many statues, they recognized me. As none prostrated themselves on the ground, it was equally clear they knew who I wasn't.

"They've seen me before," I said. "Rather, other Khraens."

The elementalist nodded. "He has been rebuilding his heart for thousands of years, though he hasn't taken a new piece in a decade."

A decade. Years before I woke in the cold mud of the north.

"If you know he's collecting the pieces of his heart," I said, "then you also know he is not a god."

"Who but a god would have a heart of obsidian?" he said over his shoulder, unperturbed at the blasphemy.

"I'm no god," I argued. "Neither is he."

"He is undying, eternal," he said, again rubbing at his lower back. "You understand who he was—who *we* were?"

"Of course."

"Then you know he died."

"Can a man who dies a thousand deaths ever be truly dead?"

I couldn't argue with that.

A caged wagon carrying a score of filthy men and women rumbled by, heading in the opposite direction. Four quadrupedal earth elementals shaped vaguely like malformed bison pulled them, a young man barking orders from the driver's seat.

Impressive as Palaq was, it paled compared to my memories of the palace at PalTaq. In part, it was the differences that bothered me. Naghron hadn't tried to rebuild what had once been. This fascination with pyramids dated back to the first real civilization that clawed its way out of the swamps and jungles of the islands. By the time I decided PalTaq would be the centre of my empire, I'd grown long tired of their sturdy simplicity. With demons and a seemingly infinite supply of souls, I could build so much more. Gossamer bridges, sweeping spiderweb expanses of stone. Twisting towers bending and reaching as if in blasphemous ignorance of the natural laws.

And yet neither was Palaq a recreation of those first cities. He took inspiration from our earliest memories and built something new. This was a city planned, built to be impressive and yet beautiful at the same time. In part, I realized, it was because he hadn't relied on demonology. Whereas PalTaq was a city of demons, alien intelligence bound to every arch and stone and door, Palaq was a seamless amalgamation of the arts. Some buildings had been built by sorcery, the practitioners spending themselves to lift gargantuan slabs of granite into place while elementalists worked their magic to keep it there. Others were entirely constructs of elementalism. Naghron hadn't scrimped on spending souls either. Travelling deeper into the city, I saw the writhing script of binding runes decorating the walls of many buildings. My judgement of the ease with which the Guild could crush Palaq had been hasty. Immense power lay hidden here.

As if excited to be home, the elementals picked up speed, rushing through the streets toward the largest of the pyramids. Pedestrians scampered from our path, turning to watch once safe. Rounding the last corner, oak wheels skidding on stone, we entered a carefully manicured garden of brightly coloured flowers, and finally slowed. Crimson robed priests hurried about their business, clumps of youths arguing animatedly, bent old men and women shuffling through the greenery.

A lone man awaited us in the centre of the paved square at the garden's heart, arms crossed. Dressed in what looked to be homespun cotton pants and a shirt, his sable hair hung loose, though flawlessly neat. Midnight eyes. Ebony skin. Thick muscle roped his neck and shoulders, swelled arms crisscrossed with pale scars. A true warrior, this wasn't a man who hid from battle. Though he carried no weapons, he looked utterly comfortable, completely confident.

I knew him.

I wanted to be him.

I hated him.

Raising his hands as if he were about to hug us, Naghron called his greetings with an infectious grin.

Nokutenda leaned over to whisper, "Even though that is every kind of fuckable, I dislike him immensely," as the wagon juddered to a halt.

The god of Palaq had eyes only for me as we clambered down.

"It's been many years since I saw that face," he said, stepping forward to study me with a raised eyebrow. "You've had a rough go of it since you woke in the north."

Having been alive much longer than I, of course, he was aware of the shard in the distant reaches of the mainland that suddenly started moving. I wanted to ask how long I'd lain there, dead. Not wanting to seem needy or weak, I quashed my curiosity.

"Of all the pieces of me," he said, placing a familiar hand on my shoulder, "you have been the hardest to track. You can't imagine my excitement and fear the first time you vanished." He spoke with unconscious ease, as if admitting doubt was nothing.

To me, he'd been some distant shard of my heart, little more than a reason to someday venture south. Older and more experienced, aware of what we were, he had been aware of me from the beginning. When that ring stole me from Shalayn, depositing me in the floating mountains, Naghron sensed my disappearance.

"Never before had a shard simply vanished," he continued. "I thought you'd somehow been destroyed by the mages. Then, when you reappeared in the same location you disappeared from, I knew what you had."

"Portal demon," I said, despite myself.

"Portal demon," he agreed with a grin of white teeth. "One that took you…" he glanced at my companions, "…elsewhere."

"It's not somewhere I remember," I admitted, not telling him the entire truth. "If you kill me, you'll lose it forever."

He gave another uncaring shrug. "After that, you bounced around the north, sometimes using the portal demon, sometimes travelling by land or water."

"It's been a busy couple of years," I said.

"Indeed. I wondered what you were up to when you disappeared from Abieszan only to reappear in Khaal weeks later. As there were no pieces of us there, I wondered if you'd gone to visit Grone. I worried you'd forgotten how much he hates us," added Naghron. "But here you are. I must ask, did you find the stone we bound him to? Does he once again serve?"

Filing the information away for another time, I shook my head with my own rueful smile. "I remembered just enough to know to avoid him."

What were the odds that stone lay somewhere in the catacombs beneath the palace at PalTaq? And if I remembered the warrens beneath the city, did that mean that Naghron didn't, or that he remembered different details?

"Well," he said, "someday we'll find it."

"You can summon demons of possession," I said, unable to help myself. "I've long wanted that knowledge."

"You'll soon have it," he said with casual ease.

"Will I? Or will you have what I know?"

"We want the same thing. In the end, we will be one man." Naghron gave me a look of confusion and concern. "These mayfly lives are nothing."

I kept my doubt that it would be so easily settled to myself and asked, "Why do you call yourself Naghron?" instead.

He blinked at me in surprise. "It's my name. It's *our* name. What do you call yourself?"

"Khraen."

"Naghron bä Khraen," he corrected. "I think Khraen meant crown or king in a long-dead language. Maybe the one we first spoke."

If he remembered that, he must recall more of our deepest past than I. As none of the other Khraens mentioned the name, he must have most of those ancient memories. And yet I possessed the memory of that golden goddess. Was that why he made himself god here, instead of trying to bring her back? Did he have no memory of her at all? It made some sense, if I was to have destroyed the pieces that remembered Nhil and my god and Henka.

Turning to the others, he said. "We're being rude. There's time for talk later. Introduce me to your friends."

Introducing them by name, I watched Naghron for any hint of recognition when I got to Henka. He showed no reaction as he clasped her hand in greeting. Nor did he make mention of her being cold, though whether that was politeness or the result of her maintaining herself, I couldn't say. Deciding the less he knew the better, I neglected to mention she was our wife and a powerful necromancer. Different as we might seem, we were the same man. The Demon Emperor could happily chat with guests before brutally torturing and murdering them.

Brenwick and Nokutenda he greeted with the same warmth.

"Come," he said, returning his attention to me. "As you are no doubt aware, one of us seems bent on our destruction. We have much to discuss." Flashing at charming grin he added, "You'll have to forgive me for sending that sorcerer after you in the necropolis. Normally, I'm willing to wait for the pieces to come to me. But there were two of you there, so close. I was impatient and acted rashly."

Good as I am at lying to myself, I've also learned to see through my bullshit. Despite ruling over his little empire as a self-proclaimed god, I didn't think Naghron had learned that lesson. Or perhaps that's *why* he hadn't. The thought raised an interesting question: If Naghron was the largest active shard, did that mean he was the most like the fallen Demon Emperor?

CHAPTER FORTY-FOUR

Maintaining a flow of comfortable chatter, Naghron led us across the gardens to a wide and flat esplanade of rust-coloured limestone. Each massive slab was set so snug I only saw the seams as I stepped over them. Tables and stalls lined the broad roadway, hawkers selling their goods to pedestrians out for a stroll. Families picnicked at granite benches or lounged on blankets spread in the shade of the buildings lining the street. Children ran and played, squealing with joy as they kicked balls around or chased one another in endless games of tag.

On the coast we witnessed scenes of blood and sacrifice, people tortured, their souls torn from bodies to bind demons. In the city, I saw a civilization putting anything the wizards had done to shame. There were no beggars, no street thieves lurking in the shadows. No one went hungry. People moved in a harmonious blend, pale northerners sheltered under parasols walking alongside islanders. Though rare, there were even a few freckled ginger-haired folks from the Crags in the western reaches of the far north. I saw none of the hate I witnessed in Taramlae. Here, all were equal.

"When is the cost of civilization too high?" I asked Naghron, interrupting him.

I wondered if it was a question he had considered.

"You've seen the sentinels I made to guard Palaq," he said, "and you've been to the mainland. The Guild was never interested in politics beyond keeping people quiet." His brow furrowed in thought. Then, "I don't know. What I do know is that there *is* a price. I know that the more enemies you have, the higher that price is. Once the world is mine—"

He laughed, slapping me on the back. "Once the world is ours, the price will be greatly reduced."

That hadn't been the case though. The Demon Emperor spent an unimaginable number of lives and souls serving his god's hunger. There had been wars unending, reaching across realities. She dreamed in blood and her appetite could never be sated.

Naghron was lying, delusional, or had no memory of our god.

Still, could he be right? If I somehow removed my god from the picture, could I unite the world and then vastly reduce the cost in souls once peace was achieved? It was a tempting idea.

I shook my head in disgust. Rather, it *would* be a tempting idea were Henka not going to destroy me once I freed her. Why was it so difficult to remember that I had no future? Planning for anything beyond that moment was pointless. Which raised another concern. Not only did Naghron have no idea Henka was our wife, once he killed me and remembered what little I recalled of her, he'd never make the same decision I had. A man who filled a city with his statues wasn't going to sacrifice himself in an act of contrition.

Two more statues of Naghron, each four times the height of a man, flanked the pyramid's entrance. We followed him into the monstrous edifice of stone. Torches lined the long hall, fist-sized fire elementals dancing their synchronized jig to light our way. The ancient pyramids of my memory were mostly solid stone with only a few narrow passages leading to sacrificial chambers, prisons where those awaiting death were held, and a space for prayer. Here, hallways branched off at regular intervals. We passed meeting rooms, prayer halls, and a dining area for the priests. There were stairways leading to higher floors and others winding down into the earth. The feat of engineering involved in such a creation staggered me. Even with demons and elementals bearing the brunt of the physical labour, the planning would have to be meticulous.

Finding an empty room decorated with colourful hangings depicting what looked like scenes from early in Palaq's history, a single large and intricately carved oak table at the centre, Naghron ushered us in. A luxurious throne of dark-stained wood and velour sat at the head of the table. Resisting the urge to claim it, I chose another seat, surprised when he did the same and sat across from me. Brenwick took the seat to my right, while Henka sat to my left.

With a cocky grin, Nokutenda collapsed into the throne and sighed.

"Food," Naghron said to the otherwise empty room. "And drink. Chilled wine."

One of the tapestries fluttered as a waiting air elemental exited. A breeze blew constantly through the room, keeping the air fresh and cool. More air elementals, I decided, ordered to circulate.

"Do you remember her dream?" I asked, knowing that if he did, he'd understand.

"I do." He blew out a long breath, eyes sad. "I remember warring in strange worlds. Killing, always killing, in her name. We don't need her. Religion is for men afraid of their mortality."

And knowing how useful religion was as a tool of manipulation, he declared himself a god.

"You think you can remake the empire without the power of a god behind you?" I asked.

"Remake? No. From the very ground up I will make something different." He leaned forward, intent. "Do you know what defines gods?"

I shook my head.

"Worship. The more faithful, the more powerful the god."

"You aim to be this world's only god."

"This and others. I can't yet reach them, but I will." Onyx eyes gleamed brightly. "You *disappeared*. You went somewhere else. You know how."

The idea of becoming a god was purest narcissistic insanity and appealed on every level.

I knew the answer but asked anyway. "Do you remember the first time we saw her?"

"No. But I remember how she used me. She gave me power and I repaid her a thousand times over. It was a debt, I came to understand, that I would never be free of."

"Is that why you've made no attempt to call her back?"

"She used us, but she was afraid of us too," he said, ignoring my question. "Deciding to betray her is the last thing I remember." Our eyes met. "Did she do this to us as punishment?"

"I don't think so." Unwilling to share what I knew, I said, "Pleasant as the chatter is, I think we have more important details to discuss."

Naghron nodded in agreement. "The piece of us bent on destroying our heart. He arrived on the north end of the island." He studied me. "He came on a rather rough-looking sloop. Shortly after making landfall, someone in white plate armour destroyed my spies and demons."

A battlemage? I couldn't believe any part of me would sail with the Guild. But then I couldn't believe something could change me so much I'd be willing to destroy my heart.

Was it Iremaire?

No. That felt wrong. If the mage had a captive Khraen, she had no reason to chase after me.

I blinked in surprise, realizing I'd been a fool.

Iremaire said Shalayn stole several powerful items and a great deal of wealth and fled Khaal. The battle mage's words returned to me: *I believe she plans on finding the other pieces of your heart so you might be destroyed once and for all.* Since escaping, I'd given little thought to the swordswoman. I knew she'd stop at nothing to kill me, but never took her seriously as a threat. She wasn't a mage, had no skill beyond being good with a blade. I thought maybe she'd stab me in the back someday, as I had her sister, but saw her as incapable of much else.

I laughed, mocking myself. "It's Shalayn." Seeing Naghron's confusion, I explained. "I killed her sister. She'll stop at nothing to get her vengeance."

"No," said Bren. "I killed her sister."

I didn't want to argue semantics. The blame was mine and mine alone.

She was the missing piece of the puzzle. Now, it all made sense. Shalayn had captured one of the Khraens and somehow forced him to betray the locations of the others. Like Henka, she realized there was a way to track me down.

"She's waiting for us," I said. "She wants to destroy us both."

Naghron's eyes narrowed. "How?"

I shrugged, helpless. Could she possibly have stolen something from Iremaire so powerful she could defeat me? The fact she managed to destroy several shards suggested that was the case.

While I was a fraction of the man I'd once been, today's mages were more powerful than anything he'd faced. I couldn't begin to guess what artifacts they'd created since my fall.

I had made a terrible mistake in coming here. Had I stayed true to my intent, passed Naghron by, and continued straight to Pal'Taq, Shalayn never would have caught up to me. We should have stopped at one of the many islands we passed over and found a boat to take us the rest of the way.

No matter how I turned the problem, I saw no way to disengage myself now. At the first hint I planned to sneak away, Naghron would kill me and take my heart. If I was honest, I wasn't sure I could leave a piece of myself behind. Even now, with Naghron sitting so close, it clawed at my consciousness, demanded I take it. I couldn't imagine how he managed to sit so calmly. Could his willpower be so much more than my own?

Or did he not feel the pull the same as I?

Now that I considered the possibility, it made so much sense. The other shards of my heart sensed each other and yet had been content to stay on their islands. Early on, before I understood who Henka was, one had fled at my approach instead of coming to kill me. The old man in the necropolis sent his undead servants instead of coming after me himself. He and Naghron had clashed over the years but neither made a serious effort to take the other. This far south, the large shard in Pal'Taq was so close its presence was a constant scream in my soul.

"You know this Shalayn," said Naghron. "How do you suggest we proceed?"

"I assume running away isn't an option?"

"From a lone woman and a single sloop? Even if it's filled with battlemages, it offers no threat we can't handle."

"Underestimating Shalayn would be a mistake," said Henka.

Bren nodded his agreement.

"I will not abandon all we have built," said Naghron, scowling at Henka. "We're less than a century from being ready to retake the mainland."

"I don't think you're going to have a decade," I said. "Never mind a century. The Guild knows about the destruction of Abieszan. I woke the city's guardian and destroyed two war galleys. They will come south to investigate, and they'll come in force. If they're cautious, we'll have a few weeks, maybe a month or two. If not…" I let the thought hang.

Naghron's eyes grew hard. "I have been infinitely patient. I remember how we did it the first time. I remember how long it took. The Demon Emperor showed us the way."

"Things have changed. This is not his world." I held up a hand to stall argument. "When the Emperor first rose, there was no Guild. The mainland was a thousand squabbling kingdoms."

"This is your fault," he said through clenched teeth. "Blundering around the world like a reckless child. Blindly destroying plans hundreds of years in the making." He shook his head in disgust. "How could you be so different? It was never about *us*. Only the Demon Emperor matters."

I snorted in amusement. "You say that, but you'll kill me for my heart as soon as you think you're safe. It's who we are."

Naghron looked genuinely confused. "Perhaps it's who *you* are. You understand nothing. I was not the man who created Palaq. I'm not the first to wear the name Naghron. Shard by shard we come. We are the same. We want the same thing. There is no need for violence. When a piece of the emperor arrives, we discuss what we remember and what we've learned since awakening. We make sure nothing important will be lost. We decide who will best serve the needs of the man we are meant to be."

Henka flinched.

"You're telling me one of you volunteers to die?" I asked, incredulous.

"Always. That is why I invited you in."

"I don't believe you."

"I expected us to have a sane and reasonable conversation, discuss what we knew and remembered." He gestured at me. "Your body is weak, but you have a portal demon. You travel to another reality, maybe more than one. You think I would callously lose that?"

It made sense and yet I didn't believe him. He talked about logic and volunteering for suicide in the same breath. It was madness.

"What about the old man in the necropolis?" I demanded.

"As I said, it was a moment of impatience. Unlike me, he had no means to extend his life. Eventually, he would have come to me, and I would have taken his heart. Not because I have to be the one to survive but because his body was too old to salvage." He shrugged. "Who knows. Had he come decades earlier, perhaps he would have taken mine."

I recognized the Demon Emperor's calm insanity in this man. He wasn't lying. He'd kill me if he had to, or if he thought it was the only way to get the stone in my heart, but he'd also sacrifice himself if he thought it moved us closer to the emperor's return. It was madness; I would never throw myself away for some distant future that would remember neither me nor my sacrifice.

"Shalayn has destroyed several shards of our heart," I said, "and we have no idea how. Perhaps she's not fighting them at all. What if she can do it the moment she sets eyes on one of us?"

"I have battalions of demonologists, cadres of enslaved wizards, ranks upon ranks of sorcerers and elementalists. I'm not going north to face this Shalayn at all. I'll send an army. Anyway, how do you know she's destroying the pieces? You've disappeared several times. Maybe she's sending them to another world."

I hadn't thought of that. Even while I prayed he was right, I hoped the pieces had been destroyed. I would go to my death in PalTaq, but the less of me left in the world, the better.

I saw in his eyes that Naghron already doubted I was worthy to become the new ruler of Palaq. If he learned I had no intention of becoming the emperor I'd be dead shortly after. He would never let me leave and my plan to free Henka would die here with me.

I wouldn't let that happen.

"Nokutenda," I said. Making eye contact, I tugged on my ear.

CHAPTER FORTY-FIVE

The sorcerer stared at me. "You've got to be kidding. Why would I help you? I told you I wanted the Demon Emperor to return. Not only is this man," she nodded at Naghron, "going to do that, but he's already started."

Rising from the throne, she backed away from me, moving to Naghron's side of the table. He remained sitting. Henka neither moved nor blinked. When Bren made to rise, Nokutenda wagged a finger at him, and an invisible force shoved him back into his chair.

"Your loyalty does you honour," she said. "Your stupidity in being loyal to the wrong man, not so much."

Bren sagged.

"Be smart," she added. "Back the right man."

Bren glared hate. "Khraen saved your life—"

"Only because he thought I was useful," the sorcerer said, standing at Naghron's side. "Anyway, I saved his life first, remember?"

Naghron examined me with a resigned look of disappointment. "Tugging your ear was your secret signal?"

"See?" demanded Nokutenda. "I told you it was stupid."

Henka sat calm and placid, hands crossed on the table before her. Though she wore a warrior's body, I wondered how much she knew of fighting. I'd seen her kill before, but she tended to rely on the fact she could always later repair herself.

"Kill him," said Naghron, "and you will have earned yourself a place here."

"Gladly," said the sorcerer.

She stabbed Naghron in the base of the skull with a stiletto, sinking it to the hilt.

He frowned, blinking in confusion, lips moving as if trying to form words. "I... I smell... burning..."

Nokutenda gave the knife a savage twist and his eyes rolled back as he collapsed forward, head striking the wood table with a dull *thud*.

She met my eyes. "I'm assuming there was nothing in his brain that you wanted."

"Nothing," I said.

It was a lie. I wanted Naghron's memories, not just those of the shard he carried in his heart. I wanted to know everything of this city he built, of the reach of his influence in the islands. Whatever plans he had to invade the mainland died with him.

Still seated, Bren looked up at her. "I knew you were faking."

"Liar."

"Why not just kill him when I gave the signal?" I asked.

"I know it seems like free power to you," she said. "But every time I use sorcery it burns part of me away. Sometimes a chunk of steel in the brainpan will achieve the same result at a much lower cost."

Giving her a small bow, I said, "I am in your debt."

"Indeed, you are. If you don't unite the islands and live up to your full potential, I swear I will crush you to dust no matter what it costs me."

"Why bother," muttered Bren, "when you can stab him in the head?"

"Drama," said Nokutenda. "And don't try to be funny. You're not good at it."

Bren shrugged. "It's my one flaw."

I couldn't pull my attention from the dead man. His heart—*my* heart—called to me, a deafening roar slamming through my blood like a tidal wave of need.

Potential. Capability. A capacity for success. Yet the more potential you had, the more you were a failure if you didn't meet it. A cruel curse, as someone else decided your potential and define what constituted success. Certainly, ruling the world seemed like an impressive achievement by any sane metric.

"My Lord," said a priest at the door, startling us.

Dressed in crimson robes and carrying a tray laden with food and drink, he bowed low, careful not to spill. We sat, stunned, as he deposited the tray on the table without so much as a glance at the corpse. Bustling about the room, he lay out plates and cups for everyone, taking a moment to pour clay goblets of wine for each person.

Task complete, he returned his attention to me. "Shall I continue with the preparations for the ceremony?"

"Ceremony?" I asked.

"For the taking of the heart, my Lord." Nodding at the dead man, he added, "Shall we have it prepared?"

I wanted it more than anything, and yet hesitated. The more of my heart I possessed when I finally freed Henka, the more of me would die at her hands.

The priest waited patiently, apparently accustomed to Naghron taking his time to make decisions. The others watched me with tense expectation, each with their own hopes, their own definitions of success and failure.

I wanted to flee Palaq, abandon all Naghron built. I could commandeer a fast ship and an elementalist and Shalayn would never catch me. I couldn't risk her killing me, robbing me of the chance to free my wife. Yet if I fled, leaving shards of my heart behind, Henka might guess what I intended.

With every passing day, I saw less difference between reasons and justifications. I wanted Naghron's heart. I wanted the knowledge it contained. I wanted to face Shalayn. I wanted her to have one last chance at vengeance, and I wanted to discover what she'd done with the hearts of the others she'd killed. And I wanted to kill her for what she'd done to Henka.

I felt trapped by my desires and the expectations of those around me. "Prepare the ceremony," I instructed the priest.

"Of course. The ceremony will take a few days—"

"Tomorrow," I said. "First thing in the morning. Make it happen."

"Of course, my Lord. I'll have acolytes sent to show your guests to their rooms."

Bowing low, he left.

Bren waited until the priest was gone before speaking. "Can we trust them?"

"I am their god."

Henka squeezed my hand, her fingers cool.

"What about Shalayn?" Bren asked. "Perhaps we should deal with her first."

"She can't touch me here. I'll be safe enough." I took Henka's hand in mine, meeting her flint eyes. "Anyway, these people won't truly be mine until after the ceremony."

I would be strong. I'd resist whatever memories lay within the Naghron shard. I'd stay true to who *I* was. No memory could change that. No memory could divert me from my goal.

"If Shalayn thought she was strong enough to come into Palaq and kill Naghron," I added, "she already would have. I am guarded by armies. That's why she's waiting for me in the north."

"She'll be ready," warned Henka. "She's already killed two of you."

Four young men dressed in crimson robes arrived. After bowing to me, they reverently lifted Naghron's body and carried it away. The growing distance between myself and the piece of obsidian nestled in his heart felt like a tearing wound in my chest. This was more painful even than leaving that earlier shard with Henka. With every piece gained the need to have the rest grew. The first bit I took from that boy who stumbled on my mud and bone hut had been a curiosity, a distant longing with none of the desperate need and hunger I now felt. When I finally had all but one fragment, the drive to attain it would be irresistible.

I couldn't imagine why. Was this some growing aspect of my personality, or was some other force at work?

Nokutenda picked at the food, popping choice morsels into her mouth and giving us a running commentary on its quality. The strawberries were good, though she said the ones grown on the mainland were sweeter. Thin slivers of salted fish she washed down with a chilled wine while musing as to whether mages were supplying the cooling magic or if some poor sorcerer was spending themselves to keep their god's drinks at a pleasing temperature. After sniffing at a selection of cheeses and declaring them some weird northern fascination, she turned her attention to the sliced fruit, picking through wedges of mango and orange.

Bren watched her with a distracted frown. He didn't seem unhappy, just thoughtful. Despite the pitchers of ale, wine, and water, he drank nothing.

More men and women in crimson arrived to show us to our chambers. Nokutenda and Bren were led off in different directions and I wondered at how much he'd changed. The nervous cabin boy was gone. He neither joked nor asked questions, instead nodding at me as he left.

A middle-aged woman led me and Henka to Naghron's suites. Deep in the heart of the pyramid, cooled by the patrolling air elementals, the rooms were a pleasant escape from the muggy heat of the tropics. Fire elementals sparked to life as we entered, dancing their synchronized jig.

Henka perched on the corner of a table while I prowled through the suite, exploring. I found none of the wealth and luxury I'd expected. The furnishings were simple and sturdy, everything of local construction. Naghron had been a man of simple tastes with little interest in displays of wealth. He was a god, and yet felt no need to lord his divinity over those he ruled. Well, beyond the innumerable statues lining the streets. Little of this fit my memories of the Demon Emperor. Even the citadel in the floating mountains was an unashamed demonstration of power and affluence. When it had been properly manned and maintained, it would have been luxurious beyond anything I'd seen in this world.

I padded through a simple dining room, with a plain table and four equally unimpressive chairs. There was a small library, most of the shelves waiting to be filled. The few books I found were history from the mainland, none dating back more than two or three hundred years. As if nothing of note happened before then. Pages and pages praising the Guild. Entire chapters discussing 'times of unprecedented peace.' The language was simplistic, no concept studied in too much detail, and I decided these were likely schoolbooks for northern children.

Beyond a few whispered horror stories, the average northerner likely knew nothing of the man who had ruled the world for near ten thousand years. The knowledge left me strangely sad. Between the shards

I'd already collected, the Naghron piece I'd take in the morning, and the large bit awaiting me in PalTaq, I would soon be the single largest piece of the Demon Emperor's broken heart. When Henka ended me, he would be forever gone. In time, nothing would remain of my legacy.

Shaking off the feeling, I continued my exploration.

The bedroom at the end of the hall was more of the same. A serviceable mattress on a raised slab of stone. A tall desk with loose papers awaiting signatures piled upon it. No art. No extravagant tapestries displaying the man's many accomplishments. Naghron achieved so much more than I and yet was so different. Was this intentional, a desperate attempt at making something his own, at being more than his memories?

"He's you and not you," Henka said from the doorway behind me. "You're all him and yet none of you are him."

"Are we more, though, or less?"

"Who can judge the value of a man?"

"His wife," I joked.

She didn't laugh. "Different doesn't mean better or worse. It only means different."

"I'm not him," I said.

"And you'll never be him. Even when you have all the pieces of your heart, you will have gained the memories in a different order than he experienced them. What's more, you have lived a very different life from his. Memories can never shape you the same way experience does. The life you live is far more important than the life he lived."

I wondered if she was right.

"You seem more willing to discuss the past," I said, still facing the blank wall. "After hiding from me for so long."

"While it was the plan to erase me from your memories," she said, "we always knew it was possible you'd remember something. Perfection is a myth. I'm glad not to have been completely erased."

A moment of painful honesty. She hadn't had a choice in any of this. *We* hadn't decided to cull her from my memories, I had. A slave, she'd done as instructed.

"You've been waiting for me to remember." How often had I told myself that?

Henka hugged me from behind. I hadn't heard her approach.

Arms roped with muscle and inked in black slid around my waist. Snakes and tigers. Swirling images telling the story of the body she now wore. Of the woman she murdered to take this form. Freeing her wouldn't change that. She'd go on killing to maintain herself long after my death. At least she would no longer be doing it to fit some juvenile definition of beauty.

For a heartbeat I wanted to ask her what form she'd take once I was gone. Would she wear something large and strong? Would she even remain a woman? I had no real understanding of necromancy. What defined her? Was her spirit tied to the bones in some way? No, that couldn't be it. Shalayn beheaded her. That body was long gone. Her skull then, or was there a magically maintained brain within?

Turning, I discovered her naked. I drank in the sight, so unlike the Henka I thought I knew. Old scars, the result of battles and hunts gone wrong, decorated her torso. Slightly lopsided breasts. Hips wide. While certainly not ugly, she was a long way from the perfection she maintained in the north.

She was a warrior now, the wife of the man who would rule the world. Henka was what I wanted, but she was also what I needed. As my needs changed, so did she. Here, in this imperfect and damaged body, I loved her more than ever. She would never let me go, never fail or abandon me. She was the perfect partner, the perfect answer for a man who can't trust.

I pulled her close, her hands sliding into my shirt, fingernails gently sketching lines on my back.

I wasn't *him*. Unlike the Demon Emperor, I had learned how to trust. I had something he never could have: Bren. Where the emperor had been incapable of loyalty, I had my allegiance to my one friend. I would never betray him. I would never let him down or fail him. No matter what it cost.

"I…"

I almost told her my plan to free her.

"I love you," I said. And it was true in a way I was sure it never had been for the emperor.

"I know," she answered.

Taking my hand in hers, she led me to Naghron's bed. She kissed me, her breath salty with blood.

Was this from the supply she'd hoarded since Abieszan, or had she already killed locals to make herself desirable to me?

I decided I didn't care.

The fire elementals didn't cease their dance until after we finished our own much less synchronized efforts.

CHAPTER FORTY-SIX

I woke to find crimson-robed priests awaiting me beyond the inner sanctuary of Naghron's chambers. Apparently, they knew better than to enter and risk interrupting him. Ignoring Henka, they laid out hastily restitched robes sized to fit my smaller build. It felt like a subtle rebuke. Naghron had been larger, muscled, and successful. He built the things I'd talked about and never got around to doing. Telling myself he had centuries more time did nothing to ease the sting.

I wanted to apologize to the priests. He should have survived. It should be my corpse awaiting him and not the other way around. Even had I wanted to unite the world as he had, my goals would have been different, my vision shaped by my life and experiences. He spoke of patience and centuries and genuinely seemed not to care if he was there at the end. To Naghron, the Demon Emperor was more important than any one fragment. That wasn't me, could never be me. Of what use was regaining the emperor's power if I wasn't there to wield it?

For their part, Naghron's clergy seemed remarkably unperturbed by his death. They bustled about me, fitting the red robes, taking in the shoulders a little more with quick stitches. No one paid Henka any attention and I wondered if Naghron had a woman in his life. I knew nothing. He could have been married. Having lived centuries, he could have sired countless children. What would happen to them now that he was gone? Would they be revered as minor godlings in this pantheon of one, or disposed of as uncomfortable reminders? I hesitated to ask. I didn't want to hurt Henka. My dead wife would never bear me children.

Their work complete, a phalanx of priests led me from Naghron's suite. I followed them through the halls of the pyramid, our way lit by a procession of fire elementals. Finally stepping into the blinding sun, I realized I'd lost all track of time. Henka pushed her way through the priests, uncaring of their startled expressions, and took my hand.

"They'll get used to it," she whispered.

The entire city of Palaq had turned out to watch the ascension of their new god. Hundreds of thousands gathered around the base of the greatest pyramid. Families huddled under parasols tilted against the rising sun. Earth elementals quit their tasks and lumbered closer. People shuffled aside, unbothered by their passage. Every fire elemental in sight leaned as if they might reach out and touch me. The monstrous flame lighting the sword of Naghron's greatest statue roared bright even in the sun. Roiling tornadoes of dust and debris circled beyond the crowd, both guarding the event, but also there to witness the ceremony.

My heart was up there, at the apex of the pyramid. It called out to me.

Sculptures of a dead man surrounded the square, all of them watching with what I now saw was a look of disappointed disgust.

"Do you think they'll remake them all to match my slighter stature?" I jokingly asked Henka.

"It'd be easier to feed you," she answered. "Give you a chance to put on some muscle."

"I'd rather knock them all down. This…" I waved my free hand at the nearest statue. "This isn't me."

She squeezed my hand. "The city is yours to do with as you will. Knock down the statues. Burn it all to ash and bones."

Constructed of staggered blocks too large to be easily climbed, I realized there was a smaller set of steps. We went up. Step after step until my legs burned. Henka walked effortlessly at my side.

Wanting a moment's respite, I made a show of stopping and turning to look out over the crowd below. Henka released my hand and stood at my side. The priests halted and obediently waited. A blissful sigh passed through the gathering; their god had seen them. Arms raised they reached for me as if I might bend and touch their stretched fingers delivering benediction. I couldn't imagine what they felt, what passed through their thoughts. How did it feel to see your god? I'd seen but the tiniest fragment of my own. While even that sliver of divinity had been enough to damage my sanity—and likely destroy Shalayn's—I still felt none of the awe these people displayed. Was it an act? Did they whisper mockingly to each other after their god was safely gone? Look at that strutting peacock pretending to be a god.

Gazing down upon them, I saw only awe and worship. No one fidgeted.

It felt good. It felt right, as if finally receiving recognition for all I'd done over the millennia. Building the first true civilization from nothing. Uniting the world in peace and harmony.

True, what I built had been imperfect, but I deserved this. I'd done more for this world than the Guild ever had, more even than my own god.

Naghron knew something I hadn't: we were meant for more than servitude. We were meant to rule, and not as kings or emperors. I was a god.

Or I should have been.

Far below something flashed bright, the sun reflecting off exposed steel, and I twitched.

Not a god at all.

I felt vulnerable here, exposed. If Shalayn wanted a chance to kill me before I took on the next shard of heart, this was it. Perhaps a magical arrow launched from a sorcerous bow or some unimaginable attack. Tien often joked about boiling my blood. Could mages enchant an item with such power?

Breath held, I waited for a bolt of lightning from the clear sky.

Nothing.

That other shard of my heart still waited on the north end of the island, and Shalayn would be there with it. No need to endanger herself by trying to attack me where I was strongest when she knew I'd come to her. She'd already had days to prepare whatever surprises she planned and would have another two days once I took the next shard. Anyway, it was me she hated, not Naghron and not the Demon Emperor. She likely wanted me to have the Naghron shard so she could kill as much of me as possible.

Nodding to the nearest priest, I once again ascended the pyramid, the others falling in around me.

Henka strode at my side. "You feel it, don't you."

Not a question.

"This is just the beginning," she continued. "Take what he started, shape it using what you've learned. Make something new."

My own lessons.

Were they truly mine though?

I loved her so completely, I would do anything for her. I couldn't imagine life without her. She was my soul, my light, and my life. Her hold over me was no less complete than mine on her. In fact, hers was stronger. Where I needed to place my hand on her heart to command her, all she need do was ask.

I shook the insane thought off, distracted by the sight as we reached the top of the pyramid.

Naghron lay dead on a stone altar stained brown with blood. Eyes closed, he looked peaceful, accepting. As if everything had gone exactly to plan. Attired in crimson robes like his priests, his chest and abdomen remained exposed. The ridged muscle felt like one last mockery. A wedge-bladed knife lay on the stone beside him. When the priests spread out to surround me, surreptitiously pulling Henka from my side, I understood. I was to hack Naghron open, sunder his corpse and dig the obsidian from his heart before the entire population of Palaq. They'd watch the shard sink into my flesh, listen to my echoing screams as I lost consciousness.

An ancient priest, sunken and wrinkled, red robes hanging loose about his gaunt frame, stepped forward to address the gathered masses.

Lifting shaking hands, he spoke in a surprisingly strong voice. "Gods can never truly die!"

The crowd roared so loud I expected to see dust shake from nearby buildings. Earth elementals stomped their feet, shaking the ground. Fire elementals burned brighter, turning a bluish white that hurt to look at. The air elementals patrolling the perimeter spun around the gathering faster and faster until a wall of upflung dust created an impenetrable wall. Every demon-bound stone whispered its worship.

All of it directed at me, I drank it in. Drinking in the Dripping

Bucket with Shalayn was nothing in comparison. I staggered, intoxicated on devotion. This was something new, something more than simply being the centre of attention. The adoration fed something in me. I felt it like the sun on my face, warming and life-giving. This was nourishment.

Do you know what defines gods? Naghron had asked.

Worship. Only now did I understand.

Though I saw no signal, the crowd suddenly fell silent.

"One lesson!" screamed the old priest, bony fingers splayed wide. "One! Lesson!"

"THAT WHICH KILLS US MAKES US STRONGER!" the crowd roared back.

"One lesson!"

"THAT WHICH KILLS US MAKES US STRONGER!"

"We are the damned of all the world!"

"THAT WHICH KILLS US MAKES US STRONGER!"

"We are the filth beneath the white foot of the Guild!"

"THAT WHICH KILLS US MAKES US STRONGER!"

"We are the murdered past!"

"THAT WHICH KILLS US MAKES US STRONGER!"

"We are the future!"

"THAT WHICH KILLS US MAKES US STRONGER!"

Taking up the knife I drove it into Naghron's chest.

Silence.

Twisting the wedge-shaped blade, I cracked the cartilage, parting his ribs. Teeth bared in a snarl, I released the blade, digging my fingers into the gore.

Wet spatter of cold blood.

With a scream, I pulled his chest cavity wide, meat tearing, bone and gristle surrendering to my will.

My breathing became deafening in my ears as I gazed down into the ruin. Slack organs. Deflated lungs. A still heart, almost half of it glistening black stone.

I touched bloody fingertips to my own chest, felt the tremor of my heart within.

How could a man live with a stone heart? Solid obsidian, there was no way blood passed through that stone. Yet here I stood. I would take Naghron's shard, and it would join my own and I would go on living.

You aren't human. People don't have stone hearts. Iremaire's mocking words. *They don't heal by draining the life from filthy rats. You are the only threat from another reality this world faces. You are the only ancient evil.*

If I was the only man in this world with a stone heart, then was I really a man *of* this world? Confused memories flitted through my thoughts. The golden god, flawlessly beautiful, dropping a lump of black stone into my shattered chest. Was I the islander boy she killed, or was I that stone?

The answer was obvious. The stone only held the memories of the Demon Emperor. Naghron's experiences died with him. They were gone.

"I am the stone," I whispered in dawning horror.

If I was the stone, then *I* was nothing. I was only the most recent host of this parasitical being. The concept of me was meaningless. He—*it*—was everything.

I swallowed my fear. "No."

Walk away. Salvage what's left of you. Don't touch that stone.

Except I knew I would. The gore-flecked black stone exposed, I couldn't resist it.

Reaching into the gaping wound, I tore the stone free, holding it aloft for the crowd to see.

"That which kills me!" I screamed at them.

"MAKES YOU STRONGER!" they roared back.

Obsidian cleaved through flesh, sank into the meat of my hand, distending the skin. Jagged stone scythed through my arm savaging everything in its path. It tore me as it burrowed to my heart. Black stone. Black life. Uncaring of the damage done.

I didn't matter. Driven to once again become whole, nothing would stop it.

Larger than the other pieces I'd taken, it ran into the bone of my ribs, unable to slip between them. They cracked and splintered, tearing my insides further. I felt a lung collapse, punctured, and gagged for breath.

The crowd bellowed their chant over and over.

"THAT WHICH KILLS YOU MAKES YOU STRONGER!"

Refusing to fall, I stood with my arms outstretched, drinking their worship, screaming my pain at them as if they might share the burden.

With each piece of heart, a little bit of the man I wanted to be died.

With each fragment I gained more power.

That which killed me made me stronger.

CHAPTER FORTY-SEVEN

A man in fragments, I dreamt scraps of memory, sharp slivers of the past.

A boy, I'd gone hunting alone and returned delirious. My tribe thought I was dying. They gathered around me, splashing my naked and sweating body with blood and chicken entrails. For days I lay insensate and unresponsive, the shaman singing prayers over me, filling the tent with caustic smoke.

I woke hearing voices in my head. They told me dire secrets, promised power and influence beyond my wildest dreams. Thinking my mind broken, I told no one, trying to ignore the endless rants of madness. But those voices knew me too well, knew exactly what to offer a youth greedy for notoriety.

I was a young man, paddling my canoe through swamps and everglades. I fished and hunted to feed my tribe, and I went to war to protect them. After each battle, I sliced my victories into my arms, jamming ash into the wounds so they healed a thick ridge of scar. The voices never left me, though I learned to parse meaning from their insane babble. They were teaching me. In a time where I couldn't understand what a 'door' was, they were trying to instruct me on how to open one.

I was not me, they said, but someday I could be.

I spent my nights in a hut constructed from the bones and skulls of those I slew in battle. I dreamt I was a god, a pillar of stone smoke. In my dreams I betrayed my pantheon only to be bested by a pitiful mortal. Some mornings I woke, surrounded by the desiccated husks of snakes and lizards and birds.

And I aged.

Desperate, I listened to the voices, followed their every instruction. I dug shallow trenches in the earth, filled them with blood. I screamed impossible sounds, my voice shredding apart. I cut throats and promised souls to incomprehensible *things*. Carving myself to expose muscle and bone, I bound demons to them for strength. I gutted myself, to do the same to my every organ. They kept me alive.

With age came something akin to wisdom. My world was filth and death. Where the young man I'd been accepted that without question, the old man I became railed against the futility of existence. Not just his own, he wanted all lives to be worth something. His people were born, lived brief brutal lives, and died, soon to be forgotten. Nothing changed. No one talked of progress. No one dreamed of a better day. You lived your father's life. You died your father's death.

I vowed then that if I was going to trade my soul, I'd get something more for it than life. Selfish though I'd been, I would serve my people.

I was older now, many thousands of years. Yet I still dreamed of spiders and stone. I dreamed of the world I wanted to create, of the world I somehow failed to make real. Somewhere, I'd become distracted. Each time I stepped toward peace I found more war. Every tribe we crossed paths with resisted our efforts to bring them civilization. Tribes banded together to fight me, and I sold more of my soul to defeat them.

Blinded by ambition at the time, only in hindsight could I see the truth: In becoming the man I needed to be to make the world I wanted, I became a man who no longer wanted that world.

The dream crumbled like ancient sun-dried clay, and I prowled through eternal fields of grass. I was the black jaguar, drinker of the night. I was the darkest hour, the storm of the north. I was war and discord, the trickster, the manipulator of man and god alike. I was the enemy of both sides, beholden only to my own whims. Five suns rose and five suns I destroyed, each time giving birth to a new age. The others were blind, unable to see that death and rebirth were in fact the same thing. I was self-serving and I was a powerless tool of fate.

I dreamt I betrayed the other gods, warred with them for possession of the only surviving city of man.

Even in my dreams I knew this couldn't be true. Here I was. Men were everywhere, living in cities and tribes beyond count. I dreamt a colossal city surrounded by a fallen world. Endless desert, bloody dust of the dead. I witnessed brave acts of selfless futility as ignorance battled to save a world already lost.

I saw the truth: Everyone fights against death, wages war against destruction, even though such things are the necessity of life.

Shattered clay dreams reformed into something newer, infinitely more recent, and yet still millennium in the past.

From the swamps and everglades of my savage tribe I united the islands of the south. First a shaman, then a theocrat, I eventually led my armies north. We discovered a civilization greater than anything we'd dreamed. The kingdoms of the mainland seemed like the pinnacle of what humanity might achieve. Sprawling cities. Roads paved in cobblestones. Priest-run schools. Sewer systems and aqueducts. Only later would I see the filth and lies beneath it all.

Kings claimed divine right, lorded their power over their peasants. They took, claiming taxes and tithes, and gave little or nothing in return. What benefits there were, weren't shared equally. Many were denied an education because of their skin colour or where they were born. Simply having parents who already owned land made you a better person in the eyes of the law.

Serfs worked the fields, died in the mud unable to write their own names. There was no chance for improvement, no opportunity to be something more. Reaching for something beyond your station was punishable by death. The landed gentry claimed a huge percentage of what the tenant farmers grew and sent it to the cities to be sold for profit. Their hands never got dirty. Unwilling to suffer the discomforts of travel, they rarely did the selling themselves, having other middlemen do the work.

The kings bickered and warred constantly, pressing the poor into service, forcing them to die to protect their ruler's interests.

I set myself to conquering this new world.

Disintegrating dreams chased teasing hints of memory, moments of time trapped in stone. Armies of crude demons lacking the finesse of my later works lumbered across the land, smashing through pitiful shield-walls, pounding defences to dust beneath monstrous fists. The first sorcerers—escaped slaves of the Deredi Giants—joined my cause. Barbaric elementalists, deranged savages worshipping the wild spirits of the land, gathered to my banner. Where the northern kings and priests spit on them as uncivilized heathens, I welcomed them with open arms. With the passage of centuries, I would mould them into the refined artists they later became.

Some part of me wondered at the lack of necromancers. Back then, it was not a word I knew. There were no undead.

After centuries of war, I united the world in a single empire. One rule. One law. Now the work of rebuilding could begin. The cost had been high, entire kingdoms reduced to ruins sinking beneath deserts born of unrestrained magical violence. The rolling grasslands to the east of the Rift were now a wasteland of cracked earth, the mighty Cralgan Empire reduced to barbarism and cannibalistic tribes.

All were now equal. There were no second-class citizens. Anyone who wanted was employed and paid a decent wage. Within a decade, the quality of life was the highest ever seen. Even those who viciously fought me were welcome in my world, though many stubbornly chose to starve in their native lands. Pride is ever the killer of men.

The voices whispered new plans, spoke of worlds beyond my own, of power I could scarcely imagine. I achieved everything I thought I wanted, and yet there was a hole in my life, an emptiness. I was meant for more. Some of the boy from the swamp remained, but I had become something new. That youth's marrow still filled what remained of my bones, his blood ran through my demon-bound flesh. But in my heart, I was something else, something infinitely older.

Somehow, somewhere, I had fallen.

I chased her dream. I opened doors best left closed, threw wide the curtain between worlds and ushered in hell.

Though she elevated me until I teetered at the edge of ascension, I hated her. In rare moments of honesty, I saw the truth. There was the world I wanted to build, and there was the world I was building. They weren't the same, weren't even close.

I bled my own people to feed her wars.

Helpless anger festered within me. The voices understood what drove me. But they'd misjudged.

Where she dreamed in blood, my own dreams were smoke and stone.

With passing centuries an idea took shape, and I began to have dreams of my own. My god made me powerful. Her armies were my armies. I would be patient. Someday, I would betray my god, drown her dream in ash. I would kill her if I could, cut her from my world if not. No longer a tribal savage, I now understood doors and I knew that they could be closed much as they could be opened.

I would smash the gates between realities, banishing her from my world.

Her dream stole what I was.

Ten thousand years a slave.

I had a dream, a vision of the world as it should be.

She tore out my eyes, replaced that vision with one of her own.

CHAPTER FORTY-EIGHT

I woke entombed in stone, the weight of centuries crushing me. I breathed cool, dry air, felt my eyes slide beneath their lids. They weren't misshapen lumps of stone; my dreams were still mine. The mattress beneath me was soft, filled with down. A single thin cotton sheet lay across my hips, exposing my chest. Eyes still closed, I uttered a small laugh, thinking of Naghron's muscled bulk. How much effort had that taken? How many years had he spent building that physique? And yet here I was, my abused and often malnourished body in his bed. He built Palaq from nothing and I, who spent my few years of life scampering madly about the world like a wilful child, would inherit it all.

It should have been him lying here, not me.

Justice, I decided, was a myth.

Despite being closer to whole, I still felt the cavernous gaps in my soul. Memories warred with regained knowledge, demanding attention. New summonings and bindings. Spirit demons capable of possessing people. I recalled the name of an elemental fire demon from a distant reality but had the sinking suspicion it died during one of my endless wars.

My fists clenched tight as I considered the possibilities. I now ruled a small empire of people who worshipped me. My priests would take care of the preparations, I wouldn't have to shed a drop of blood. No doubt, Naghron already had Soul Stones kept at the ready, though of course, his memories were lost to me. I understood now why he liked to chat with the other Khraen's before killing them. Whatever secrets he had died with him. Hidden chambers buried beneath these pyramids.

Demonic weapons. All gone because he died without a chance to pass along what he knew.

Though I now remembered being Naghron bä Khraen, the man who carved an empire from the savage island tribes, I still thought of myself as Khraen. Loosing a breath, I concentrated on the pull of my heart. The piece on the north end of the island was still there, still waiting. There were a few small shards far off to the east, farther than I'd travelled. With the memories in Naghron's heart, I recalled more of the world. Another land lay far beyond Khaal. On the southern tip there was Aszyyr. I remembered it as a thriving city, the hub of trade with that part of the world. North of Aszyyr lay an endless tangle of impassable jungle so fierce that few who entered were ever seen again. Beyond the jungles lay the Krsak Mountains, breeding grounds for the most terrifying species of dragons. As Emperor I'd maintained aviaries there, hidden in the mountains, run by my priests, and staffed by demons. I had no idea what, if anything, remained. Hidden in the southern range of the Krsak Mountains lay the Mines of Azal Sil from whence the steel used to forge Kantlament was mined.

Beyond the Krsak Mountains—

"I wanted you to be awake," said Shalayn. "I wanted you to know it was me."

Eyes snapping open, I found her standing over my bed. Pale blue eyes icy with hate, she wore a strange cloak I couldn't focus on. I saw through her as if her legs and body were a distorting mist. Where she was still, she became perfectly invisible. With her sleeves pulled up to expose her hands and the brutal sword she held, and the cowl thrown back, she was a disembodied floating head and hands.

"Shalayn," I said, blinking up at her.

How many times had I thought about seeing her again, about how she deserved her revenge? Or at least, her chance at revenge. I thought that if I ever saw her again, she'd be encased in white plate mail. If, that was, I saw her at all. I'd have been less surprised had she stabbed me from behind, driving her sword through my guts.

"You aren't wearing your armour," I added stupidly.

"Too noisy," she said. "The cloak makes me invisible, not silent."

She stood loose and easy. Knowing her speed, I understood just how fast she'd stab me if I twitched. Instead, I lay as if relaxed, mind racing for an escape, looking for my chance. If I yelled for guards, they'd find my corpse in an apparently empty room.

What about the air elementals? If they passed around her, they must know she was there. Unlike my guards, they didn't rely on eyes to see.

"I knew you couldn't resist killing Naghron," Shalayn added. "I knew you'd take his heart. Remember the wizard's tower, how you passed out for two days leaving me to think you were dying?"

"I'm pretty sure I warned you what was going to happen before I touched that stone," I said.

She shrugged, unmoved by my defence. "The moment you took his heart I knew I had two days to reach you and kill you."

"Your captive Khraen told you when I took it," I guessed.

"I thought it was going to be harder," she admitted. "I guess while the Guild have been honing their craft since the fall of the empire, the demonologists have been stagnating."

"To be fair, they've been crushed under the loving thumb of the Guild." I darted a glance at the door. Nothing.

"Even were I not about to kill you, you could never retake the world. The cast-off trinkets of the mages are already more than you can handle. I stole a few small things and have hunted and killed you with ease. Over and over." She shook her head, cold eyes never wavering. "You're so predictable."

"It's my one flaw," I said before realizing she wouldn't get the joke.

She grunted a laugh. "One flaw? All you are is flaws."

"I don't want to retake the world," I admitted, stalling. "I have no interest in being the Demon Emperor."

Not entirely the truth, but not a lie either. I wanted to explain how my time with her influenced me in ways no one could have predicted. It was no great exaggeration to say that my desire to be a better man stemmed from my time with Shalayn.

A time Henka let me have. Could she have planned even that?

"Happy times, then," said Shalayn. Stepping closer, she lifted the sword. "Let's just make sure you don't change your mind."

"Wait," I said, not moving.

Tensed and ready for me to attempt escape, she twitched in surprise.

"There's something I have to do before I die," I said. "I did something horrible. I have to make it right."

"You murdered my sister, turned her into an undead slave, and got her incinerated in a pointless battle you had no chance of winning." She grinned death. "Go on. Make it right."

"I enslaved my wife. I have to free her."

"That woman whose head I tossed into the ocean?"

"She's surprisingly difficult to kill."

"Not to worry. When I'm done here, she's next. I'll burn her to ash. I'll set her free for you."

"Air elementals," I yelled, rolling off the far side of the bed, "I command you to attack!"

Nothing happened and Shalayn and I stared at each other, her with a quizzically raised eyebrow. I stood in the slim space between the bed and the wall, just wide enough to fit the small side-table nestled there.

"Worth a shot," I said.

Looking past Shalayn, I spotted my laundered clothes neatly folded on a desk. My sword sat atop the pile.

"Go for it," she said.

"You'll let me get my sword?"

"Sure," she purred. "You can trust me not to stab you in the back."

Right.

I judged the distance separating Shalayn and I. The bed wasn't much more than a cot and I damned Naghron and his minimal tastes. She could impale me with one good lunge.

If I could reach Adraalmak, its influence alone might end the fight. At least I'd have a chance.

An idea, insane and dangerous.

"You'll never escape," I said, stalling while I memorized that side of the room.

This was madness. Using a portal demon required hours of careful study, locking every detail in your memory. One mistake and I'd end up in the wall or torn away to some distant hell or trapped gods knew where.

About to strike, Shalayn's arm tensed. I fed Frorrat, the portal demon bound to Iremaire's ring, a soul.

Behind me, Shalayn lunged across the bed, stabbing the wall and cursing. Guts twisting, I puked, retching. My knees gave, and I found myself at eye-level with the folded clothes.

Sword, I thought. Get the sword.

Hands shaking and palsied, I grabbed the sword and rolled away, wrestling with the scabbard as it had become tangled in the laundry. On her feet, Shalayn kicked the bed aside and was on me in an instant, sword stabbing at my heart. I rolled away, suffering a long gash in my right arm. Finally finding the pommel, I ripped Adraalmak from its scabbard, exposing the demonic blade.

Light and colour curled like burnt leaves and died. The room became dead and grey, leached of all joy, drained of life.

Freckled skin pale and damp, the swordswoman looked from the sword to me. She didn't quiver, didn't fold under the onslaught of its foul influence. Instead, a slight smile curved the corner of her mouth. I understood in that fraction of a heartbeat: Her world was already dead, drained of life and joy and colour the moment I murdered Tien. Adraalmak's influence was nothing.

"Fine," said Shalayn, "you can have your sword." Retreating a step, she motioned for me to rise.

"I beat you once," I said, standing on wobbling knees.

I attacked, a blindingly fast combination ending in an angled thrust meant to take her in the throat. She knocked aside my attacks and feints as if they were nothing, never moving more than the absolute minimum. Her sword was everywhere, bright steel singing with every contact. She punched me in the jaw with her left hand, sending me staggering back, ears ringing.

Shalayn followed.

Calm. Deadly.

Faking high, I stabbed low, intending on slashing her femoral artery. Her sword swept up, tapped aside my feint, and then snapped down impossibly fast to bat aside the real attack. She hit me again in the side of the head, a punch I only knew about when I looked up from where I knelt on the floor drooling blood down the front of my naked chest.

I lunged from my knees, trying to stab her in the guts. Shalayn smashed Adraalmak from numb fingers and slashed a deep wound along my back from shoulder to hip.

Wheezing from the effort, I rolled away, clumsily regaining my feet. She followed, that small smile never leaving her lips. Where I sucked air, desperate for every breath, already exhausted, she remained calm and balanced, untouched by her efforts. I looked around the room in dazed confusion.

"Your sword is under the bed," said Shalayn. She stepped close, her sword rising in a decapitating arc.

Having already done one stupidly suicidal thing that morning, I did another. Sketching the library in the floating mountains in my thoughts, I fed Frorrat another soul.

CHAPTER FORTY-NINE

Kneeling in the library, I vomited all over the floor.

"Disgusting," said Nhil, standing before me.

"I need a—"

He handed me a loaded crossbow. "I do think—"

I ignored him. I had to get back before Shalayn gave up on me and went after Henka or Bren. Building Naghron's bedroom in my imagination, remembering how the clothes got scattered from the table when I grabbed the sword, I fed Frorrat another soul.

I appeared behind Shalayn, my guts feeling like they'd been stuffed full of warring snakes. Choking down the need to puke again, I lifted the crossbow and fired. She spun as if dragged by her sword and knocked the bolt from the air with the blade.

Another soul. Back to the library. The bedroom and the floating castle swam in my thoughts, the differences between the two blurring. I roared, crushing my focus in the vice of my will, until I saw the library floor.

Kneeling, I retched over and over, screaming until my voice tore and I coughed bloody bile.

"This is unhealthy and unwise," said Nhil.

Making an incomprehensible bubbling noise, I spat on the floor. "She has a magical sword."

Squatting at my side, Nhil handed me a ring of simple steel. "There's a demon—"

I snatched the ring from his fingers. "Why didn't you give this to me the first—"

"The demon's name is Brisinder," he said. "You'll need to—"

Another soul and I was back in Naghron's bedroom, twitching on the floor. Reality twisted around me, enraged at my abuse. With nothing left to vomit up I sobbed and pissed myself. Barely capable of seeing the room through my tears, I knew I wouldn't survive another transition.

I reappeared in the same spot. This time, Shalayn was waiting.

Agony. The grate of steel on stone behind me where the blade punched through my back to grind against the floor.

Shalayn leaned close, grinning into my face. "Got you, fucker."

Pinioned, I reached up, touching the ring to the hand holding the sword. Adraalmak was nothing. For a heartbeat, the rotting stench of unadulterated evil filled the room. And was gone. I recognized the scent from ancient memories.

Shalayn hunched over me, unable to move. "No," she whispered. "No, please."

"Brisinder," I whispered, coughing. "Take the ring."

Shalayn took the ring with her free hand.

"Put it on," I managed, lips bubbling blood.

She slipped the ring onto a finger. Frowning down at me as if noticing the sword for the first time, she pulled the blade free.

Blood came faster now, splashing the stone beneath me. I slumped to the floor

Shalayn blinked and tears fell.

I couldn't move, gasped for breath, my strength draining away. "Shalayn?"

She dropped the sword and it clattered at her feet. Arms hanging loose, she stood relaxed and easy as if she hadn't just tried to kill me.

"Master."

In that moment I hated Nhil more than I'd ever hated anyone in this or any past life.

"Brisinder," I said. "You're a demon of possession."

Shalayn bowed.

Closing my eyes, I sagged back against the wall. Why, Nhil, why?

I knew the answer. Shalayn had information and knowledge I needed. Having worked for Iremaire, however briefly, she knew more of the current state of the Guild than I. And she knew what she'd done with the other shards of my heart. If she hadn't destroyed them, I'd need her to get them back.

"I don't need them," I said. "I don't want them."

It was a lie. Even now, bleeding out in this bedroom, I knew I had to go north and claim the piece of me waiting there. Nothing would stop me.

"It'll just mean there's more of me for Henka to kill."

Ignoring my babble, Shalayn said, "Should I get you help before you bleed to death?"

"Yes."

Stooping, she lifted me easily, held me cradled like a baby.

CHAPTER FIFTY

I woke in the same room, back in bed, the sheets clean, my chest wrapped in white cotton. Henka stood at my side, one cool hand on my arm. Bren and Noketenda were behind her, looking worried.

Shalayn stood beyond them all, arms crossed. Dressed in a loose shift, she wore the magical sword strapped about her hips. She looked bored, ignoring Bren's darted guilty glances.

Feeling the presence of something in the bed with me, I looked to the side, discovering the sunken and withered corpse of an old man. The sight reminded me of the husked animals littering my grave in the north.

"You needed to heal quickly," said Henka.

I winced as I sat up. Considering I'd been run-through, I had little to complain about. "Was anyone else hurt?"

"Just you," answered Brenwick. "As usual."

I grunted a pained laugh.

"Is it true?" he asked. "Is Tien's sister possessed by a demon?"

I nodded. "It wasn't what I wanted, but I had few options."

"I didn't know you had a demon of possession bound," said Henka.

I ignored the unspoken question. "Shalayn," I said, getting the swordswoman's attention. "Or Brisinder? What do I call you?"

"Either," she answered. "Most find it easiest to continue using the host's name."

There were many kinds of spirit demons capable of possession from different realities, but all were parasitical in one way or another. I didn't know the specifics of this type of demon. Some fed off sanity, drained memories, or devoured the host's ability to feel emotions. The longer Brisinder remained in possession of Shalayn, the more damage would be done to the woman's mental state. Once again, I was the cause of her suffering.

Bren turned to face Shalayn. "I'm sorry," he said. "I didn't—"

"Piss off," said the demon, voice flat. "The woman in here no longer matters. I am in control. This is *my* body."

The scarred man wrang his hands. "Shalayn is still in there?"

"Indeed. I have access to her memories and skills and can replicate her personality with ease."

"She's still alive?"

"For now."

Bren turned on me. "We can't do this. We have to let her go."

"She has information I need."

"Not to mention, she came here to murder us," Henka pointed out. "She almost killed Khraen."

Hearing Henka speak of murder made me want to laugh. I allowed none of it to show.

"It's not like she doesn't have reasons," said Bren.

"I don't want to be killed by anyone," said Nokutenda. "No matter how good their reasons. Letting someone go who is actively trying to do you harm is stupid."

Bren ignored her. "Maybe we can free her once you have what you need."

I didn't see how. Nothing would come between Shalayn and her vengeance. Even if I somehow managed to extract a promise that she'd leave, someday she'd be back to try again.

"Maybe," I said, not wanting to lie.

Bren accepted that. "Can we at least give her some freedom until then? I can't imagine the horror of being trapped helpless in your own body, not able to communicate. It'd drive me crazy."

"You're actually pretty shit at communicating," said Nokutenda. "You mostly grunt and point and look at my tits when you think I'm distracted. I doubt anyone but me would notice if you were possessed."

Bren blushed, the ridged burn scars turning pink.

"How much freedom does Shalayn have?" I asked Brisinder.

"As much as I decide to let her have."

"Meaning as much as *you* want her to have," Bren said to me.

He wasn't wrong.

The demon accepted the correction with a slight bow in my direction. "I can let her wander free," said Brisinder, "or I can crush her to nothing. Or anything in between. Want me to rule the body while she has free run of the mouth?" The demon leered, a look so unlike Shalayn.

"Keep her silenced," said Henka. "We can't chance her saying something dangerous at the wrong time."

Brisinder ignored my wife as if she hadn't spoken and I wondered if that was Nhil's doing. Come to think of it, where had he gotten this ring? He'd said he could neither summon nor bind demons, that the pacts weren't written for his kind. Brisinder obeyed me without hesitation. Had I bound the demon long ago, giving it to Nhil to hold for such a day?

"Brisinder," I said, "allow Shalayn to speak freely."

"Of course."

"Shalayn, what do you want?"

"Free me or kill me." Though I heard the hate in her voice, her expression remained oddly blank.

"I need you," I said. "For now. If I free you after…"

Henka looked from me to Shalayn. "She already tried to kill you twice."

Nokutenda nodded. "I'm with your wife on this one. Releasing her would be stupid."

They were right. Freeing Shalayn only made sense if I was planning on dying anyway, and I couldn't let them know that.

"Shalayn," I said. "I don't want to kill you. What happened to your sister wasn't entirely my fault." Her face remained expressionless. "I know you could never forgive me, and I don't deserve it."

"Don't even bother," she snapped. "Somehow, someway, I will kill you." Then she added, "No, she won't," with a different inflection. "*I* rule this body."

Bren raised a tentative hand. "I have an idea. What if you partially free her once you have what you need? Tell the demon to stop her from interfering with us, but otherwise leave her free to live her life."

Glancing at my friend, I saw the desperate hope in his eyes. "That might work," I said. Not quite a lie, it certainly wasn't the truth. As long as Brisinder remained within Shalayn, the woman would suffer, slowly crumbling as the parasitic demon fed.

"I'm going to kill you both," said Shalayn. "I will find a way. Nothing can stop me."

Lips twitching, she managed a sick grin of cracked and broken teeth before her face again became slack. Laughing, she drew her sword, and cut a long line in her left arm. "She is harmless," said Brisinder. "I promise."

Henka touched Bren's shoulder, gentle and apologetic. "I'm sorry. We can't chance it. If the Guild ever found her, they might remove the demon. There are a thousand ways letting her go might harm us and no way it helps. The most merciful thing we can do is end her suffering."

Bren bowed his head. No matter what he wanted, what he believed, or thought was right, he would never argue with Henka. I didn't know if it was because she was my wife, and thus the Empress, or if he had other reasons.

The draw of the piece of my heart on the north end of the island demanded my attention. Try as I might, I couldn't ignore it forever. I shivered, thinking of the pieces of me slowly disappearing as that Khraen hunted them.

"Shalayn, what did you do with the shards of my heart you killed?"

"Destroyed—" She shook her head. "Shalayn has a box she stole from Iremaire. They're inside."

I sagged, emotions warring for dominance. Relief. Disappointment. I loved Shalayn. Or used to love her. I wasn't sure anymore. I was the cause of her pain. I couldn't hate her for craving vengeance. I knew that nothing I did could save her. Even were I to free her and hand her a knife so she might slaughter me, Shalayn would be forever broken. Revenge would heal nothing. She'd be dead within a year, either through drink or bad decisions.

I knew I should find out where this box was and kill her, but hesitated. She might know some of Iremaire's secrets. Certainly, retrieving the box with the shards of my heart would be easier with Shalayn at my side.

"For now," I said to Bren, "we need her controlled. Later... I'll free her if I can."

Always hopeful, always expecting the best of people, he accepted my doomed promise.

Shalayn's lips twitched. "You lying motherfu—"

"Silence her," I instructed Brisinder. "I want you in control at all times."

Bren winced and left the room, Nokutenda following him.

Henka stayed a moment longer. "We'll get the pieces the swordswoman collected." She smiled. "For all she plotted against you, all she really managed was to collect your heart and bring it here to you. She couldn't have served you better had she done it on purpose."

I watched Henka leave, thoughts racing. She couldn't have planned this. Not even Nhil could manipulate events so perfectly. Closing my eyes tight, I shook my head. Distrust was a worm. It burrowed deep, gnawing at the support structures in your life until your world collapsed.

Only Shalayn remained, relaxed, sword once again sheathed.

"You have her skills?" I asked.

"I do."

"That cloak she wore?"

"Stolen from Iremaire along with several other items. It's on the table." She gestured at where my other clothes once again sat folded.

She paced the room, rolling her shoulders with a slight frown. A prowling cat, she moved with deadly grace. "It's an excellent body."

"Shalayn used to stomp about like a caravan driver."

"That was an act. She did it on purpose so men wouldn't notice her on the road. Eventually, it became habit. She loves you."

"Still?"

"Loved?" Brisinder shrugged. "Difficult to tell. That's why she hates you so much."

I understood. Sometimes I wondered if that was how I felt about Henka. I loved her so much it terrified me. The Demon Emperor must have felt the same; he loved her so much he enslaved her so she could never betray him.

But love wasn't the only reason for my fear. There was something else there I didn't understand.

Maybe it was hate.

Shalayn continued talking as she paced. "You were the first man who accepted her for who she was and made no effort to change her. She was strong, a fighter, and that didn't intimidate you. She wanted to get drunk and fuck and take risks and feel alive and you were all of that for her. Instead of telling her something was too dangerous for a girl, you asked her to come with you. You never told her to smile when she was down, or to talk quieter or be demure. You never told her she couldn't have another drink. You put more effort into making her happy than any man before. Even the one she'd thought she might marry; the one Tien stole."

When I first met the little wizard, I'd known the women shared a history and there was tension between them. I hadn't understood they were sisters until it was too late. It felt like finding the missing piece of a puzzle you'd long since given up on.

Shalayn stopped, stood studying me with a raised eyebrow and quirked lips. Though she talked more than Shalayn ever had, the demon had indeed mastered the swordswoman's mannerisms.

"She took that invisible cloak from Iremaire as well?"

"Correct. It's folded atop your shirt."

Looking to the table, I saw only my clothes, a padded gambeson, and a chain hauberk.

"This body," she cupped a breast, rolling the nipple between her fingers until it hardened. "I remember what you did to it, how it made her feel. You liked it and she liked it. If you want—"

"Leave. Now."

Shalayn bowed and left.

CHAPTER FIFTY-ONE

 Rising from the bed, I went to the table where my clothes and weapons waited. I found Shalayn's invisible cloak by feel. The material was soft as silk and yet felt cold, as if weaved from impossibly fine metallic thread. I stared through it at my hands. When I moved there was a slight blurring, but if I held still the fabric became perfectly invisible. I considered ordering a priest to fetch me a set of crimson robes so I might wear the cloak beneath, a last resort in case of trouble. I couldn't do it; the Demon Emperor dressed like that. I remembered him stalking long halls, bloody robes sweeping the floor, priests fleeing before his stone eyes.

 Touching the armour, I found demons bound to both the gambeson and chain. Someone had fetched Adraalmak from under the bed and sheathed the demon sword.

 I dressed, surprised to find myself comfortable in the heavy armour despite the tropical heat, and strapped the sword about my waist. A few experimental movements demonstrated the chain's impossible lack of weight and the fact it made no sound. The cloak I jammed into my pack. Slinging it over my shoulder, I went in search of Henka.

 An old woman, thin and frail, awaited me beyond my chambers. She bowed low, red robes hanging loose, grey hair tied back in a tight braid reaching past her hips.

 "My Lord," she said, straightening. "I am Phaoro, your High Priest. Unless you should choose to replace me."

 "Show me to my wife and friends," I commanded.

 She set off down the hall at a surprisingly brisk pace and I hurried to catch up.

"Is it strange?" I asked. "Serving one man and then another and pretending nothing changed?"

"You are my third." She winked. "I'm older than I look." She paused for a heartbeat then, "Usually there is more ceremony and less murdering during a meal."

"Naghron really did talk with the other pieces, decide who was best to move forward?"

"Yes."

"That is no longer the case," I said. "I will be the last. All shall become part of me."

"Of course, my Lord."

"How old are you?"

Her brow crinkled in thought. "I've been High Priest for near five hundred years."

"Demonologist?"

"Of course. All your priests are."

"Five hundred years. I suspect you could rule in Naghron's place."

"I do. Gods have little interest in the petty affairs of men and only somewhat more interest in the affairs of young women."

"Do you always speak to your god this way?"

"I've outlived several. I figure I've earned it."

"Fair enough. You'll remain my High Priest. For now."

There didn't seem much point in replacing her, and perhaps she could keep the city together when their god abandoned them.

Phaoro continued down the hall, leading me through the labyrinthine passages within the pyramid. Finally, the passage sloped upward, exiting into the sun.

The sprawling gardens and courtyard had changed. The people who came to witness me carving the heart from their god were gone. In their place stood ranks upon ranks of soldiers, cadres of demonologists and elementalists. There was even a squad of haggard looking sorcerers milling about. Foot soldiers armed with halberds and clad in boiled leather sweat in the sun. Mounted cavalry in gleaming chain hauberk sat ready, lances rising in salute when they saw me. Beyond the gathered mortals, lumbering demons shuffled in loose formations. A hundred different realities were represented there. Hell-eyed nightmares of mist and bubbling flesh. Carapaced insects standing no taller than knee-high, capable of reducing a plate-armoured man to gibbets of flesh in a heartbeat, stood in the shadow of elephantine monsters sprouting tusks and teeth from every visible surface.

Shadows flashed past, a formation of colossal Quetzal demons, fifty-foot wings stretched wide, circling above. Deep in my stone heart the Demon Emperor gloried at this show of strength. While nothing compared to the armies he'd commanded, this was the greatest gathering of demons the world had seen in millennia.

Henka, Brenwick, Nokutenda, and Shalayn all wore new clothes and stood beside saddled horses. A black stallion in crimson livery awaited me, stamping with impatience to get moving. A waiting priest took my pack and attached it to the horse's saddle.

"Who are we invading?" I asked Phaoro.

"Your wife said you'd want to ride north the moment you woke."

She knew I'd need to chase after the shard there the moment I was able. "Of course."

I wasn't sure if the amassed strength was a miscommunication or an overreaction and decided I didn't care. Much like that moment on the pyramid, feeling the waves of worship wash over me, this felt right.

"Is this everything?" I asked.

Phaoro glanced at me from the corner of her eye, gave the slightest shake of her head.

"A lot more?"

The slightest nod with a hint of a pleased smile.

Interesting. Though my High Priest seemed willing to obey my wife, she also kept things hidden.

"You have enough ships to transport everything?"

"Wouldn't be much use if we didn't."

"Was Naghron planning on invading the mainland?"

"Not for another century or two. He didn't want victory, he wanted absolute domination. He wanted the Guild crushed to nothing."

I wondered if I could ever be so patient.

Though the gathered armies stood ready, eyes locked forward, I felt their attention. Less intense than at the pyramid, their worship still warmed me. It felt like standing in the sun, or the way I imagined a child felt when their mother rubbed their head and told them they'd done well. People spent their entire lives living for those brief moments when they got to be the centre of attention. Having thousands of people believe in you was a special kind of intoxication.

And it was poison.

It would be too easy to think the faith of all these people somehow made you right, or that their worship elevated you beyond the person you were before. This was how egos became inflated and tyrants born.

Good as it felt, it changed nothing. I still had to free Henka and all the worship in the world couldn't save me from her wrath.

New memories rattled in my skull, settling like pebbles and sand in a shaken jar, each searching for its place. Perhaps our memories don't define us, but the memory of butchering thousands, harvesting their souls, couldn't help but alter how I saw myself. I could say, 'That wasn't me, it was the Demon Emperor.' But the fact was, I remembered holding the knife.

I joined my friends, Phaoro following a step behind. Shalayn stood in a shiny hauberk and unadorned grey livery. Hip cocked to one side, hand resting on the pommel of her sword, lips bent in that crooked smile she wore when pleased with herself, she could have been the woman I first met. Guilty as I felt for my part in her misery, I missed the pain in her eyes.

Brenwick, a scarred and hulking brute of a man, wore the chain armour I brought back from the floating mountains. It stretched tight across his chest. I wanted to promise I'd find some way of making him whole again. I said nothing.

Nokutenda stood at Bren's side, shoulders almost touching. Her new clothes accentuated her curves and yet the young man refused so much as a glance. Arms hanging loose at her side, her fingers moved as if she wanted to take his hand. She said something out of the corner of her mouth, and he stifled a smile. I prayed she was patient enough to wear down the walls he built after Tien's death.

Clothed in a gossamer dress, sword slung across her back, Henka was stunning. She nodded as I approached, flint eyes fierce. Strong and beautiful, imperious in bearing, she was the perfect island queen. I had no doubt she'd chosen everything for exactly that effect.

It struck me she had the only grey eyes I'd seen since coming south. Like Nokutenda, Bren, and myself, all islanders had brown eyes only varying in darkness. I'd thought she'd taken the body of a single woman, but she'd clearly found a mainlander to harvest too. Had she left the woman alive and eyeless?

No. Of course not. I'd never once seen her leave a victim alive. Like me, she never left an enemy behind her.

"What did you look like before we first met?" I asked.

"That me is long gone."

"Were you always beautiful?" I couldn't picture her choosing an ugly form.

She laughed. "If I was a huge and slimy undead slug, would it matter now?"

Her question startled me. It never occurred to me she could be anything other than human. But then I had memories of a time before necromancers. Aside from that one memory of the hall of pedestals, I still had no recollection of my wife. Yet I recalled many thousands of years where Henka was not part of my life. Had I found the necromancers on some distant part of this world, or were they from some neighbouring reality?

When I failed to answer Henka said, "I have always been beautiful, though standards of beauty change with the passing centuries."

And a slimy slug might still be beautiful to other slugs.

Mounting our horses, we set out, the great host moving with us. Wanting some space, I urged my horse to the front. My friends matched my pace and soon we had nothing but cobbled road before us.

We rode past spiked trees decorated with demon-bound corpses. Heads lifted at our approach, empty eye sockets following our progress.

"It's been too long since I led an army," I said to Henka.

"Soon," she said.

My hand squeezed into a fist, imagining the feel of Kantlament. An end to sorrow. A sword to conquer worlds, or a coward's attempt at abdicating responsibility for his crimes?

It was somewhere in PalTaq.

The pleasure of the sun's heat, of finally finding a place in the world where I was welcomed instead of reviled, distracted me from my spiralling thoughts. We rode for hours, Nokutenda dragging Bren into a conversation about the different kinds of ships and their advantages and disadvantages. She wasn't subtle, but he didn't seem to mind. Soon he regaled us with increasingly far-fetched stories from his youth involving pirates, sea dragons, and an island princess his captain rescued from mainland slavers. Either Bren's life had been one of non-stop adventure prior to meeting me, or he was a fantastic and imaginative liar. Either way, he threw himself into every story, telling it with heart-felt emotion. As always, he was never the hero and though he wooed every buxom woman to take the stage, each ended with him nursing a broken heart in some run-down tavern.

We travelled for two days. In no rush, we stopped for long and elaborate meals prepared by a team of chefs travelling with the army. Each night squires scampered about the camp erecting tents and delivering ale and wine.

On the second night, after weaving yet another story about how he signed onto a pirate ship that ran afoul of an enraged patch of ocean, Bren retired to his tent. Running her fingertips around the rim of her beer mug, Nokutenda watched him leave. Frowning, she downed the rest of her pint and rose to follow. At the entrance to his tent, she hesitated, shoulders hunched. Then, she ducked and entered.

"Are you drunk?" I heard him ask, voice muffled through the fabric.

"Yes," she answered.

"You're in the wrong tent."

"I don't think I am."

"You are," he said. I'm not—"

"For the love of fuck, shut up. I need an orgasm if I'm going to sleep tonight."

Henka touched my shoulder. "She's not the only one."

"You don't sleep," I said.

She ignored Shalayn as if the woman were nothing, completely beneath notice. "I didn't mean me."

CHAPTER FIFTY-TWO

The next morning, we continued north. A myriad of expressions waged war to claim space on Bren's scarred face. His lips would curve in a pleased grin even as his eyes crumpled in pain. He alternated between dashing looks of puppy dog gratitude and guilt at Nokutenda.

Finally, becoming frustrated, she moved her horse alongside his and reached out to take his hand. "I can see I haven't quite managed to fuck you stupid. I must be slipping. One is usually all it takes." She kissed his palm, uncaring and oblivious to the audience. "Not to worry. A couple more nights and you'll be too brainless to be unhappy."

When he opened his mouth to protest or argue, she told him it was impolite to refuse a lady's offer to dance.

Shalayn chatted amiably with Nokutenda, the two women joking about how only a man would bring an entire army to deal with a ship of small-time pirates already loyal to one of the women in the group. Brisinder played the swordswoman perfectly, a master of every nuance. Had I not known she was possessed, I would have thought we'd been visited by the woman I first met on the caravan.

Early mid-afternoon, Shalayn raised a hand and pulled her horse to a stop. "It's not far now," she said. "A couple more hills, and we'll see the coast and the ship. Assuming the crew hasn't abandoned me."

Phaoro rode forward to join the conversation. "She's correct. My spies have reported the ship is anchored just off the coast. They've set up a small camp with a few guards littered around."

"If the crew sees that mob," Shalayn said, gesturing at the army gathering behind us, "they'll weigh anchor and flee."

"Bringing the ship down would be no great challenge," said Phaoro.

"There are things I need on board," I said. "I'd rather not sink it into the ocean."

"In that case, we could have demons and elementals in among them before they knew they were there."

Shalayn arched an eyebrow, an incredibly familiar expression of poorly concealed self-satisfaction.

"Yes?" I asked.

"It's a ship. It has a crew. As much as untrustworthy cut throats and murderers can be considered loyal, they're loyal to me. I think the five of us should go ahead, have the army follow along maybe an hour behind us. I'll tell the crew everything is fine, and the army is expected and bringing supplies to restock the *Katlipok*."

"I know that name," I said.

I recalled a demonic race of carnivorous man-sized insects reminiscent of praying mantises. Someone joked about them being *preying* mantises, but beyond that I remembered nothing.

Shalayn shrugged. "The original captain named it after some ancient island trickster god."

Had I killed that god?

"Any mages among the crew?" I asked Shalayn.

"One half-assed air elementalist. Nahlan's a drunk, couldn't find work on any other ships." She flashed a grin. "But I was frantic to chase you and bought the first ship I found. As the saying goes, desperate times call for desperate bedfellows."

"I don't think that's the saying," said Bren.

I looked to my friends, dangerous each and every one. A crew of pirates wouldn't be much trouble.

"We'll go on ahead," I decided. "Phaoro, give us an hour head start and then follow along."

"And my spies?"

"Leave them in place. If it looks like we've run into trouble, have them come to our aid."

"Of course."

We set out at a trot. Half an hour later we crested the last hill and looked down upon the coast. As promised, a ratty looking ship floated not far offshore, sails furled. A few ragged and stained tents had been set, and a cooking fire lit. A handful of well-armed men and women sat awaiting their lunch.

Seeing them, Shalayn stood in her stirrups and shouted, "Hey, you lollygagging goat fuckers, fetch your captain some ale!"

"Was that how Shalayn was with her crew?" I asked, surprised.

"I like the old Shalayn better," Brisinder answered. "The new one is a psychotic depressive bent on murdering anyone and everyone who ever did her wrong. Her list goes well beyond your own considerable crimes. She often dreamed of returning to Iremaire and killing the mage for lying about what she planned to do once she captured you. Then there was the man she loved that Tien stole. She was going to skin him alive and boil him in cat piss."

"I like the old Shalayn better, too," said Nokutenda. "She's funny and probably won't stab me."

Bren stared at the back of his horse's head and said nothing.

As we rode toward the camp, the crew of ruddy sunburned northerners scrambled to draw weapons and form up in a military formation sloppy enough to have been embarrassing. Happier to be at something close to a safe remove, those still aboard the *Katlipok* made no move to join those on land.

"They're all mainlanders," I mused, surprised.

"Shalayn discovered a dislike for islanders after you murdered her sister," said Brisinder.

Maintaining a relaxed pace, careful not to make threatening moves, we approached the crew. Their hands never strayed far from weapons, though their tension eased somewhat when Shalayn greeted each by name and demanded a report. One of the women stuttered something about the fishing being good and otherwise all was quiet.

"You brought a bunch of filthy darkers," said one of the men.

Nokutenda studied him with pursed lips. "Your shirt is a lovely yellow. Is that piss, sweat, or both?"

When the sailor bristled, reaching for his sword, Shalayn stepped between the two, "This lovely young lady is a sorcerer. Be polite or she'll peel you like an orange."

Nokutenda smiled sweetly.

The sailor spat, mumbling under his breath, but retreated.

Much as the crew disliked the sight of my companions, I bore the brunt of their loathing. They glared hate, sneering, and making those foolish signs over their hearts.

The woman who'd reported the fishing nodded at me. "Isn't he the one? I thought…" she trailed off, noting my attention.

"He's like the other," said Shalayn. "I need this one alive."

The woman glanced back toward the ship and nodded, apparently pleased with the answer.

Shalayn strode among her crew, barking orders to prepare the skiff. She said the five of us would board the *Katlipok* and that the rest were to build up the fire and prepare a good meal. "In the morning," she barked, "we sail!"

The crew grinned, slapping each other on the back, pleased to be leaving the island.

"We going north finally?" demanded yellow shirt. "We already been gone two months longer n' what I signed on for."

Shalayn waved him away, ignoring the question.

The others kept their distance but couldn't keep their eyes off me.

"They know who you are," whispered Shalayn, when we had a little space. "She told them everything. How you are the Demon Emperor reborn and how you murdered her sister. She promised them they'd be heroes. Parades, wealth, and fame. They're gullible morons. Though she did pay well since she stole a pile of diamonds and whatnot from Iremaire. She also sold off a few of the lesser magical trinkets." Brisinder shook her head in disgust. "You know, she could have lived out the rest of her days in luxury but instead came after you. What's really funny, she's in here screaming about how she'll somehow break free and kill everybody."

I'd half thought to use Shalayn's crew to sail south but now understood that could never happen. They hated me, would never take orders from a stained soul, and I couldn't trust them with knowledge of PalTaq. At the first chance, they'd run to the Guild to sell what they'd learned.

AN END TO SORROW

I wanted to feel some guilt at what was to come and found nothing, not the slightest hint of regret. Just as they hated me, I'd come to hate them too.

When the skiff was ready, we set out toward the *Katlipok*, Bren and Shalayn taking the oars.

"How many crew still aboard?" I asked.

"Twenty," answered Shalayn.

"We're going to kill them."

Henka and Nokutenda nodded as if this were the only reasonable course of action. Bren's shoulders hunched for a moment, and then he too nodded.

CHAPTER FIFTY-THREE

A caravel that had seen better days, the *Katlipok* sat low in the ocean, her hull heavy with crusted salt and barnacles. Once white sails hung sloppily furled, showing their age in the many crude stitch jobs and stains. The masts were of two different colours, the forward one having been replaced in the last century or two. The crew gathered at the rail to watch our approach. I saw hate on every face.

"There's a poxy batch of rodent scum," muttered Nokutenda under her breath. "Funny that such filthy specimens have the gall to look down on us." She wrinkled her nose and glanced at me. "You folk do most of the killing. I'm not much for physical violence and would rather save myself for the important stuff."

"Having a sorcerer is less useful than I thought," I joked.

"I'm plenty useful." She nudged Bren with a booted toe. "Isn't that right, big man?"

Bren coughed and concentrated on rowing.

Shalayn waved and the crew hesitantly lowered a rope ladder for us. We clambered onto the deck, the men and women retreating to make space, but staying close. I realized they thought they were being protective of Shalayn.

"Where is that drunk, Nahlan?" the swordswoman demanded, hands on hips.

"Sleeping," answered a boy who looked no older than thirteen.

"You think I asked just to sate my never-ending curiosity?" she demanded. "Fetch him."

The youth nodded and dashed below decks.

For several minutes Shalayn fielded a barrage of questions about what she'd found, why I hadn't yet had my heart cut out, where the *Katlipok* was heading next, and when they might be going home. She deflected her crew's queries.

When a shaggy old man with a tangled mop of greasy white hair tied back in a disintegrating queue staggered up the steps, the cabin boy in tow, Shalayn waved everyone to silence.

"Nahlan. Here." She snapped her fingers, pointing at the deck in front of her.

Nahlan shambled forward, filthy bare feet dragging as he scratched at his exposed belly. "Look," he said, "we're not sailing so you don't currently require my services. What I do in my time is my business."

Shalayn stabbed him through the chest, enchanted steel punching effortlessly through meat and bone.

Pulling the sword free, she said, "There. That's the elementalist out of the way."

Nahlan took a step back, one hand rising to touch the growing red stain on his shirt. "I didn't…" His knees folded, and he landed in an awkward heap, still blinking up at us in shock.

For a heartbeat, silence, as everyone gaped at Shalayn, trying to decide if this was swift ship's justice, or an insane captain turned murderous.

I drew Adraalmak, the demon devouring the world's colour for a score of paces. Instead of drawing their weapons, the crew fled, scampering in every direction like startled rats. For all their talk and bluster, these were not hardened warriors.

"Fucking hell," muttered Nokutenda, looking pale. "Perhaps carry two swords in the future. One for fighting wizards and demons, one for butchering old men and boys."

"Split up," I said, ignoring the sorcerer. "Kill everyone you find. Nokutenda, stay here and protect the skiff. If anyone tries to leave the ship, kill them."

She said nothing, but remained where instructed as Bren, Henka, Shalayn, and I headed off in different directions.

The crew on the shore roared in anger at what they'd seen, drawing weapons like they meant to swim over and fight us. The timely arrival of my army worked wonders as a distraction and soon they too were fleeing. Some tossed aside their weapons and sprinted into the ocean. I don't know where they thought they were going, but they didn't get far. Archers peppered them with arrows, turning the water red with blood. Others fled up the coast and were pursued by brutally swift demons and torn apart.

Ignoring the horrors occurring on the beach, I set off toward the rear of the ship, following a trio of sailors. Spotting me, they disappeared into the captain's cabin beneath the quarterdeck, slamming the door behind them and bolting it. Without slowing my pace, I chopped through the door and kicked aside the splintered ruin.

Entering, I stopped. Like the rest of the ship, Shalayn's cabin was a disaster, showing all the signs of a splintered mind. Crumpled maps and scraps of paper littered the floor. Empty whiskey bottles rolled, clattering with each swell. Sea-stained windows at the rear of the room let in a murky yellow light. Words had been carved into every wooden surface in a jagged and angry script: *My dreams are blood. Infected, filth soul. She's inside me. I'm sorry, Tien. All my fault. Destroy the heart. Save the world.* Over and over, *Destroy the heart. Save the world.*

Two men and a woman faced me. The men held cutlases, the woman a long three-pronged fishing spear that looked as old and poorly maintained as the rest of the vessel. Spacious by crew's standards, the captain's room was still a cramped place for a sword fight.

Adraalmak devoured what little colour there was, turning the sepia light into a foggy grey. The pirates flinched but held their ground; there was nowhere to run.

"What did you do to the captain?" asked the woman, voice cracking.

Seeing no point in answering, I closed the distance.

The men went wide, making use of what little space there was so they might attack my flanks. The woman, in the centre, hesitated, spear clutched in shaking hands.

Batting aside a clumsy attack, I cut down the man on the left first, the demon sword crashing through him from shoulder to hip. He fell in two separate directions, splashing the floor with blood and entrails. As I turned to engage the second man, the woman saw her opportunity, and lunged to stab me in my exposed side. My demonic armour stopped the impaling thrust, the impact staggering me, and the ancient wood of the spear splintered apart. Ignoring her, I stabbed the other sailor, punching Adraalmak through his chest. The woman dropped what was left of her spear and fled out onto the deck. The man I'd stabbed made wet choking noises on the floor as his lungs filled with blood. His lips moved, trying to curse me. I felt nothing at his pain.

Leaving the sailor to bleed out in peace, I followed the woman from Shalayn's cabin. I found her sprawled on the deck halfway to Nokutenda, leaking blood from one eye.

"You do know you were supposed to kill them," grumbled the sorcerer, "Just about wet myself."

Nudging the woman onto her back, I found no other wounds. She stared blankly at the sky and then blinked.

"She's not dead," I said, as the sorcerer ambled over to join me.

"Might as well be." She held up a sharpened iron spike the length of her little finger, too hefty to be of use as a sewing needle. "Old sorcerer's trick."

"I didn't think there were old sorcerers."

"Funny. Pushing one of these is a lot easier than crushing skulls, but they're difficult to aim. Not much use in a big brawl, but if someone is polite enough to run straight at you, and if you can keep your cool, they'll punch through an eye socket easy enough."

I frowned at the woman still blinking stupidly at the sun. "You killed her with a little iron needle?"

"Well, it's somewhere inside her brain right now. Sometimes they die quick, but sometimes it takes days. I heard of a thief who crossed a sorcerer and spent the next three decades with a sliver of steel in his head. Last I heard, he'd joined some crazy cult and was wandering the streets of Aszyyr proclaiming the return of the Demon Emperor." She wrinkled her nose, brow crinkling. "I hadn't thought about him in years. Funny, eh?"

The others returned from below decks, splashed in gore, but unhurt.

"All dead," reported Shalayn, face expressionless.

Looking over my shoulder I said, "Sorry I made a mess of your cabin," and immediately felt stupid. The woman I was apologizing to was trapped within, helpless and unable to express whatever she felt

"I figure it's your cabin now," she said. "I'll take one of the now vacant officer's rooms."

On the shore, my army had made short work of the pirates.

Shalayn wiped her sword clean on the woman lying at our feet and sheathed it. "I suppose you'll want to see Shalayn's pet Khraen?"

I sensed the presence of the man somewhere beneath me but nothing of the other shards.

"Yes. And after that, the box where she keeps my heart."

For reasons I couldn't explain, I didn't want Henka with me.

I was there when the shaman cut your heart out, Henka had said. *There were already pieces missing.*

If I collected every shard I sensed, would I still be incomplete?

I shook the thought off, angry at how easily I forgot I had no future.

"Henka, take Bren and Nokutenda and go ashore. Find Phaoro, tell her to ready supplies for a long journey. We'll take this ship. I want it ready to leave in the morning for Pal'Taq."

Henka gave me a quick hug and returned to the skiff with the other two, Bren helping her into the boat with an offered hand as if he were a gentleman and her a lady of the court.

"Shall we?" asked Shalayn.

"Lead the way."

I followed the swordswoman across the deck and down the creaking steps, the incredible pull of my heart growing in strength, filling me with need. We passed through the lower deck, ignoring the corpses littered there, and into the hold below. Everything stank of rotting fish, mouldy bread, and sweat. Emptied barrels and crates littered the open space, tossed aside once no longer needed. This crass dereliction was not the woman I knew, though truth be told perhaps I never knew her that well.

Shalayn gestured toward the rear of the ship. "She keeps him chained in the ship's locker." She glanced around, frowning. Spotting an oil lantern hanging nearby, she collected it. I waited as she spent several frustrating moments searching before finding a flint and steel and a box of sulphur-infused pinewood matches. Using the flint to spark the match, she then lit the lantern.

"There we go," she said, hefting the lamp.

Leading the way, she fished heavy keys from a chain around her neck and unlocked the door. Swinging it open, she stepped aside and raised the lantern so I could see into the windowless room beyond.

A wall of stench assailed me, shit and piss, puke and the sour diseased stench of rot. A naked man lay curled foetal in the filth, shivering despite the tropical humidity. Scores of desiccated rat corpses and half-eaten fish littered the floor, floating in the sewage.

"Things got really bad for him," said Shalayn from behind me, "when she realized she could beat him to the edge of death over and over."

"He's so young," I mumbled in shock.

This Khraen was barely beyond boyhood, a thin fringe of sparse stubble darkening his chin. Suppurating sores littered his body, bruises and poorly healed scars decorating his familiar flesh.

Shalayn wrinkled her nose in disgust. "She barely feeds him enough to keep him alive, never brings fresh water. Mostly he lives off the dead rats his body drains to heal itself."

Hearing Shalayn's voice, he twitched, crawling as far from the door as the chains allowed. Eyes clenched closed, he whispered, "Please, please, please," over and over. At least two teeth were missing, several more shattered and jagged in unhealthily pale gums.

For all I'd suffered and starved, I'd never been this bad.

"Sometimes she tortures him," said Shalayn. "She screams at him or beats him with an oar. Other times she cries and apologizes and tells him she still loves him. Those are the worst, because then she'll kick his ribs until they break and his breath rattles. She's quite insane."

"My fault," I said.

Because Brisinder knew everything Shalayn knew, it was oddly easy to converse with the demon. On some level I think I was pretending it was Shalayn I talked to.

"Probably," agreed the demon. "I have memories of her life before you. I remember you murdering her sister, driving that sword up through her back. Shalayn watched her die, they were looking into each other's eyes."

"I didn't know," I said, praying Shalayn heard.

Brisinder continued, uncaring. "Then you raised her sister and threw her into a fight with battle mages. That broke what remained of the woman she'd been. Kind of impressive, really. Few people get a chance to murder someone in front of their family twice! After that, your god destroyed what was left." She examined the cowering youth with pursed lips. "She hates you more than anything. If you think you can ever free her, you're wrong. She would sacrifice herself without hesitation to kill you because she thinks she's saving the world."

"I'm not sure she's wrong," I admitted.

Brisinder didn't care. The worries and concerns of mortals from another world were nothing to the demon.

This young man had been tortured over and over for reasons he probably barely understood. She hurt him because it was the closest she could get to hurting me.

Her suffering was my fault, as was his.

All the disgust and pity welling up within me was nothing compared to the need. He was pathetic and weak, the most disgusting Khraen I'd met. He reminded me too much of my moments of weakness in Iremaire's underground bubble. I wanted to say that I would have escaped, that somehow, I always did, but all too often I'd been rescued.

"Killing him would be a mercy," I said.

Hadn't I recently said that to someone else?

Desperate hunger crushed the thought to nothing. Much as I wanted the stone, I hated the need. Who was in control here, me, or the obsidian?

I reached for my sword and hesitated. Unsheathing the demon to kill this wretch seemed somehow disgusting, an insult to the steel. For the first time, I was glad none of our memories survived; I didn't want to know what broke him.

"Kill him," I ordered Brisinder.

She drew her sword and stabbed him neatly through the heart. No emotion. Cold inhuman action. Shalayn never would have done that. Even now, broken as she was, she'd cried when torturing this Khraen.

Causing pain should cause pain, I decided. Empathy.

"Cut out his heart," I told the demon. "Wrap it in cloth."

I watched as Shalayn did as instructed, folding the bloody sliver into a kerchief she kept in a pocket. She stood relaxed, awaiting further instructions, splashed to the elbows in gore.

"Show me to the box."

Shalayn's face twitched, lip curling. "She's fighting me," said Brisinder. "She was fine with killing this boy but doesn't want you to have the box. Morality among mortals is such a weak and tenuous thing, more delusion than reality."

I didn't want to discuss philosophy with this demon. "You remain in control?"

"Of course. Though she is surprisingly strong willed."

"She can't break free?"

Shalayn grinned that familiar grin. "Never."

"Where is the box?"

"In her cabin," said Shalayn, turning and heading back up the steps to the main deck.

I followed, stunned. I'd been in there and felt nothing.

Back to the captain's cabin, Shalayn tutting as she stepped over the ruin of the door. "Shame I killed the ship's carpenter."

Weaving between the corpses—the man I'd stabbed lay dead and still, frowning at the cobwebbed ceiling—she approached the bed. She knelt, drawing a slim-bladed dagger, and pried open a secret compartment that would only fool someone who wasn't looking for secret compartments. She withdrew a small box made of polished white oak bound in bright and untarnished steel.

"It carries several permanent enchantments," Shalayn said, holding the box out in offering. "There's a stasis spell within, and some kind of protection against scrying on the exterior."

"Scrying?" I knew the word, but not in relation to mages. "Isn't that when shaman look into the spirit world?"

"Shalayn overheard Iremaire yell at an apprentice because he wasn't wearing the scry-warded robes she made him. She said that if her enemies wanted to see what she was up to, all they had to do was spy on his stupid ass. She made him cry."

Iremaire had kept me in a stasis spell when she transported me from Abieszan to Khaal. Then, when she held me trapped underground, I'd been unable to sense the other shards of my heart. Was that the result of some new protective wizardry?

Taking the box, I turned it in my hands, feeling the smooth surface, studying every whorl in the lustrous wood. A simple clasp held it closed. It was a work of art. I felt nothing of the hearts within. The shard Shalayn held wrapped in cloth was a constant distraction, scraped at my every thought: Take. Take. Take!

"Am I protected against scrying too, now that I'm holding the box?" I asked.

Shalayn grunted and shrugged.

Cracking the box open, screaming hunger and need drown all thought. Unable to breathe, I stumbled backward, snapping the lid closed and hissing in startled rage.

The swordswoman watched with a raised eyebrow as I steadied myself, steeling my resolve. Again, I opened it. Ready this time, I managed only a low moan of desperate desire. Two pieces of jagged obsidian lay inside. Pain stabbed through my skull like Nokutenda had driven one of her iron spikes into my brain. I closed the box, gently this time as a show of will.

"It wasn't that bad when we were in the wizard tower," said Shalayn. "Ever feel like free will is an illusion?"

Looking up from the box, I said, "Who bound you? Was it Nhil?"

"You did. A long time ago."

"What happened after?"

She made Shalayn's 'how would I know?' face. "I was in a ring in another reality."

The demon could be lying. I had no way of knowing. Nhil had told me he could neither summon nor bind demons, and while I had some doubts, I tended to believe him. He had, after all, helped me at every turn. He saved my life at least twice, the most recent time being strangely prepared with first a crossbow and then the ring containing Brisinder.

Was that it? Maybe Nhil couldn't summon and bind demons, but he'd never mentioned wizardry. Was he using the magic of the filthy mages to spy on me from another reality?

I handed Shalayn the box. "Put your piece in there."

She did as instructed. The instant the lid clicked shut, my head cleared, the pain fading. I laughed, shaking my head. Iremaire had inadvertently given me a great gift. Though I could never resist the pull of my heart for long, I could drop it into this stasis box. No longer would I be a slave to the hunger. I would take each piece if, and when, I wanted.

She handed me the box, saying, "Shalayn didn't like that!"

I left Shalayn's cabin, box tucked under one arm.

"Right then," muttered the demon before following.

CHAPTER FIFTY-FOUR

We made camp one last evening in Palaq. Fires were lit, tents erected, and a feast prepared. My army spread out around us, my priests working to replace the demon-bound sentinels Shalayn and her crew destroyed. A team of earth elementalists and demonologists worked on the *Katlipok,* repairing damaged beams, and strengthening the hull and masts against the storms we would no doubt face.

Bren sat near enough to be protective and yet separate from the rest of us. Leaning back against a sack of grain not yet loaded onto the ship, his legs stretched out before him, he watched the strange host go about their duties. Odd as the sight was, he seemed unperturbed, as if nothing could surprise him after all he'd seen. Nokutenda made no attempt to join him, apparently unconcerned by his distance. Instead, she chatted with Henka about the world as it once was, long ago. My wife wove stories of beauty and grandeur. When she spoke, it sounded like the world had once been perfect, all mankind united in purpose. Perhaps, as the Empress, that was how it appeared.

Out of sight out of mind was more than just a cliché. It explained all human existence. If you didn't personally witness the horror, did it even happen?

"And he's going to bring that back, right?" I overheard the sorcerer ask.

"Only the best parts," said Henka. "It won't be the same. Nor should it be. One must learn from the past and strive to do better."

That was exactly what I intended, though not in the way she envisioned.

AN END TO SORROW

Aware that both Henka and Nokutenda were within earshot, I summoned Phaoro. The high priest arrived moments later at the fire. Frowning at a chair that had been set out, she sank down to sit in the dirt at my side.

"The romance of lounging at a fire is greatly dwarfed by the discomfort," she grumbled, shifting to pick a rock out from where she sat.

"You will rule Palaq until my return," I said without preamble.

"As you wish. Any idea how long you'll be gone?"

"Two months to reach PalTaq. A week in the palace, assuming we face nothing unexpected."

She snorted. "What qualifies as unexpected in a place that hasn't seen humans in thousands of years?"

"Call it five months round trip, then."

I was lying, but for a good reason. I would accept my punishment, but these people need not suffer for my crimes. I would make sure they were prepared to face whatever the Guild threw at them. Maybe the islanders weren't ready to conquer the world, but they could at least carve out a place for themselves. Independence was better than nothing.

"The Guild will come south in force," I said. "Many mages died in Abieszan, so they'll go there first, but expect them here soon after." The Guild would want someone to punish.

"I had thought that someday it would be us invading the mainland, not the other way around." She frowned at the fire. "We will prepare."

My fist clenched around the imagined pommel of my sword. An army gathered and awaiting my command and I was going to abandon them. I wanted so much to crush the filthy mages I was tempted to forestall my promise to free Henka until after. Defeat the Guild. Pacify the world. Secure a lasting civilization. Make sure this world was safe against the depredations of gods from other realities.

On and on.

Forever.

There would always be reasons to stall.

"Call the banners. Mobilize the islands. I go to PalTaq to reclaim my sword," I added loud enough to be sure Henka and Nokutenda heard.

"Kantlament," Phaoro whispered. "An end to all sorrows."

All sorrows?

I told myself that at least Palaq would be ready to defend themselves when the Guild came south.

With the memories gained from the Naghron shard, I now knew that every town, village, and city left from the old world had a demonic guardian hiding within, awaiting the call of the emperor. I'd seen countless abandoned villages. An army of demons were hidden in the very heart of the wizard-ruled world. And I was going to turn my back on them and go south to my doom instead.

Shalayn wandered over to join us at the fire. The swordswoman sank to her haunches in that loose and easy way she had, elbows resting on her knees. Phaoro watched with the annoyed envy of someone whose joints were long past such behaviour.

Finding a stick in the dirt, the swordswoman poked at the fire, rolling a log so sparks stuttered into the night air. "Shalayn is hiding something." Spotting a worm wriggling in the earth at her feet, she dug it free and dropped it at the edge of the fire. We watched it writhe. "Maybe *hiding* is overstating it. Let's say she has a suspicion she's never liked but could never shake."

"And?" I asked.

"She was terrified of how smart the mage is. Iremaire worked in layers, every plan concealing three others all of which were distractions from her real intent." Shalayn rolled her shoulders. "She worried stealing that stuff was too easy."

I will always be smarter than you.

"The mage thought a lot of herself," I said.

Phaoro listened with interest.

The swordswoman looked doubtful. "Iremaire once told her that you'd have to escape at some point. Shalayn got angry. She wanted you dead. The mage tried to calm her, saying you'd never *really* be free. That was when she decided to betray Iremaire."

The rest of the conversation with the mage returned to me.

Keep the ring as a reminder that I will always be smarter than you, she said, *always be ahead of you.*"

Opening my hand, I looked down at the ring on my finger. *I'll keep the ring,* I'd answered, *as a reminder that one should always strive for freedom from oppression.*

I'd been an idiot.

I'd bound Frorrat, my only portal demon, to that ring and gone to the Black Citadel. If Iremaire could scry into other realities my ego had endangered Nhil.

Mind racing, I kept my face expressionless.

I had the stasis box, which Shalayn said was protected against scrying. Did it now hide me from the mage? Had she made a critical error? I had to assume she'd not only seen and heard everything but was still scrying.

"Wizards aren't renowned for their humility," I said, in case the mage was listening, "and Iremaire is smugger than most."

I'd thought to go to the Black Citadel to prepare myself to face whatever dangers awaited us on PalTaq. That hadn't changed, but now I needed to be ready to face a powerful battlemage as well. I couldn't let Iremaire interfere with my plans. I might be prepared to die at Henka's hand, but no way the filthy mages were getting PalTaq. The palace was mine.

Shalayn used the stick to nudge the worm closer to the flames and I scowled at its twisting agony. When had I stopped thinking of it as the castle in the floating mountains? I felt sure it was after taking on the Naghron shard. Searching my new memories, I still found nothing of the place.

Turning to Phaoro I said, "Slight change of plans. I only have a few souls in my Soul Stone. I'm going to need more."

"How many?" she asked.

The memories Naghron carried in his heart were still settling into the nooks and crannies of my life. He'd known more summonings and bindings than I. How many souls would I need? Hundreds? More?

"One thousand souls," I said. I realized I had no idea how large the blood elemental under the castle was. Nhil had said it was meant for emergencies. I couldn't chance depleting it. "Blood too."

Phaoro gave a curt nod. "It will be here first thing in the morning."

I sat silently stunned. No argument. No appalled shock that I wanted to spend one thousand souls. Not even a hint of inquisitiveness as to my intentions. This was how it was supposed to be. For the first time I truly felt like what I was meant to be, an emperor, the leader of men.

A god.

"Get me clothes," I added. "An entire wardrobe. Henka too. She is my empress. Bren!" I called. "What do you want?"

"Ale."

"Get him some new boots," said Nokutenda. "I can see his toes."

"These still have some miles in them," he argued.

The sorcerer rolled her eyes.

"Get him ale and a wardrobe befitting a ship's captain," I instructed my High Priest.

Again, she nodded.

I turned to Nokutenda with a raised eyebrow.

"I'm tired of being dirty," she said. "I want a bathtub in my room. I want a hot bath every morning and then I want to fuck someone until I need another bath." She nudged Bren with a foot. "Eh, big boy?"

He blushed, scars turning pink.

"My love?" I said to Henka.

"Nothing for me."

"New clothes?"

She shook her head. "I'm enjoying the simplicity of tribal attire."

Phaoro stood and bowed low with a slight wince. "I'll see to everything."

We spent the rest of the evening drinking and eating, chatting around the fire. People and demons came and went, refilling mugs, and delivering platters of food. Right as this felt, and anxious as I was to get moving, my mood soured my enjoyment. Iremaire outsmarted me and that stung. What else had I missed?

At some point, Nokutenda staggered upright and held a hand out to Bren, which he accepted. She dragged him to his feet and the two stumbled to her tent.

"She's good for him," I said, hoping it was true.

"Perhaps," said Henka, rising and circling the fire to sit leaning against me. She felt solid with muscle, warm and alive. "But is he good for her?"

"Probably not," I admitted. "But they're both adults; they make their own mistakes."

She said nothing and my mind wandered.

When I made my desperate escape to the Black Citadel during Shalayn's attack, Nhil had been there, waiting with a crossbow. Somehow, he'd *known*. Was Iremaire not the only one spying on me? He said he was effectively trapped there. As he'd remained in the library for thousands of years, I had little reason to doubt him. But that apparently didn't mean he couldn't influence events here. When the crossbow failed to kill my assassin and I returned, Nhil immediately handed me a ring with a bound demon of possession. That hadn't been luck. He knew I'd need Shalayn alive and controlled.

I hated him for that.

A thought hit me so suddenly I felt sure it was true: I'd often wondered how my heart could have been broken with such perfect accuracy. I'd thought a shaman, skilled in reading souls, might have done it. That wasn't the case at all. Nhil was the only creature I'd met with an intellect terrifying enough to achieve such results.

"Nhil helped shatter my heart," I said to Henka. "No one else would know where to break it and what was in each shard. And I wouldn't trust anyone else."

She sat silent.

"You said I promised to destroy Nhil, and that he would never agree to breaking my heart." Was this the first time I'd caught her in an outright lie? "You said he would never allow me to escape my god's dream."

"He wouldn't," she said. "But we needed his help and so we lied about the reason it had to be broken. But we knew we couldn't trust him, that he'd try and manipulate whatever you became after."

"He has helped me where you have spied and manipulated."

Flint eyes turned in my direction. "The one thing you know—the *only* thing you know—is that I love you and will always act in your best interest."

"In what *you* see as my best interest," I corrected.

"That's true of everyone. You trust Bren. You trust he will act in what he sees as your best interest."

"Bren has never spied on me. He has never attempted to manipulate me."

"No?" she asked. "What is loyalty and friendship if not pressure to act in a certain way? The more loyal he is, the more he sacrifices to help you, the more you will do anything for him. He was nothing, a stupid cabin boy, until you saved him from drowning. Now he's a ship's captain. Later, he'll be admiral of the entire fleet."

"He's more than earned it."

Still leaning on me, I felt her shoulders shrug. "Perhaps. And what have I earned? You promised Nhil would be destroyed once your heart was broken. You said you'd arranged it. You had this *thing* in the Eye of Gods you took from a dead reality. It was some kind of elder deity, madness and savagery. It was going to do the deed."

Though until now I hadn't recalled the name, I immediately knew what she meant. I'd worn a stone bearing imprisoned gods in one of my eye sockets.

"And?" I demanded. "You know I remember none of this."

"Do I? You were going to destroy Nhil. You were going to carve out the pieces that remember me and your god. And yet Nhil is alive, you know I'm your wife, and you've already called upon your god. Who else cowers in the Black Citadel? Thalmitus?"

"Who?"

She pulled away to sit upright.

Too many questions wrestled for attention. She wasn't wrong, and yet the accusations felt like a distraction. "How did I never order you to always tell me the truth?"

"Because you didn't have to! You already ordered me to love you forever." She snorted a sarcastic laugh. "Anyway, you never much liked the unadulterated truth."

I blinked at her, unsure whether her words hit too close to an uncomfortable truth, or if she was simply lashing out in anger.

"You don't like me, do you?"

"Like you?" She smiled, sad and sweet, grey eyes softening. "You fool, I love you more than anything in this or any world. I would topple kingdoms and murder entire realities if it would make you happy." She took my hand in hers. "And I have done so."

It wasn't an answer. It was, I knew, entirely possible to love someone you didn't like.

As always, she was right. She loved me and had no choice but to act in my best interest. And yet I'd lied to her about killing Nhil, hiding the demon away. Unless Nhil had somehow escaped the god I sent after him and fled to the Black Citadel. What if the only reason he hadn't returned was because that god still hunted him, awaiting his return?

I searched for clues in my interactions with the demon, some sign of anger or distrust in him, and found nothing. Either Nhil escaped and knew I'd tried to kill him, or I'd lied to Henka. Either I could trust my demonic friend, or he'd been plotting revenge for the last three thousand years.

No, I decided. Nhil could have easily killed me in the Citadel many times over. I'd been weak with starvation and thirst, an easy victim. I spent countless nights sleeping on the library floor at his feet. When I took the heart from the other Khraen who'd somehow stumbled upon the bubble reality, I was helpless for days.

Unless Nhil plotted something far more sinister.

I saw only one answer that made sense: At one time I'd trusted both Henka and Nhil enough to let them play their parts in breaking my heart, but later lied to my wife. Something must have changed, and I'd decided I trusted the demon more than my enslaved lover.

Or I was wrong about everything.

Could they be working together against me, Henka pretending she still had no choice but to love me, Nhil feigning friendship?

My skull hurt, worries chasing each other in endless circles.

CHAPTER FIFTY-FIVE

I woke the next morning hungover and feeling like a mouldering washcloth left out in the sun. Rolling over with a groan, I found myself alone. I crawled from the sweltering oven of my tent on hands and knees in search of water. A priest stood waiting with a full skin, handing it to me the moment I croaked at her. Apparently, such behaviour wasn't uncommon among gods.

Regaining some mental faculties, I managed to stand. Most of the camp had already been broken, tents packed away for the trip back to Palaq, wagons loaded, carthorses chewing cud, waiting with the kind of enviable patience I only achieved when this hungover.

I resisted the urge to ask the priest what happened last night. She wouldn't know, and whiskey-fogged memories were creeping back to me. In what was either cowardice or wisdom, I'd decided against chasing Henka for more answers. Since I had no means of telling truth from falsehood, there seemed little point. It would wait until I was back in PalTaq and could coerce her to truth.

At least, that was last night's decision. Now, in the light of a rising sun, I remembered the truth didn't matter. The truth didn't change what I had done to the woman I loved. I understood any questions I might ask were a distraction, a search for reasons not to go through with what I promised.

The *Katlipok* sat lower in the water, loaded with supplies for the journey to come.

Phaoro appeared at my side. "The ship is ready to go. Are you sure you wouldn't rather wait for a more trustworthy vessel? Give me three days, and I can have a war galley crewed and ready to leave."

I shook my head and winced. "We leave now."

"Of course." She lifted a small leather pouch tied closed. "Soul Stones. The largest has ninety-six facets, and there are three of those. All told, one thousand souls."

I accepted the bag of diamonds. Ignoring the souls, there was enough wealth in this pouch to keep me and my friends in the lap of luxury for the rest of our lives. Bren could own a fleet of ships and open a few taverns as a hobby. We could forget our various dreams of vengeance and redemption and live in comfort.

I wanted to laugh, but it would hurt too much. How many times had I held wealth enough to support myself and turned my back on the easy path?

"There are several barrels of blood in the hold," said Phaoro. "I've assigned a sorcerer to your crew. His job is to keep the blood chilled so it doesn't go bad before you can use it. I've also ordered KriskOrke to travel with you. He's a talented demonologist and will aid you as needed."

I'd have to make several trips to carry the barrels to the Black Citadel. Happily, that would be less of an issue now that I didn't have to worry about running out of souls.

A wave of dizziness and disgust washed over me. I closed my eyes, trying to understand my emotions. I felt nothing at the thought of the people who died to fill the barrels. Bleeding slaves was nothing, though I didn't want to have to do it myself. The souls in the stones were a valuable resource, and I was happy not to have to be quite so miserly in spending them.

A small chuckle escaped me as I understood. I was disgusted by my lack of disgust. The revulsion I once felt was gone. In taking on the Naghron shard, I murdered yet another part of myself.

More of my heart waited in Shalayn's stasis box. What would be left?

I had a choice to make, and it had to be made now.

The young man who met Shalayn would never enslave someone he loved. Her freedom and willingness were a large part of what he loved about her. The emperor, on the other hand, thought nothing of shredding souls. He was so terrified of trust he stole Henka's freedom to protect himself. I realized how close I'd come to succumbing to the lure of his power. I kept saying I was going to PalTaq to free Henka, and yet constantly thought about the treasure awaiting me there—Kantlament, my stone eyes, ancient artifacts beyond count—and what I might do with them.

If I took on even one more sliver of his heart, I would fall to temptation.

I was a young man who wanted good and evil to be black and white, a hard line delineating the two so there could be no confusion. I was an old man who knew the words were meaningless, more useful as tools of manipulation than viable concepts. The moment you accepted that truth, you were reduced to arguing shades of grey victim to subjective interpretation. Kill a man and his brother will say you are evil. Kill a man to save another, and the one you saved will say you've done a good deed.

"Keep Palaq safe," I instructed Phaoro. "Prepare for war."

I left without another word, unable to look back at the people I was abandoning.

Once onboard, I retired to the captain's cabin, which Bren refused to take despite my insistence. He claimed one of the officer's rooms instead, saying he wouldn't know what to do with more space. Someone had carried my pack onboard, depositing it on the table.

Henka joined me, sitting cross-legged on the bed in silence with her eyes closed. With no need to rest, I wondered what she was doing. Most likely communicating with distant spies, I decided.

"Are you in communication with any dead on PalTaq?" I asked.

She shook her head without opening her eyes.

"You left spies on Palaq though?"

Eyes still closed, she nodded.

I frowned at her. "What are you doing?"

"I have spies in WestWatch and EastWatch. Any fleet leaving Taramlae will stop at one of those ports before heading south. When they do, I can warn Phaoro that the Guild is less than a month away."

An hour later, we were sailing south, following the coast. Bren, dressed in his new clothes, polished black leather boots rattling the deck as he walked, knocked on our door, entering when I invited him in.

He carried a map, laying it out reverently on the table for me to see.

"This is the most detailed map I've ever seen," he said. "I can't guarantee its accuracy, but the parts I'm familiar with—" He pointed out the many islands east of Palaq "—look very good."

Henka forgotten, I moved to stand at his side. The detail was incredible, the work of a dedicated artist and cartographer. Coloured ink, faded with time, differentiated grasslands from forests and deserts. The far north was a range of ice-locked mountains reaching across the world to the Deredi homelands, where it ran into a younger range of sharper peaks and ridges.

"How old is this map?" I asked.

"The Grand Admiral gave it to me on Phaoro's orders. He said it was over one hundred years old and copied from a map that was closer to two thousand years old."

This ancient map was likely made one thousand years or more after the Demon Emperor's fall.

Seeing my expression, Bren added, "Some of the city names have changed, but they're still recognizable."

It was a world of ruins. Much of the eastern coast of the mainland to the south of the Deredi appeared to be shattered cities.

I pointed one out. "Even stuff like this?"

"Few venture to such ruins and fewer still return. I've heard stories of ancient magics run amuck. The Guild got desperate in the last days of the war. Spells were attempted by massive circles of mages pooling their power. Some failed catastrophically, forever savaging the very fabric of reality." He pointed out a desert south of the Deredi Mountains labelled *The Undying Lands*. "This was the site of one of the largest battles. Hundreds of thousands died here, men and women, demons and elementals. A necromancer tried an experimental spell, attempting to raise them all in a single go. She succeeded but was slain shortly after. Now the entire area is populated by the dead."

I glanced at Henka, wondering if she controlled all of them. Eyes closed, she showed no sign of listening.

"Dead demons," continued Bren. "Dead elementals. Entire armies of corpses. I heard a madman in a tavern tell a story of a band of freebooters who ran into an undead fire elemental." He shivered. "Maybe he was crazy, but I just about shit myself."

Leaning close, I squinted at the map. There were hints of structures hidden in every forest and jungle.

"The Guild don't care enough to update the maps," Bren said. "The ocean is too dangerous."

The ocean we were about to spend two months sailing.

I focussed on the islands. Palaq was much larger than the others, Khaal and Jhalaal included. PalTaq was bigger than all of them put together. The map showed it as a land of black mountains and smouldering volcanoes. Located on the eastern coast, the palace took up too much of the island. It had to be a fanciful exaggeration.

Bren pointed out scattered islands between Palaq and PalTaq with a blunt and scarred finger. "They're not all shown, but there are enough islets littered about we shouldn't have any trouble restocking our water supply. As long as we avoid the local tribes; most are cannibalistic."

Henka stood, unfolding like a cat, and joined us at the map. "You have the pieces Shalayn collected?" she asked, knowing the answer.

"I do." I didn't mention the box. She either already knew or didn't need to.

"Will you take them before you go to the Black Citadel?"

"I don't think so," I said as if only now thinking about it. "I'll do it as soon as I arrive. I want to know what new summonings I'll remember."

Henka's unhappy expression twisted my gut. It hurt to disappoint my love.

Hoping she'd refuse, I said, "Come with me."

She blinked in surprise, and I wondered how much of such reactions were conscious manipulation and how much was ancient habit left from her previous life.

"No," she said. "The dry air is murder on my skin."

"I have plenty of blood," I said, tempted to see how far I could push her.

"No," she repeated. "There are things here needing my attention. I need to prepare for PalTaq."

I suspected I'd be returning to an undead crew. It was probably for the best. They'd be harder to stop, if it came to violence, and would work tirelessly. With barrels of blood in the lower hold, she'd have no trouble maintaining them.

Inspiration struck. "Bren, how about you?"

"What?" he asked, startled.

"Come to the Black Citadel. I'd appreciate the company."

"Well, I mean…I'm the captain…"

"Please," I said.

"Of course."

"Ask Nokutenda to join us, if you want."

He brightened at that.

After he left, Henka pulled me into a tight hug. "Be careful, don't attempt anything too dangerous."

It felt like a subtle warning to be on my guard around Nhil.

"I'll be careful," I promised.

I spent the rest of the day memorizing one corner of the cabin I shared with Henka, and then flitting back and forth between the *Katlipok* and the library delivering food, wine, ale, and barrels of blood. The first time I appeared, Nhil looked up from the book he was reading and then ignored me after that. I took my time, resting between each transition so as not to distress myself as I had last time. I made no attempt to keep track of the number of souls I spent transporting luxuries to the Black Citadel.

It was all so easy.

Would anyone be different? If I trapped the most moral person in the world in the Black Citadel and told them the only way to save themselves was to spend the immortal soul of another—someone who was already dead—would they hesitate? I thought not.

Once everything was delivered, I went back once for a wine bottle opener, and a second time when I realized I'd forgotten to pack socks.

Late that evening, I took dinner in the cabin with Henka, and she convinced me to stay one last night and leave in the morning. After, she took away my worries, made every doubt and suspicion seem foul.

As I lay in a blissful fog, my mind wandered. Henka gave and she gave, and I took, and I took. Even now, knowing what I'd done to her, knowing she had no choice but to try and make me happy, I'd taken advantage of her. Would I have been better to refuse her advances because, at some level, they weren't genuine? I mocked myself for the stupidity of the question and loathed the man who only realized such things after he'd sated his needs. I told myself that, had I resisted Henka's advances, she would have been suspicious. The truth was I hadn't given it a thought. I wanted to ask her if an innately selfish man could aspire to be better but worried that too might cause suspicion.

Unable to find an answer, knowing I'd succumb to her charms every time, I slept.

Bren and Nokutenda were packed and ready when I woke. After kissing Henka goodbye, I collected my own pack and asked them to step close. I'd never brought anyone else to the Black Citadel like this but felt sure it would work. Holding one in each arm, I closed my eyes, picturing the library.

Nhil looked up from his book when we appeared, violet eyes doing their mistimed blink. "I see you've brought company."

"It's a bit late to pretend you're surprised or that you don't know exactly what's going on."

"Do I look surprised?" he asked. "No, I don't think I do."

I introduced the demon to my friends. Nhil was flawlessly polite, dipping a bow to each before I led them from the library. Trailing me through the long halls, they peered into every room we passed, awed by the extravagant wealth carelessly displayed. Finding an empty suite that looked like it had been tidied and dusted but moments ago, I waved them in.

Spotting the window at the far end, Bren crossed to look out. He stared at the nightmare sky spiralling in to be swallowed by the imprisoned Lord of Hell hanging like a reverse sun above the floating mountains.

Nokutenda joined him, peering over his shoulder. "Where are we?"

"Different world," I said. "Past that, it's difficult to explain."

It would have been more honest to say that I hadn't a clue where we were. Of what value was a concept like geographical location when discussing alien realities. I left them there to unpack and get settled, promising to collect them on my way back, and headed to the chambers at the top of the highest tower.

The rack where the crimson armour had hung sat empty and accusing, and I was glad for it. The room felt cleaner for the absence. Dumping my belongings on the floor, I walked the room, pausing at the oil painting of Henka caught in the act of turning away. Familiar because I'd been here many times, and yet also strange. Naghron knew nothing of this place and no new memories crept to the surface.

I sat for a long while on the edge of the bed, contemplating the many demons now available to me. Assuming Iremaire couldn't spy on me here, I had a chance to arrange surprises. The most tempting option would be to summon and bind several massive and deadly manifestation demons to travel with me as bodyguards. Unfortunately, she'd see them and be able to arrange her own magical responses, likely nullifying their powers. If the Guild kept any kind of records, she might be able to research each demon to find its weaknesses. Something subtler was in order. I considered several possibilities but wanted to check with Nhil first to make sure I was safe from scrying.

I also wanted to confront him on his own spying.

Deciding I'd given Bren and the sorcerer enough time to unpack, I returned to their room, taking a longer more circuitous route because I wanted to refresh the Black Citadel in my memories. I found them sitting on the bed, facing each other.

Nokutenda saw me first. "I keep worrying that I'm an idiot for believing you might be the Demon Emperor returned to save his people, and then you do something like this." She waved vaguely at the sprawling citadel beyond.

"I'm not sure me being the Demon Emperor reborn saves you from being an idiot," I joked.

Bren snorted. "I told you his sense of humour was terrible."

"The worst," she agreed.

"Come," I said, turning away. "Let's see if we can squeeze some truth out of a demon."

They followed me back to the library. Nhil was as we'd left him, standing with a massive tome open and held in one hand, the other rubbing at his smooth chin.

"I thought you knew every book in the citadel," I accused.

"Sometimes I like to read the more beautiful passages again."

"Why reread something you've memorized?"

Lifting the book, he stuck his nose into the crease, inhaling deeply. "I like the feel of the paper and the smell of old books."

"I think a Guild battlemage has been scrying on me," I said.

Focussing on me from between the pages, he raised a single eyebrow. "Why and how."

I lifted my hand with Frorrat's ring, fingers spread.

"Oh," he said. "Shit."

Whatever rejoinder I'd had in mind died. "Are you sure?"

"Quite," he said.

"Can Iremaire scry on us right now?"

For the first time, he looked uncertain. "I'm a little out of date on Guild advancements," he admitted. "But I'd say no, probably not."

"Probably? What happened to the great and all-knowing demon of knowledge?"

"I haven't set foot in your world for three thousand years."

"Hmn," I grunted. "Speaking of my world, care to explain how you knew I was going to need a loaded crossbow?"

Violet eyes studied me.

"Iremaire isn't the only one spying on me," I said.

"You and I," he said, "exist on different levels. We see things differently, time included."

"You're telling me you know the future?"

"Don't be ridiculous. Predictable as you are, there are still too many variables at play to calculate the outcome of so many mortal indecisions."

"You mean decisions," I corrected.

"No, it's the things you waffle on that make the calculations difficult."

"For that matter," I continued, talking over him, "why didn't you give me the ring the first time?"

Nhil handed me a loaded crossbow, and I stared at the thing in shock.

"Where did that come from?" blurted Nokutenda. "And can I have—"

He handed her one as well.

She immediately began looking around the room for something to shoot at.

"Not the books, please," I said.

Nhil said, "Many of the demons in the citadel obey me," offering Bren a crossbow as well. "Many of us are either much faster than humans or acting on a different timescale altogether. I told you I hadn't left the library in several millennia, but you also knew that I was able to give orders to some of the other demons here and many of the elementals. Whenever you needed a sword or armour to bind a demon, there was always one ready. Not once did I sluggishly wander off to fetch it for you." He sniffed with disdain, as if appalled that I might question his loyalty. "You arrived wounded, naked, and desperate. I saw you needed a weapon and since you left here with a demon sword, I assumed it hadn't been of much help. In the fraction of an instant I had, I decided a ranged weapon might be of more use and handed you the first thing that came to mind. Understand that while I went nowhere, the crossbow was delivered to me by a minor portal demon with a very specific set of instructions. You immediately vanished without a hint as to what you faced. Well, now that I had more time—several seconds to be precise—I decided it would be wise to have something else ready in case the crossbow failed. I gambled you faced a human enemy and hopefully not another powerful demonologist, and ordered the ring fetched. You returned and I handed it to you. I was about to explain the limitations of the demon and query as to your struggle but you, as you so colourfully like to put it, fucked off before I had the chance."

"So, you aren't spying on me?"

He snapped the book closed. "You aren't that interesting."

I wasn't sure if I was relieved or disappointed. If he was spying, he could have told me everything Henka was up to.

My hope I might turn the tables by spying on Iremaire died. "And you aren't lying?"

He rolled one eye.

"Ew, yuck!" said Nokutenda, looking queasy. "Please don't do that again."

Deciding to take Nhil at his word, and knowing I had little choice, I said, "Nokutenda, I apologize, but I need to talk with Bren and Nhil."

She looked from me to Bren. "Fine, but I'm keeping the crossbow."

"You know your way back to your room?" I asked.

She nodded. "I'm going to find something to shoot on the way back."

Plucking Bren's crossbow from his hands, she left. I considered telling her not to shoot anything valuable and decided I didn't care.

Bren watched her leave with a confused blend of fondness and glum acceptance. "I'm not sure I can be what she wants me to be."

I felt much the same about Henka. "I'm not sure either of us understands what women want."

"She's terrifying."

"All women are. I have a plan," I said, changing the subject. "Nhil, you're not going to like it, but I need your help. My mind is made up. Promise you won't try and convince me to change it."

"What is the point of having a demonic advisor if you're going to limit the advice he can give to that which you want to hear?"

"Promise," I said, "or I'll discuss this with Bren and forgo your council altogether."

Thin grey lips pursed in thought. "Fine," he said.

"Say it."

"This is foolish."

"Promise me."

The demon looked away, shaking his head. "I promise not to attempt to dissuade you from whatever stupidity you have planned. And let it be noted, the fact you are asking this of me means you already know it's stupid."

"He has a point," said Bren.

"Listen to your friend. He's smart."

"I'm going to free Henka," I said.

"I was right," said Nhil.

"Hey!" I barked. "You promised!"

"Factual statements are not attempts at persuasion."

"Why would freeing Henka be stupid?" I demanded.

"You already know the answer."

"Because she'll kill me?"

Crossing his arms, Nhil said nothing.

"I'd say I've more than earned that punishment."

Still, he said nothing.

"Unless there's something you're not telling me."

Grey face expressionless, he didn't move.

"I still remember almost nothing about Henka," I said, watching for a reaction. "I don't remember first meeting her, or how I got her heart, or who she was before I met her."

Nhil could have been a statue.

"You know more about her than I do. Tell me what I've forgotten. Tell me why freeing Henka is a bad idea."

When he opened his mouth to speak, I added, "Beyond the fact she'll kill me, which I already know."

His mouth snapped closed.

"You can't tell me," I said. "Or you won't?"

No reaction.

He once told me I'd freed him and had ignored my commands on several occasions. Had he long ago made promises to me he was now forced to keep? Was I once again my own worst enemy, or was this something I'd foreseen and planned for? That seemed unlikely, such foresight being more Henka's strength than mine.

"I *need* to do this," I said.

Violet eyes stared into mine, unblinking.

"I wanted you to be the emperor," said Bren, "to free the islands from the choking grip of the Guild. I wanted you to give islanders a reason to walk proud, to show the world we're not stained souls, force the mainlanders to see us as equals. I didn't much care what it cost." He made a fist, stared at the scarred knuckles.

"Please don't say a pointless act of love is more important than all of that," said Nhil.

"A pointless act of love is more important than all of that," said Bren, releasing the fist. "I suppose I'm a romantic. It's my one flaw."

"Who is Henka?" I demanded of Nhil. "What is she?"

"She is the Queen of the Dead," he answered. "Once, long ago, you chose to lock her in chains of servitude."

Terrible memories scratched at the edge of consciousness.

"You know something that will change my mind about freeing her and either can't or won't tell me."

Nhil said nothing.

Henka would remain my enslaved wife forever.

Nothing could make that right.

Knowing I couldn't coerce the demon, I turned away. Lurching into the hall, picking a direction at random, I walked. Enslaving someone you love is wrong. It had to be wrong. If Nhil changed my mind and I accepted the one crime still haunting me, what would be left? What kind of man could do all of that and feel nothing?

Hours later, Bren found me slumped in a massive leather chair in one of the citadel's many libraries. He carried an unopened bottle of whiskey in each hand.

Hesitating at the entrance, he said, "May I join you?"

I nodded.

Sitting across from me in another leather chair polished to a buttery shine, he cracked open both bottles and handed me one.

When I accepted it, he raised his in salute. "To those infinitesimal parts of ourselves we still like. And to the women who find those little bits and peel back the shit so we can see them for ourselves."

We drank.

Did Henka do that for me, or did she feed the parts I hated? It was strange to know that while she wanted what was best for me, I didn't know what she thought that was. The suffering of others in no way entered the equation. She gave no thought to right and wrong, good and evil.

"There was a woman," said Bren. "I knew her a long time ago." He took a long drink. "Well, a long time ago for some, not so long ago for others."

He told me a story of love and pirates.

BREN TELLS A STORY

Captain Luscane, an unrepentant pirate and one of the angriest women I've ever met, once told me that falling in love is a lot like buying a new pair of boots.

You start off head over heels. These are the best boots you've ever owned! But then, inevitably, they start to chafe. They're uncomfortable and feel like they're trying to force your foot into some awkward new shape rather than conforming to the bones defining you. They look so good though you hesitate to let them go. And what's a little discomfort? You go through this with every pair of boots anyway, right? So, you give them a little time. Maybe your foot changes a little where the leather won't give, and the boot gives where your foot refuses. Soon, you have the best boots you've ever owned. They're comfortable and still new enough they look great. All you see is what's right about them.

But as the philosophers say, time wounds all bootheels. Your new boots become scuffed and ragged. They lose their lustre, the leather worn and cracked. Maybe they don't look quite as good as they used to but they're comfortable. They might even be the most comfortable pair of boots you've ever worn. Where at first, you loved them for being the beautiful and shiny boots they were, you now grow fond of them in a way that's surprisingly much deeper than what you used to feel. These boots have become a part of you, and you swear that you'll never let them go. If anything goes wrong, you fix it. Heel worn to nothing? No problem. You treat them to an expensive evening at the best cobbler in town. Laces fray and break? That too is soon fixed with some flashy new ties, though perhaps you frown for a moment at how out of place these new laces look on your old boots. But you shrug it off because they're still more comfortable than anything you've previously tried on.

At some point, someone will point out your boots are looking a little scruffy. Pretty them up as you might with spit, polish, and a good bit of friendly rubbing, they'll never look as good as they used to. You become more aware of your boots and notice that, while they're comfortable, there are certainly a lot of better-looking boots out there. So, you step into a shop, just for a moment, to try on something new.

Good as they look, they rub you in all the wrong ways and you rush back to your comfortable old boots having learned your lesson.

Here's the thing with boots though. Unless you baby them, constantly careful not to step in shit or drag your heels, eventually they become damaged beyond repair. But you love these boots. You walk in the memory of their comfort, at first unaware that they're no longer quite so comfortable. Even when you finally notice they're hurting you, you still refuse to part with your trusty boots. You've been through a lot together and they've been good boots; you're not going to abandon them just because of a little discomfort. You get desperate. You take them to better cobblers, spend more and more money trying to get back that old feeling. Sometimes they hurt so much you begin to look fondly at some of the old boots you used to enjoy wearing still piled awaiting your attention in the closet. Maybe you even slip one of them on for a bit, though inevitably you remember why you stopped wearing them.

The sad truth is, we are creatures of habit, addicted to simple comforts, slow to change even when the current situation is doing us harm. You will wear those ragged old boots long after you should have cast them aside. They'll cause you endless pain, doing permanent damage, if you're stubborn enough. It's not easy, but as you age, you learn to see the warning signs earlier.

Now, different people deal with all this in different ways. Some like to have several pairs of boots and cycle between them, wearing each for a while and then setting them aside before they become too worn.

I see no reason why a woman can't have several pairs of boots, she told me. And that doesn't mean you value them any less. Let's face it, there are boots good for stomping about the deck and other boots more at home dancing a jig in a tavern.

Others, like my ma, pick that one pair of boots and wear it until they die. By the end, the damned things are held together by twine and goat-gut glue. They say they're happy with their crumbling old boots, but you'll notice they never take them for long walks. I suppose it's possible there's some way to get your boots past that uncomfortable damaging stage when they first fall apart, but I've never mastered it.

Personally, I think folks should try on as many boots as they like. See some nice boots? Take them for a walk! Find a pair you really like? Keep them until they become annoying.

Lying on the bed in her cabin, I looked up at Captain Luscane and asked, "Why are you telling me all this?"

"Ain't exactly the shiniest pair of boots, are you?" she said. "Look. You're a lovely new set of boots and I tried you on. Even went for more than one walk because I liked them so much. But you're desperate to be comfortable boots and I'm not much interested in just having the one pair."

"What?" I'm not proud, but there may have been a slight quiver to my voice.

"There are several other pairs of boots on this ship I'd like to take for a walk," she said.

"I don't mind," I lied. "You're the captain."

"You do mind, and that's what I like most about you. It's dumb but sweet."

"So why don't you—"

She cut me off with that imperious hand-wave-thing all captains have when they get tired of explaining something to a stupid deckhand.

"You're a fine pair of boots and I like the way you look on me, but I'm not looking to invest in any long-term footwear at the moment. So put your boots on and get out of my cabin."

I stared at Bren, confused. "I'm not entirely sure I understand the point of that story."

"Do all stories have to have a point?"

"Yes, I think so. Otherwise, what's the point?"

"Fine. I guess the point is that I'm not a nice shiny new pair of boots and Nokutenda deserves better."

"Isn't that her choice?"

He took a long drink from the bottle. "Too many times I've been the boots causing the damage."

That struck too close to home, and I too drank.

"I come out of every relationship with a broken heart," Bren continued, "and you probably haven't noticed, but sometimes I set myself up for the pain."

"I hadn't noticed," I lied.

"It's like I'm desperate for the drama." Bren swirled the bottle, frowning at the liquid within. "It's my one flaw. But I've never given much thought to what I left behind. I was always focussed on how wrecked *I* was. It wasn't until Tien that I realized—" He stopped, glared at the bottle, and took another long swig. "I don't want to be the one that damages Nokutenda. She's suffered enough. The Guild. Her family. I don't need to add to that."

"I think this might be a conversation you should have with her," I suggested.

"I did. She told me I was a fool, that love is nothing like boots. She said it was more like a smelly cheese. I didn't really understand what she was on about."

CHAPTER FIFTY-SEVEN

The next morning, I told Bren and Nokutenda to entertain themselves as I would be busy. I promised we'd take evening meals together any time they wanted company, but to otherwise enjoy themselves. We had plenty of food and booze.

I found Nhil waiting for me in the library. We didn't speak, and he stood motionless, eternally patient, as I paced the room in thought.

One thousand souls.

I asked, and Phaoro handed me a bag of diamonds the next morning like it was nothing. Had my priests been busy all night rounding up the city's unwanted and sacrificing them, or had Naghron kept such a supply on hand?

One thousand immortal souls I would feed to demons, forever destroying them. Less than a thousand, I realized. I'd already spent several travelling back and forth between the *Katlipok* and the Black Citadel with supplies. I had no idea how many I spent. Somehow, I'd gone from counting every soul, feeling the crushing burden of each, to spending them like flinging copper coins at the poor.

Rather than being upset at what I planned, I found myself annoyed at the limitations forced upon me. Instead of surrounding myself with monstrous bodyguards, I could only use demons Iremaire couldn't see. And there were still demons I couldn't summon, even with one thousand souls. Some required live sacrifices, pain and torture being part of the ritual.

Someday I would restock the Black Citadel's larders, keep a supply of living—

I stopped pacing, angry at myself.

"I used to have robes with demons bound to every thread."

Nhil said nothing.

"We have robes here I could use?"

"Of course," he answered.

"How many threads in a typical set of robes?"

"The full-length robes in storage all have over two hundred and twenty-five thousand threads," he answered without hesitation, as if keeping track of the thread-count in each article of clothing in the Black Citadel were simply part of his job.

"Exactly how many threads does my shirt have?" I asked.

"If I answer, you'll have to count to see if I'm lying. The only way to do that accurately would be to pull the shirt apart. Let's not waste time."

"But you know, don't you?"

"Of course."

"Smug—"

"Fucker," finished Nhil. "Careful, you're becoming predictable."

As emperor I'd owned scores of robes like that. My wardrobe alone represented millions of sacrificed souls fed to demons. They weren't all human though. There were sentient souls in an infinite number of worlds, and I'd harvested many. There were at least three worlds I'd stripped of life in wars of genocide to feed one Lord of Hell or another.

Fine. I didn't have to bind demons to each individual thread to make decent armour. With perhaps three layers, each with a different demon, I could make a protection that looked like normal clothing but would be invulnerable to most attacks. Iremaire would have no idea how well-protected I was until it was too late.

Searching through the summonings I knew, I found my memories jumbled and chaotic. Not only had I rediscovered them out of order, but key moments remained missing that would connect them in a more meaningful tapestry. It felt like walking into a library of a thousand books I once read. I couldn't list them, but if someone mentioned a title, I would know that I'd read it. Likewise, if someone described a book, I'd remember details but likely not the title.

That Nhil knew the title and contents of every book just made him more annoying.

"I have one thousand souls," I said. "I remember countless summonings but can't decide what to start with."

"Your first thought should be to ward yourself against scrying."

The moment he spoke I remembered demons who could do that. The basements beneath the palace in PalTaq were warded against spying of any kind.

I understood: That was why Iremaire let me go. If I carried this ring into the basement, I'd effectively bypass all the wards keeping her out.

"Of course," mused Nhil, "the simplest thing you can do to protect yourself is destroy that ring and bind a new portal demon. If she can't find you, she can't attack you."

"I don't like leaving an enemy behind me," I said. "As long as she doesn't know I'm aware of her spying, I can arrange a trap and kill her."

Making no attempt to be convincing, Nhil gave me a look of confusion. "But why? You've already said you're planning on dying. Why waste time with the mage when you can easily avoid a confrontation? Why risk losing to her and missing out on the chance to go through with your stupid plan?"

All good questions. He was right, it was the smart thing to do.

"She interfered."

"You mean she angered you and you want her to feel your wrath. Foolishness. Even if you defeat the battlemage, the cost will be high. Ward the ship and your crew—"

"The crew?"

"You have to assume the mage is scrying on others as a backup to spying on you. If you're protected, but the person next to you isn't, she can still keep tabs on you. Teleport spells are not like using portal demons," Nhil explained. "Where you can memorize and visualize a location, wizards need to see where they're teleporting to."

"Know a lot about wizardry, don't you, demon?"

"What kind of advisor would I be if I didn't?"

I decided not to answer that. "You're wrong. There's more at stake here than my need to punish a mage. If I vanish, Iremaire will get curious. I can't chance her turning her attention on Palaq. Phaoro needs more time to prepare before she faces the Guild. I will buy her that time. Given the chance, she will lead the islands to freedom."

"Such benevolent self-sacrifice," he said.

"Such smug self-satisfaction," I answered.

"You're not going to ward yourself against her spying?"

"No. I want her feeling safe and in control. I want her to come to me so I can kill her."

Nhil crossed slim arms. "Which is more important, freeing Henka or protecting the islands?"

"I can do both."

"Maybe," he said. "But your chances of success will greatly improve if you focus on a single goal."

"You're trying to convince me to give up on freeing Henka?"

"Not at all. I am simply pointing out that if you work at cross purposes, you reduce your odds of success. When you are dead you will no longer care what Iremaire does. When you are dead, she can pillage the palace to her heart's content or drown the islanders in blood and it will not matter to you."

"It matters to me *now*."

"Short-sighted."

"That mage almost ruined everything. People I care about suffered because of her interference. She thought she could use me. She thought she could outsmart me."

"She did."

"Get out."

For an uncomfortable moment I glared at him while he studied me with calm detachment.

Then, with a small bow, Nhil left.

"I don't need your help!" I shouted after him. "I'm the damned Demon Emperor!"

Alone with the musty smell of old books, my rage filled the room, a tangible force.

"Smug bastard doesn't know his place," I muttered.

Except he did and he was dangerously intelligent. Had that been exactly what he wanted?

I couldn't see what he might hope to gain.

Leaving the library to echo with the memory of my emotions, I descended to the summoning chambers in the lower level. Nhil was right, the smart thing to do would be to avoid all confrontations and focus on freeing Henka. Everything else was a distraction.

And yet, I couldn't.

Mages should know their place. Iremaire had let slip that she was born not long after the fall of the emperor. She never knew me, grew up hearing only the Guild's version of events. Had she been a few decades older, she would have known better.

Unwilling to ask Nhil for help, I spent hours lugging barrels of blood to the basement. I could have summoned one of the citadel's many earth elementals to carry them for me but needed to work off my frustrations. By the time I had the third barrel in place, my arms shook, sweat soaking my shirt. The physical labour had done nothing to improve my mood. Instead, I'd worked myself into a seething rage. Lungs heaving, I studied the summoning chamber, gaze tracing the pacts engraved in the granite.

I'd show him.

I didn't want another sword, or spirit demons warding me against attack. I didn't want rings that spat hellfire or demonic gloves that would give me the strength to shatter stone in my fists.

I wanted to shake the world. I wanted the very fabric of reality to quiver in terror before my wrath.

One thousand souls.

Why settle for a handful of demons when I could bind something truly horrific?

It was a shame King Grone, the elemental Demon Lord, had apparently taken up permanent residence in my world. He would have been perfect. There was only one elemental Demon Lord more terrifying than Grone, and that was…

I grinned at the rune-carved floor. "Karatal."

I'd banished the elemental demon to some distant hell three thousand years before the empire fell. Iremaire would have no concept of the power she faced. Even a circle of battlemages was no challenge to something like Karatal. Like that library, once I'd spotted the cover of the book I wanted, its contents came rushing back. I knew the summoning and binding spells and I had enough souls, though there wouldn't be many left over. The more I thought about it, the more perfect the idea became. A spirit demon, Karatal had no physical form, though she could appear as a maelstrom of fire. I could bind her to an object, trapping her within until I called.

Iremaire could spy all she wanted and see no hint of the demon. The instant the mage appeared, I'd free Karatal with a single word.

Decision made, I worked fast, pouring blood into the grooves sunk in the summoning room floor. Nhil would be appalled, but even he'd have to admit the brilliance of my plan. Once the mage was dead, I could give the ring to Brenwick and instruct Nokutenda to deliver him to Phaoro in Palaq. Or I could command the demon to obey my friend, and he could be the man who freed the islands. That seemed just and fitting. Bren deserved to be a hero.

Rage honed my will to a vicious stiletto.

I called Karatal to this pocket universe, trapping it in the wards, and prepared to bind the elemental lord to one of the diamonds I'd emptied summoning her. The others, still containing their burden of souls, I held in my other hand, ready for the binding. Searing light filled the room, blinding me, heat climbing until sweat ran off me in rivers. Eyes clenched, I retreated a step. Through my lids I saw twisting snakes of red so bright they seared traces on my retinas.

Something was wrong.

"I bind—" My voice cracked, throat parched.

I drew breath to try again, and my lungs burned. The stench of singed hair filled the room as I retreated another step, confused. This wasn't right, the wards should contain Karatal and her power. Sheltering my face with a hand, I cracked one eye open, squinting at the wards.

Steaming, bubbling blood.

I'd splashed blood on one of the symbols in my haste, causing an imperfection in the protective ward.

YOU! Karatal filled the area defined by the sigils, pressed against the defences until the wards crackled, buckling beneath the assault.

"No," I tried to say, my lips splitting and weeping.

Savage hate throttled thought, crushing evil leeching the air from the room. Karatal was destruction and chaos, a feral force of nature, entropy personified, anathema to life.

YOU. I WILL BURN YOU FOR AN ETERNITY.

It was impossible. I'd summoned and bound things ten thousand times more powerful than Karatal. I knew every detail of the binding, had spent centuries learning and then practicing it. I retreated another step in stunned confusion.

When I summoned the pathetic little demons for the swords and armour, I'd crawled around on the floor searching for imperfections. I'd been meticulous and careful. This time, summoning an elemental Demon Lord, I'd been sloppy and careless. I wanted to somehow blame Nhil for this, but the bastard wasn't here.

The vision in my open eye turned white, then red, and then nothing. Not even black, it was just gone, a hole in a non-existent reality.

The sweat in my hair steamed, hissing, and then was gone.

With a deafening *crack*, the granite floor shattered.

YOU WILL BURN!

I ran, fleeing blind with a hand thrown out before me. Rebounding off walls, I lost all sense of direction. I hit something low, a table perhaps, and sprawled on the floor. In trying to catch myself, I dropped the diamonds, heard them skitter across stone. The heat was everywhere and climbing with each heartbeat. The floor felt like a woodstove. Though one eye saw nothing, the other saw pink-tinted white through the clenched lid. I dared not open it. The stink of smouldering fabric joined the smell of burning hair. Crawling, I felt for the diamonds, my hands burning with each touch. Finding one, I grabbed it tight, and screamed in pain. Reason fled and I knew only one thing: I had to leave, had to get somewhere cooler.

I built the cabin I shared with Henka on the *Katlipok* in my thoughts and fed Frorrat a soul.

Nothing happened and I roared in agony.

BURN!

Had I missed some detail in my panic? Were there no souls in this stone?

    I tried again.

    Nothing.

    Sobbing and whimpering, my hands and knees searing and then going numb and cold, I crawled until I found another diamond and tried again.

    Nothing.

    BURN!

    Stone exploded, peppering me with sharp shards. Building the library in my thoughts, I fed the portal demon another soul.

CHAPTER FIFTY-EIGHT

Cool darkness. The fire elemental torches lining the library walls sparked to life. This time, there was no joyous synchronized jig. They quivered in terror, flinching and twitching. Lurching to my feet, I promptly collapsed back to my knees. Half the world had ceased to exist, everything appearing oddly flat and blurry. My right eye had been destroyed, and the left badly damaged. I didn't have time to worry or panic. If I survived the next few minutes, they'd eventually heal.

Why had I been able to come here, but not return to the ship?

"Nhil?"

Regaining my feet, leaning on the leather chair, I turned a complete circle, finding the library empty.

The floor shook, and I felt the grinding of stone, a deep bass rumbling, in my guts.

"Nhil!"

Though cooler than in the summoning chambers, the temperature rose quickly. The sound of exploding stone echoed long halls.

"Bren!"

Praying he was in his chambers with Nokutenda, I ran. The world tilted, and I spun into the wall. Half-running, half-crawling, I clambered along the leaning floor. Torches flared and spat, growing as they strained against the bindings trapping them. I couldn't tell if they were attempting to flee or join with the fire demon. The floor angled further, and I slid backwards before arresting my descent. I clawed my way up the floor, fingertips finding narrow seems in the stone, grabbing at torch brackets and anything else to help propel myself forward.

My stomach did a little flip and for a heartbeat I was grateful to feel lighter. Then I understood: the floating mountain was falling. And still, the floor tilted further. I crawled until I climbed.

Bren and the sorcerer were in their room, clinging to the edge of the window, staring out. They flinched when I climbed through their now sideways doorway.

"Tell me this happens all the time," shouted Bren.

I shook my head, joining them at the window. Peering out I saw that strange sun, the colour of rotting blood when I first came to this bubble reality, now engulfed in raging flames. It was smaller than I remembered and shrinking.

"Not a sun," I mumbled, remembering Nhil's explanation.

It was the last surviving god of this reality, and I'd bound it in the sky. Karatal appeared to be devouring the trapped god.

"How long before we land?" asked Nokutenda.

Realizing she'd never seen the floating mountains from the outside and had no idea of the strangeness of this reality, I said, "I'm not sure there's anything to land on."

"We can't fall forever," said Bren.

Despite Karatal having left the citadel to war with the imprisoned god, the temperature still climbed. Sweat soaked us all. Certain we'd be cooked to death before the mountains hit anything, I said nothing.

Nhil clambered through the door, hung on the frame with grey fingertips. He carried my pack slung over one shoulder. Violet eyes glanced out the window and an eyebrow climbed further than would have been possible were he human. "What happened?"

He tossed me my pack, and I caught it.

"Everything went exactly to plan," I said.

"You summoned a fallen sun god to a world with no sun."

"If you hadn't angered me—"

"Right," snapped Nhil. "Nothing is ever your fault."

I blinked, mouth opening and closing. This wasn't the time for self-examination. "Can we stop it?"

"The Demon Emperor could," said Nhil. "Maybe."

Looking out the window, I saw the shrinking sun slide from view and felt everything shift in my stomach. The citadel had begun to spiral as it fell, gaining speed. We'd soon be pinned to a wall, helpless to move.

"Everyone to me!" I barked. "Grab hold tight. I'm getting us out."

Nokutenda and Bren, already at the window, clung to me.

I held out a hand to Nhil. "You can't stay here. Jump!"

The trapped god died, plunging the world into perfect black.

Stuttering red slashed the darkness, and a new sun was born. Karatal's fury lit the sky. Heat blasted through the open window, singeing us. The falling mountain struck something, and we were slammed against a wall. Bren hit hard, leaving a long bloody smear. Dazed, he hung loose in Nokutenda's arms.

"I can buy you time," said Nhil. "Give me the cloak."

Understanding what he meant, I dug Shalayn's invisible cloak from my pack. About to toss it to him, I hesitated. "You brought my pack."

"We don't have time for this."

"I never mentioned the cloak, yet you knew about it."

The grinding explosion of superheated stone drowned his response.

I threw the cloak at him, saying, "I knew you were spying."

No more than a translucent mist, he caught it easily. "Of course I was spying." Releasing his grip on the doorjamb, he shrugged into the cloak and disappeared. "You can never return. Karatal rules here now."

I laughed, a parched cough of burnt lungs. Once again, I was my own worst enemy.

Nhil said, "I'll slow Karatal until you're out."

"It'll only take a moment!" I shouted.

There was no answer.

I couldn't understand. We'd be gone in a heartbeat!

I couldn't figure out how this went so wrong. I knew the summoning. I understood the dangers and had completed more difficult summonings many times, though admittedly all in the distant past. Could I be so different than that man? I didn't know whether I should count this a victory or yet another catastrophic failure. Somehow, I'd been so unbelievably careless I'd missed the spilled blood. That wasn't me! Even rushed, I was never sloppy. I was a man who, in the middle of a sword fight I was losing, could build the memory of a room so perfectly I could go there. I didn't miss details!

Had Nhil planned this? He commanded many of the demons and elementals in the tower. He could have ordered one to splash a little blood on the ward when I was distracted.

"Nhil," I said. "Did you betray me?"

Again, there was no answer.

"Hold on to me," I said. "I'm getting us out of here."

"About time," mumbled Nokutenda, dragging the still dazed Bren closer. Clinging to him with one arm, she grabbed me with the other.

I built the cabin in the *Katlipok* in my thoughts, filling in every detail until it was perfect. The damp salt smell of ocean-soaked wood. Decades of mould. Every whorl and crack in the furniture.

I fed Frorrat a soul.

"Was something supposed to happen?" asked Nokutenda.

Opening my one eye, I found we were still in the falling mountain. The air felt thick and stunk of sulphur. My throat and lungs, already damaged, voiced their protest at the acidic burn.

"No," I said in rising fear.

Somehow, Nhil had known I'd fail.

I'd tried to return to the ship earlier and put my failure down to pain and distraction. Despite plummeting to a certain death, I was calm, centred. It should have worked.

I tried again, taking longer to make every detail perfect.

Again, I failed.

"No, no, no."

Henka wouldn't have willingly allowed something to change. She would have done everything in her power to ensure I returned to her. My calm shattered, panic building. Facing my death was one thing, but I'd left Henka behind. If she was in danger—

Possibilities bubbled up from the dark recesses of my mind. The *Katlipok* had sunk. Iremaire decided to strike while I was away, possibly freeing Shalayn from Brisinder's thrall. The swordswoman would have butchered the crew, chopped my love to pieces and tossed her into the ocean. Henka somehow learned of my intention to free her and decided I was beyond saving. She'd trapped me here thinking I'd eventually starve to death, and she could collect the shard of my heart to lay her obsidian path and try again. Some ancient enemy—

"Khraen!" yelled Nokutenda. The room darkened quickly, the world beyond the window a swirling hell of clouds. "We have to get out now!"

Focus.

I built the cabin in my thoughts. I willed it to be real. I made it real. I was the Demon Emperor, and nothing could stop me. I was a goddamned god! I was the smoke in the stone, the soul trapped in glass.

Nothing.

We remained trapped in the citadel, the mad spiralling plunge crushing us all against one wall. Each breath hurt, seared my throat and lungs. Thick tears ran from my one eye, vision collapsing in a blurred tunnel.

Somewhere else. Anywhere else.

The room in the basement beneath the mummer's headquarters? The chambers beneath the pyramid in the necropolis? Every location I thought of was weeks from where I left Henka. If she was in trouble, I had to get to her now. Anywhere other than the ship and I'd lose her.

"I'm sorry," I said to Bren and Nokutenda, not explaining.

I wouldn't abandon my love, no matter what it cost me. My life. Their lives. I would get to her, or I would die trying.

Focus.

Thoughts sodden and crushed, suffocating.

Again, I built the cabin in my thoughts and fed the portal demon a soul.

CHAPTER FIFTY-NINE

Opening my eye, I saw the cabin. For a single instant everything looked normal. And then the wall lurched in my direction like the hand of a god smashing an annoying bug. I flopped about on the floor, boneless and loose, bordering on unconscious, thoughts swimming in confusion. Someone cursed and a weight fell atop me, crushing what air I had from my lungs.

"Sorry," mumbled Bren, standing only to fall again when the ship lurched in the other direction.

Nokutenda clung to the bed, eyes wide in terror. The world beyond the small window was a smear of black and grey punctuated by barbed forks of lightning stabbing down over and over as if trying to smite the ocean.

"Can we go back?" the sorcerer shouted.

I couldn't pull together enough thought to know if she joked.

The ship rolled with another wave and again Bren ended up piled atop me. The walls shuddered with the crash of pounding rain and roaring winds. In a moment of clarity, I realized what had happened: I hadn't been able to make the transition because everything loose in the cabin rolled back and forth with each wave. I'd got lucky, timing the last attempt when everything was heaped against the far wall.

Crawling to the door, I managed to regain my feet. My right eye remained an absence in reality, a hole in the world. Pushing through the door, I saw an ocean lost to madness. Waves reared up to lash at the roiling black clouds. The sky above screamed hate and war, jagged bolts of crackling lightning lancing the ocean.

The elements, woken three thousand years ago by insane elementalists acting on orders from the Guild, still waged war. The *Katlipok* was caught in the middle. With each curling wave the ship threatened to roll, only the demons bound to her hull keeping her upright.

An iron grip caught my wrist, pulled me into a sodden and frigid hug. Henka clung to me, ice-cold face buried in my neck. Caught between disgust and overwhelming gratitude to discover her alive, I held her tight. She screamed something and the wind whipped her words away, hurled them far out into the ocean. A few crewmembers clung to the mast or anything else solid. There were less than there should have been. I hoped the rest cowered below decks.

Unable to roll the ship, the ocean changed tactics and hammered the hull with watery fists. Through the blinding rain I saw someone clamber from the hold only to be swept from the deck the moment they stepped out. Eyes wide, arms windmilling in panic, they disappeared without a sound.

Henka yelled something else I couldn't hear and dragged me back into the cabin, slamming the door closed behind us. Bren and Nokutenda, who'd remained inside, sat on the bed, braced against the ship's movement. Henka and I joined them there, and the four of us huddled together.

"How did we get here?" asked Bren, groggy and confused. "Are we sinking?"

Henka shook her head, dark skin faded and grey. She been wounded, the skin of her hands abraded to show muscle and bone. Her left forearm bent at an odd angle, flopping with each roll of the ship. She ignored it, focussed on my face.

"No," she said. "I don't think so." She touched my cheek below my blinded right eye. "The ship should survive."

If anyone else noted the oddly specific answer, they said nothing.

Henka brushed hair from my face, looking me over for more damage. "What happened?"

"I…"

I made a terrible mistake. Overconfident, I tried to bind an elemental Demon Lord when a few smaller demons would have sufficed.

Instead of simply blocking Iremaire's ability to spy on me and getting on with what I planned, I'd chased vengeance.

Unbridled hubris.

Forever my own worst enemy.

"You're burnt," she said, seeing my hands.

Glancing down I saw the palms charred to white ash, the fingers blackened and cooked. I hadn't noticed, the pain distant and unimportant.

Seeing Bren and Nokutenda's dazed expressions, the way they held each other as if stunned to be alive, she said again, "Khraen. Tell me what happened."

"The Black Citadel is gone. It... it fell."

She stared at me in shock. "Fell?"

"I summoned Karatal," I admitted.

"Oh no."

"I wanted..." I made a fist, charred flesh flaking off. "I wanted to *crush* Iremaire."

Henka looked from me to Bren to Nokutenda, and then around the room. "Nhil?"

I shook my head. "He died there." My heart broke. "I left him."

Pulling me into a hug she cried. No matter what she felt for the demon she knew he was my friend.

Clinging to my wife, I too cried, though not for the reasons she thought. She loved me so completely she had no choice but to be saddened by my loss. I'd stolen even the freedom to have her own genuine emotions.

For hours the ocean and sky battled on. Unceasing rain pounded the deck as waves crashed against the hull in a constant roar like thunder.

Bren said he was still the captain and had to see to the crew. Opening the door, he found the deck abandoned. The crew had either been swept overboard or were hiding in their quarters. Dark and heavy storm clouds choked the sky. We couldn't tell if it were day or night, and it never got any brighter. Wind and rain whipped the ship, reducing visibility to a couple of feet. He wanted to try to cross the deck to search for survivors, but I wouldn't let him. Making the short distance to the stairs leading to the crew quarters and hold would be impossible.

None of this should have happened. Not the destruction of the citadel, and not the raging elements. The Guild in their mad hunger for power had pushed the elementalists beyond reason. Either the mages hadn't given the repercussions any thought, or they hadn't cared. Thousands of years later, the world still suffered for their sins. I wanted to crush them like the insects they were. I wanted them to understand true power, to realize they'd only ever lived on my mercy. A mercy now dead and gone. In my darkest moments, I considered using the portal demon to take me and my friends back to Palaq and Phaoro. I could mobilize Naghron's armies. Perhaps I wasn't ready to conquer the mainland once again, but I could certainly earn the islands their freedom.

When Henka held me, cold and dead and loving me despite my crimes, I knew I could never turn my back on her.

I asked her where Shalayn was, and she said she thought the swordswoman was below decks, though couldn't be sure.

With nothing to draw sustenance from, I didn't heal. On the second day I went in search of a mirror. I found one of polished bronze, tarnished around the edges. I found my face drawn and sunken, skin pallid. My right eye was a charred and empty, the flesh around it a raw, swollen wound. I laughed and laughed until my chest hurt, the words *atone, atone, eyes of stone*, running over and over through my thoughts. I had the mad desire to find something to cram into the gaping space.

Water leaked through the walls and ceiling, poured around the small porthole windows, and soaked everything. Savage winds buffeted the ship, the rumble and groan of wood audible even over the constant thunder. At least we wouldn't die of thirst.

Bren and Nokutenda bickered and apologized and bickered and apologized and fell asleep holding each other every night. Only the tight-tucked blankets saved them from being tossed to the floor. Henka never slept, and the throbbing pain in my skull kept me awake too. Wedging myself into a chair, I planned everything from what I would say when I finally gave Henka her freedom, to how I would torture Iremaire's soul for a thousand years. But here I was, trapped in a little room, utterly vulnerable. I imagined the mage laughing as she watched.

On the fourth day, the sun broke through the clouds and the *Katlipok* sailed on calm waters. Exiting the cabin we blinked in the harsh light, shading our eyes with sodden and wrinkled hands. Anything not protected by bound demons had long been smashed to splinters and washed overboard. For all the devastation, the deck was spotlessly clean, scrubbed by an enraged ocean.

Bren went to check on the crew and take stock of our situation. When he reported back a short time later, the news was not good. We retreated to our cabin to hear the details.

Of the thirty or more who set sail with us, nine remained, and three were wounded. The sorcerer in charge of maintaining the food supplies had been washed overboard on the first day. KriskOrke, the demonologist Phaoro sent with us, was alive, though he'd struck his head and was in and out of consciousness. Everything in the hold had been soaked in sea water and was quickly rotting in the tropical heat.

"Can you fix that?" Bren asked Nokutenda.

She shook her head. "I'm not that kind of sorcerer."

To make matters worse, most of the barrels in the hold had been smashed by the ship's mad tossing. Only two unbroken water barrels remained. The kegs of blood were gone, smashed to kindling, their contents soaked into the wood of the hull.

"And so," said Bren, glancing at the now cloudless sky, "despite all the rain we just suffered through, it's now a race between starving to death and dying of thirst."

"There are thousands of islands out here," said Nokutenda. "All we need to do is find one and replenish our supplies."

"Easier said than done," said Bren. "Most of them are feral, cannibalistic tribes living in ruins. Elementals running amok. Anywhere big enough to have something edible will have something living on it."

"Nothing we can't deal with," I decided.

Bren looked doubtful. "Few of these smaller islands are mapped, and all we have is a two-hundred-year-old copy of a two-thousand-year-old map. We could sail the rest of the way to PalTaq and never spot a hint of land."

Avoiding the sodden bed, I paced the room, thinking. At each turn the situation looked worse. If we got lucky and found an island, we'd have to face its dangers with our dwindling crew, and if it took more than a few days, we'd be weak from hunger and thirst. With our store of blood gone, Henka would either decay or be forced to bleed the crew. Already damaged, she'd want to harvest someone to repair herself. Of the nine survivors, four were women, not counting Shalayn, who Bren said had survived unhurt. I might be their god, but would they willingly sacrifice themselves for my wife? On top of all that, Iremaire could still scry on me, and I'd destroyed the only place I had to escape her spying.

I considered summoning a new portal demon and throwing Frorrat overboard, but a ship like this was no place for such an intricate ceremony. While not impossible, the odds of something going catastrophically wrong were much higher than when working in an environment like the summoning chambers within the Black Citadel. With my last failure, my confidence was shaken. One mistake out here, and the ship would be destroyed, the crew doomed.

It felt like the world plotted against me, striving to bend me from my path at every opportunity. I still had the portal demon and could return to one of the other places I'd memorized, but all were far away. I could take my friends somewhere safe. With a few trips, I could save the entire crew. I didn't want to. I'd come too far and was too close to admit defeat and turn back now.

The crew spent several hours dragging everything soaked onto the deck to dry in the sun. Mattresses, bedding, and clothes hung on every rail and line. Once my own meagre belongings were hung, I went to the bow to look south, scanning the ocean for islands.

Pauper emperor. Lord of nothing. Failure at every turn.

This time, I would not be distracted.

If the world worked against me, it would lose.

Henka joined me, the scent of spoiling meat following her. She stood downwind and I wondered if that was a conscious choice.

"I won't turn back," I said. "But I have an idea."

She touched my arm, the briefest hesitant, cold contact.

"I can return to the necropolis for supplies. Assuming your necromancers have maintained it, I have a room under the pyramid memorized."

"It won't work," she said. "The day after we left Palaq a white war galley arrived. They burned the island to nothing. One or two of my necromancers escaped but were later hunted and destroyed."

"You didn't say anything!"

"Do you really want to go backwards?"

I didn't.

Picturing the outdated map as best I could, I figured the necropolis was a month north of Palaq. We'd been at sea for weeks. Between the floating mountains, and the storm, I'd lost track of time.

"Have they reached Palaq?" I demanded. "I thought we'd have more time. Is Phaoro already at war?"

"Not yet," Henka answered. "My spies say the High Priest is aware of the threat and preparing. Nothing the mages do matters. Once we reach PalTaq, nothing can stop you."

That wasn't quite true; she didn't know about Iremaire's spying.

I toyed with the ring, spinning it on my finger. It was my escape and yet its use was limited. Anywhere I fled to, Iremaire could follow. If I couldn't use it to feed the crew, what use was it?

I slipped the ring from my finger. "They say you should never burn bridges behind you," I said.

Henka looked from me to the ring.

"But if you do burn them," I added, "you're left with no choice but to continue forward."

"Having some means of escape is always wise," she said.

"I'm done escaping. I'm done retreating."

I threw the ring into the ocean. It disappeared with the tiniest *bloop*.

For a mad instant I wanted to dive in and retrieve it, if only to apologize to the demon for the callous treatment.

Henka placed her hand on mine, and I resisted the urge to pull away from the touch of cold, dead flesh. I considered telling her about Iremaire, but with the ring gone there didn't seem much point in admitting my stupidity.

Bren rallied the crew, dividing the tasks among the survivors. The sails were raised and once again the *Katlipok* caught the wind, heading south. Two of the crew were ordered to construct nets, poles, and lures for fishing, while two more worked on solving our water shortage.

Dragging the remains of the barrels up from the hold, they built makeshift buckets in the hope it might rain. Though after the fury of the storm, the sky remained depressingly clear. The rest worked on salvaging what little food remained, gathering it together so it might be shared out equally. God and emperor, I might be, but I refused more than my share.

That evening we dragged our sun-dried mattresses and crusty salt-stained clothes back into our cabin.

South. Ever south.

A hot and impatient wind pushed us on our way, hurrying us along. No hint of clouds teased the horizon, and the fish were few and far between. Those we did catch were strange, pale and twisted creatures with too many eyes. Instead of fighting over who got to eat them, the crew argued over who needed them more, everyone claiming they were fine, and that someone else should have their share.

That only lasted until our few salvaged supplies ran out. When staring into the face of starvation, the fact your fish has fur and looks like it may have been the offspring of some bottom dweller and a demon, ceases to matter. They tasted the way a wet dog smelled.

When we woke to find the demonologist, KriskOrke, dead, his stomach having burst and his guts writhing with furry white worms, no one wanted to eat the fish anymore.

The sun burned overhead, shrinking the boards, and darkening already dark flesh. Thirst and hunger sharpened eyes to angry slits and shortened tempers. The industrious crew became increasingly lax with their duties. Why scrub the deck when each day dragged you closer to a painful death? Filth piled up, chores going unfinished, and I couldn't bring myself to care. Where they once viewed me as their god, I saw growing hate. I did this to them. I killed their beautiful Naghron, I murdered his plans. I kicked everything he spent centuries building to dust and ruin. Searing winds blew us south and we slouched across the ocean.

Our mid-day shadows dwindled, each day hotter than the last.

Water in every direction, as far as the eye could see.

Parched throats and croaking voices. Cracked lips seeping thin blood. Even as thirst became a single monotonous note hummed beneath every thought, I felt increasingly at home. The crew took to gathering at the rails, searching the endless ocean for signs of land. We saw no birds and the foul stench of the polluted waters grew until each thick inhalation tasted of putrescent fish.

Weakened by hunger, all but the most critical tasks were left undone. Day and night we headed south, taking turns at the ship's wheel. When the sun was up, we huddled in the shade, scanning the horizon for land. Each night we slept fitful and exhausted though we'd done nothing.

One morning Henka joined me on the bow as I searched the seas in vain. Skin peeling, leathery muscle showing through, she stood at my side. She stunk like rotting meat. She'd made no attempt to harvest any of the living crew to repair herself and hadn't asked for blood. The crew regarded her decaying state with fear and disgust, refusing to talk to her or remain in her presence.

"You have a difficult choice to make," she said.

I closed my eyes. "I'm tired of difficult choices. Give me an easy one."

She studied me with a look of concern. "All right," she said, and left me alone at the rail.

CHAPTER SIXTY

That night I dreamt I was Naghron bä Khraen, and of the floating mountains as they once were, centuries before the emperor built the Black Citadel. An elemental reality, it thrived with life. The floating islands wore a heavy mantle of earth, rich with strange flora and fauna. Like my home reality, everything was alive. Colossal rock elementals slumbered as they flew through an endless void. Herds of vine-like trees shambled about the islands in idyllic peace. The sun was a god, the air a living entity giving life to the world. Heavy clouds, laden with water elementals, clustered around the islands. It was a world of lush green.

A race of flying reptiles had risen to dominance. They ruled their world, squabbling amongst themselves as all such species do, ignorant of the dangers beyond the existence they witnessed. They were a tribal people, loyal to their shaman, hunting from island to island, gathering the wings of their foes so they might display them as grizzly trophies. To me, they were demons. To them, I was the demon.

They reminded me of my own past and my heart hurt thinking of such simple days.

Hunt. Kill. Eat.

Defend the village.

But my god dreamed, and her dream was ever ravenous.

Sometimes she sent me to worlds demanding a specific life, insisting I kill one particular priest or god. Each time I had to split their chest wide and cut their heart out so I might bring back the sliver of obsidian as proof. Unlike the shards of my own heart, these didn't call to me.

I tried to catch the thought and lost it to the imprisoning logic of

Naghron's dream.

Sometimes, however, she wanted more than one death. I visited worlds and enslaved their people, binding them to my service so I might later call upon them in times of war. In other worlds, I butchered the dominant race, leaving the reality otherwise untouched. I never knew why, or what drove my god's decisions. Perhaps she knew some people would never serve and, like me, refused to leave an enemy behind her.

This time, my god wanted something special.

She demanded suffering on an untold scale.

After studying the world, I planned their pain. It would be easy. For all that everything was alive, the inhabitants possessed no power as elementalists. In a reality of impossible floating mountains, there were no wizards, sorcerers, shaman, demonologists, or necromancers. They were entirely without magic.

I returned with my most powerful elementalists. We bound the mountains and the air and the clouds. I bound their sun god, trapping it helpless in the sky to watch. The great herds of trees were ordered to walk off the edge of their mountains forever plummeting into the nothing below. The imprisoned sun god I ordered to sear the water elementals and clouds to dust. Every rock and speck of dirt on the mountain was slain or fell into the nothing until only the bare obsidian bones of the mountains remained. The dragon-folk I saved for last, milking every moment of horror for my watching god.

Then, I made the parents decide: If they willingly sacrificed themselves and their eternal souls to my god, I would clip their children's wings and let them fall forever. Or at least until they starved or hit something. I promised the souls of such offspring would be spared, given the chance to be reborn.

Many fought and I butchered them. Most of the rest surrendered or took their own lives. The rest I forced to witness the mutilation of their offspring before murdering all of them, ripping their souls free and feeding them to my—

I woke to find Henka curled against me, naked, warm, and whole. She kissed me and I tasted blood on her lips and tongue. A smear of jaundiced light struggled through the filthy portholes. Still half-asleep, I traced the lines in her flesh where the colours didn't match, reached up to cup a breast different than what I remembered. She straddled me, grinding and insistent, until we became one.

Alertness hit me like a slap.

I couldn't do this knowing she had no choice.

"Stop," I said, lifting her off me.

She frowned in the yellow light. "You need this."

I wanted it, but to Henka my every want was her need. I would not be the man who was unbothered by such a crime. Yet that hateful little voice in my head argued I had to let her continue so she wouldn't grow suspicious.

"Did you kill one of the women?" I asked.

It was a stupid question.

Pulling her legs in tight, wrapping her arms around her knees, she retreated from me.

Crime upon crime. She harvested women to be appealing to me because she had no choice. And I attacked her for it.

"Sorry," I said. "That was unfair."

"She was dying anyway," said Henka, shrugging off the apology. "Poisoned."

As if that somehow excused killing and harvesting the woman.

Except my love needed no excusing. She was what she was because of me. This was my crime and not hers. I pulled her close and held her, desperately wanting to beg forgiveness, and knowing I dare not hint at what I felt.

We stayed like that for a while. I wanted the moment to last forever. She was mine and I hers. We were eternal.

Raised voices out on the deck caught my attention. Pulling on a faded pair of threadbare cotton pants and a loose shirt, I strode out to see what the excitement was. Stripped to his underclothes, a rag stuffed in his mouth, Bren knelt in the middle of the seven surviving sailors. Hands tied behind his back, blood trickled from a cut in his brow. I saw no sign of Nokutenda, and my heart fell. The sailors all carried drawn cutlasses. Shalayn stood with them, her own sword drawn.

I cursed, realizing I'd been going unarmed for weeks as carrying the damned sword about was too much effort. Rather than show weakness by fleeing back into my cabin, I approached the mob.

"Explain yourselves," I demanded.

They flinched back, brandishing their weapons in fear.

At the sound of my voice, Bren's head came up and he blinked blood from his eyes. "Clubbed me when I was sleeping," he said groggily.

The largest of the men, a scarred brute with a squished nose, stepped forward. "We're done." He pointed over my shoulder, and I glanced back to see Henka exit the cabin behind me. "I saw what she did. She skinned Bhnaiir alive and then drained her of blood."

It was unlike Henka to be so sloppy.

"The necromancer goes overboard," the big man said, "as does anyone unwilling to sail north." Then, as if needing to defend this little mutiny, he added, "We sail until we find fish we can eat."

"No," I said.

He raised his cutlas over Bren, threatening. "You're no god. I've watched you piss into the ocean. I've listened to you cry out in your sleep. Phaoro was wrong."

"We continue south."

"You're in no position to negotiate! I decide—"

I silenced him with a raised hand. I was so tired, so thirsty. Each word hurt. These mortals thought their lives mattered. They wanted to flee destiny, return to their filthy islands and cower from the Guild.

"Brisinder," I said.

Standing among the mutineers, sword already drawn, three were dying, stabbed neatly through the gut, before I finished the name. Brisinder, uncaring of the swordswoman's thirst or weakness, pushed Shalayn hard. She danced and spun, blade flickering out to leave small but deadly wounds. Glorious grace. Murderous intent.

In Shalayn's eyes, I saw the horror of her actions.

Bodies littered the deck, each with a single neat hole in their torso.

"Anything else, master?" Brisinder asked, face again devoid of emotion.

Something about the precision of the kills bothered me. I'd seen Shalayn fight before, and this wasn't her usual style. She was deadly, but never missed an opportunity to inflict damage on an opponent in favour of waiting for a killing blow. Not that any of her opponents were dead yet. Each lay curled about their wounds. Some sobbed or begged for aid. Others, too lost to the agony, drew ragged hissing breaths, each weaker than the last. Not one of the wounds was instantly fatal. None had been stabbed to the heart. Each having received a perfect thrust to the gut, none of them bled much.

"Take Bren back to his cabin," I ordered Brisinder. "See if the sorcerer lives, and report back."

She pulled him to his feet, but he resisted being pulled away.

"What happened?" he asked, confused from the blow to the head.

"They mutinied. I killed them."

"Technically," said Shalayn, "*I* killed them."

I ignored the demon. "This was not what I wanted." Though already I saw how this was to my advantage.

Touching a growing lump on his head, he winced and let Shalayn lead him away.

Henka joined me on the deck, pulling my arm around her waist. Feeling the warmth of her through my shirt, seeing the mottled patchwork repaired flesh, the pieces fell together.

"You did that on purpose," I said. "You told Brisinder to be ready, to pretend to be with the mutineers. I'm surprised the demon obeyed—"

Henka interrupted me. "There wasn't enough food and water to keep everyone alive all the way to PalTaq."

Looking down, I studied the neat, near bloodless wounds. "You're going to bleed them and raise the dead."

"We need a crew."

She hadn't simply taken advantage of the situation, she made it happen, planned the moment to the last detail. "You made sure there was a witness. You pushed them into this mutiny."

"It was the only way Bren would be all right with killing and harvesting them."

She thought of everything. "You should have told me."

"You said you were tired of difficult choices and to give you an easy one."

"And what's my easy choice?"

"Whether or not to forgive me."

I wanted to yell at her. Something could have gone wrong. She couldn't know the mutineers wouldn't murder Bren in his sleep, or that they'd accept Shalayn into their numbers. I still didn't know if Nokutenda survived.

Was I not giving her enough credit, or were these possible losses she was willing to accept?

Seeing my expression, Henka said, "I raised the first woman I killed and harvested. She watched over Bren and the sorcerer, was ready to step in if things went sour. And I have dead rats all over the ship spying for me." She nestled against me. "They're both fine. The sorcerer took a nasty blow to the head and was gagged and tied up. She'll have a headache for a few days; nothing worse."

I hugged her close. It was that or scream. She was right, the choice to forgive her was effortless. She understood what I needed and did whatever was required to make it happen.

As Nhil said, she left nothing to chance.

CHAPTER SIXTY-ONE

In the first day after the crew's doomed mutiny, Henka harvested what she thought useful and worked her necromantic magic. After, she brought me to the ship's locker where Shalayn once kept her imprisoned Khraen. One of the mutineers, his wound sloppily bandaged, lay chained on the floor.

"Drain him so you can heal," said Henka.

My wife missed no detail.

That night, I slept in the locker. When I woke, the man was dead, and I once again saw through two eyes.

Though making no attempt to become the striking beauty she'd been back in Taramlae, by the end of the second day she once again looked like the perfect island warrior. Corded ropes of iron muscle wrapped her arms, her stomach a ridged plane.

By the third day, when the crew were shambling corpses bloating in the sun, their hair falling out, the patchwork of her flesh had become uniform.

On the fourth day, the crew, while still haggard and decaying, suddenly looked sunken. I didn't know if Henka worked more magic, or simply drained their distended bowels to stop them from bursting. KriskOrke made a reappearance, the dead demonologist's burst guts hidden by heavy fabric. Henka said she'd raised him on the off chance he might prove useful.

She apologized for not being able to better care for the crew the way she had Chalaam so long ago but said there wasn't enough to work with. Not knowing how long the trip would be, she jealously hoarded the remaining blood. The dead worked tirelessly, silent and uncomplaining, though I saw the misery in their eyes. She must have ordered them to silence. Where it had once bothered me to so use people, I was now glad for the quiet.

No longer needed to work the ship, Bren and Nokutenda spent most of the time in their cabin. When they did come up on deck, they avoided the dead and were careful to stay upwind. Henka and the sorcerer spent more and more time together, which surprised me. My wife had never expressed much interest in the lives of others. Perhaps, like me, she too was changed by our trials. It was an odd thought. she didn't seem the type to change. There was something permanent about her, immutable. There was no horror I couldn't imagine her shrugging off. Maybe it was a consequence of age. Having lived as long as she had, survived countless deadly situations and no doubt lost innumerable friends, it made sense she'd be hardened to tragedy.

The Demon Emperor had been like that. It seemed that my every decision moved me a step closer to once again becoming that man.

Had breaking my heart been an attempt at regaining something long lost?

Two days later, I woke to find Bren up in the crow's-nest, peering through a battered eyeglass. When he noticed me, he waved me up to join him. My heart fell as I wondered if he'd spotted land and Henka hadn't needed to kill the crew. Looking out to sea, I saw nothing but endless blue water and an even bluer sky.

Climbing to the crow's-nest, I asked, "What have you seen?"

"Nothing," he answered, handing me the eyeglass, "but pretend to look anyway."

Confused, I did as instructed.

I saw only endless ocean.

"I didn't know where else we could talk," Bren said.

Still scanning the water, I said, "What do you need to tell me?"

"I'm not sure. Maybe I'm being paranoid. A couple of times, I found a rather haggard rat hiding under the cot in our room."

"Right." Probably one of Henka's spies. Bren must have figured it out.

"And then the rat disappeared, and Nokutenda started asking

about what happened in the Black Citadel that day you sent her away."

Henka's interest in the woman suddenly made sense. Hurt by the loss of my friend, I'd been unwilling to talk about my time away. Curiosity and the need to take care of me must have pushed her to look for answers.

"What did you say?"

"Obviously I left out everything about your intent to free Henka. I told her we talked about old times and that the demon fellow told embarrassing stories about you."

I felt a sharp pang of loss at the mention of Nhil. So many times, he told me he was my friend, and just as often I doubted him. In the end, he sacrificed himself to save me.

"He actually did," added Bren. "You were off having dinner, and he told me about the time you bound a demon and ordered it to obey some friend. They turned it against you. Because of the wording of your command, you didn't know until it was too late."

I had no memory of that.

Shading his eyes with a scarred hand, Bren peered out to sea too. "Nokutenda's not a romantic." He sounded disappointed. "She thinks nothing is more important than freeing the islanders from the Guild. Not friends. Not love. Sure as shit not happiness. Ever wonder if some people are incapable of happiness, or do you think they just don't want it?" He grunted and continued without waiting for an answer. "Love and loyalty should matter. Friendship should mean something. That's not to say I don't have doubts," he added. "It'd sure be nice if we could do both though, free Henka and save the islanders."

It was rare for young Bren to say so much and so I listened.

"Every now and then," he continued, "some king or duke declares himself ruler of some puckered asshole of useless land that no one wants, and the Guild go in and burn it all down. Centuries later, the land is still dead, nothing growing there. They go in with a certain glee, as if grateful for the chance to finally test out the new magic they've been working on."

"What about the Crags?" I asked. "Didn't you say Queen Maz Arkis rules there?"

"She does, but the Crags still pay tribute to the Guild and do their dirty work when it comes to patrolling the shipping lanes. Being pale northerners, they're considered a better class of person than islanders."

I wasn't surprised. Those mages in their pristine white robes would avoid the filth of responsibility and rulership at any cost.

Bren dropped his hand, frowning at the twisted fire-scarred knuckles. "There's got to be a way we can free Henka *and* save the islands. What if, before you freed her, you ordered her not to interfere? That way we can return to Palaq and she can get on with her life."

It was tempting. "Freedom with limitations on what choices you're allowed to make isn't freedom at all."

"What if we *mostly* free her, save the islands from the Guild, and then give her total freedom after?"

"Mostly free her." I laughed, lowering the looking glass. "I know me. There will always be a reason to put it off. There will always be one more thing I must do. I'd free the world from the Guild, but then all those kings and queens would fight over territory. What kind of man would I be if I turned my back on the suffering of the common people? Then, I'd be busy building a new civilization, making sure everyone was safe and treated well, mainlanders and islanders alike. I'd be making a new empire."

"Doesn't sound terrible," he pointed out.

And that was the problem.

"Assuming she didn't destroy it herself, how long would my new empire last once I freed Henka and died?"

"It must be possible to find someone who could run it for you."

"You?" I asked.

"Gods no. I want to run a little pub, tell tall tales, and die fat and old and thinking about oral sex."

I wanted to tell him he'd have all of that, but if he stayed with me, Henka would kill him too. And yet, I couldn't send him away. Having lost Nhil, I couldn't bear to part with my only friend. Without him at my side, reminding me what was right, I'd spiral into old behaviour.

"I wish I could talk to Nokutenda about this," he said. "She's going to feel betrayed."

"She's going to *be* betrayed." I realized that much as I feared the answer, I had to at least offer him a way out. "If you love her, when we get to PalTaq, you can drop Henka and me off, take the ship and dead crew, and return to Phaoro."

"I can't."

I didn't push and hated myself for a coward.

Bren plucked the looking glass from my hand and peered south. "Is that clouds, or mountains?"

We took turns squinting through the glass. Despite it being midday, the sky to the south grew dark, though it didn't look like clouds.

"If it's another storm," said Bren, "I'm going to jump overboard and get it over with."

Over the next two days, the southern sky changed. Mountains seemed to rise out of the ocean, smoke and ash spewing from gaping mouths. By the third day we sailed in gloom, the morning sun turning the world a muted cinereal smear. Ash rained from the sky. Stealing the last of our dead crew's colour it piled high on their heads like grey snow, clung to their lashes. The rest of us wore layered strips of cotton wrapped around our mouth and nose to filter the air.

Much had changed and yet I knew this place.

Home.

Nearing the north end of PalTaq and swinging around the east coast, we saw scores of dim shapes circling the highest peaks. Smoke, ash, and distance robbed all detail.

"The offspring of your aviaries," said Henka, standing at my side. "The dragons will remember you, remember the oaths their parents swore."

Spotting us, two of the dragons broke formation, veering away from the mountains and heading out to sea. Massive wings spread wide, they rained ash in their path.

"I hope you mean 'remember' in a good way," said Nokutenda, joining us. "Fondly would be nice. Tasty, less so."

"More fear than fondness," said Henka. "Though the end result is much the same."

The two dragons disappeared, diving beneath the waves.

Seeing us gathered at the rail, Bren sauntered over. "What's so interesting?" he asked.

"Nothing," said the sorcerer. "We just really like looking at grey shit."

We stood for a minute or more looking west toward the island.

"Well," said Bren, "I guess—"

Not more than a hundred strides away, the two dragons burst from the ocean in an explosion of white froth.

Bren flinched, cursing. "I may have pooped myself a little."

Cleaned of soot, they displayed a stunning array of shimmering oil-slick colours. The larger of the two, blood crimson shot with coils of emerald fire, looked big enough to swallow the *Katlipok* whole. The smaller of the two, midnight blue so dark it crossed into black, would have needed two bites. Gaining only a little altitude before flying overhead, the wind gusted with their passage, rocking the boat.

"I think the red one was trying to scratch his balls on the mast," muttered Bren.

Nokutenda shook her head in mock disgust. "Reptiles don't have balls."

"Actually," said Henka, "they do. But they're internal, next to their kidney."

I wondered how many dragons she dissected before learning that.

"I've seen forest dragons," said Nokutenda. "Wingless runts sneezing smoke. And I think I once saw an ocean dragon kill a full-grown whale, though I didn't see much more than an explosion of entrails bubbling up from the depths. But that…" She glanced at Henka. "I could die happy having seen real dragons up close."

"I'd rather die with clean underwear," said Bren.

Henka turned, watching the dragons climb into the sky. They circled the ship a few times, curious but unthreatening, before returning to the mountains. "Anyway, those two were female."

Memory is a timid beast, only crawling from the dark recesses of your mind when lured forth. Henka's words triggered a spilling cascade of scenes ripped from different parts of my life.

I stood on the pinnacle of a living mountain, having roared across the land crushing villages and cities beneath me. Thousands of dragons gathered below, necks stretched in obeisance. I flew over jagged, white-peaked mountains with a wing of sorcerer-mounted ice dragons behind me. We battled a mammoth god who thought to dominate my world. Though he stood, head in the clouds, we left his corpse to rot in the mountains to the west of the Deredi hives. Dead dragons choked the skies, tens of thousands of rotting corpses held aloft by will and stinking magic. They were the shadow blanketing the earth, blotting the sun.

"Look," said Bren, pointing south.

The memories crumbled, too disjointed to fit into the jigsaw of my splintered past.

Far to the southwest, barely visible through the smog, the mountains changed. Those nearer remained jagged and harsh, a ruptured and impassable wasteland of blasted stone. Beyond, hinted at through the haze of distance and thick tropical air, they became strangely uniform and blocky.

"The palace," said Henka. "It's taller than the tallest mountains. Had the air been clear, we would have seen it days ago." She sighed, a small and wistful smile curving her lips.

The palace at PalTaq.

Impatience plucked my nerves. I wanted to scream at those distant dragons to come fetch me, carry me home.

Henka took my hand, ducking under my arm and nestling against me. Together we watched the coast slide past. My forever love. My imprisoned heart.

My end.

CHAPTER SIXTY-TWO

The next day the palace and surrounding city grew in detail. Where Taramlae was the largest metropolis I'd seen, and Abieszan the most impressive—though King Grone's insane Khaal, thrust from the very mountains, was a close second—PalTaq dwarfed both. The palace alone was larger than either, an entire city unto itself. If PalTaq had a voice, it spoke one word: permanence. Colossal walls towered over even the neighbouring cliffs, wards and runes carved into every surface. Here, time was helpless. Ten thousand years of ocean wind, tropical storms, crashing waves, and thundering volcanoes hadn't dulled a single edge.

Dark shapes streaked from the distant harbour, lancing through the ocean with impossible speed on a collision course with the *Katlipok*.

"I think," said Nokutenda, "I'd rather go out in a blaze of life-devouring sorcerous glory than be eaten by whatever those are."

The dead crew, continuing their tasks with dogged determination, didn't bother looking out to sea.

As the creatures approached, they split up and circled the ship. Murky ocean waters hid all detail, leaving us to guess at the monsters' size and shape. Nothing about them suggested native origins. Impossibly agile, they twisted and turned beneath us with gut-churning speed and ease, a swarming tangle.

Dim memories bubbled up. "Demonic guardians," I said. "They're here to guide us into the harbour and sink us if we seem unfriendly."

Bren shouted at the ocean, "We're all friendly in here!"

We followed our escorts south, the demons easily matching our pace and remaining dim shapes beneath us. Maybe they knew their emperor had finally returned. Or perhaps they did this with every vessel daring enough to approach PalTaq. Knowing the wizards' dislike for oceans, I guessed it had been centuries or more since they'd seen another ship.

Late in the day we cleared the harbour wall, finally getting our first real look at the city. Pristine, untouched by time, the motionless silence was disquieting. Stone docks for thousands of vessels of all sizes sat empty. Nothing moved in the streets. No garbage littered the city.

"Something is missing," I mumbled, confused.

"People?" asked Bren.

"Birds," said Henka. "It was an unexpected side-effect of the demons bound to protect the city. They saw birds crapping on walls, roofs, and streets as an attack."

She was right. No raucous mob of seagulls battled in the air for scraps. No bird shit stained a single surface. Every harbour I'd seen since reawakening had been swarming with seabirds, screaming and fighting and shitting on everything.

"Can't say I miss them," I said.

Henka leaned against me. "That's why you never changed their orders. Eventually, everyone got used to not being crapped on, to not having to hide their catch when they returned to the harbour. You could eat a sandwich on an open-air patio without fear of avian thieves."

"Sounds nice," said Nokutenda. "I miss taverns and drinking ale in the sun. Though a city this big should smell worse."

Drawing a deep breath, I realized she was right. Even the usual tropical scents were muted. I caught no hint of rotting fish or fruit.

Henka smiled up at me. "Elementals sweep the stench out to sea, pulling fresh cool air in from above. Anything left too long is tidied away and they keep the city free of dust, ash, and detritus."

"I lost a war," I said. "I was expecting more damage." I saw none.

"You didn't lose," said Henka. "You stopped fighting."

"Still... The wizards never came?"

"I'm sure they did," she answered. "And I'm sure the defences of PalTaq came out to greet them, and they decided to leave well enough alone."

Something didn't make sense. "The Guild were part of my empire. There would have been thousands of mages already in PalTaq. They had an entire wing of the palace to themselves. And the people who lived here, tens of thousands—"

"Hundreds of thousands," she corrected. "Just shy of one million souls at the last census."

"They could have stayed. The demons would have protected them. Why is this not a thriving metropolis, streets busy with commerce?"

Henka nibbled on her bottom lip, glanced from Bren to Nokutenda. "I heard from a survivor that you ordered the city emptied."

A survivor? Picking through my fragmented memories I realized she hadn't been here with me at the end. All she had was rumour, myth, and hearsay. "How could the entire population be moved? There couldn't possibly be enough ships."

"You told your priests to harvest every single soul in PalTaq 'for the war to come.'"

"Hadn't we already decided to break my heart at that point?"

She nodded. "And then you ordered your high priests to harvest the lower ranks, and finally the demonic guardians to slay the high priests. Some escaped. I heard from one you'd decided you wanted the city polished of life, all PalTaq's souls stored in a single impossible demon-cut diamond with one million facets."

Why would I do that if I'd already decided to shatter my heart and remake myself?

For later? For the war to come?

The chunk of obsidian hidden somewhere in the palace called to me. My heart a magnet, my soul was cold iron.

The winds dropped to the gentlest breeze as we entered the harbour, the *Katlipok* suddenly accelerating toward one of the berths. Bren shot me a wide-eyed glance and shrugged as the ship brushed against the dock and stilled as if locked in stone. No wave jostled us.

"This," said Henka, "is what cities were. This is what humanity achieved with the right leadership. None of the mud hovels of the islands. None of the filthy castles of the mainland. No one starved. This was humanity united."

And I, presumably the right leader, had killed them all.

"The cost was too high," I said. Realizing I tread dangerous ground with Henka, I added, "Next time it will be different. I will make something better. Something true to what the Demon Emperor wanted before his god tore out his eyes and replaced his vision with her own."

I swallowed, suddenly uncomfortable with my own strangely familiar words.

After cleaning our mouldering armour, untouched for weeks, and strapping on our weapons, we packed what few supplies remained and left the *Katlipok*. Bren swayed as if still accounting for the relentless roll of the ship. Nokutenda's attention rarely left the distant dragons, little more than floating specks, circling the slumbering volcanoes to the north. She looked like she half-expected them to suddenly veer off and come racing toward us. For a moment, no one moved or talked, everyone taking in the scene. Countless miles further inland, the palace loomed over the city, throwing much of it in shadow.

Shalayn joined us on the deck. She wore the brilliant white plate armour she stole from Iremaire, her sword hanging at her hip. Helm in place, she had the visor raised.

"A little hot for that, isn't it?" I asked.

"I'm fine," she answered.

PalTaq awaited me, impatient stone promising to reveal her every secret.

Henka ordered the dead crew to remain on the *Katlipok*. They did so without grumble or complaint, never looking up from their tasks.

"As long as they remain on the ship," she said, "the demons will leave them alone. If they wander off, they're likely to be tidied and disposed of as garbage."

We headed into the city. No one spoke, the scrape of boots on stone the only sound. A cool breeze stole the tropical heat, left us refreshed and comfortable after our weeks in the relentless sun. Ghosts of a forgotten past teased, memories of memories. I imagined bright and colourful parades filling the streets, happy children squealing in delight as demonic jugglers, contortionists, and acting troupes entertained them. Families with money purchased brief rides on elderly dragons, retired from my war menageries. Canopied stalls sold candied fruit and savoury meat served wrapped in fried bread. Clean streets teemed with pedestrians, traders and politicians strolling alongside musicians and artists peddling their wares. I remembered unsurpassed wealth and splendour. Free to all, the greatest schools and libraries the world had ever known lined the streets. The students gone, murdered and harvested on my command, the buildings remained spotless and waiting. PalTaq felt like a breath held in anticipation, though for what I couldn't be sure. The return of people, or perhaps another genocidal ruler to slaughter its population.

Bren twitched. "Did you see that?"

None of us had seen anything.

"I thought…" He shook his head. "I thought I saw an old man following us, but when I turned to look there was no one."

Empty street after empty street. We walked in the shadow of giants, a civilization unrivalled in the millennia since its fall. Soaring towers, shaped like curved swords, stabbed into the sky. Some leaned drunkenly, windows looking down upon the city below. Others bent and twisted and became walkways to the far side of the street. Despite the impossible architecture, everything felt secure and permanent unlike anything in Taramlae. Even the grand Guild Hall was a sad hovel in comparison, and we had yet to reach the palace.

Nokutenda stopped suddenly. "Fucking hells."

"You saw the old man?" asked Bren.

"What? No. A young man, looked like a blacksmith. He was missing both arms."

Gaping windows showed empty rooms lined with spotless shelves. The forge sat cold and dead, tools hanging neatly on the wall. A huge black anvil took up the centre of the room, ready and waiting for use.

"There's no one—" I stopped, catching movement in the corner of my eye. Turning, I saw nothing. "It's just—" A young priest, book bag thrown over his shoulder, hurried past on his way to some lecture. I saw him and I saw through him.

"The ghosts of PalTaq," Henka said cryptically.

Stopping, I let my eyes become unfocussed. All around, people seemed to seep into the city as if slowly transitioning from some neighbouring reality. Many were priests, others were scholars or librarians. All looked to be educated or skilled in some craft or trade. I saw no children anywhere.

We stood watching as more and more of the ghosts became visible.

An old woman wearing the robes of a teacher slowed to a stop. Turning, she stared at me. Her bored expression changed to one of shocked surprise as we made eye-contact.

"I can't see them," said Henka. "Never could."

Shalayn stood relaxed in her plate armour, blinding in the sun. She ignored the ghostly figures.

"Ghosts?" Bren asked.

The old teacher pointed at me and said something I couldn't hear.

"Those with valued skills," Henka explained, "were given the opportunity to sell their afterlives. Shaman would trap their souls here. They'd stay on as teachers or lecturers and in return their children or grandchildren would be paid a stipend. It was a way of supporting your family from beyond the grave."

"Why would anyone do that?" asked Nokutenda. "As if working your whole life isn't enough?"

"Contracts were written up detailing the duration. Many would stay on for a decade or two before being released. Otherwise, eventually the city would have been overrun by ghosts."

The old lady grabbed at another passing ghost, her wrinkled fingers passing through his shoulder. She babbled at him in silence, and he too turned to stare in shock.

"The last generation of ghosts," continued Henka, "those under contract right at the end. They must have been forgotten or deemed not worth the time."

Scores of ghosts gawked at us, eyes wide, mouths moving in silence.

"They've been trapped here for three thousand years?" asked Bren, focussed on my wife.

"Yes."

"Doing *what?*"

Henka pursed her lips in thought. "Going insane, I suppose."

We were the centre of ghostly attention, thousands of spirits gathering around us, more pouring in from every street and alley.

"They're harmless, right?" Bren asked. "Immaterial or whatever? Nothing they can do to hurt us?"

"Not physically," agreed Henka.

"We need to move," I said, as the dead souls pressed closer, growing in clarity and detail.

At first hesitant, they grew bolder, pleading hands reaching for us. Many displayed the wounds of whatever killed them. Some showed the ravages of disease, faces pocked with sores, limbs withered with rot. The rest, likely those who'd died peacefully in their sleep, were uniformly elderly in appearance.

Watery eyes, pleading.

Bony fingers, reaching.

Desperation in the increasingly panicked faces.

"It's maybe almost possible," said Bren, "that I'm ever so slightly shit-water terrified of ghosts." He retreated, hand reaching for his sword, useless as it would be. "It's my one flaw," he admitted.

"I thought wanting to sleep with your face tucked between two large breasts was your one flaw," said Nokutenda.

Bren backed away another step. "It is."

"Have they seen you?" asked Henka.

"They have," I answered.

"Run," she said. "Run now."

The ghosts mobbed us, mouths stretched in silent screams, clawed hands reaching, eyes wide and insane. Bren hauled his sword free and swung, cutting through the spirits to no effect. They pawed at him, fingers sinking into his eyes and past his clenched teeth. They tried to grab his hair and turn him to face them so they might mouth their silent pleas. He staggered away, swinging the demon blade with mad abandon. I lost him in the swarming throng of spectral shapes, and then they were on me too, broken souls submerging themselves in my flesh. I tasted them, smelled the foul madness of their thoughts.

Free me.

Shalayn watched with detached interest, unperturbed by the dead. Sword raised, Bren froze, muscles locked rigid. "I am Tik

Gnarlson," he said in a voice like dry parchment, his accent strange and yet so familiar. "I taught demonic wards to the first-year students—"

Another ghost slammed into Bren, shoving Tik stumbling from the body. "I am Rydk Nashto!" Bren bellowed, voice scaling up an octave. "Elementalist to the—"

Nokutenda, unmolested by the ghosts, pled with Henka to help us. I wondered why they ignored both her and Shalayn, and then a soul forced its way into me. I gagged on the stench infusing my being, foreign thoughts filling my skull.

I understood now why no one came to PalTaq. The island was haunted. Even wizards would be powerless against such an assault. Any living thing stepping foot in the city would be mobbed until their mind broke under the strain. Later, the demonic streetcleaners would sweep up the corpses.

"I am Rarice Ich Oughl," someone said through my voice. "I had a five-year contract—"

Another ghost barrelled into me, sending Rarice from my body, and I babbled about the tensile strengths of various types of steel, gloriously happy to finally have purpose. We danced like marionettes controlled by children battling each other for control. Bren begged in the wavering voice of an old lady to be put out of his misery.

A demonologist, I was no stranger to the battle of wills. Demon after demon had thrown themselves at me, seeking to dominate my spirit. I crushed all thought to a seething pinpoint of rage and yelled, "I am Khraen, and I command you to stop!"

They ignored me, soul after souls shoving itself into me and my friend for its moment of glorious life.

My control wavered and I screamed, "I am Naghron bä Khraen, the Demon Emperor! I am the ruler of this world and I command—"

My throat choked closed, a soul clawing past my defences and causing me to bite my own tongue so it might feel something. Staggering to my knees, I drooled blood. Bren flopped on the stone like a beached fish, eyes and mouth gaping, every muscle locked rigid.

The shamans did this, not me. I had no control over the dead.

The guardians!

Wrestling my own mouth for control, I mumbled, "Demons," through mush lips, frothy blood bubbling my words. "Demons!" I managed, stronger. "I command you to protect us! Stop the souls!"

Spirit demons and hellish wraiths slid from every stone and devoured the swarming souls in a feeding frenzy. The ghosts fled as far as their bonds allowed, but each had been bound to a location to do its work. I watched in horror as my demons slaughtered PalTaq's survivors and the dead died one last death, never to be reborn.

In saving myself and my friends, I'd opened PalTaq to the Guild, though they wouldn't yet know it. With the ghosts gone, there was nothing to stop the filthy mages from plundering my island.

"It doesn't matter," I whispered.

Or at least it shouldn't. Henka wouldn't leave enough of me to care what the wizards did.

"We should go," she said. "If we hurry, we might reach the palace before dark."

CHAPTER SIXTY-THREE

We saw no more ghosts that day, the city's guardians having ended their misery. As the sun sank behind the monolithic palace, throwing us first into shade, and then deepening dark, we travelled through hushed streets, all the more haunted for the lack of ghosts. Empty schools, homes, and churches watched our passing with vacant eyes, accusing. Within minutes of returning to PalTaq I'd finished the pogrom begun so long ago. Yet dead as it was, life remained. Cats stared from alleys or glared down at us from rooftops with distant disdain. Five hundred generations ago their ancient ancestors had been pets and cherished family members. These new lords of the city missed none of that. Curious but unafraid, they made no attempt to follow or approach us. We weren't worth their time, grooming and chasing mice being infinitely more interesting.

We passed through the outermost palace gates as the sun touched the horizon. Travelling through immaculately maintained gardens, those of us still living breathed deep the sweet scents of anacardiaceae and citrus. Trimmed hedgerows and sprawling vineyards lined arrow-straight paths. Planned forests, trees planted in perfect lines, were home to all manner of rodents. And, of course, cats. Lanterns mounted atop polished poles of black steel lit our way, fire elementals sparking to life and dancing their mad joy for probably the first time in thousands of years. Overhead, stiletto stars cut a cloudless night sky.

"Is it just me," said Nokutenda, squinting into the trees, "or is everything here cute?"

"The demons cull the uglier pests," said Henka. "To be allowed to live here an animal must be attractive or useful. Preferably both."

As if I needed more proof of how colossally shallow the Demon Emperor was.

Bren hadn't spoken since the ghosts, and remained quiet, eyes like wounds as he contemplated the flashing moments of long-dead lives that had passed through him.

We reached the palace entrance to the grand hall around midnight, mentally exhausted from our struggle with the city's ghosts, and physically tired from the walk. Staggering a few paces into the cavernous expanse of granite and marble, we stopped to listen to the fading echoes of our footsteps.

"We can rest here," I said, "or go in search of guest quarters. I think I remember where they are."

"How far?" asked Bren.

"Maybe half an hour."

With a grunt, he began digging the sleeping roll from his pack. No one else looked much interested in walking further, so we made camp on the stone floor. It wasn't the worst place I'd ever slept. Not even close.

The sorcerer lay her roll beside Bren's and after a few half-hearted attempts at drawing him into conversation, curled up and went to sleep. Still wearing his armour, Bren lay on his back, fingers laced over his chest, staring up at the ceiling. Shalayn, also so still armoured, sat with her back to a pillar. She closed her eyes and was gently snoring moments later. I remembered that soft purr, the way she slept with her mouth open when drunk, drool staining her pillow. Pale, freckled skin. Strawberry hair hacked short and yet still managing to always be a mess.

After turning a complete circle, examining our surroundings, Henka said, "I suspect we're safe, but will keep watch anyway."

She had changed during the weeks since we murdered the crew. Still beautiful, she'd put on considerable muscle. Shoulders broader than I recalled, her biceps were coiled iron. She had worn the body of an islander warrior for months, but only now truly looked the part. My wife had remade herself for war so slowly, so subtly, I hadn't noticed.

Seeing us hunkering down for the night, the fire elementals lighting the hall flickered out one by one until we appeared to be silver-limned ghosts.

We might be safe here, but none of us knew what awaited beneath the palace. Many of those memories remained lost to me or so scattered I couldn't place them in time. I once dreamed of the hall of pedestals, but in truth had little idea where it was. The only thing I knew for sure was that we'd have to descend deep into the bowels of the world.

After laying out my sleeping roll, I tossed and turned. That large shard of obsidian called from deep below the palace, demanding my attention. Though Henka phrased the retaking of my heart in terms of doing it in the right order, it was clear she wanted me to have them all. There'd been no mention of avoiding some pieces because of what they contained.

Though he wouldn't say why, Nhil also wanted me to claim all my heart before deciding whether to free my wife. That most certainly meant there was knowledge in there that would change my mind.

It was a trap. To keep my promise, I would have to make a decision in ignorance. Yet I knew that if I ended that ignorance, I would not keep my promise. Whatever that insight was, I dare not achieve it. Too often my resolve wavered, tempted by thoughts of domination, conquering the world, and returning to the vision which first set everything in motion.

But could I resist?

My fingers found the stasis box.

It would take every last shred of will, but maybe, if I got it in there fast enough.

Seeing my restless tossing and turning, Henka sank into a relaxed squat at my side. She said nothing, offering comfort with her presence.

"With the ghosts gone," I said, "people can safely return. I wonder if that was what Iremaire wanted."

"I don't think so," said Shalayn from where she sat, eyes still closed. "I think she wanted something more specific."

Kantlament, my sword to end all sorrow. The stone eyes I once wore, jammed into my protesting skull by my god to replace those lost serving her will. The hall of pedestals, each displaying its trophy of leathery heart. Perhaps there was a Soul Stone somewhere in the palace with near one million souls trapped within, waiting to be spent. There was more, too. Endless catacombs and hidden basements wormed through the rock beneath the palace. I'd spent millennium collecting and hoarding artifacts of power. Though I remembered little of it, there were things down there that terrified even the Demon Emperor. Any of these would have been of interest to Iremaire. Or all of them. Why stop at just one world-shattering relic?

I must have drifted off because I woke with morning's first timorous light. The sun had yet to breach PalTaq's outer wall and the cloudless eastern horizon was lit in golden fire. As I sat up, Henka strolled from the darkness deeper into the cavern.

"It's been a long time," she said. "So strange how some memories remain crisp with detail while others fade. I found a kitchen where I remember you taking your morning coffee. You only did it the once, usually preferring to drink it…" She laughed. "Elsewhere. I don't know. That, I can't remember."

Somehow, *immortal* seemed such an incomplete and shallow word for the true reality of living forever. Immortal didn't save you from pain or guarantee that you'd remember your past. Even those doomed to perish left something behind with the ceaseless march of days. No one got to choose what was forgotten. Important lessons were as likely to fade as long moments of boredom. We remembered useless slivers of time, like that one cup of coffee, and forgot where we left our wife's heart. Of course, having been rudely meddled with, my memory was more fractured than most.

Bren groaned as he woke, sitting up to rub his eyes like a child and peer blearily about the hall as if confused about how he got here.

"Did you dream about boobs again?" asked Nokutenda.

He shook his head. "I remember killing someone, bleeding them into a bowl bigger than a bathhouse, and trapping their soul in stone."

He looked up at me with ancient eyes, tinged red with lack of sleep and haunted with the memories of murderers long dead. Little remained in that gaze of my young friend, and nothing of the cabin boy I saved from the wreck of the *Habnikaav*.

Anathema to innocence, bane to happiness, I was killing him.

My own ghosts surrounded me, most still living. Henka, my

enslaved love. Shalayn the victim of my need for vengeance. Bren, clinging to me out of a sense of loyalty I intentionally fostered because I needed him more than he needed me.

Only Nokutenda seemed untouched.

At least so far.

After eating the last of the food we scavenged from the *Katlipok*, we set off, heading deeper into the palace. Once again, the fire elementals lining every hall and chamber sparked to life to light our way. I followed the pull of my heart and my friends followed me.

I flinched. I kept thinking of them as friends, but Henka and Shalayn were slaves, Bren tied to me by misguided and youthful loyalty, and the sorcerer because she thought I would bring back a world that had never existed.

We traversed long miles of echoing hallways, passed through rooms larger than colosseums, saw libraries lined with shelves disappearing into the distance, and stopped to marvel at indoor amphitheatres built to seat tens of thousands. The Black Citadel was nothing in comparison, the tiny private bolthole for a man who loathed most of humanity.

"When I saw Naghron's pyramids," said Nokutenda, "I thought I was looking at the shining pinnacle of islander civilization. It was like looking into the past, seeing what we'd once been capable of. It was all so grubby compared to this." She glanced at me. "We should bring everyone in Palaq here. The Guild can smash themselves stupid against the city's defences. If they could have conquered PalTaq, they would have long ago."

"We will," I lied.

She accepted me at my word, flashing Bren a satisfied grin. His own answering smile carried a hard edge and he looked quickly away.

The deeper we went into the palace, the more I remembered. Hallways became familiar, having been traversed so many times over thousands of years. Soon, I hurried ahead, no longer needing to heed the call of my heart. I knew where it was.

My friends hustled to keep up, my own excitement mirrored in their eyes.

The emperor's personal chambers lay at the heart of the palace, the massive demon-bound stone doors recognizing me and swinging open at my approach. Through another library, and I jogged down a long hall of guestrooms set aside for visiting dignitaries. My heart screaming at me to run, I found the doors to my inner sanctum.

A hulking mountain of a man in plate armour shaped from some strange jade stood blocking the way, sword held point down, gauntleted hands resting on the pommel.

Eyes the colour of his armour studied me through the visor's narrow slit. "Master."

I remembered. A manifestation demon called from some war-torn world and clothed in demonic armour rivalling the emperor's own, I once trusted this creature with both my life and my privacy.

"Miktel HanVoose," I said. "These are my guests."

The demon bowed. When he gestured at the granite door, it swung silently open.

"Oh, thank fuck," muttered Bren.

The room beyond looked too much like the summoning chambers in the Black Citadel for my liking. The walls and floor were polished granite of gleaming sable cut with veins of bloody crimson. Everything was cold stone. A massive marble desk, a single stone chair before it that could no more be comfortable than it could be moved.

I staggered as I entered, Henka catching me in strong hands, holding me effortlessly until I regained my composure.

There, on the desk, a jagged sharp-edged lump of obsidian. It stole my breath, robbed me of thought and will. I stumbled forward on unsteady legs, Henka still guiding me.

Take it.

Take it.

Take it.

The size slowed me. It was too large to be a human heart, particularly when combined with the stone I already possessed.

Take it.

Henka said that when we first cut out my heart to break it, pieces were already missing. How could that be possible? This could never be the heart of a man.

I hissed with rage, discovering my hand already reaching for the stone of its own volition. The hand hesitated but refused to return to my side.

Take it!

"Take it," said Henka. "Remember."

Take it and remember why I placed my hand on her heart and commanded her to love me forever. Take it and remember why I couldn't free her.

I sobbed with hunger, triggering some of the Demon Emperor's old rage. A man of iron determination and cold purpose, he saw need as a weakness. He was never a man to be manipulated. The emperor gripped destiny in his fist and bent it to his will. He conquered worlds and killed gods.

"Take it," repeated Henka.

What if she guessed my intentions? Her love guaranteed she couldn't want to be free because that freedom would hurt me. That, combined with Nhil's insistence I know everything before deciding, made up my mind.

"Not yet," I said through clenched teeth. "It will incapacitate me for days, and there are still things I must do."

"You need to remember everything," she said, voice desperate. "Only then can you make the right choices."

I wanted to laugh at the irony of my own slave trying to dance me to her will.

I forced that errant reaching hand to close. "I'll take it when I'm ready. I promise," I lied again. "I will be whole."

Digging the stasis box from my pack was an act of incredible will, my hands shaking. When I opened it, and the combined pull of the obsidian fragments shrieked at me I almost cracked, tears streaming from my eyes.

"Bren," I managed to whisper. "Please."

Lifting the stone heart with awed care, he placed it in the box.

Snapping the lid closed, I collapsed to my knees. I felt like a puppet with its strings severed, deprived of volition, boneless and gutted of purpose.

"Why not take your heart now?" asked Henka, a comforting hand on my shoulder. "We're safe. What else is there to do?"

Always questioning. Never trusting. Planning and scheming, never leaving anything to chance.

But I was ready, had spent months thinking about this moment and what must follow.

Putting the box into my pack, I said, "My sword. I remember where it is."

It was a lie.

"Kantlament," breathed Nokutenda in awe. "The Guild will fall before us!"

I gave her a weak grin as Bren and Henka lifted me to my feet.

Once I felt steady on my legs, I said, "Come, my sword is in the basement."

CHAPTER SIXTY-FOUR

I walked with no idea where I was going. We passed long halls lined with warded doors, none of which called to me. At every opportunity, I led us down. Sometimes the stairs were straight, a sudden plunging into a darkness unsullied by light for thousands of years. The fire elementals lining every hall flickered into life, spasming in joy, as we approached. Some stairways were hidden behind secret doors I only remembered as I reached them and curved down in tight spirals barely wide enough for Brenwick to pass through.

Memories returned as I walked and I'd slow as I approached a warded and demon-bound door, recalling the artifact hidden within. So much I wanted to explore. I'd spent millennium pillaging worlds, stashing their most powerful magics here. Some were put away for later. Others were locked up so they might never be used against me. The deeper I went, the more I remembered, the more I knew the Guild played no part in my fall. They couldn't have toppled me then and, should I decide to reclaim the world, they couldn't stop me now. They would only rule as long as I allowed.

Down.

We walked long corridors littered with the bones of fallen gods, behemoth skulls mounted like trophies.

Ever down.

The temperature dropped as we plunged ever deeper. Dressed for the tropics, we shivered as our sweat-drenched clothes cooled. The last of our food finished, we paused briefly for water before continuing. There was no stopping now and I would not return. I would die down here one way or another. If I failed to find the hall of pedestals, I'd starve. If I succeeded…

Another set of hidden stairs led to a short passage ending in a single door.

"Is this it?" asked Bren "Or did we miss something?"

Not answering, I opened the door. Beyond stood an empty room of plain stone. There was no marking or blemish of any kind, nothing to memorize. No torch-bound fire elemental lit the interior. I'd never be able to use a portal demon to come here. Was that the point?

Everything about this room felt wrong.

"Everyone in," I said, entering.

"But it's empty," said Nokutenda, following.

Large enough for the five of us, it would have been uncomfortable with twice our number. Taking a deep breath, I closed the door, plunging us into perfect darkness.

"Now what?" asked the sorcerer.

Though so much had returned to me as we walked the halls beneath the palace, a lot remained missing. Something felt deeply wrong here. Not like I'd forgotten something critical, but rather that some key understanding eluded me.

I opened the door, stared down that same short passage, and closed it again.

Spirit demons could be bound to any object. A ring. A sword.

A doorway or room.

There was a portal demon here, awaiting my command. But it wasn't as simple as telling it to take me to the hall of pedestals because that wasn't where it went. Or rather not quite.

The words, I remembered them.

My hands shook and I clenched my fists to hide it.

No, no, no, no.

This couldn't be right.

I remembered binding this demon and the phrase that would trigger it. I didn't, however, know *why* I'd chosen those three words. That piece remained missing.

Henka stood behind me, silent and patient. Had she taken it, or had I carved it out myself before we broke my heart?

I was there when the shaman cut your heart out. There were already pieces missing.

"Take me home," I said.

When I once again swung the door open, the short passage and the fire elementals lighting it were gone. Hot, dry air hit me with concussive force, staggering me back. I felt strangely heavy. All hint of the ever-pervasive tropical scents were gone, my sweat-damp clothes drying in moments.

Though I couldn't see, no fire elementals having sparked to life as I opened the door, I knew we'd gone somewhere new.

"We need light," I said. "Nokutenda, can you do that?"

She hesitated for a moment, shooting a glance at Henka. "I'd rather not."

"Making a small light barely costs you anything," I snapped, annoyed. As the words came out, I knew they were true.

"Still, that's my life you want to spend. If there's any other way…" She sounded uncertain.

"I got this," said Shalayn.

I heard her sword slide from its scabbard, and then a warm, yellow light filled the room and lit the hall beyond.

Where the many basements beneath the palace were all polished granite, perfectly smooth, I now saw a long passage of simple stone. Everything looked ancient, rough and rounded, and had none of the palace's crisp angles. Red sand dusted the floor. Shalayn's sword lit a score of paces. Beyond that all was dark.

"I didn't know your sword did that," I said, glancing over my shoulder.

"Never needed it to."

Henka stepped forward to stand at my side. "I've never been here before."

"This is where I keep my most valued possessions."

It was true, but why here?

Because Henka could never find this place, never travel here without me. If I'd gone through such lengths to keep this place a secret, had I made a terrible mistake in bringing her?

"Where are we?" Nokutenda asked.

Ignoring her question, I headed into the hall. Once again, my friends followed, huddled in the pool of light. I wanted to laugh. A sorcerer, a demon-possessed swordswoman, a powerful necromancer, and the Demon Emperor all suddenly afraid of the dark.

The red sand stopped abruptly at the first intersection. Though strangely devoid of sand and dust, the stone beyond remained the same. Rough as it was, there wasn't a single seam anywhere. I knew this place, and yet as was so often the case, cursed the gaps in my memory. On some previous trip, I'd spent days exploring and found a stairway leading up, to the surface. We were in a basement hidden far beneath a temple unlike anything in PalTaq. That church sat in the very centre of the ruins of a colossal city. The world was dead, endless blood red sands reaching beyond the horizon in every direction. In some ways, it was the perfect hiding place. Nothing lived here so no one might stumble upon my hidden prizes. The likelihood of anyone first finding this dead world and then bothering to explore it was beyond slim. Time had erased every trace of the inhabitants. I had no idea what they'd looked like or how they lived. Nothing but broken stone and half-buried structures remained.

Stepping into the intersection, I frowned at the sharp line of sand stopping where the first hall ended.

"A long time ago," I said, speaking as the memories returned, "I brought an air elemental here. I ordered it to keep the halls free of sand so my footprints wouldn't betray the location of—" I caught myself about to mention the hall of pedestals. "The cache of treasures," I continued. "I ordered it to avoid the hall with the portal door because I didn't want it somehow dumping everything there or accidentally leaving."

Someone—a close friend, maybe Nhil—had cracked a rare joke: What's dumber than an air elemental? Two air elementals!

And then we'd laughed and laughed like it was the funniest thing. I laughed until I cried, tears streaming down my face, and still I laughed. We then shared stories about all the times air elementals misunderstood directions or confused the messages they were supposed to deliver. I told my friend about the time a bunch of elementalists gathered for a conference and one ordered the elementals in the room to circulate and keep the air fresh. At some point they all wandered over to the same corner and everyone died from asphyxiation.

Blinking, I realized I'd been silent, lost in memory for some time. Tears stained my cheeks.

"Left," I said, knowing it was the right direction.

We stalked through long halls devoid of sand, Shalayn's sword our only source of light.

"I can't believe I'm going to say this," said Bren, sweat dripping from his nose, "but I miss being cold."

I too was soaked, though I was too distracted to care. The oppressive heat didn't seem to bother the women, though in Henka's case I understood why. Sweat was just one of the many inconveniences that didn't plague the dead.

The pressure changed, my ears popping. A gust of hot wind tugged at my hair.

"Do you hear something?" asked Bren.

A low rumble, felt first more than heard, built as the wind picked up. Henka looked back. "I think something is coming."

Something too stupid to ever think to do anything other than follow its last command.

"Run!" I shouted, shoving everyone into motion.

We managed no more than a few strides before it overtook us. One moment my feet pounded stone, legs pumping as fast as they could, and then the ground disappeared, and I was lifted into a choking tangle of sand, hair, dust, and unidentifiable detritus. Something hit me from behind and I tumbled head over heels, all sense of direction scrambled. I caught a flash of Bren's armoured elbow as it slammed into my face and then he disappeared into a snarled morass of collected garbage. Grit filled my teeth, clogged my nose closed. Empty shells and the husked corpses of insects caught in my hair as I rolled over and over as if caught in an ocean riptide.

Coughing.

Gagging.

Tiny sips of air, always polluted. The air elemental barrelled around a corner, unheeding of its new cargo and I bounced off a wall, one of my shoulders taking the brunt of the blow. Peering through narrowed eyes I saw bones, some looking human, others oddly twisted, float past, caught up with everything else. A sword of black stone tumbled beyond my reach, coated in powdery grime. Struggling to turn, swimming in a chaotic sea of dross, I tried to catch sight of my companions. The world blurred, turning foggy and indistinct, as my lungs fought for breath.

Some madman cackled at the thought of being collected along with all the other garbage, my corpse spending the rest of eternity trapped within the air elemental I'd summoned.

I summoned.

There was no way I would have trusted an elementalist to do this for me.

Drawing breath to speak, I choked on dust and hair. Retching, I lifted the edge of my shirt and inhaled through the fabric.

"Stop," I managed, voice throttled and weak.

I hit another wall, skull bouncing off rounded stone. Bright sparks danced behind my eyes, swirling purple traceries drawing drunken pirouettes.

Low buzzing filled my ears, and then I found myself spat out and sprawled on the floor. Coughing up a tangled hairball, I stared at the heaving monstrosity before me. Hawking thick phlegm, I puked mud, head slow to clear. I felt like I'd been stored in the mouldy corner of an unused closet, clothes caked and chalky.

"The others," I managed. "Spit them out."

The dust elemental throbbed, a foul wind ruffling my hair, and I heard its ancient language: *What others?*

"The others you picked up!"

Tremors ran through the chaotic tangle and several dry bones tumbled out. They must have been caught in there for a thousand years.

"The living ones!"

Hunching like a cat about to vomit a hairball, it expelled Bren and Nokutenda.

"Next time," grumbled the sorcerer, sprawled in an ungainly heap, "a little warning would be nice." She coughed a cloud of reddish dust. "And maybe shout 'run' about ten minutes earlier."

AN END TO SORROW

Bren lay on the floor, eyes bright in his filth-caked face. "That hurt."

I realized, dim as it was, I could see. From deep within the elemental came the faintest yellow glow. Shalayn's sword!

"All of them!" I commanded. "Dead and living!"

After regurgitating more bleached bones, it finally deposited Henka, and Shalayn.

The swordswoman, still gripping her glowing sword, rose to her feet, hair a rat's nest of twigs and splintered bone. She stood waiting, as if being swallowed by a massive dust elemental and almost dying was beneath notice. Our eyes met, and for an instant I saw the pure hate she held for me.

Once we were upright, I turned a complete circle, trying to get my bearings. The elemental blocked my view in one direction, but I felt sure what I wanted wasn't back that way.

"I know where I am," I said, realizing it was true. "Not far now."

"Tell me there's water there," said Bren.

"Sorry." He wasn't going to survive this any more than I was. We were all doomed. Perhaps that was why I hadn't insisted we pause to refill our water skins and collect food from the gardens before descending. "Sorry," I started again, "you'll have to wait until we get back."

We locked eyes and he nodded, understanding. "That's fine," he said. "I don't mind."

After ordering the dust elemental to stay where it was, I set out. Two corners later, I found what I was looking for. A twenty-foot-tall door of polished obsidian filled the end of the hall. Approaching, I saw my smoky reflection, warped and twisted in the stone. I stopped, unable to continue. I hadn't paid much attention to my appearance in a long time, never bothering to look in mirrors. My hair, long and black and unkempt, hung to my waist in riotous coiled knots. My crumpled and threadbare clothes looked like I'd walked through a torrential downpour and then been rolled in dried shit. My face... so impossibly youthful. No wrinkles. No iron-grey hair. I couldn't remember ever being this young. Everything about me was so wrong I wanted to scream at him, smash the black stone so I didn't have to see that face I hated so much.

I *am* the smoke, I thought, not this ebony flesh.

I was the death of light, the murderer of sun gods. I brought destruction with my left hand, ended epochs with my right. There could be no birth without death, no beginning without an end.

"I am that end," I said.

I never saw anyone with skin like mine because there was no one. Midnight flesh. A heart of cold obsidian shattered and remade over and over. Nothing about me was natural.

"Take me home," I said. "Take me home."

Half request, half desperate plea for understanding.

Stepping forward, I placed my hands against the obsidian door, my reflection doing the same. For a heartbeat we stared at each other, and then I pushed the door open.

CHAPTER SIXTY-FIVE

I entered the hall of pedestals and my friends followed more slowly than before.

Eyes narrowed, Henka scanned the great room, attention flicking from pedestal to pedestal. She approached the nearest, bending to read the name on the plaque.

Straightening, she reached out to touch the leathery strip of desiccated heart. "You still live," she said, voice soft. "Gather the others."

Confused, I watched as she moved to the next pedestal, fingers caressing its grizzly trophy.

"I have returned," she whispered. "Gather in the ruins south of the Undying Lands."

"What are you doing?" I asked.

Henka turned to face me. "My heart is here?"

I readied myself, physically and mentally. She'd either attempt to convince me I was making a mistake or kill me and start again.

"It is." I gestured into the dark beyond the reach of Shalayn's sword. "At the back."

Sadness bent her.

"I have to do this," I said. "I can't live with the crime of what I did to you."

Henka looked from Shalayn to Nokutenda and back to me. "You never understood. My love is terrible and complete."

"No worse than mine."

"I would destroy worlds for you. I *have* destroyed worlds. I will do anything to make you happy." She smiled then, though it was an expression of loss and regret. "At least this world is already dead."

"You knew I'd bring you here." My chest tightened in fear. "You *want* me to free you."

"Not quite," she said. "My vengeance would rob you of any chance at happiness."

"I don't understand."

"I murdered entire realities. The dead worshipped me with a fervour the living could never manage, unsullied by doubt or free will." Her eyes became wistful. "I was close to becoming a god."

"You were the threat from beyond." Nhil had hinted as much, but why hadn't he spoken clearly?

"I came to your world to cleanse it of foul life. We fought, and you, with the help of your god, won. But instead of destroying me, you decided to use me. With my undead armies, you thought to betray your god."

I could see it happening. Defeating Henka, I laid my hand on her heart and ordered her to love me. It was the only way to guarantee she'd never betray me.

I asked, "Do you still love me?"

"More than anything in any world," she said.

"Then how—"

She silenced me with a raised hand. "You are happiest when in danger, when facing almost certain defeat. You *like* being cornered. You live for those mad thrills. You once told me the last time you were happy was when we battled."

Finally, I understood. Henka would do anything to make me happy, including hurl an entire reality into a terrible war. She wouldn't let me free her, because then she'd be free to destroy me, but she needed to know where her heart was so she could ensure I could never return, never again lay hands on it to change my last order. She would kill me, shatter my heart, and again scatter the pieces. Then, she would destroy the portal demon leading to this world. Without it, I would never find my way back. She would love me forever, destroy me over and over, always pushing me to the edge I craved so I might know those rare moments of happiness.

I have returned, she'd said. *Gather in the ruins south of the undying lands.*

She'd given a last command to her remaining necromancers. They would await her return, begin building her army for the war to come.

"I'm sorry for the pain this will cause you now," Henka said, "but later you will not remember. Nokutenda, make sure Bren doesn't interfere. Crush his skull if he does. And Shalayn, my dear, please kill my loving husband."

The swordswoman's casual disinterest fell away, raw hate twisting her features. "With pleasure."

Nokutenda turned on Bren, saying, "Stay!" as if commanding a dog. When he reached for his sword, she waggled a finger at him. "Do that, and I'll squish you like a bug."

The big man hesitated, looking to me for guidance.

"Bren," I said, seeing that raised finger, recognizing the ring Shalayn no longer wore, "do as she says."

"But—"

Backing away from the swordswoman, I said, "It's not Nokutenda anymore. It's Brisinder."

It wasn't difficult to guess how Henka gained command of the demon. She'd raised KriskOrke, the demonologist who died when his stomach burst, and ordered him to sever the binding on the ring. With the wards broken, he rebound the demon, commanding it to obey her.

"Cut Khraen's heart out when you're done," ordered Henka. "But don't further damage it."

The visor of her white helm still open, Shalayn advanced, grinning cracked and broken teeth. "I told you I'd kill you."

I drew Adraalmak, the demon finding little colour in this dead world to devour. If Nokutenda wore the ring containing Brisinder, how was Henka commanding Shalayn?

That too was obvious. My wife must have murdered the possessed swordswoman the moment I left for the Black Citadel. The demon, incapable of possessing a corpse, would have retreated to the ring, which she then brought to KriskOrke. I wanted to laugh, to complement Henka on her planning, and to tell Nhil he hadn't been wrong. She thought of everything. She needed the sorcerer's power, but the dead couldn't fuel sorcery with their lifeforce. She needed Shalayn's sword and skills but couldn't command the demon possessing her.

That was why Henka became so desperate to kill off the last of the crew and harvest them; she needed blood and flesh to maintain two undead such that they passed for living.

So many small and ignored mysteries made sense. The way Shalayn obeyed Henka when she barked orders. The way the sorcerer and my wife began spending more time together after we returned from the floating mountains. The dust elemental hadn't spat Shalayn and Henka out until I specified I wanted the dead ones too.

Shalayn attacked with a series of feints and stabs, testing my defences. I knocked a few aside, suffered a shallow wound, and hit nothing when I tried to decapitate her. Her sword, the only source of light in the hall of pedestals, left yellow lines seared into my sight.

My emotions were a chaotic maelstrom of confusion. Henka wanted me to bring her here the entire time, and her protestations otherwise were all manipulation. Even insisting I take the large shard had been a trick. She knew the more she pushed, the more I'd resist. The last thing she wanted was me taking on the piece that knew better than to trust her. I was what she made me, the piece that loved her so much I'd bring her here in a misguided attempt to free her.

Shalayn attacked again, lunging to impale my gut, and I batted her sword aside with mine. Weaving a web of defence, I retreated, creating space. Last time we fought, I'd been unarmed and barely awake. This would be different.

I flashed a grin. "Even with your magical sword and armour you can't beat me. You know it's true."

She screamed in rage and attacked, smashing at me without finesse, hacking like she meant to fell a tree. For all Henka's necromantic control, without Brisinder, this was once again Shalayn. And I'd murdered her sister. She might not be allowed to damage my heart, but she'd been given free rein to otherwise butcher me. Powerful as her enchanted sword was, it could never damage Adraalmak. The demon blade sang savage joy as the mageblade shed sparks and fine slivers of metal.

I saw my moment.

Sword coming up in preparation for cleaving me from shoulder to hip, she left herself open.

I stepped in, drove Adraalmak through the breastplate of her white armour so hard the sword's tip punched through her back as well. Transfixed, weapon still raised, she blinked at me.

I remembered the way she looked when I murdered Tien. Heartbreak and betrayal.

"You were never going to win," I said. "You—"

Shalayn landed a front kick in my gut doubling me in agony and crumpling me to the floor. Adraalmak, lodged in her armour, was torn from my hand. Eyes watering, I wheezed for breath as she drew the sword from her chest and tossed it contemptuously aside, sending it skittering into the dark. I crawled backward, trying to escape, and she planted an armoured boot in my ribs, cracking several. Curled foetal, I sobbed in pain.

"You're not going to remember this," said Shalayn, "but I will." She stomped on one of my hands, shattering the bones. "She promised I could torture you. She said that if I served well, she'd let me kill you each time you came back. Over and over and over."

She stabbed me, careful not to hit anything critical. "And so," she said, "I will serve."

Through my pain I heard Bren say, "I never showed you my necklace, did I?"

"You don't want to do that," said Nokutenda as he reached a hand into his shirt.

"It's not a weapon," he promised, hand still moving.

"I'm going to skin you," Shalayn told me.

Since the sorcerer knew Bren would never lie to her, so did Brisinder. "She doesn't want to kill you," the demon said, "but I won't hesitate."

"I never told you about the jaggler god," Bren said, pulling out the rounded stone talisman.

"The *what* god?"

"I'll sharpen my sword on your teeth," continued Shalayn, ignoring the others. Leaning forward, she pushed the tip of her sword into my shin. "I'll core the marrow from your bones."

Bren clutched the stone in his fist. "Ak'b'al."

I wanted to scream at Bren to stop, that the pathetic talisman would be powerless here, but was too busy roaring in agony as Shalayn drove the sword between the bones in my shin and then twisted it. Gods, however, are not bound by the mortal rules. They exist, shattered, wearing a million guises in a million worlds. Like me, they were littered across realities. In one world, Ak'b'al was all but forgotten, worshipped only by a single savage tribe. In another, he was an aspect of the Lord of the Night Sky, a small piece in the broken puzzle that was the God of Strife.

That talisman, once painted shiny black and no larger than a child's thumb, represented something like me, something that existed both back in my world, and here. Little more than a ghost itself, that dead jaguar god still haunted the endless red sands beyond this fallen church.

It heard Bren's call, sensed his need, his utter faith it would come, and answered.

Bren pounced, crossing the distance between him and Nokutenda before she could blink. Twice her weight, he crushed her to the ground. Wrapping his huge, scarred hands around her neck, he lifted her head, slammed it down against the stone.

She made a noise, small and confused, eyes struggling to focus on her attacker.

"Stop," he said, hissing between his teeth.

Her hand rose, forefinger and thumb coming together, and Bren made a retching wail as his eyes bulged from the pressure.

"Something is wrong," Henka said. "Shalayn! Kill him! Kill him now!"

Even as Shalayn bellowed denial, her sword slid from my leg, lifting for a killing blow. She had no choice but to obey. From somewhere I heard the sodden crunch of pulverized bone.

A voice rang out, echoing through the hall of pedestals. "Command Shalayn to protect Khraen and then be still and silent!"

I knew that voice.

Shalayn's sword descended in a decapitating swing, as Henka yelled, "Protect Khraen!" and stopped, edge leaving a thin line of blood in my flesh.

The swordwoman stared down at me, jaw clenched with hate and rage, as she fought the necromancy. There was no winning; Henka owned her.

"Let me kill him!" she begged. "We both want this! Let me kill him!"

But Henka remained silent.

"Someday," Shalayn whispered, standing over me, eyes already scanning for threats, "I will kill you."

Crawling from under her, I struggled to my knees, peering about the hall in confusion. Nokutenda lay dead and limp, crushed skull still gripped in Bren's hand, blood pattering on the floor below. Henka stood rooted, mouth clamped shut, eyes wide and locked on something behind me. Turning, I saw Nhil. Still wearing the cloak of invisibility, only his face exposed, standing before a pedestal barely visible at the rear of the hall.

Stunned to see my friend alive, I could only think he must have used the cloak and returned with me when I escaped the Black Citadel with Bren and Nokutenda. For some reason, he hadn't wanted me to know he survived. Though the first thing I'd done was share my grief at the loss with Henka. Perhaps that, instead, had been his goal.

"I worried I couldn't do it," he called, words echoing. "Working such manipulations from another world is—"

A blinding blue light interrupted him, drowned the yellow of Shalayn's sword. The air crackled with power, stuttering sparks hissing. The hairs on my arms and neck stood shivering, frigid goosebumps pimpling my flesh despite the desert heat. Henka, visible only as an unmoving silhouette, remained locked in the act of turning toward the pedestal at the rear of the hall.

The light dimmed and I blinked away the flowering lines seared into my vision.

There, in the centre of the hall, stood Iremaire in robes of harsh, actinic white. She floated in the air, pale blue flames creating an oval shield around her.

"I told you to keep the ring as a reminder that I would always be smarter than you," the mage said. "I see that you threw it away."

CHAPTER SIXTY-SIX

Brenwick looked up from where he crouched over Nokutenda. Still under the influence of the totem, his eyes were a pale green, pupils narrowed to slits by the bright light. His lips rolled back in a cat-like snarl. The sorcerer lay limp beneath him, head twisted at an unnatural angle, the back of her skull crushed flat. Blood soaked her hair, dripped from Bren's clawed hands.

Shalayn, under orders from Henka to protect me, moved faster. She launched herself at the battlemage crossing the distance in an instant despite the plate armour. Striking Iremaire's shield, the force of the impact staggered the mage back several paces. Iremaire gestured with her right hand, a slight flick of fingers, and something flashed out to pass through the swordswoman. Too fast to focus on, it looked like harmless wisps of fog.

Shalayn fell, one leg suddenly missing from the hip down, the other gone at the knee. Dead, she felt nothing. Still driven by Henka's command, she scampered forward like an ungainly three-legged dog, leaving a trail of thick blood behind her.

Surprised, the mage retreated, and lashed out again. This time, Shalayn saw it coming and rolled away. She lost her left arm and most of her torso below the ribs. Undeterred, she advanced, intestines spilling out in looping coils as she dragged herself with one arm, sword gripped in the fist.

"Oh," said Iremaire, surprised, though unconcerned. "I must have missed this little turn of events."

Again, she gestured with her right hand, a thin line of fog drawing a neat line across Shalayn's throat, and the swordswoman's head rolled away, eyes wide with surprise. The body fell still, sagging as the will left it.

Taking advantage of the mage's momentary distraction, Bren leapt, and was smashed to the ground by a gesture with Iremaire's left hand. He landed with bone-crushing force, blood spraying from his mouth with the impact. Dazed, he lifted his head, still trying to move, and the mage made a pushing motion with her left hand. Pressure crushed him down and he screamed, pinned. Blood leaked from his eyes and ears. He sagged, wheezing in agony, as if someone had dropped an elephant on him.

"Stay there," said Iremaire.

Looking for my sword, I turned in time to see Nhil flip up the hood of the cloak and disappear. Spotting Adraalmak, I crawled toward the weapon.

"How about you stay where you are," drawled Iremaire. "Stop this silliness, and I won't paint the floor with your young friend."

Her left hand twitched and Bren was dragged several strides, leaving a long red smear behind him.

With little choice, I stopped.

The battlemage flashed a smug grin as she surveyed the hall, gaze lingering on the various pedestals. "You thought I'd let you go with only a single scry focus?" She tutted, shaking her head. "I made sure I had several planted on the swordswoman, that sword and armour for starters, and more on your scarred friend." She smiled sweetly. "Unless you all stripped naked and replaced virtually everything you carried, there was no way I'd lose you. I must admit, I was disappointed at how long it took you to figure out the ring. It was meant to be obvious, so you'd feel secure." She frowned at Henka, still standing silent. "What's wrong with her?"

"She underestimated her opponent," I said, "and is now paying the price."

Iremaire wrinkled her nose, studying my motionless wife before returning her attention to me. "You're not quite what I expected. I thought I was going to have to demolish you in battle before you'd bend to my will. But you genuinely love this corpse," she nodded at Henka, "and care for that dim-witted lump of scar tissue."

I shouldn't. The old me wouldn't have. But in breaking me and selecting only the piece that loved her enough to bring her here and free her, Henka had weakened me greatly. The man who could casually toss aside friends, feed them to gods and demons or sacrifice them on the battlefield for the slightest gain, was gone.

When I didn't speak, Iremaire said, "Please remove my stasis box from your pack."

I did so, and it skidded across the floor to stop at her feet.

"Fetch your wife's heart for me, and then we'll go get that sword."

I didn't move. "You could scry here," I said, stalling. "Even though this is a different world."

"Of course. The art has changed a lot since your fall. I watched you in your bolthole reality too. The demonic wards there were all outdated, protecting against a form of spying the Guild hasn't practised in a thousand years."

Bren whimpered and coughed blood.

"If you're so powerful, why do you need Henka?" I asked.

Iremaire gave me a patient and amused half-smile, as if she had all the time in the world. "You really don't know?"

I shook my head.

"Henka was the first necromancer. Before her, this world knew nothing of undeath beyond shaman speaking to the spirits of their ancestors. She is the first and she kept the heart of every necromancer she made." The mage gestured at the pedestals surrounding us. "Those are the hearts of the most ancient and powerful necromancers. Some are gone, destroyed during the war, or fallen to the Guild in the millennium since, but many escaped. They fled to bolthole realities like your Black Citadel or disappeared into the jungles."

Somehow, long ago, I had taken Henka's heart and commanded her to give me the hearts of her necromancers. I knew then they played a larger role in my early domination of this world than I'd remembered. Later, the undead had been but a small part of my armies, but in the beginning, they were my hidden advantage. They were my spies, my unkillable shock troops.

"You aren't here on Guild business," I said, trying to keep the mage talking so Nhil could do whatever he planned.

Iremaire snarled. "They've been complacent for centuries. The islanders have been building cities, gathering armies, and pillaging ruins for artifacts. I warned the Guild about Naghron and Palaq and they laughed! They said the situation was 'under control' and that the darkers were nothing to worry about. Old men with heads up their wrinkled asses, lost in researching useless esoterica." She waved a hand as if gesturing at the world beyond. "You've seen how it is. Poverty and filth. The Deredi once again growing in power."

"You need a war," I said, understanding. "A common enemy."

"One who obeys," she agreed. "Henka is perfect. Through her I can control when and where the necromancers strike. My opposition in the Guild will fall first. Then, when they see I've been right all along, I'll begin predicting Henka's next moves, turn the tide of war against the foul dead."

She'd either use that to better her position in the Guild or replace it completely; I didn't much care. All too well I recognized her lust for power.

Nhil had shouted an order and Henka obeyed, which meant he must have placed his hand on her heart. I'd thought he'd come to my aid, but he could just as easily have come for his own reasons. Much like Iremaire, he needed me to bring him here.

I wanted to scream with frustration, rage against my helplessness.

Except I wasn't helpless. Even now, this mage underestimated me. I called my god once, I could do it again.

Or could I? Last time, I'd been in the hold of Iremaire's ship, in an entirely different world. My god answered my call, possessing the body of the mage left to watch over me. He hadn't survived the experience. The shear proximity of her divinity had shattered what remained of Shalayn's sanity. Would she come if I called from this world, or had I chosen this as the hiding place for Henka's heart because she couldn't?

The idea seemed worse and worse. There were only two people here my god might possess, Bren, and Iremaire. Knowing the perversity of her dream and her dislike of what she deemed my weaknesses, she'd choose Bren. Calling her would doom my only friend.

Iremaire sighed, a world-weary exhalation. "I'm not just one step ahead of *you*," she said, "I'm a step ahead of all your friends as well."

"My friends?"

Nhil appeared, the once invisible cloak bursting into flames. He writhed and screamed on the floor, boiling from the inside, grey flesh bubbling and blistering. Violet eyes burst into steam, ran down his cheeks like scalding tears.

Iremaire watched, head tilted. "*I* made that cloak, foolish demon. You thought I couldn't see it?"

Nhil's screams turned to mad cackled laughter. "Not at all," he hissed between teeth cracking from the heat. "Rather, I counted on your overconfidence." He reached into his robes.

Panicked, the mage dumped power into the spell, turning the demon into an expanding cloud of bloody steam. Even as he came apart, my most ancient friend sent what he'd kept hidden all these years rolling across the floor toward me.

Focussing all that energy on Nhil must have distracted Iremaire. Bren was back on his feet with a wheezed roar or rage, limping toward her like he meant to tear her apart with his bare hands. One side of his chest bent inward and down, the ribs no longer lined up on both sides. His left ankle was broken, the foot bent at a gut-twisting angle. Blood ran from his ears and between his bared teeth.

As the mage turned her attention on my last friend, I stopped the rolling stone with my left hand.

With the other, I reached up to claw out my right eye.

AN END TO SORROW

CHAPTER SIXTY-SEVEN

Once, thousands of years ago, my god tore out the first of my eyes. Fragments of that memory still haunted me. The incredible pain as divine fingers slipped through my flesh, gripped the orb, and dragged it from my skull. The stuttering sparks filling my head as the nerves were stretched to snapping. Watching with my remaining eye as she crushed it in her fist. The agony of losing that eye was nothing compared to having a jagged and too large gemstone immediately crammed into the still raw wound.

It was the moment I lost the vision I'd nurtured for so long. The vision of a united world, of justice and prosperity for all.

It was the moment my vision became hers.

Something inside shrieked in mad laughter as I dug my filthy fingernails into the corner of the socket. No sane man tears out their own eyeball; every part of you rails against the blasphemous assault of self. Your own body betrays you, hesitates, resisting your deranged intent.

Never a man, sane or otherwise, I dug the eyeball from its nest, tearing the now useless lid in the process.

Searing pain, and a bright flash. Then, nothing.

I tossed the eye aside, heard it land, gelatinous and sodden, on stone.

The Eye of Gods felt cold in my fist. Sharp edges cut my palms. It would never fit in the orbital socket.

Atone, atone, eyes of stone.

Kneeling, tears of blood spilling from the gaping wound in my face, I crushed all doubt with savage intent. From the moment I crawled from my earthen grave, I'd left behind a trail of destruction and soul-torn corpses. Over and over, I paid lip service to the idea of being something I wasn't, of being a better man.

Atone, atone.

For all Henka's machinations, for all she remade me into someone capable of loving her, I'd changed in ways she never could have predicted. A capacity for love meant I was not only capable of having friends but would need them. Loving someone meant caring what they thought and how they felt. It was both strength and terrible weakness.

Bren was my friend, but I was his too.

I would sacrifice myself for him.

I slammed the Eye of Gods into the empty socket. When it stopped, stuck, I lunged forward to smash it against the stone floor, driving it the rest of the way.

Bone cracked, my skull breaking so my forehead bulged, distended on the right side.

Iremaire swatted Bren like an insect, smashed him to the ground. The dregs of the jaguar god, Ak'b'al, were nothing in the face of a battlemage prepared for war.

Still kneeling, I saw the hall of pedestals and I saw the *things* imprisoned in the facets of the gemstone eye. Deities. Lords of Hell. Mighty demons. Divinities I, with the help of my own god, defeated and bound like demons. The only difference between gods and demons was scale.

No mortal mind could stand this, and on some level, I understood how deeply wrong it was that I could.

Most of the gods I didn't recognize, the memories of trapping them likely in the last shards of my heart.

One god, I remembered.

Sanity shivered, splintered. I'd been the Demon Emperor, whole and powerful, last time I laid stone eyes upon the foul god. And the emperor had quailed, mind crumbling.

Bren made a retching tearing scream as his ribs compressed, skull grinding against stone under the growing pressure of Iremaire's magic.

"Azagothoth," I said, voice shaking. "Come."

A seething bubbling nightmare tangle of snakes and slugs knotted with a thousand-legged spider answered my call. It filled the hall, reality shivering around the god, flinching in horror. A damp cavity opened in the bulbous grey flesh, fat, greasy lips forming as it shaped a mouth. Glistening worms wrestled to create a misshapen tongue.

"Emperor," the god said.

Something within me broke.

I'd half hoped Iremaire would flee, and I could return Azagothoth to his prison. She didn't. Perhaps she hadn't recognized what I called, or maybe she was overconfident after having so easily bested me. With a word, the battlemage triggered scores of prepared spells. Bright shields of light sparked around her, shoving the god back several strides. Wispy blades of smoke encircled her, lashing angrily at any part of Azagothoth that came close. The god wailed in pain and surprise. Jagged forks of lightning stabbed out, impaling mucilaginous flesh, leaving deep smoking craters. Fires raged forth, searing the god, snakes and worms writhing as they crisped black and fell to ash.

I watched the display in stunned awe. The last time I'd seen magic like this, an entire circle of battlemages had been pooling their power to make it happen. That a single wizard could attack a god and force it to retreat showed just how badly I'd misjudged their power. Unfettered by the emperor's laws, they'd experimented with abandon, pushing the boundaries of their chaotic art.

Enraged, Azagothoth struck back, smashing through Iremaire's shields. Suction-cupped tentacles attached themselves to the mage, coiling about her like a thousand slimy snakes. The god tore away great swaths of skin, pulled her apart, scattering limbs and bloody gibbets of flesh across the hall. She didn't have time to scream.

In a heartbeat, the wizard was gone, a gory ruin all that remained. Powerful as she was, she was still just a mage. All too human. And Azagothoth was the fallen lord of a greater hell.

I left the god to its victory, and it slumped about the hall slurping up the bloody mess, leaving polished, glistening stone in its wake.

Checking on Bren, I found him alive and unconscious. Most if not all his ribs broken, one leg bent badly beneath him, I decided this was likely a mercy.

Nokutenda lay dead, the back of her skull smashed in, and I

wondered if there was some way I might save her too. She betrayed me, though not by choice. She still wore the ring carrying Brisinder. The demon of possession had said it learned everything its host knew, could mimic every personality trait. Could it remember the sorcerer so perfectly as to fool Bren if I put the ring on another woman and told him it was Nokutenda?

Undecided, I collected the ring, pocketing it. It would be a terrible, evil thing to do to an innocent victim, but might make Bren happy. At least, if he never knew the truth.

Henka remained standing motionless and silent. Nhil's corpse, still bubbling and steaming, lay a few strides from her.

I staggered to my wife. "Was this what you wanted?" I demanded.

My skull burned and ached, throbbing pain pulsing along the right side of my face.

She didn't so much as twitch a look in my direction.

After Nhil laid a hand on her heart and ordered her to be still, she had no choice but to obey. Limping to the back of the hall, I found the pedestal with her heart. This time I could clearly read the plaque: Queen of the Dead.

The emperor hadn't used her name. Back then she was a tool, a weapon. He never loved her. Or at least not as I now did. Collecting her heart, I carried the wizened leather back to Henka.

I paused before her, hesitating. Even with her heart in my hand, she was dangerous. She would do anything to make me happy and in trying to do so, had near destroyed me. She tricked me into bringing her here, all part of her plan. I reeled from the implications. All this because I once told her I was happiest when we'd battled, and I faced impossible odds. It was exactly the kind of thoughtless bravado I imagined the emperor saying.

Loving me as she did, being willing to do anything to make me happy, she plotted to become my great enemy once again. She would kill me the moment she was free, and she couldn't let that happen, as doing so would cause me misery. At the same time, she couldn't allow me access to her heart so I might command her to stop. She needed to first trick me into showing her where the hall of pedestals was hidden, and then bring her here so she might awaken her necromancers and destroy

AN END TO SORROW

the portal.

"You would love me even while we fought," I said.

Henka didn't react.

"You are free to speak, but nothing more. I command you to answer my questions truthfully."

"It's not too late," she said, still staring into the rear of the hall. I hadn't allowed her the freedom to move. "I can still make you happy."

"My happiness isn't worth the misery of the world."

"It is to me."

I tried to swallow my pain. This was my wife, my Henka. She was my soul and my life. She was my world. And I was hers. Somehow, we'd done this to each other, trapped ourselves in an insane love. Knowing the truth changed nothing. I loved her and I always would.

I decided on a question that felt safe. "Why did Nhil command you to be silent after ordering you to protect me?"

"He didn't want to give me the chance to command him."

"He told me I freed him."

When she didn't answer, I added, "Why did he lie?"

"You were unhappy. It hurt that I couldn't be what you needed. Realizing what must happen, I convinced you I required a demonic advisor of my own. You bound Nhil to my service. He was never your demon. For millennia I worked with his help, manipulating your closest people, turning the Guild against you. In time, you and Nhil became friends." Only her lips moved, the rest of her locked rigid. "How could I not suspect ulterior motives on his part? He was always one for the long game. Then, when you asked me to free him, I knew he'd manipulated you. I ordered him to lie and tell you he was free, and that he remained out of friendship."

"He could never tell me what you'd done, because you commanded him not to."

It wasn't a question, and she didn't answer.

"He helped you plan this," I added. "Every last detail. He had no choice. And yet, he managed to leave hints."

"I made mistakes," Henka admitted, "was sloppy in the wording of some commands."

"Explain."

"We were at war, the Guild having risen against you when I goaded them into rebellion. They'd been so slow to act I was surprised at the ferocity of their response once in motion. I worried you might flee and ordered Nhil to destroy your boltholes like the Black Citadel. There were dozens." She made a sound like a laugh, her face expressionless. "My mistake was telling him not to return until he'd destroyed the last one. Had I not been distracted, had I worded the command differently, I could have avoided his meddling. He destroyed all but one, remaining in the last, beyond my reach."

Alone, Nhil waited three thousand years for my return.

In the end, he'd followed Henka's command, not returning until the last bolthole was gone. I told her he was dead, and she believed me. I understood then how deep his plans went. Nhil had to destroy the Black Citadel before returning and had to return the moment he did. He subtly goaded me into summoning Karatal and then made sure the binding failed. He couldn't tell me what he was doing or why and followed Henka's orders while still trying to save me.

When I first told Henka Nhil was still alive and in the Black Citadel, there was little she could do. If she was too obvious in trying to turn me against him, I'd become suspicious of her. She knew he couldn't tell me anything. Trapped, my demonic friend did what he could, returning hidden in the cloak, waiting for his chance.

"He died saving me," I said.

"I was wrong," admitted Henka. "He was your friend."

Unable to tell me the truth, he let slip so many hints. He told me there was a threat from beyond the world and that I was the only one who could stop it. I'd briefly thought he meant me, but it was Henka, my wife.

'You can believe one of two things,' he told me. 'Either Henka and I both want what is best for you and disagree on what that is, or one of us has ulterior motives.'

Then, when I refused to distrust her, he insisted I take a sword.

'You really think I need a sword to confront her?' I'd asked

'You must find the rest of your heart and remember yourself. Otherwise, your world is doomed.'

Over and over moments I'd barely noticed flickered through my thoughts.

Me, trying to corner him on why he called her the Queen of the Dead. Nhil, neatly evading my questions and distracting me. He once said that if Henka wanted to rule the world, it would be hers. When I asked why she didn't, he said it was because she loved me more than she wanted to rule. Later, when I demanded proof of why I shouldn't trust her, he said nothing, refusing to answer.

'She loves me,' I'd said, as if that won the argument.

'Nothing,' Nhil answered, 'is more dangerous than Henka's love.'

Because I remembered nothing else of my wife, I'd thought my memories of the hall of pedestals a mistake, something missed when my heart was broken. They weren't. Rather, they were exactly what I needed to push me to want to free her. The guilt caused by those memories was why I brought her here. Once again, my love planned everything.

"You can't free me," said Henka. "I'll kill you, shatter your heart to dust. I'll murder your world and enslave the dead. Even you can't be that selfish."

Even me.

She was right, I couldn't free her.

"I can still make you happy," she repeated. "We'll leave together, destroy the portal so neither can return. I'll gather my necromancers and be the enemy you need."

"I'd be happier with you working *with* me."

"If that's what you need."

Nokutenda's battered corpse caught my eye. Bren couldn't take another loss like that. With Henka at my side, maybe he wouldn't have to. I could save my friend a great deal of pain and not lose my love—

I realized I hadn't asked a proper question and the wording of my last command meant she only had to answer *questions* honestly.

"If we leave here together, what will you do?"

Still unable to move, Henka gazed unblinking into the dark. "As I always have."

Truth, yet still an evasion. "You'll keep trying to make me happy."

"I love you. How can I do otherwise?"

"Will you shatter my heart again?"

"If I must."

"If I order you not to?"

"I will do my best with the man you are now."

I thought that over. Could I give her enough ironclad commands she'd be the companion I wanted rather than what she thought I needed? Perhaps, but Nhil often said she was smarter than me. I'd have to be careful not to leave a single loophole.

I caught myself contemplating intricate commands to forever lock my wife into obedience. What a beautiful trap she'd concocted. I loved her and couldn't keep her enslaved, and yet I could neither free nor destroy her.

"I made you," she said, perceptive as ever. "I designed the man you are. You can't be happy without me."

I knew she was right.

"I can't do it," I admitted. "I can't destroy you."

"I know."

I laughed, a mirthless chuckle. "Because you made me this way."

"Indeed."

Take me home. The words haunted me.

"That isn't my world, is it?"

"Your world is dead."

"Who killed it?" I asked.

"I think you did."

We stood beneath a temple in the ruins of a dead world.

Take me home.

I swallowed. "This is my world. I killed it." I struggled for calm. "Who am I?" Who? I had a shattered heart of obsidian. I died and returned, over and over. I bound gods to my stone eyes. "*What* am I?"

"Your god once called you the Death of Suns."

The words meant nothing to me.

"When I cut you open," continued Henka, "your heart was already broken. I wasn't the first to shape you."

My god's own words: *Find the pieces of you that matter. The piece that understands power. The piece that drives you to master your world.* Like Henka, she'd chosen the fragments she could use.

"She dreams in blood," I said, "but I have dreams of my own."

"Command me to make your dream a reality. We will conquer world after world, searching for the rest of your heart."

Bren groaned in pain.

My friend.

My hope to be a better man.

I asked, "What is the life of one friend worth?"

"Having someone you like more than yourself is the greatest gift," Henka said. "The luckier mortals achieve it through their children. Those like us don't have that option. We're trapped in an endless cycle of selfishness. I am a slave and happier in my slavery than I ever was ruling worlds."

"I have you," I said.

"You love me but don't like me."

She said it without emotion, as if my feelings for her were irrelevant. Much as her casual observation hurt, she was right.

"I turned the swordswoman and the sorcerer against you," she said, "but Bren was always safe."

"You couldn't use him because hurting him would make me unhappy."

Brenwick Sofame. Flawed as he was, I both liked and loved the man. There was no one else I could say that about in all the world. He took chances I dared not, exposing his heart for the breaking at every turn, willing to suffer to feel those rare moments of joy.

"He would do anything for me," I said. "Can I do any less for him?"

"You could," said Henka.

"What if grey is an excuse, a way to avoid black and white?" I asked. "If slavery is evil, then it's always evil; there can be no excusing it. I must free you. Whatever happens after, at least I will have kept that one promise."

"Don't," said Bren from where he lay. "I was wrong."

I stared at him in shock.

"I was wrong," he repeated. "What you want and what I want doesn't matter. *You* want to free Henka. Doing so and turning your back on the islands is an act of selfishness. If you want to be a better person, you must save your people."

I wanted to laugh and to cry. It was the perfect way out: be a better man by embracing the stained soul I was. It gave me everything I wanted. Henka would remain mine; she'd love me forever. Bren would remain at my side, as long as he thought I was doing the right thing. He could guide me, be my conscience where mine failed. I'd conquer the world to save it from the neglect of the Guild.

"With the dragons," Henka said, "we can reach Palaq before the wizards. My necromancers already mass for war. While the Guild is looking south, we can strike from the heart of the mainland."

I could awaken the demons of PalTaq, bind the mighty King Grone to my service once again. All the islands would swear fealty to their emperor returned. I would find my sword, Kantlament and perhaps even my other stone eye. Queen Maz Arkis of the Crags loathed the Guild and I felt sure she'd join in my war. I would bring the Deredi to heel.

"Worlds of dead still await my command," said Henka. "Entire realities of demons amassed for a war that never came. They will answer your call."

That knowledge and more lay in the stasis box, awaiting me.

"And my god?" I asked. "What of her dream?"

"If I can't be your enemy, she will have to do."

I could keep my Henka and have the enemy she thought I needed. First, however, before I faced my god, I'd bring the world to heel. The Guild spent millennia honing their craft, but I would crush them.

All of it would be mine, with no god dancing me like a marionette.

She dreamed in blood, but I dreamed in war.

Can't lament, a terrible joke.

If the end of sorrow was the end of knowing, there was but one escape.

I was a coward.

"We have to help Phaoro," I said, stooping to collect the stasis box from where it lay. "I must save the world."

CHAPTER ONE

For an eternity I was nothing but animal hunger. Small lives, skittering and slithering, fed me. I wanted more, needed more. Always more. Buried in sand I fed off the tough desert grass above me. I was voracious, insatiable, a devourer. Snakes and scorpions crossing my ravenous grave stiffened and fell dead.

With each life I grew.

Blood.

Blood soaked through the earth. This was a large life, a bright spark of existence, wounded and dying. It collapsed upon me. Even buried, I felt its weight impact the soil above. Sucking the life from it, I regained some shred of what I was. What I had been.

I woke suffocating, choking on sand and clawing in mad panic. I fought free of my prison. Pale roots hung from me, the veins through which I fed. I watched them squirm and writhe their way back into my flesh and wondered what I was.

Naked and filthy, I stood in the morning sun. Thousands of tiny corpses, husked and dried, littered the ground. Translucent shells of insects. Fragile birds, skeletal and empty. Countless remains of rodents, twisted with agony. The corpse of a man, long rotted to bone and gristle, lay nearby, his throat cut.

A woman with yellow hair and pale green eyes wearing the spotless white robes of a mage stood nearby. Tossing stained clothes at my feet, she said, "Get dressed."

Blackest hate filled me, left no room for thought. Snarling, I crouched, ready to pounce and tear her throat out.

AN END TO SORROW

"The Demon Emperor is risen," she said, looking unafraid. "Only you can stop him."

Something far to the west called me. I wanted it.

EPILOGUE

Shatter me.
Put me back together.
Shatter me, praying for change, and put me back together.
Your efforts are doomed.

He begs and pleads that you not become what he was. But he was nothing, a sliver too small to reflect more than a glint of light.

I *am* the mirror.

Ten thousand deaths cannot stop me.

For I am the Death of Suns.

And tomorrow, a new day must dawn.

HERE ENDS THE FIRST OBSIDIAN PATH TRILOGY

WORLD MAP

These full colour versions of maps can be found at:
http://michaelrfletcher.com/the-obsidian-path-maps/

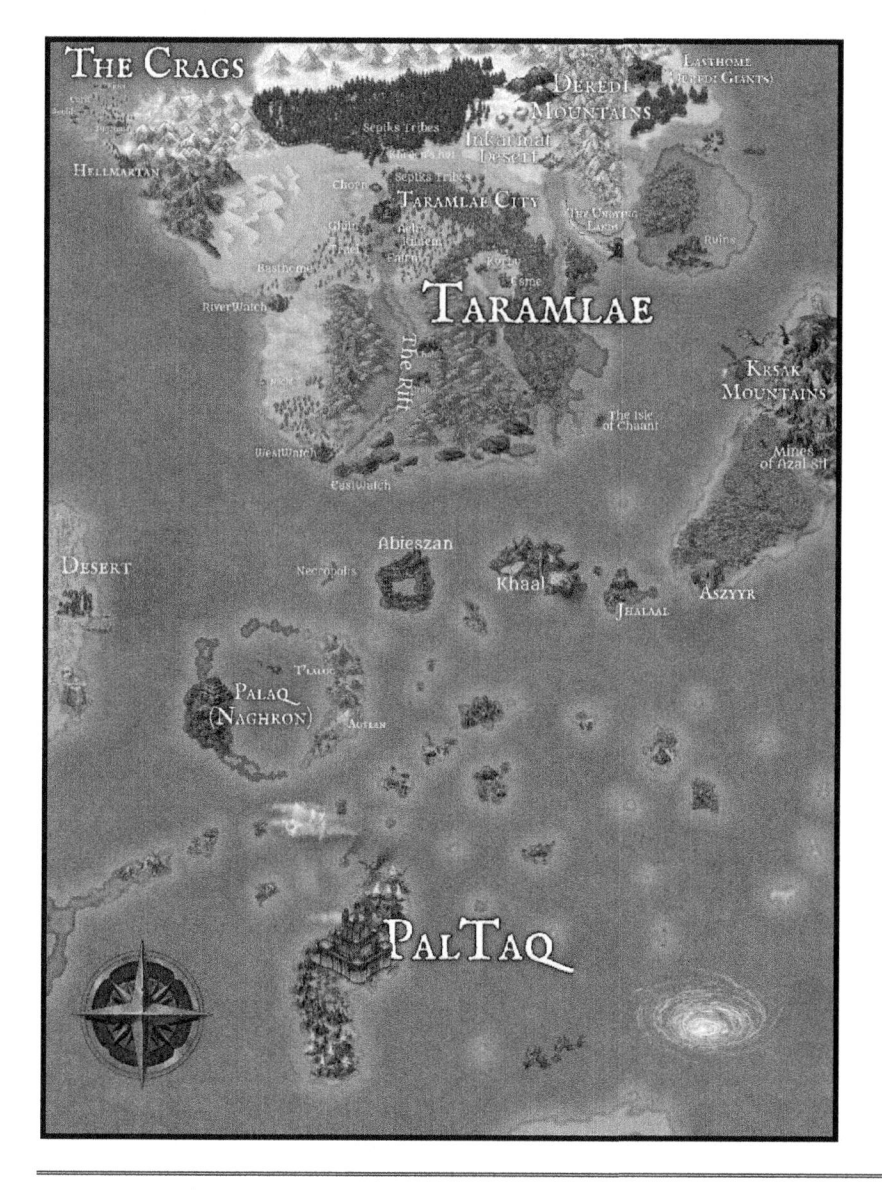

TARAMLAE AND THE CRAGS

SOUTHERN ISLANDS

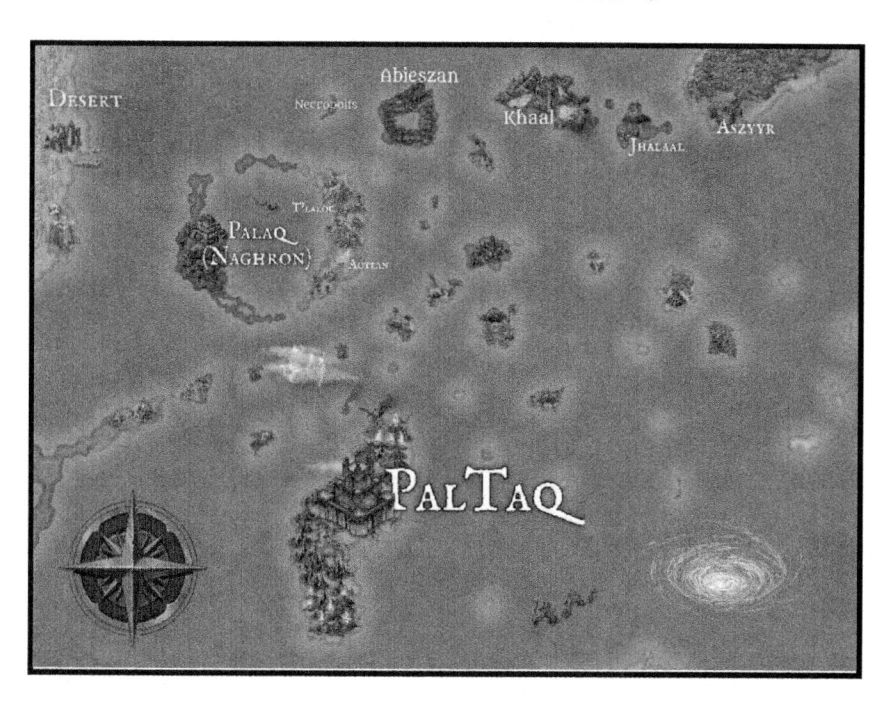

SOUTHERN ISLANDS

THE EASTERN LANDS

ACKNOWLEDGMENTS

With every book I release there are more people I need to thank. It's a strange life. I sit huddled at my keyboard or hunched over a pad of paper scribbling like a madman. While so much of the process is just me, it's all the stuff that happens once it's not about me that really matters. I can scrawl my deranged little stories all day (and often do) but without the people listed here, no one would ever know. Hell, let's be honest, without the occasional kind word or kick in the ass, I would have given up long ago. It's because there are crazy folks like you that I'm still here, still doing this. Your name might not be listed here, but the fact you're reading this means it should be. If you've read any of my books, thank you! Mind, if this is the first one you've read, you've really fucked up.

Where to start…where to start?

Probably at the beginning. I've said it before, but without my parents, I wouldn't be here, literally or literarily. They instilled in me a love or books and words, and I will forever be grateful for that. Though if they hadn't, maybe I could have been a race car driver or a ninja or soccer player like I originally planned.

Anyway.

I don't feel like planning or putting thought into this. My brain is pretty cabbaged right now as I'm currently writing two books while getting this one ready to go live. So…all hail the Lords of Chaos!

Wait! I have to take a moment to thank Bruno Catais Costa for all his many contributions over the years. He has been a source of wisdom and sage advice. Dude. The next pint shall be raised in your honour.

I've had the same small group of close friends for over thirty-five years. These are the dudes I used to roleplay with before writing devoured all me time, and we still hang out at every opportunity. 88, Zed, Kenio, Hop, Spin, and Dave (who for some reason doesn't have a nickname), you are better friends than I deserve. {EDIT}: Since the first draft of these acknowledgements, we've started the weekly gaming sessions again. I'm GMing a campaign set in the *Obsidian Path* universe.

At some point an extremely polite Australian with nice hair reached out and asked me if I wanted to do a weekly podcast with him. I was about to tell him to fuck off when he mentioned Rob Hayes and Dryk Ashton had already agreed. Not wanting to be left out, I jumped on board. In hindsight, I think he told us all the same lie. Either way, thanks to Jed Herne, author of *The Thunder Heist*, for putting together the Warriors Wizards and Words Podcast and tolerating the fact I show up hungover most days because we record the damned thing at 8:30am Saturday mornings. And I guess I should thank Rob and Dyrk for being awesome co-hosts and great humans. Wait a moment. Did they have anything to do with this book? Yeah, I don't think so. To hell with them!

Focus, damn it!

Mark Lawrence, author of the amazing *Broken Empire* books runs the SPFBO (Self-Published Fantasy Blog-Off) every year. *Black Stone Heart* came in second the year it was entered, and the attention it received played a huge part in the book's success. A massive thanks to Mark and to all the amazing authors I met during the process.

There isn't a secret cabal of authors. There just isn't. And if there was, they'd still be writers and totally useless at cabal-type stuff. Thanking them for being awesome would be a terrible breach of security.

There are so many bloggers/reviewers I need thank (all the sites who take part in the SPFBO, Adrian and the folks at Grimdark Magazine, David and the team at FanFiAddict, Mihir and the folks at Fantasy Book Critic, Booknest, The Queen's Book Asylum, and so many more!) it'd take an entire book to thank them all.

This book had more test-readers than any of my previous releases. First, though, I must thank Carrie Chi Lough. Carrie has been First-Reader for all my recent releases. Her initial feedback helps shape what the books become. Thank you!

AN END TO SORROW

Björn, Mitchell, Brendan, Justin, Chris, and Nikolas (all Patreon supporters) beta-read the book. I received great comments from everyone, and their efforts helped fine-tune the end result.

A huge thanks to Julia Kitvaria Sarene for being all-around awesome. Julia is a champion of everything fantasy and is always the first person to beta-read/listen to my audiobooks.

Sarah Chorn edited this and my last several releases. She's recently become Grimdark Magazine's staff editor and is always a pleasure to work with. Thank you!

Felix Ortiz is an art god. This is the fifth cover he's done for me, and the dude just keeps getting better. Art. God. Though please don't hire him to do your books because I already have to book him a year in advance. I booked him for the cover of my next release before I wrote the first word.

Petros Triantafyllou. Dude.

Ooh. Massive thanks to Nokutenda Rebekah Nzira for agreeing to lend me her awesome name. I thought the sorcerer was going to hang around for a chapter or two before dying a horrible death, but she turned out to be surprisingly stubborn.

There are an insane number of writers out there who have helped me in countless small ways. Kind words of support. A shoulder to scream at. Someone who sees the humour in this mad world of publishing.

I want to thank everyone who took a moment to write, email, message, or tweet to me about their reading experiences. It doesn't matter how brief the message is, each one has a real impact. I want to write, but hearing you enjoyed a book, connected with a character (seriously, consider seeking help), or were in some way moved or impacted, lights a fire in me.

And finally, a heart-felt thanks to everyone who reads my books. Without you, I'd probably be a ninja or a race car driver.

A HUGE THANKS TO THE FOLKS ON PATREON!

I have a Patreon!

If you are so moved to help support me in my endless quest to bring darkness and cynicism to the world, feel free to join me at: https://www.patreon.com/michaelrfletcher

My solemn oath is that I will not pocket a single penny of the money made there. Everything goes toward cover art, editing, interior illustrations, maps, and anything else I can think of that might in some way improve your experience.

A MASSIVE thanks to my current Patreons who made the cover art and illustrations within this book possible. Many of them beta-read an early release as well (yeah, one of the perks) and I'm grateful for their efforts.

And finally, a hoisting of the pint glass to my high-tier Patreons Carrie Lough, Nick Carlson, Colin Tavares, Mitchell Van Hoose, Chris Corke and Jackie Bannerman. I shall endeavour to deserve your faith in my work.

ABOUT THE AUTHOR

Michael R. Fletcher is too lazy to write his own "About the Author" and has promised me a bottle of whiskey to do it for him. I know several things about the man and I'm sure I can string these out to fill the space. He's Canadian, he recently placed 2nd in possibly the most prestigious literary contest for fantasy, and his middle name is just the letter R.

His debut book tops all the charts that rate books by grimdark content. So, open this one with tongs and leave at least an hour after meals before reading. Surprisingly, he has a wife and daughter!

To conclude. I was not coerced into writing this. Mr Fletcher is a real person. And this book contains not only a decent number of words but also all the letters.

—Mark Lawrence

Printed in Great Britain
by Amazon